THE PERILOUS TOWER

THE GATES OF GOOD & EVIL BOOK 3

IAN IRVINE

SANTHENAR PRESS

THE GATES OF GOOD & EVIL QUARTET
Book 3 – The Perilous Tower

Ian Irvine

PART OF THE SOUTHERN HEMISPHERE
OF SANTHENAR

LEGEND

Mountains
Hills
Desert
Salt Lake
Marsh, Swamp
Conifer Forest
Broadleaf Forest
Tropical Forest
Grassland
Reef
Main Road

Banthey

Fankster Huccadory
Gendrigore Bel Torance
20° Nys Taranta
FARANDA Strinklet
Tar Gaarn & Roros
Havissard Twissel
SEA OF Mistmurk Mountain Guffeons
PERION Jepperand
Gosport
30° Katazza
Flude Maksmord
Ashmode
Nithmak CARENDOR KALAR STASSOR
Tifferfyte
40° Zile
MELDORIN Morrelune
Thurkad Fadd
Nennifer
Great Mountains
Burning Tirthrax Triki
Mountain
Fiz Gorgo LAURALIN MIRRILLADELL
50°
KARAMA MALAMA OOLO
(Sea of Mists) LUUMA NARTA
HA-DROW Ogur
SHAZABBA
Steppe
60°
KARA AGEL Noom
(Frozen Sea)
Grinding

N
W   E
S

SCALE
KILOMETRES
0 100 200 300 400 500 600 700 800 900 1000
0   40   80   120   160   200
LEAGUES

70°

Maps by the author

CONTENTS

1

THE MOST DISTURBING THING

The sky galleon, an absurd craft with an equally silly name, *Three Reckless Old Ladies*, streaked north along the coast of the Sea of Thurkad. There had been no further sign of the enemy and Llian allowed himself to hope that the Merdrun's great Crimson Gate had failed. That they had not succeeded in invading Santhenar after all.

Even the best-designed gates were dangerous, and all who entered them did so at their peril. The enemy could be undone by bad luck too.

He looked west, in the direction of Karan's former family estate of Gothryme, and sighed. After being banned from working as a chronicler or teller he had done his best to learn about farming and forestry, but from the beginning Karan had made it clear that the estate was hers, not *theirs*, and she would not let him manage the smallest aspect of it. He had seldom been happy there.

Now Gothryme was gone, and good riddance! She was no longer the owner of a great estate, impoverished though it may have been, handed down mother to daughter for more than a thousand years. And Llian was no longer a eunuch of a man, forbidden to pursue his calling. Finally, they were equals again.

And not before time. Dark times needed a great Chronicler of the Histories, and a surpassing Teller of the Great Tales, and he could be both. With Gothryme and his tarnished reputation confined to history, the burden of the past ten years had lifted. He could make a new start here.

So many tales needed telling, but ... Karan was not going to be happy.

~

Karan's eyes were wet as she gazed at her sleeping daughter, the most perfect thing in her life, yet the least explicable.

The black pill Rulke had given Karan, which had allowed her to become pregnant in the first place, had greatly enhanced Sulien's natural gift for *far-seeing*, though not in a good way. Four months ago, she had far-seen the Merdrun's one fatal weakness in a nightmare, and since then she had been stalked, betrayed, hunted, lost, rescued, recaptured with Karan and condemned to death –

Until, in an act so reckless and desperate that Karan got chills every time she thought of it, Llian, a clumsy scholar who was incompetent with any kind of weapon, had saved Sulien and herself. The scar low on Karan's belly, from the stab wound that had almost killed her that day, burned.

When they'd escaped to the future she had thought the danger over, but two days ago Sulien had far-seen a Merdrun army at the Crimson Gate, and Rulke had managed to extract part of her nightmare.

A child of a lesser race can defeat us if her mighty gift is allowed to develop –

Develop what? No one could guess. Not even Rulke had been able to recover the rest of the nightmare, and that was bad for two reasons.

Whilever the secret was buried in Sulien, the Merdrun could protect themselves by hunting her down and killing her. A nine-year-old girl's life meant nothing to them; they saw their enemies as subhuman.

And Sulien felt guilty that she could not remember this vital secret. She would not give up trying to find it, and she had a bad habit of acting without thinking things through – like her mother!

Instinctively, Karan looked to Llian, who was slumped against the rear wall of the cabin, next to the closed hatch that led below. There was ink on his fingers and the front of his shirt, and the journal that never left his side was open on his lap, but he was asleep.

Her heart went out to him. How he had suffered these past years. How she had *made* him suffer, controlling cow that she was. Lording it over him because she owned Gothryme and he, being banned, could not earn a copper grint from his calling. Well, everything had to change now.

But how? She felt torn out by the roots.

She took the front door key to Gothryme Manor from her bag. The black iron, heavy and worn, was as old as the manor itself. The bow was a cloverleaf, flecked with orange rust in the interstices, the shank as long as her hand, and the key wards were crescent moons. It was all she had left.

Before she, Llian and Sulien had found a way to flee 214 years into the future, Karan had given Gothryme, the drought-stricken estate that she'd loved with every atom of herself and had planned to pass down to Sulien, to a stranger.

But the Santhenar of today had been ground down by the 160-year-long Lyrinx War and the west had suffered worst. The cities and towns of Meldorin had been emptied long ago, its estates great and small abandoned, Gothryme among them. It was her binding duty to get it back and leave it to Sulien, whatever the cost to herself.

Karan put the thought aside. They had come to the future to save Sulien from Maigraith, but Maigraith was still alive and as vengeful as ever, so what had it all been for?

And it had always been Karan's role to provide, though how was she to provide for Sulien and Llian now? Or Wilm and Aviel, who had also ended up here in some mocking twist of fate. Karan's purse would soon be empty and then they would be dependent on charity.

Yet in a world exhausted by war followed by civil war, and facing another war, how long could charity last? Were they doomed to become serfs, slaving all the hours of the day just to feed themselves, and at the mercy of every predator, human or beast?

No chance for a second child then. Her eyes stung. She had abandoned the idea years ago and turned away whenever Llian mentioned it. But if they had a proper home –

'Xervish?' she said.

'Mmm?' said Xervish Flydd. A small, greatly scarred and hideously ugly man, he was seated in the far rear corner of the sky galleon's overdecorated cabin, reading a small book of tales.

'Can we go to Gothryme? It's only half an hour out of your way.'

'What for?'

'I'm no use to you. I'm going to take my estate back.'

Llian woke abruptly and twisted around, staring at Karan. *What?*

'Meldorin is an empty land,' said Karan. 'We can go home.'

'It's not home anymore.'

'Where else can we go? You can't provide –'

'Thanks for reminding me,' he said bitterly.

'Meldorin is a dangerous place,' said Flydd. 'I don't think –'

'If the Merdrun come,' said Karan, 'everywhere will be dangerous.'

'What about Maigraith?'

'If she comes near my family again,' Karan said ferociously, *'she's dead!'*

Flydd closed the book and rubbed his twisted fingers. 'You can't hide from her, or the Merdrun, in your former home.'

'Then we'll go up into the mountains. We can live off the land. It'd be a lot better than –'

'Being dependent on me?' Flydd shrugged and called forwards. 'M'Lainte, would you?'

M'Lainte, a big, saggy, cheerful old woman, stood behind the binnacle at the front of the cabin, holding the stubby levers that controlled the speed and flight of the uncanny craft. She turned it west towards the range of mountains called the Hills of Bannador.

The sky galleon was the most ridiculous vessel Karan had ever seen. It had the deep keel and curving sides of a seagoing ship, though the timbers were sheathed in brass interleaved with black metal and swirling strips of silver, and the interior was decorated with even greater extravagance. From the high bow, scalloped metal shields extended along both sides of the deck in place of rails. A heavy, spear-throwing javelard was mounted behind the bow shields, and a catapult on another swivelling platform at the stern. She had no idea what allowed such a heavy craft to fly, but then, she had not understood Rulke's construct either.

As she gazed upon the familiar, snow-tipped peaks of Bannador, her eyes misted. Home. How she loved it. It had come to her when her mother, Vuula, died when Karan was twelve, and giving it away had meant abandoning the one good thing she'd had from Vuula. She had to get it back. Llian would just have to get used to it.

Karan's eyes don't shine like that when she looks at me, Llian thought. She cares more about that drought-struck expanse of rock and dirt than she does for me.

He tried to see her side but the anger that had smouldered in him for years was too strong. He jumped up. 'No, Karan. Not again!'

Flydd gestured to M'Lainte, who slowed the sky galleon and hovered above the aromatic coastal heath.

'What are you talking about?' Karan hissed.

Llian hesitated. Was this the time? It had to be now, or he would lose the courage and end up a pathetic, bitter old man. 'I can't do this again.'

'Do *what*?'

'Follow you back and sit at your feet like an adoring little lapdog, waiting for the occasional bone, but never allowed to do anything worthwhile.'

Karan snapped, 'You couldn't *do* anything at Gothryme.'

That hurt. 'I could have written the records, kept the accounts, learned to help plan the crops and the rotations –'

'Those were my jobs.'

'*Everything* was your job. You wouldn't trust me to do anything.'

'Daddy's right, Mummy,' said Sulien, in a *let's be reasonable* tone. 'You are a bit, um, controlling.'

Karan softened her voice. 'Not now, darling.'

'I lost ten years of my life,' said Llian.

'Are you saying the last ten years of your life, *with your family*, have been wasted?' Karan hissed.

'You know what I'm talking about.'

'I didn't get you banned. You managed that all by yourself.'

'Supportive of you to say so, for the hundredth time.' He took a deep breath. 'Well, I'm sorry, Karan, but I'm getting my life back.'

'What's that supposed to mean?'

'I'm not going back to cringe and cower at Gothryme. I'm going after another Great Tale.'

'You've got a family, Llian! Why isn't that enough? Why can't you be an ordinary Teller?'

'Because I'm not an ordinary Teller. That's what drew you to me in the first place, if you remember. My retelling of the greatest of the Great Tales – the *Tale of the Forbidding*.'

Karan's anger faded and her green eyes took on a dreamy look. He knew she was reliving the magical night when she had first set eyes on him, when he'd retold the tale at the Graduation Telling and caused such a sensation. That night had changed both of their lives.

'Well,' she said softly, 'I'm sorry, but we all have to make compromises.'

You never have, he thought, but everyone was staring at them and he said no more.

'What's the decision?' Flydd said to Karan.

'Gothryme.'

She was studiously avoiding looking Llian's way.

Karan had just resumed her seat when Sulien's eyes rolled up and her breath whistled out between her teeth.

'*It's in an amber-wood box,*' she said in the grating Merdrun accent, '*and amber-wood is famously lucky. It could have survived. Find it!*'

Icy needles crept through Karan like frost spreading across a windowpane. 'Xervish, *they're here!*'

Flydd leapt up. 'M'Lainte, down!'

The sky galleon descended rapidly. 'What is it?' she said calmly.

Nothing seemed to faze the old woman. But then, she had been an important figure during the last decade of the Lyrinx War, and through all the turmoil since. Karan supposed M'Lainte had seen it all.

Shrubs creaked and snapped as the heavy craft settled. She smelled crushed leaves, thyme and rosemary, dust, and the salty tang of the nearby Sea of Thurkad.

'The most disturbing thing I've heard all year,' said Flydd. 'Sulien?'

Her eyes were unfocused, her mind in a far-off place.

Karan was trembling as she took Sulien's hand. 'Are you having a *far-seeing*?'

Nothing.

Flydd touched her forehead with a gnarled fingertip. Sulien jerked and her eyes sprang open. 'A foggy mountaintop,' she said in her own voice. 'Big pieces of white metal sticking up. And bones! Bones and skulls, *everywhere*. It's pouring with rain.'

'Thuntunnimoe,' hissed Flydd, looking meaningfully at M'Lainte. 'It's worse than I feared. Far worse!'

'What's Thuntunnimoe?' said Llian, leaning forwards eagerly.

'Mistmurk Mountain. A high, cliff-bound plateau in the rainforest west of Guffeons – away in the tropical north. I spent nine years trapped up there in my former, badly-aged body.'

Karan gazed at Flydd, wondering. The body he had now was nothing to inspire the poets.

'Dozens of Merdrun in bright red armour!' cried Sulien. 'Wading through bogs and pools. They came through a *gate*.'

'Why are they looking for an amber-wood box?' said Lilis, a white-haired, little old lady who had once been Librarian at the Great Library in Zile. 'Xervish, what's going on?'

'Please, no!' Flydd's warped hands were clenched, the battered knuckles standing out.

'What's all the white metal?' said Llian.

'Wreckage of the God-Emperor's sky palace. He flew it there four years ago, hunting his renegade son, Nish, a hero of the war. Maelys had broken him out of prison. I – I had no choice; I cast the forbidden renewal spell on myself –' pain shivered Flydd's raddled cheeks, '– and got a younger, stronger body. In the ensuing battle the sky palace fell out of the air and smashed to bits. We only escaped, Maelys, Nish and I, by a whisker.'

'Skald!' whispered Sulien. 'Skald Hulni.'

'What's that, darling?' said Karan, taking her small, cold hands.

'The Merdrun I'm ... *seeing* through. A young battle mancer ... He reminds me –' Sulien frowned as if chasing a lost thought, then shook her head. 'He's using a *seeking* spell.'

'Clever fellow,' said Flydd. 'Pray he fails.'

'He's desperate to find the box. He's shaking.'

'Why does he want it so badly?' said Llian.

Sulien's eyes closed again. Karan sat beside her, still holding her hand. Was going home the right thing to do, with Llian so opposed? How could she rely on her own judgement when she had made such colossal blunders these past few months? Like coming to the future.

Llian had never felt he belonged at Gothryme, because she was such a controlling bitch! What if he'd had enough of her? If he discovered the secret she'd been keeping from him all this time he would be gone in an instant.

Would Sulien stay, or go with him? Karan thought she would go. Feeling a scream building up, she suppressed the dangerous thoughts. If they left her, she would surely go mad, like her poor mother. But where else could they be safe?

After pacing for an interval, Flydd said to M'Lainte, 'It'll be dark soon. How far are we from Thurkad?'

'Hour and a half.'

'Get us there, fast as you can.'

'What about Gothryme?' cried Karan.

'The enemy have invaded, and you want to *run away*?' Flydd snarled.

'They want Sulien dead. Will you protect her, every hour of the day?'

Flydd didn't answer. He didn't care!

'Take your seats,' said M'Lainte, standing at the controls with impressive calm.

As the sky galleon heaved itself into the air and hurtled north, the sun went down behind the mountains to their left, streaking the sky with light and shadow. Home was so close Karan could almost smell it – but she wasn't going to get there.

Sulien's *far-seeing* went on, in fragments, for the best part of an hour. The enemy searchers scoured the rain-drenched plateau in straight lines, an arm's length apart, ploughing through chest-deep pools and sucking mires. Three soldiers were taken by swamp beasts that lunged from the brown water, their massive shearing blades crunching right through the Merdrun's crimson armour. Two more were dragged into giant carnivorous plants and submerged in viscous yellow digestive acids.

'They're screaming for help,' whispered Sulien. 'But the other soldiers are just ignoring –'

Whatever was in the amber-wood box, the enemy were desperate to find it.

Sulien shuddered, wiped her running eyes and continued. 'The water's all red. Red everywhere –

'*I've got it!*' she cried in a young man's voice that lacked the harshness of the other Merdrun. '*I've got it!*'

She opened her eyes very wide. 'That was Skald, in a gully on the edge of the mountain. He's holding up a big wooden box.'

'But what's *in* it?' said Karan irritably.

'The greatest folly of my life,' said Flydd in a dead voice. 'Something I'd assumed to be destroyed when the sky palace crashed.'

Stupid man! What had he done?

'I'd love to hear your story,' said Llian, bright-eyed, his pencil hovering over his journal.

'Put that away,' snapped Flydd.

'Tell us!' Karan yelled.

He scowled at her. 'You can't imagine what it was like being trapped up there, with no way down.'

'Then how did you climb up in the first place?'

'Fourteen years ago, I went there to a secret rendezvous, to plan the fightback against the God-Emperor, but none of my fellow conspirators turned up. Turned out they'd all been imprisoned or killed. The body I had then was old, well past sixty. I broke my ankle and it healed so badly I couldn't climb down again.'

'Must be lonely up there,' said Llian.

'The top of Mistmurk is surrounded by mile-high cliffs on all sides, and it *never* stops raining. I was stuck there, waiting for my allies to appear. Then, after it became clear they weren't coming, waiting to die. More than nine years I spent there, and they were hard times ... I was rotting alive. I – I had to keep my mind active or I would have gone insane.'

'Arguably, you did,' said Karan waspishly.

'Not helpful,' said M'Lainte without looking around. It was dark now, for the waning moon had not yet risen.

'I'd always planned to write the truth about the Lyrinx War,' said Flydd. 'Someone had to. Everything the Council of Scrutators wrote was propaganda ... or outright lies.'

Llian stared at Flydd, his eyes shining. Irritating men, both of them!

'So you wrote some books,' said Karan. 'So what?'

'I made paper from reeds, and ink from soot and rotgut spirits I distilled to numb the endless nights, and in five volumes I set down my *Histories of the Lyrinx War*,' said Flydd. 'At least, the vital last thirty years. It seemed important at the time – every node of power had been destroyed, and the depraved God-Emperor controlled the world with his sorcerous quicksilver tears, Gatherer and Reaper.'

'I don't see –'

'If you'll shut up for a minute, I'll tell you.'

Karan shut up, flushing.

'My fifth book described the last two years of the war, and I named all the key names: the top scrutators and generals, the greatest mancers, the most skilled artisans and artificers, and people with every other skill vital to such a war. I listed our most important mines and manufactories and training colleges, told the stories of the most important battles and how they were won or lost ...

'Imbecile that I am, I even described our magic-controlled weaponry, the flying thapters and armoured battle clankers, and how they were powered by the fields surrounding natural nodes. I drew dozens of maps showing battlefields, mines, manufactories ...'

He put his head in his hands. 'And fool, *fool*, I reproduced Tiaan's priceless charts of the locations of nodes and fields throughout Lauralin and Meldorin ...'

The skin on the back of Karan's shoulders crawled. 'Why would you do such a thing?' she whispered.

'So the future can learn from the past.'

'The future never learns from the past,' said Llian. 'It always thinks this time is different.'

'At the time, we believed the nodes of power were gone for good,' said Flydd.

He ground his grizzled head into his spread hands and went on. 'Our brilliant advances in mech-magical weaponry, and the fields that powered them *and are now regenerating*, are our only advantage in the coming war. If I'd thought there was a chance the books had survived, I would have raced to Thuntunnimoe the moment we saw the Crimson Gate open.

'But now the Merdrun have them, and my Histories will tell them everything they need to know to master our mech-magic ... and utterly expunge us from Santhenar.'

Karan rocked back and forth in her seat. Coming to this worn-out future had made things disastrously worse and there was nothing she could do about it.

And Sulien had far-seen this gifted young Merdrun battle mancer, Skald. What if he had also seen her?

2

WHERE ALL HIS BODIES ARE BURIED

F lydd would never take them to Gothryme now, but it was only eighty miles from Thurkad; they could walk it in a few long days. The mountains and forests west of Gothryme were vast and Karan knew them well – they could hide there for years. It would be a hard life, but they would be as safe there as anywhere. Assuming she could convince Llian to give up his dream, which would not be easy. Impossible to pursue another Great Tale while hiding in the wilderness.

But her duty to get Gothryme back, and pass it down to Sulien, was paramount. Llian had known it from the moment she was born, but he no longer cared. When had his love died?

It had been coming for a long time. Years, despite his recent heroics. What had been the catalyst? Her refusal to allow him any part of Gothryme? Or did it go deeper? Had he discovered her wicked secret?

Shivers ran up the back of Karan's neck. As a great chronicler, Llian had a close-to-perfect memory, and chroniclers were also skilled detectives, adept at noticing clues, linking facts together and sorting truth from lies. Reading faces, too.

The sky galleon lurched violently, throwing her off her seat and dragging her back to the present. If Skald had far-seen Sulien, the enemy's magiz could already be looking for her. Could Karan protect her family from him, in a world at war? Could anyone?

She had no way of deciding what to do, and little hope that she could make the right choice this time, when she had blundered so badly in the past.

Llian had gone to the port-side rail. *Probably sulking*, she thought waspishly, but regretted it at once. He was just as tormented. More so, if he *knows*. Sulien lay on the floor, wrapped in a blanket, asleep after her traumatic far-seeing. Flydd was sitting in a rear corner of the cabin, at a bolted-down table, whispering into a glassy sphere, the size of an orange, mounted in a semi-circular brass frame.

'What's that he's using?' Karan asked Lilis.

She had known Lilis as a twelve-year-old waif, and more recently as a junior librarian at the Great Library in Zile. Karan could not come to terms with her as an old woman with white hair, a scratchy voice and a beak of a nose. After Lilis succeeded Nadiril, the magic that went with the Librarian's position had greatly extended her lifespan, but she had retired a few years ago and was now looking for adventure. She might get more than she planned.

'It's a farspeaker,' said Lilis. 'He's telling our allies to prepare for the worst.'

Every so often Flydd consulted a notebook, rotated the sphere of the farspeaker to a new position and bent over it again. Each time he spoke, it glowed mustard yellow. Karan glared at him. He ignored her.

The sky galleon dropped sharply as M'Lainte settled it onto the cracked roof of a mansion of long ago and climbed down, carrying a box lantern. Decrepit buildings stood all around, some more or less intact, others reduced to chimney stacks, sections of broken wall and piles of rubble. Across a broad avenue, a line of once great public buildings stood empty. Many were roofless, with gaping window openings, and some were a few keystones away from total collapse.

Before the Lyrinx War, Thurkad had been the greatest city on Santhenar, home to a million of the most corrupt and venal people in the world, and Karan had no good memories of the place.

Emmant, an outcast half-Aachim who had conceived a murderous lust for her, had nearly killed her here. Tensor had shattered the Great Conclave with a forbidden potency here, driving her out of her wits. Llian had been imprisoned and sentenced to death here, and had been lucky to escape.

But the Lyrinx War had almost emptied Thurkad, and when the Dry Sea filled to become the Sea of Perion again, causing sea level to fall everywhere else, the coastline had retreated fifteen miles east. Thurkad was now a vast ruin on a salt-scalded plain, home only to a few thousand renegades and desperadoes, preying on each other and on the early settlers returning to Meldorin.

Flydd looked up at Karan. 'You might as well know the worst.' He lifted the hatch and yelled, 'Wilm? Aviel?'

Wilm climbed the ladder. A tall, strong youth, but thin after slaving for the enemy on the Isle of Gwine, and missing half his right ear from a near-fatal brush with the summon stone several months ago. He wore a black-handled sword in a copper sheath, though it looked wrong on him. Since he and Aviel had been dragged into the future, Wilm had been out of his depth.

Aviel was head and shoulders shorter, slender, with a sweet, heart-shaped face, fine silver hair that drifted in the slightest breeze, and a determined set to her small jaw, though she stood behind Wilm as if using him as a shield.

Llian came in, glanced at Karan and looked away. She knew the signs. He was steeling himself for another argument.

M'Lainte heaved her bulky body back up from the roof, panting.

'What is *the worst*?' said Llian.

'Merdrun armies have gated into Roros, Guffeons, Gosport and Fadd,' said Flydd, naming the four largest cities on the east coast of Lauralin. 'They took Guffeons and Fadd without much of a fight – after they slaughtered hundreds in the market squares, the citizens got the message. Gosport is still fighting but my informant says it'll be over within hours.'

'And Roros?' said Llian. 'We've been there, many years ago.'

'Two hundred and twenty-six years ago,' said Karan softly. It must be changed out of all recognition by now.

'Roros is the greatest and proudest city on Santhenar,' said Flydd, 'and they don't take kindly to outsiders telling them what to do. Since the time of the God-Emperor they've been prepared, under Governor Yulla Zaeff –'

'The third "Reckless Old Lady",' said Lilis with a fond smile.

'Yulla is a greedy old woman, but she loves Roros and she had two days' warning. It was long enough to activate every trap that human cunning has been able to devise, and hide many of the people the Merdrun are likely to target. They've suffered ten thousand casualties, from an attack force totalling sixty thousand, and they've only taken a quarter of Roros.'

'The Merdrun will make them pay tenfold for every casualty,' said Wilm in a quiet voice.

He had seen first-hand their savagery. Aviel took his hand in both of hers, a touching gesture from someone who normally kept her distance.

'They've probably invaded other cities, but not all of my informers have fars-peakers,' Flydd concluded.

'And they aren't reliable at great distances,' said M'Lainte.

'That all the bad news?' said Karan.

Flydd snorted. 'Thousands of Whelm have renewed their oath of service, this time to the Merdrun's leader, Durthix. And there's another thing. I don't know if it's good or bad ...'

'Spit it out, then,' said M'Lainte.

'They've driven the townsfolk out of Guffeons, locked the gates, and Merdrun civilians are coming through the Crimson Gate in their tens of thousands.'

Karan shivered. 'Does that mean they're here for good?'

Flydd packed the farspeaker into its battered case and rose stiffly. 'Get your gear. We'll be here for a day or two.'

'What is this place?' said Llian.

'Flydd has spies and boltholes all over the land,' said Lilis, smiling. 'He can't let go.'

'Once a scrutator ...' said Flydd.

He led the way across the roof and down a broad stone stair. As Karan followed, something crunched underfoot. The steps were littered with regurgitated owl pellets, full of grey fur and small, fragile bones. How easily they were crushed.

Flydd stopped on a landing several levels above the street and unlocked an iron-reinforced door, using three keys one after another. He went carefully along a dark hall, opened a second door, and the light was dazzling.

He swore, shaded his eyes and snapped, 'What the hell are *you* doing here?'

The room had once been a grand chamber, with high ceilings, large windows and intricate mouldings painted in many colours, though the plaster had come away from the laths in places, the ceiling and walls were mouldy and stained, and the broken windows had been crudely boarded up.

A mellow, slurred voice said, 'Toasting the end of the world.'

Flydd laughed. 'Even at the end of the world it's good to see you, old friend.'

On a long leather sofa, once magnificent but now battered and grubby, three scantily clad women sat around a handsome man of middle age, a dwarf with a wooden left foot. He raised an etched-glass goblet brimming with dark red wine. Empty bottles lay all around. A scarred redwood table bore a platter of pastries and two more bottles.

'Won't get up if it's all the same to you,' said the dwarf. 'Not sure I can stand at the moment.' He turned to the dark-skinned lass next to him. 'Open the best bottle, Telia my dear. Flydd's not an adaptable man; he can't abide the cheap stuff.'

'I think not,' said Flydd. 'We must talk privately. Right away.'

When Klarm had paid his companions and they were gone, Flydd said, 'This disreputable wretch is my old friend, the former Scrutator Nuceus Klarm, a mighty mancer and a good man to have on your side. I can't tell you how many times he's saved my life –'

'Twenty-three times,' grinned Klarm. 'And I only regret twenty-two of them.'

Flydd turned to Karan. 'This is –'

'Karan Elienor Melluselde Fyrn,' said Klarm softly. 'Well, well, well.'

'How did you know?' Karan cried, alarmed.

'I used my knoblaggie –' he held up a small brass object like three intergrown plums, '– to gate us to the top of the tallest tower of Shazmak, a couple of years ago.'

'What for?'

'To try and discover what had happened to you.' His eyes roved over Llian and Sulien, then Wilm and Aviel. 'Sadly, I overdid things; can't make gates anymore.'

'Who can?' Flydd said curtly. 'Apart from the enemy.'

Klarm did not reply.

Karan wasn't sure what to make of him. He looked like a drunken reprobate, but clearly there was much more to him. If Flydd wouldn't help her, maybe Klarm would.

Flydd introduced the others. Klarm rose, a trifle unsteadily, and shook hands with everyone. Karan noticed Sulien eyeing him apprehensively.

'You look out of place among all these scoundrels, my dear,' he said to her.

'Mummy and Daddy aren't scoundrels,' Sulien said hotly. 'And Wilm and Aviel are ... really nice.'

'But not Flydd,' Klarm said sagely. 'Don't worry, child, I can tell you where his bodies are buried, in case you ever need a hold over him.' He tapped the side of his nose and winked.

Sulien managed a smile.

'My daughter's around here somewhere,' Klarm added. 'Jassika's ten; I'm sure you'll get on famously.'

Sulien looked dubious. 'Is she ... um ... like you?'

'Unfortunately, not. She's disgracefully tall.' He raised his voice. 'Jass, Jass?'

'You have a child?' said Flydd in rank astonishment. 'I know you have a way with the ladies, you rogue, but ... *a child!*'

'And a lovely girl she is too,' said Klarm. He beamed. 'Here she is now.'

A girl clumped in, scowling. She was a foot taller than her father and seemed to have nothing in common with him. Her shoulder-length hair, ruler-straight, was the glossy black of a freshly shone boot. Her face was oval, her skin dark amber and her eyes almost purple. She would have been pretty, save for her furious expression.

'What do you want, *stumpy*?' she snapped.

'Don't hold back,' said Klarm. 'Say what you really think of me.'

'You're a lazy, irresponsible, drunken *womaniser.*'

'I've never understood why *womaniser* is supposed to be an insult.'

'You wouldn't! It's lucky you had to hack your left foot off.'

'Why is that, Jassika dear?'

'If you had two feet, the smell would be unbearable!'

Sulien's eyes were as wide and round as green plums. Karan fought down a smile.

Klarm grinned. 'Sulien, meet Jassika. She's refreshingly direct. Jass, show Sulien around and explain what's safe to do in Thurkad, and what's not.'

'Nothing's safe in Thurkad,' said Jassika. 'It's full of crooks and Father is one of the worst.' She offered her arm and, after a long hesitation, Sulien took it.

'Sulien, I don't think –' said Karan.

'Jassika is surprisingly responsible,' said Klarm. 'Compared to me, at least.'

Jassika rolled her eyes. 'An hour ago you called me a vexing little witch.'

'You were picking on my lady friends.'

'I wouldn't call them friends – or ladies.'

'Off you go. I'm busy.'

'You're always too busy for me.' She led a reluctant Sulien out.

'What's the bad news?' said Klarm, drawing Flydd aside.

'The Merdrun have inv–'

'Roros, Guffeons, Gosport and Fadd. I've got spies too. But that's not what's bothering you, is it?'

'Open a bottle, Klarm. I'm ... out of my depth.'

Karan found this alarming. Up to now, Flydd had been so commanding.

Llian sat on the other couch, next to Wilm and Aviel. Lilis went through the far door. Klarm extracted the cork of the nearest bottle and waved it at Karan. She shook her head.

'No, thank you,' said Aviel for herself and Wilm.

'I'll have some,' said Llian.

''Course you will,' said Klarm. 'Tellers! Pisspots, every one of you.'

He poured half the bottle into a none-too-clean goblet and handed it to Llian, then gave Flydd a small serving. Flydd scowled.

'Need your wits about you. Such as they are,' said Klarm.

'I – I've made a disastrous mistake, Klarm. Not sure we can recover from it.'

Klarm did not speak. Flydd summarised what he had said earlier about the state of the invasion, then paused.

'What else?' said Klarm.

'Two hours ago, Sulien had a *far-seeing*. The enemy gated a company of troops to the top of Mistmurk Mountain and searched it minutely.'

Klarm examined his broad hands. 'What for?'

'My *Histories of the Lyrinx War*. I wrote them while I was trapped up there. Very – detailed – Histories.'

'Judging by your doleful expression, they found them.'

'Yes,' Flydd croaked.

'So they'll soon know all about our battle mech-magic, and the names of the key artisans they'll need to take, to use it for themselves.'

'Plus all the people to kill, to gravely weaken us.'

Klarm sat back, suddenly looking sober. 'Whole battlefields and manufactories full of clankers, and other machineries of war, were abandoned after Tiaan destroyed the nodes, because without power they were useless. But now the fields are regenerating –'

'The enemy will take them and use them against us,' Flydd whispered. He was leaning forwards, his hands clenched and his bony jaw knotted. 'But that's not the worst.'

Klarm set his goblet down with a crash that snapped its stem. He quaffed the contents and tossed the bowl and stem at the fireplace, which was littered with broken glasses. 'Please tell me you didn't mention the scrutators' lost secret weapon.'

Flydd groaned.

YOU WORTHLESS LITTLE WRETCH!

P *lease, please let it work!*
   Battle Mancer Skald Hulni wiped sweat off his face and hands, then checked his makeshift scrying device again. He had cobbled it together following a design he'd glimpsed in the fifth book of *Histories of the Lyrinx War*. In the years preceding the invasion every Merdrun had been ordered to learn the enemy's common speech, and he could read it fluently.

But after discovering the amber-wood box at the bottom of a fern-covered ravine there had only been a few minutes to examine the books before Senior Sus-magiz Pannilie realised the *Histories* had been found. She snatched the book from Skald and sealed the box.

The enemy's mech-magical arts were foreign to the Merdrun, who had never seen anything like the complicated mechanisms they made to draw power from fields and control their mechanical contrivances and weapons of war. Skald did not expect his contraption to work but, if it did, it might give him the chance he so desperately needed.

His device was a jumble of crystals, wires, dials, toothed wheels and amber rods and other bits and pieces, surrounding a glass bowl shaped like an eggcup, which he had mounted above the centre of a pair of black concentric discs like compass roses. Heart beating very fast, Skald clamped a thick copper wire against one end of the yellow crystal and fixed a thin silver wire to the other end, then slowly rotated the small upper disc, and the larger lower one as well, *tick, tick, tick*.

Pinpoints of white light drifted back and forth across the curved base of the eggcup, climbed the sides, circled the base again – then a beam of brilliant green light burst upwards, scorching a path through his cropped hair. He sprang backwards, beating at it, and the smell of burnt hair filled the small room. The beam blinked on and off a dozen times and went out.

That wasn't supposed to happen. What had he done wrong? Leaning out of harm's way, Skald rotated the discs back to their previous positions. Again the searing, pulsing green beam.

It had worked – though not in the way he'd hoped. He marked the spot the beam had come from, wrote down the positions of the two discs, checked his map of Santhenar and located the source. Then sat down, shivering, though it was a hot day. He rubbed his hair, which was standing on end, and charred fibres drifted down onto the bench.

Skald had hoped to find a natural source of power. Or, if he was very lucky, locate an enemy adept using the Secret Art. But the pulses of light weren't a power source, or an adept. They appeared to be a signal or beacon, a powerful one, and it came from Alcifer, the long-abandoned city built for their great enemy, Rulke, in ancient times. But who had made the beacon? Who were they signalling, and why? Skald choked; this was *big*. This could finally give him the chance to rise above his family's shame.

Taking Santhenar was going to be bloody; tens of thousands of Merdrun would die, and dozens of sus-magiz, the magiz's deputies. Seven had been killed already. Yet every death created an opportunity, and there would be many opportunities for a determined, *worthy* young battle mancer.

Assuming he could climb the first, very difficult step and become a sus-magiz himself. The magiz, Dagog, hated Skald and would never agree to a trial – unless his hand was forced. *Dare I?* Skald thought. *I must!*

He packed the scrying device into a box and carried it out onto the main street. The air reeked of smoke, charred flesh, foul drains and ordure, human and animal. He hardly noticed – it was the same in every city the Merdrun attacked and, though he was only twenty-four, Skald had been part of many such attacks on a variety of worlds over the past half-dozen years.

He strode by hundreds of ruined and burned buildings, up to the squat watchtower on the highest of the five hills of the subtropical city of Guffeons, which the Merdrun had taken three days ago. After a modest slaughter, by their standards, the inhabitants of Guffeons had been ordered to leave or die, and most had fled. A few hundred, out of a city of 150,000, had refused to leave their homes or businesses and had paid the price, but once the city had been cleared the magiz reopened the Crimson Gate and the Merdrun civilians had come through.

The sight had brought tears to Skald's eyes. They had been hidden on a barren worldlet in the void for aeons, for their protection, but the Day of All Days was very close now.

He had not yet taken a breeding partner, but it was wonderful to see his people reunited at last. It meant that they were close to the goal they had ached for, ever since they were cursed and exiled by Stermin at the dawn of time. Skald was determined to be one of the few who finally gained the Merdrun's greatest desire. The yearning burned him – *only months to go.*

He suppressed the forbidden emotions that would fatally undermine him and strode on, clutching the box.

At the gate of the watchtower he saluted the ever-watchful guards. 'Battle Mancer Skald Hulni. I bear important news for High Commander Durthix.' His stomach throbbed. What if Durthix would not see him? Skald dared not go direct to the magiz, who would curse him and take all the credit.

'Captain Skald?' said the senior guard, 'who found the enemy's secret box the other day?'

'Yes, sir.'

'What is your news?'

'It's a military secret, sir.'

The guard pursed his cheeks. 'The High Commander does not wish to be interrupted.'

A senior sus-magiz appeared, a big, square-faced fellow called Widderlin, fourth below the magiz. 'What is it, Skald?'

'I've discovered something that could turn the war, sir.'

Widderlin drew him aside and Skald told him what he had done and found.

Widderlin looked in the box, then said to the guard, 'I'll take responsibility. Come with me, Skald.'

Widderlin escorted Skald through two more checks and he was allowed into a circular room, thirty feet across, at the top of the watchtower. A stair ran up to the guard post. The chamber contained six officers, an adjutant, High Commander Durthix and, to Skald's dismay, the magiz himself.

Dagog was small, wiry, hairless and none too clean, with glittering black eyes and a faint reek of decayed meat, none of which mattered a damn. A magiz could be man or woman, big or small, old or young, handsome or hideous. The only requirements were a brilliant gift for the Secret Art and an utter indifference to human suffering in enemy or friend.

Skald hastily turned his back. If the magiz recognised him he would be sent away unheard. Dagog hated Skald because of his father's cowardice in battle, and because Skald, who was big and strong and hairy, looked like a true Merdrun hero.

Widderlin had a quiet word to Durthix and after half an hour Skald was called over. The high commander was a large man, black-bearded and shaven of head, as all the senior officers were, though Skald was pleased to note that he topped Durthix by an inch and was equally broad in the shoulder. In the Merdrun army, size mattered. As did body hair, the more the better. On both sexes.

'Skald Hulni?' said Durthix. 'Who's he?'

'Battle mancer to the Ninth, sir,' said an adjutant, a slender, narrow-shouldered fellow, too meagre to ever qualify as a field officer. 'The young fellow who did such clever work on Mistmurk Mountain.'

Dagog bridled. 'Damn you, Widderlin! Skald's father was executed for cowardice and he's tainted too. Skald, get out!'

Skald fought the fatal emotions. The magiz was trying to break him, publicly.

Durthix turned a cold eye on Dagog. 'We're at war, Magiz, and this is *my* command.'

'There was a time –'

'And that magiz's harshness and obsession led us to the brink of ruin. That's why *I* am supreme, Magiz – and you are subordinate.'

'Fairness, justice, *mercy!*' the magiz spat, standing toe to toe with Durthix, though the high commander was twice his size. 'Your army is soft. We must return to the old ways.'

'An army ruled by fear cannot be a great army.'

'If *I* were supreme –'

'Are you challenging me?' said Durthix in a low voice.

Dagog took a step backwards and bowed. 'No, of course not.' His eye fell on the senior sus-magiz. 'Widderlin!'

'Yes, Magiz?'

'You are to gate to Ogur, deep in the south, within the hour. Prepare yourself and your company for a long stay.'

'Why Ogur?' said Durthix. 'It has nothing of strategic importance.'

'Are you questioning my authority over my sus-magizes?' Dagog asked coldly.

Durthix smiled thinly but said no more. Widderlin trudged out, his broad shoulders slumped.

Ogur, Skald knew, was a frozen wasteland. For supporting Skald, Widderlin was being sent into exile. That's the kind of man the magiz was.

Durthix gestured Skald across. 'Well, Battle Mancer?'

Skald, who had lost focus, was about to gabble when he saw the magiz's chilly eye on him. His smile exuded malice.

Sweat, Skald's personal affliction, oozed down his chest and sides. He waited for three painful heartbeats, then said, 'I've built a scrying device, High Commander, loosely based on an enemy design – and it's detected a strange signal or beacon that appears to be coming from Alcifer, the abandoned –'

'We know what Alcifer is,' hissed the magiz. 'Give it here!'

He held out his hand. His fingers, stained manure-brown, stank. Skald handed him the box and Dagog opened it, took out the scrying device and laid it on a bench.

'Would you like me to explain how it works?' said Skald.

'*I–am–magiz!*'

Dagog fixed the wires to the ends of the crystal and rotated the graduated circles one way then another, and back again. 'I see no signal.' He rotated them further, a tiny crystal winked, then the beam of green light roared upwards and began to pulse. He yelped, scrambled backwards and fell onto his back, thrashing like a four-legged crab. Skald fought to control his face; a twitch of the lip could doom him.

Dagog got up. 'Something amusing you, Skald?'

'No, Magiz.

The magiz returned to the device and studied it for several minutes, scowling.

'Well?' said Durthix.

'Clear the room, High Commander. We must talk.'

'What is it?' said Durthix.

'He's not dead,' the magiz whispered. '*He's back!*'

Durthix ordered everyone out. Skald went reluctantly. *Who* was back? And what should he, Skald, do? Questioning an order could mean a black mark on his record, but it wasn't forbidden, and he had to know more about his discovery.

Sweat dripped into his eyes. He wiped his forehead on a black-furred arm. Outside the door, he turned. 'High Commander?'

'Return to your post!' snarled Dagog. '*This–is–not–your–business.*'

'No, wait outside,' said Durthix, and closed the door.

It proved a long wait. Had Skald made some stupid blunder? Wasting the time of the magiz and the high commander might mark him as a troublemaker, someone expendable. Skald believed passionately in *One for All* and was almost as ready to sacrifice his life for the good of the Merdrun as the next man, though such a fate would prove his mother had been right about him. Pain stabbed him in the kidneys.

A memory struck him, one he had not taken in before. Someone had touched his mind when he was looking for the amber-wood box. An enemy; *a little girl.* He strained to recover the details but the memory vanished like mist in sunlight.

The door was wrenched open and Durthix said, 'Enter, Battle Mancer Skald.'

As Skald went in, his knees felt disturbingly weak. The commander's face showed nothing; it seldom did save after victory in battle, for triumph was an *allowable* emotion. The magiz looked sour and malicious; nothing new there.

'You have done well, Skald,' said Durthix. 'You have revealed something at Alcifer that could be an opportunity – or a threat.'

'May I ask what –?'

'You may not.' Then Durthix smiled, a fierce baring of big, square teeth. 'This is the second time you've impressed me, Battle Mancer. After your success at Mistmurk Mountain, you made a request to the magiz, I understand? One that was refused.'

'Yes, High Commander.'

'Do you wish to make the request again?'

'Yes, High Commander.'

Durthix jerked his head towards the magiz, whose face twisted in fury. Skald caught his breath. This would give Dagog the excuse to destroy him.

'Magiz Dagog,' said Skald, 'I request a trial to become a sus-magiz.'

In the past, the Merdrun had only had a few sus-magiz but, because their armies were spread across Lauralin, many more were needed for this invasion and for the Great Purpose to follow. Skald had dreamed about becoming a sus-magiz since he was a little boy, training with a slate sword on the barren rock in the void that the Merdrun nation had called home. Until now.

'You are aware of the risks?' said Durthix.

'No,' said Skald. 'The trial is secret.'

Dagog said, with a malicious grin, 'Those who fail the trial – *two out of every three* – are damaged and no use to anyone. They are staked through the belly, disembowelled alive and left for the dogs.'

A dishonourable and agonising death. Skald's mother would be vindicated. Accept or withdraw – he only had seconds to choose. Above all, a sus-magiz must be decisive.

Her voice echoed in his mind from a time she had flogged him as a little boy, after his father was executed for cowardice under fire, and Skald had committed the unforgiveable crime of asking his mother if she loved him. *Hide your emotions, you worthless little wretch, or you'll be put down too.*

'I will submit myself to the trial,' he said, voice rasping in his dry throat. 'I am determined to succeed, to the glory of our people. How long do I have to prepare?'

'There is no way to prepare for the trial,' said Dagog, 'and it will be held immediately you have learned the two spells. You have one hour to master them.'

'T-thank you, Magiz,' said Skald, shivering inside. 'I am proud to be one of the chosen few. And whether I succeed, or ... fail and must be ingloriously slain ... I am honoured at the chance to serve my people in a greater way.'

But inwardly he was consumed with treasonous rage. Oh, to have the magiz in his power, just for one minute. One day, Dagog!

A pair of red-robed acolytes escorted him down through an empty cellar and down again to a sub-basement, where the first acolyte handed him a sealed spell scroll. They backed away and waited by the steps. He wiped his face and broke the seal. The spell, inscribed in faded green ink on stained leather, looked as though it had been written a thousand years ago.

The basement was large, semi-circular and lit only by oily brown candles. Corpse candles, made from fat freshly rendered from the dead of Guffeons. If Skald failed, what was left of him would illuminate the sus-magiz trial of the next fool to beg for the chance.

It was hot, airless, and so humid that the walls were sweating. He felt an urge to shoulder the acolytes aside, bolt up the steps and run for his very life. But that would also be fatal – once the trial began the only way out was to succeed at it.

One chance in three.

Besides, running would prove the one thing about himself that he was desperate to deny.

Skald longed to sit and study the spell minutely, but a Merdrun never sat when he could stand, never stood when he could walk and never walked when he could run. He started to pace but each turn at the end of the room was distracting, so he walked in a figure-eight, struggling to commit the first spell to memory. As a battle mancer, he was used to learning spells in a hurry, but this one was longer than most, complex, and some of the words were difficult to make out. Yet he had to do it perfectly, first time.

He read the second spell, which was even more difficult. Panic choked him; how could he learn both spells in so little time?

His head throbbed, the thick air clotted in his throat and sweat had puddled in his boots, but a sus-magiz must be able to work under the most difficult of circumstances. As a battle mancer, Skald could draw considerable power from within himself, and also from the *im-har*, a little cubic box engraved with glyphs, on his left hip. But there were times when a sus-magiz needed greater sources of power – power that could be obtained wherever there were victims.

A sus-magiz had to be able to drink lives. That was the purpose of the first spell.

4

BRING IN THE VICTIM

All too soon Dagog entered. 'I despise you, you stinking son of a coward,' he said venomously. 'Nothing would give me greater pleasure than to flay your hairy pelt off you and drink your shitty little life.'

Was this part of the test? 'Yes, Magiz.'

'And when I find your weakness, I will.'

'Yes, Magiz.'

'But if by some miracle you pass the test, you're mine, body and soul.'

'Yes, Magiz.'

'Have you learned the spells?'

'Yes, Magiz.' If he said *no* he might be killed on the spot.

Dagog called outside. 'Bring in the victim.'

His eyes had a sickly gleam; he was looking forward to the spectacle. The magiz had drunk hundreds of lives, and rumour said he revelled in every one. The thought made Skald feel ill, but he had to prove himself worthy, or die.

A young woman was hauled in, a prisoner taken during the attack on Guffeons and probably kept alive for this purpose. Her hands were bound, her long dark hair tangled, her yellow gown stained and torn.

She looked from Dagog to the acolytes, then to Skald and back to Dagog, and her hazel eyes were large and wild. She did not know what was going to happen, but she was very afraid, and he felt a tickle of feeling for her. He suppressed it.

One truth was beaten into every Merdrun boy and girl from an early age – their enemies were subhuman. Their lives did not matter.

The magiz ordered the acolytes out and sealed the door. 'Because this is a trial,' he said, 'I will cast the protective charm that blocks the personality and,' he grimaced, 'the sad little *emotions* of the victim from coming through to you. *You* don't feel emotions, do you, Skald?'

'No, Magiz.' After Skald's father had broken and run in battle, his mother had taught him to utterly deny them. Skald's back still bore the scars.

The young woman reached out to him. 'Please let me go,' she said in a cracked voice. 'My kids got no food, no water ...'

Despite everything, the plea tugged at Skald's heartstrings. He suppressed the fatal emotions.

'If you succeed at the trial,' said Dagog, 'next time you will master the protective charm and cast it yourself. Are you ready?'

'Yes, Magiz,' Skald said hoarsely.

Dagog gestured to the young woman. 'Stand up straight. Don't speak your name.'

She looked desperate now; she must have guessed what was coming. She clenched her small fists in futile defiance and shrieked, 'Damn you! My name is Tataste!' She pronounced it Tar-*tass*-tay.

The magiz cursed her, cast the protective charm and gestured to Skald. *Now!*

He hardened his heart – whether he succeeded or failed, Tataste was doomed. No outsider could witness a sus-magiz's trial and be allowed to live, and if he displayed the smallest trace of empathy for her Dagog would flay him and drink his life. Skald had to become a sus-magiz. For the son of a coward, it was the first step to being safe.

He cast the spell on Tataste – no, *the victim* – and knew he had done it perfectly. He had established a magical link between her and himself, and within seconds the life force was flowing out of her into him, weakening her and strengthening him.

And he had never felt anything like it! His gift for the Secret Art was swelling, power surging through his veins like hot oil until the whole world of magic opened to him.

Tataste's freckled face crumpled and twisted as the life force was torn from her. She fell to her knees, reaching out to him in a last despairing plea, then raised her head and looked him in the eyes. He could not look away.

'Please,' she whispered. 'My little kids –'

With a sickening wrench the magiz's protection charm cracked and the *who* of her struck Skald so hard that he was almost overwhelmed: her hopes of returning to the home town she had left years ago; her longing for the young man she had foolishly turned her back on; her terror of the war and what it would mean for her parents and sisters; her desperate love for her little girl and boy, still huddled in the basement where she had hidden them when the invasion came. They must be hungry and frightened, crying out for the mother who would never come back.

He even saw their faces – the girl only three, with bowl-cut brown hair and soft eyes like her mother's, holding the little boy's hand and speaking to him soothingly, taking the responsibility seriously. 'Mummy will be back soon, I promise.' The boy, not yet two, small and pale and utterly bewildered.

Skald's own long-denied emotions surfaced and he was wrenched to the heartstrings, but Dagog's eyes were on him and if he showed any feelings he would die. Using the iron self-control beaten into every Merdrun from the day they could walk, he managed to suppress his horror and pity.

He had to end this before he cracked. He drew all the life Tataste had left in her in a single gulp and she fell dead at his feet, withered and shrunken and entirely pitiful.

Instantly he was overwhelmed by the power her life had given him, power far greater than anything he had ever felt before. It was exhilarating and seductive, but he had control of himself now. He needed it; he had to use that power and cast the second spell – a mighty enchantment only magizes and sus-magizes were allowed to learn – to create a gate from one place to another. It was massively more difficult than anything he had ever attempted before but with so much power at his disposal, and such golden inner confidence, he knew he could do it.

He cast the gate spell. Nothing happened. He cast it again. Not even the hint of a gate. The malicious smile reappeared on Dagog's sallow face and he drew a thin-bladed flaying knife. It had wavy brown stains from the last time it had been used, and smelled of rotten blood.

Sweat trickled into Skald's eyes. He dashed it away. The trial allowed three attempts at the gate spell; if he failed this time, the magiz would gleefully use the knife.

Using all his senses, Skald focused on the one destination he could visualise clearly enough, the dining hall of his barracks – stained wooden tables and benches, a haze of greasy smoke from the kitchens next door, the acrid smell of charred offal, the clatter of cutlery on wooden plates, the taste of leathery water buffalo meat and stringy banister beans – and cast the spell a third time.

A ragged porthole appeared in the centre of the room, crackling and rimmed with jumping blue sparks, and through it he saw the fifth table in the middle row, the place where he took his meals. Warm air hissed through the hole, carrying the reek of stewed cabbage, another staple of the disgusting diet here, then the gate collapsed in a shower of sparks.

The trial was over. His uniform was drenched in rancid sweat, his head throbbed, and he was so exhausted he was swaying. He had made a gate of sorts, but was it enough? And had Dagog noticed Skald's little slip before Tataste died?

Dagog seemed grudgingly pleased, though was he pleased because Skald had succeeded, or failed? Skald's gaze slid to the body of the young woman, crumpled on the floor like a deflated balloon, and flicked away. He could not afford to look at her; he forced himself to meet the magiz's eyes.

'You made an error,' said Dagog.

Skald's heart skipped a beat, then began to pound slowly and painfully. One chance in three. 'Magiz?' he croaked.

'You're sweating like a hairy pig, Skald. Are you feeling *emotional*?'

'It's this wretched climate,' he lied. 'I'm not used to the heat and humidity.'

Dagog smiled sourly. He knew it was a lie.

Skald straightened his shoulders. If he had failed, he would die on his feet with his head high. 'My error, Magiz?' he said, and this time his voice sounded true. 'What was it?'

After another drawn-out pause, Dagog said, 'You did not take power smoothly. You drank most of the victim's life in a single gulp.'

'I was too eager, Magiz.'

'Gulping a life is wasteful; inevitably, much of the victim's life force will be lost. Next time you will do it properly. You will savour that life as if it were a fine wine.'

Skald's heart gave another heavy thud. Next time? But there was no next time in a trial.

'Are you saying I've passed the trial, Magiz?'

'Are you suggesting that I've missed some critical failing in you?'

'No, Magiz.'

The magiz took a palm-length shard, an oily green in colour, from a locked case and held it up. 'This will be your *rue-har*. Look straight ahead. Make no sound. Do not flinch – that also counts as a failure.'

Skald swallowed, then stared over Dagog's head at a skull-shaped patch of mould on the far wall. The shard was as sharp as a flint blade and came to a wicked point on the end. Dagog raised his hand and for a hideous moment Skald thought the shard was going through his right eye, but Dagog touched it to the black Merdrun glyph tattooed in the middle of his forehead and thrust hard. Skald felt the tip of the rue-har embed itself in bone.

The magiz subvocalized a spell. Pain shrieked through Skald's forehead and it took all his self-control not to move or cry out. Power surged through the shard and into him; his head grew so hot he expected steam to gush from his nostrils. The magiz wrenched the shard out, dripping blood, put it in a small leather case and handed it to him.

'Guard your rue-har, Sus-magiz Skald. Lose it and you die disgraced.'

'Thank you, Magiz,' Skald said stiffly.

'I loathe and despise you, Sus-magiz, but I concede you have skill, courage and self-control, and I must accept you. Go to your barracks; prepare yourself for the morrow. You have many spells to master and much secret knowledge to learn. And remember this – as the lowest of my sus-magiz, you are *always* on trial. Always subject to the ultimate penalty if you fail me ...'

Dagog smiled, a sickening sight. 'I hope you do, Sus-magiz. I ache to drink your life. Clean up this mess.'

As if to demonstrate his own mastery of the Secret Arts, he made a small secret motion with his claw-like left hand and disappeared. Skald was about to let out a whoop when he thought better of it. Dagog had vanished silently, which probably meant he had just turned invisible and was still here, hoping Skald would reveal some fatal failing. If the magiz had transported himself away via any kind of gate, there would have been a hiss of air or a little *pop*.

Skald picked up Tataste's sad little corpse and carried it down the street to the nearest body pile, for burning. He ate and drank and went to the bathing chamber, then to his bed, his feet barely touching the floor. He was a sus-magiz – one of the chosen! In the next weeks and months, should he survive, he would learn secrets that not even Durthix, who had been a battle mancer of considerable power and subtlety, was permitted to know.

Secrets that had been handed down, magiz to sus-magiz, from Merdrax the First at the dawn of the Merdrun's existence. And one day, if he worked hard and had good fortune, and Dagog failed or was killed in battle, which Skald devoutly hoped for, he might achieve the ultimate honour and be made magiz in his stead. He would finally have escaped the family shame, and he would be safe at last.

On that happy thought he fell asleep.

In the darkest hour of the night he woke to hear someone groaning. Nightmares were not uncommon among the Merdrun, especially after they'd taken a fortress or city with slaughter and atrocities, but Skald was horrified to discover that the groans came from his own throat.

The nightmare came home to him with overpowering force as he saw deep into the mind of the helpless young woman he had killed, *for power*. Again he experienced Tataste's emotions, though this time there was no protective charm to shield him, and he felt her inner hopes and fears and terrors as deeply and desperately as she had, because they had come across the link as he drank her life and he did not know how to erase them.

As a true Merdrun, Skald had always seen outsiders as vermin to be destroyed, but now he knew Tataste had been a human being like himself, save that she had been good, kind, loving – and innocent. If he had ever been innocent, he did not remember it.

Then he saw her children again, as clearly as if they were right in front of him. *Mummy will be back soon, I promise*, the little girl had said to her brother.

Skald's gorge rose and he sprang up and vomited into the bucket at the foot of the bed. All around him the other sleeping soldiers stirred and muttered. He rose and dressed in his sus-magiz gown, took the bucket down to the privies and washed it out, then went to the dining hall and slumped on a stool, gasping.

A sentry came in, off the night watch. 'You look pale, Sus-magiz.'

'Something I ate,' lied Skald.

'Put your finger down your throat and get it all out. The muck they eat in this accursed city doesn't agree with me either.'

After he had gone, and Skald sat alone in the dimly lit hall, Tataste's face reappeared, pleading for her children. They had neither food nor water, and he could not have them on his conscience as well. Could he spirit them out of the city and leave them somewhere safe? Would that redeem him in some tiny way?

With the power stolen from her it would be easy to find out where she had been captured. He went out into the dark streets and, though he encountered many sentries on patrol, no one would question the doings of a sus-magiz.

Save another sus-magiz! Skald froze. What if the magiz was having him watched, waiting for the mistake that would doom him? Skald had to take the risk; in this hot climate the children would not last long without water. After taking extra precautions he cast his spells.

He found the street and identified the building where Tataste had lived, a crumbling rooming house, four storeys high, that had been emptied when the inhabitants of Guffeons were driven out three days ago. He located the basement, opened the door with an effort, for it was stuck, and went down ten steps.

And there he found them, the three-year-old girl and the little boy, huddled together between mouldy old chests and empty barrels, but they were dead. They must have tried the door, found they could not open it, then clung to one another until they died of thirst. It would not take long in this heat.

Tears welled in Skald's eyes and this time he did not fight them; he sank to his knees on the dirt floor and howled. He was a monster, a murderer of innocents, and for a mad instant he contemplated breaking into Dagog's apartment and choking him to death. He would fail, of course, and Dagog would torture him to the brink of death before drinking his life, though was even that enough to cleanse Skald's tainted soul?

He took the little bodies down the dark street to the burning pile and laid them beside their mother. Tears flooded his cheeks. He wiped them away and looked around in case someone had seen, but there was no one around at this time of night.

It would not do. He carried Tataste and her children to a park and found a pretty spot between three trees. Skald used a minor spell to dig a hole and laid Tataste in on her back, the girl clasped in her right arm and the boy in her left. He closed their eyes, wiped his own, carefully replaced the earth over them and covered the grave with stones.

He trudged back to the barracks but did not sleep for hours; he kept seeing the dead faces of Tataste and her little children. He would *never* drink another life!

What have we become? he thought. *No – what have we turned ourselves into?*

Skald woke in the pre-dawn with his body afire and the blood singing through his veins. Ah, the seductive feeling of taking all that power for himself, of drinking a life! He could not wait to do it again.

5

BEWARE OF THE SWORD, WILM

Hardly anyone here knew about Llian's banning by the College of the Histories two centuries ago, and surely no one cared. And the Santhenar of today was ripe for his talents. There were few chroniclers and tellers anymore and, after writing propaganda for the scrutators in the Lyrinx War, and for Jal-Nish the brutal God-Emperor after that, most were held in low repute.

A lifetime of fascinating work awaited Llian, stripping the Histories and the Great Tales of all the lies and exaggerations, and restoring them to their rightful place at the centre of human life on Santhenar. And crafting new tales that could well become Great Tales – stories from the Lyrinx War and the God-Emperor's monstrous reign, Llian's unfinished tale of the Merdrun's invasions ...

It felt as if he had struggled out of a raging sea into a paradise. And only the small matter of the Merdrun army standing in his way, he thought wryly.

The daydream now seemed foolish, a kind of denial. He looked around the faded magnificence of the great chamber, which might once have been a ball-room. Flydd's face was so pale that the criss-crossing scars stood out like basket weave. What had he and Klarm been talking about?

Klarm had said, 'Please tell me you didn't mention the scrutators' secret weapon.'

'It was destroyed in an air-dreadnought crash at the edge of the Sink of Despair,' Flydd said grimly. '*Wasn't it?*'

'What's the secret weapon?' Llian said eagerly. His instincts were aroused; there was an important tale here and he would not rest until he knew it.

'I can't tell you,' said Flydd.

'Where's the Sink of Despair, then?'

'North of the Great Mountains. A desert of sunken land, blisteringly hot in summer and freezing in winter, surrounded on three sides by mountains.'

'Can I be your official chronicler?' said Llian.

'*What?*' cried Karan.

'We have to eat!' Llian muttered. Why was she always undermining him?

'I don't need chroniclers,' snapped Flydd. 'I need mancers and armies, and a gigantic war chest. None of which I have.'

'I've never thought of you as a reckless man, Xervish,' said Klarm, filling another goblet. 'What possessed you to write about the secret weapon?'

'As a warning – that some devices are too dangerous to ever be used. It seemed safe to do so, since it had been destroyed –'

'But it *wasn't* destroyed.'

Flydd lurched to his feet, gaping at the dwarf. '*How come?*'

'Everyone on the air-dreadnought died in the crash, but when we went there to recover the secret weapon it couldn't be found.'

'Why not?' Flydd whispered.

Klarm shrugged. 'Perhaps it hid.'

'*Hid?*' croaked Aviel, her grey eyes huge. 'What kind of a device is it?'

It had to be an *intelligent* weapon. A device not just capable of assisting its owner, like Wilm's enchanted black sword, but of independent action and movement. Llian's mind raced through the possibilities, and most were dark. People were bad enough; how much worse would thinking machines be?

'It was the greatest secret of the war,' said Klarm. 'How did you find out about it, Xervish?'

'How the hell did it get past the scrutators' so-called ethics group?' said Flydd.

Klarm laughed hollowly. 'They weren't told; they would have forbidden it.' He rose, scowling at Flydd, and Llian was surprised to see that Klarm was the dominant man here. 'The Merdrun learned our languages last time they were here, and as soon as they read your *Histories*, they'll hunt the spellcaster down.'

'Don't say the name, damn you!'

'Bit late now.' Klarm sipped his wine and smacked his lips, ostentatiously.

'If they find it, they could reopen one of our abandoned manufactories and make thousands of copies.' Flydd paused for a long time. 'Then *erase* human life on Santhenar.'

'Then it has to be found.'

'And destroyed.'

'Brought back,' said Klarm.

'No, *destroyed*!' Flydd paced for a minute. 'You know more about it than anyone. Put together a search team. I'm flying east for help. I'll drop you at the Sink of Despair on the way.'

'Where are you off to?'

'If you don't know,' said Flydd with a flinty smile, 'you can't be forced to tell. Who will you take?'

'M'Lainte, if you can spare her. There's no one better when it comes to devices, mechanical or magical.'

'All ... right,' said Flydd, with great reluctance. 'Who else?'

'I came across a clever young artisan a while back, Ilisial. She can be M'Lainte's apprentice – if she agrees to take her on.'

M'Lainte frowned but said nothing.

'Half a dozen guards, and I'll need an assistant. Someone steadfast who can think on his feet.'

'You need Wilm,' said Llian, without thinking.

'No!' cried Aviel.

Wilm squeezed her hand, then rose. 'We're at war. I have to do my bit.'

Klarm looked dubious. 'You look a trifle young for this job, lad.'

Aviel's high voice rang through the room. 'Wilm's got the stoutest heart you'll ever meet. He taught himself sword fighting, then beat Cumulus Snoat's best assassin to save Llian. Then, defending me, he killed Unick at the summon stone; that's how Wilm lost half his ear. And on the Isle of Gwine he led the slave revolt that helped to beat the Merdrun army.'

'If you don't want him to go,' said Klarm, smiling at her passion, 'why are you promoting his qualities so vigorously?'

Aviel's cheeks had gone a charming pink. 'Wilm's the bravest man I know, and the kindest,' she said. 'If he wants to go, that's all that matters. *And* he's got Mendark's enchanted sword.'

'You've got *Akkidul*?' said Klarm.

Llian made a mental note of the name. That dark blade was mentioned a number of times in the Histories, though not during the time Mendark had held it.

Klarm held out a hand and, after a long hesitation, Wilm drew the black sword and handed it to him. Klarm felt along the blade with his fingertips, rubbed the hilt and put it to his ear. His heavy eyebrows rose, he stared at it for a moment, then gave it back. Wilm sheathed it.

'Press it right down,' said Klarm.

Wilm pushed the sword in until it would go no further.

'When it's all the way in, Akkidul can't hear,' Klarm added.

'Why does that matter?'

'An enchanted blade is, if you'll permit so feeble a pun, a double-edged sword.'

'I don't understand.' Wilm absently moved it up and down in its sheath.

'When an inanimate object is enchanted, this sometimes forms a *persona* – a kind of intelligence – within it. But the persona is trapped and can never escape, and if it feels unappreciated or ill-used it may withdraw its aid, or even deceive or betray its user. Beware of the sword, Wilm.'

Wilm looked down at the hilt, uneasily.

So much to learn, Llian thought. *Does any tale ever end?*

Klarm turned to Aviel. 'What can you do for us, my dear?'

Aviel, her eyes now downcast, whispered, 'I make scent potions.'

'I thought that art was lost long ago.'

'I – I've got Radizer's book,' she said, almost inaudibly.

'Master Radizer's lost grimoire? Where the blazes did you get it?'

'Shand gave it to me ... after I kept ... um, borrowing it.'

Klarm rolled his eyes. 'Come now. A master's grimoire is way beyond the capabilities of a half-grown girl.'

Llian was about to correct Klarm when Wilm interjected.

'Aviel's brilliant!' he cried. 'She made the scent potion that located the summon stone, and she can do alchymy, too.'

'Is that so?' Klarm was smirking. 'Is there anything this *little prodigy* can't do?'

'Don't you dare insult my friend!' Wilm said hotly. 'Aviel also made a batch of nivol to destroy the summon stone.'

Klarm stared at Flydd, then Wilm, then Aviel again. '*You – made – nivol?*'

'Twice, but I don't like alchymy,' said Aviel. 'I just want to be a perfumer.' Her eyes shone in the lamplight, then she looked down and the gleam went out and she was a timid girl again.

'Extraordinary! We must have a long chat before I go.'

Aviel did not look thrilled at the prospect. Llian wished Klarm would favour him with a long chat. He must have lived through a hundred tales.

'So must you and I, Klarm,' said Flydd. 'Do you happen to have a key to the ancient Magisters' spell vault?'

'What happened to your key?'

'Lost it.'

Klarm turned back to Aviel. 'Why are you here, my dear?'

'We – we came to the future by accident.'

His dark blue eyes narrowed. 'Not a sentence I hear very often.'

'Maigraith had hunted Karan and Llian and Sulien, and us, through Shazmak.' Aviel closed her eyes for a moment. 'We were on the wall at the top of the tallest tower, and Yggur had just materialised the construct. Llian and Sulien were inside, and I was telling Karan how to use the scent potion to see the right future –'

'I unbuckled the sword.' Wilm moved it up and down. 'And tossed it down to Llian, for luck.'

'You gave away an *enchanted* sword?' said Klarm.

'Llian needed it more than I did. But a bubble formed around the sword, and Aviel and me, and pulled us down into the construct. It was too late to get out.'

'Maybe Akkidul resented you giving it away. After all it had done for you.'

'More likely it resented being given to me,' Llian said with a rueful grin. 'When it comes to fighting, I'm a clodhopper.'

'I'm sure it would have helped you,' said Wilm loyally.

'It's marvellous how you've changed in the time I've known you,' mused Llian, remembering the nervous lad Shand had asked him to escort to Chanthed to sit the college scholarship test, only four months ago. 'You've utterly transformed yourself.'

Without my aid he'd be a shit-shovelling yokel! a reedy voice sneered from the copper scabbard.

Wilm had not pushed the sword all the way down. He flushed. Klarm gestured to him to draw the weapon and he laid it on the table between the empty bottles.

'Got something to say, Akkidul?' said Klarm.

The sword did not speak.

'Wilm's transformation came from within,' snapped Llian, offended for his friend, 'and it started long before we found the sword. Which Mendark had buried in a rusty old box in the desert. Why did he dump such a *famous* blade, I wonder?'

The sword rattled on the table. *Since you still haven't realised how Mendark duped you as a boy, your opinion is worthless.*

Llian stiffened. 'What are you talking about?'

Leaving home so trustingly *with him when you were twelve, to take up his scholarship at the College of the Histories.*

'I wasn't duped,' Llian said slowly, caught up in old but still painful memories. 'Mendark made the offer, and I talked it over with Mum and Dad, and we agreed I'd take it. I didn't want to go so far away, but we were poor and the scholarship was too good to refuse ...'

Llian's time at the college had transformed him. It had given him the opportunity to become a great chronicler and teller – perhaps the greatest of the age – though the cost had been a lot higher than he had expected.

You didn't choose freely at all, sneered Akkidul. *I was there.*

'I don't know what you're talking about,' Llian said dazedly.

You were going to say no, weren't you?

'Well, yes ... but I changed my mind.'

Mendark could never take no *for an answer. He cast a compulsion on you to make you change your mind. And another on your parents to allow you to go.*

'That's not true!' cried Llian. 'He was good to me ... at least, in the early days.'

When you got to Chanthed, Akkidul continued relentlessly, *what did Mendark say to you?*

'"Never forget how much you owe me."'

Then he ordered Master Wistan to persecute you for being an accursed Zain, and make sure letters to and from your family never reached their destinations, so you'd forget them and focus all your energy on your studies.

'You're a stinking liar!'

Did you receive a single letter from your family in the sixteen years you spent at the college?

It was a hammer blow to the gut; Llian barely had the breath to speak. 'No,' he choked. 'But –'

You thought they were angry with you for going.

'A little, but ...'

And you never went home.

'I missed them desperately ... and everyone hated me because I was –'

A treacherous Zain!

Llian flushed. 'But it was a six-month journey home to Jepperand, and cost a fortune ... and my stipend was just enough to live on ...'

Mendark made sure of that.

'I – I finally got home twenty years later,' said Llian, the old guilt rising until it choked him. 'But Dad and Mum were dead ... Mum of grief, the neighbours said. My two sisters were long gone, no one remembered where. And it all was my fault! How could I have believed they'd turn their backs on me?'

The sword sniggered. *The proud chronicler is finally humbled. Never thought I'd see the day –*

'Damn you!' cried Wilm, thrusting the sword into its sheath and pushing it all the way down. 'Llian, don't take any notice.'

What a fool I've been, Llian thought.

How betrayed his family must have felt. His little sister, Alyz, only six at the time, had pleaded with him not to go. *Llian is never coming home again*, she had wailed. *Never, never, never!* It had nearly broken him. The long journey south, then west to Chanthed, had been the worst six months of his life. His only consolation had been that his family wanted him to get the best education he could, and he had been determined to make them proud.

Why had Mendark done such a monstrous thing? So Llian would be forever in his debt, of course. What a bastard! No favour without an eternal obligation.

Alyz, Alyz, how could I have hurt you so?

'You said you'd corresponded with your family,' Karan said quietly. 'You told me several times.'

'I couldn't bear to admit that they'd never answered my letters,' he muttered.

'How could you keep such a thing from me?'

He lowered his voice further and said pointedly, 'Says the woman whose whole life is built on secrets. And I'll bet they're a lot darker than mine.'

A pink flush moved up Karan's throat. His intuition was right; she *was* keeping something from him. Something really important.

'Well, you left home twenty-eight years ago,' she said. 'We've got to focus on what matters now.'

How could she be so indifferent to a revelation that had torn his life apart? It proved that she no longer cared about him; she was just pretending for Sulien's sake. Llian stalked to the far corner of the room, flung himself down in a grubby armchair and stared at the boarded-up windows, thinking bitter thoughts. Perhaps it was for the best. It made his decision more justifiable, at least.

'I'll get organised,' Klarm said quietly, and went out.

CRACK!

A small square gate opened beside Llian, its edges glowing like plaited red-hot wires, and hot, humid air hissed out. He scrambled backwards but crashed into the wall. A dark hand appeared in the opening, pointing at him.

Zzztttt! There came a bright blue flash and he was jerked off his feet and drawn towards the gate.

He tried to catch the edge with his left hand but there was another flash, a blinding pain in his little finger, a wisp of smoke, then he was drawn through the gate and flung into darkness.

As he tumbled through nowhere, Llian clutched his throbbing left hand with his right. The little finger was gone, severed by the side of the gate. He landed hard on an unseen floor, raising dust, and the gate disappeared. Where was he? Why would the enemy take him, of all people? What did they want from him?

He crouched in a dark space, shivering. The Merdrun had a rare mastery of torture and he was not good at enduring pain. This was going to be bad.

6

YOU FINALLY SHOWED SOME SPINE

As the gate snapped shut, something arced through the air, trailing smoke, and landed with a plop on a plate of pastries in front of Karan. Llian's left little finger, cauterised as if by a red-hot knife, was pointing at her as if accusing her.

She shrieked and ran for the gate, but it had vanished. She came back and picked up the finger, shivered and put it down again. The air reeked of charred flesh, Llian's flesh. Who had taken him? What were they going to do to him? Her knees wobbled and she had to sit down. Why had she been such a heartless bitch?

She clutched her head with both hands, shaking it. Her stomach heaved and she thought she was going to throw up. Where had they taken him? She tried to get up but could not; there was no strength in her legs or arms. She was failing him again.

'M'Lainte,' rapped Flydd, 'I need the gate-scrier, quick.'

M'Lainte was already lumbering towards the door.

Karan watched numbly as, with the tip of his staff, Flydd traced faint silver lines, the edges of the former gate, and studied them from both sides until they faded. He returned to the couch and sat down heavily, scowling at his staff, which was as battered and gnarled as the rest of him. 'So it begins.'

Karan's throat was so tight she could scarcely draw breath. 'Where'd they take him?'

Flydd did not reply.

'I saw a hand. A big, dark hand.'

'Most of the enemy are big and dark.'

Sulien burst in. 'What was that noise?' She looked around. 'Where's Daddy?'

'Don't – know,' Karan whispered. The loss of him was unbearable; she could not think; she was lost.

'He was dragged through a gate,' said Flydd. His eye drifted to the finger. 'At least, *most* of him.'

'They cut off Daddy's finger?' Sulien said shrilly. 'You've got to find him!'

'We don't know where to look,' Karan said numbly. 'Come here.'

She reached out and Sulien ran to her, clinging desperately. Everything was falling apart. Why had she brought her family to this dreadful future?

Sulien wrenched herself away. 'Mister Flydd, can't you do something!'

'He could be a thousand miles away, child,' said Flydd. 'In any direction.'

How had the enemy known he was here? Why had they taken Llian, of all people? And, terrifying thought, they could take Sulien just as easily.

'Why did they chop Daddy's finger off?' said Sulien. She picked up the empty bottles and stacked them near the door. She always tidied when she was upset.

'I think it was an accident,' said Karan.

'Could a healer grow it back?'

'Not unless we can recover Llian in the next hour,' said Flydd.

Karan's bad leg was hurting again. She went to one of the grimy windows, pulled a moth-eaten curtain aside and peered out into the darkness. Even abandoned and crumbling, Thurkad retained an air of ancient wickedness. Now it was home to plunderers picking over the ruins, thieves preying on anyone foolish enough to come back, and outlaws of every description. Plus a brace of ex-scrutators, up to who knew what villainy.

Why had she fought with Llian? Gothryme was gone and there was no going back. To do so would prove that she was in thrall to her heritage. But her love of the land was bone-deep. It was her spirit, her soul, her place. It was her duty to work the land and look after it, and hand it down to Sulien who would love it and protect it in turn, and pass it to her own daughter one day.

She trudged back. 'Did you have fun with Jassika, darling?' Karan hoped Sulien had made a friend.

Sulien crashed two round wine bottles together, breaking one of them. 'She's very rude.'

M'Lainte burst in, red in the face. 'The gate scrier's gone!'

Flydd raced up to the sky galleon. Karan, M'Lainte and Lilis followed.

He was rifling through the storage compartments down below, and cursing. 'Field scanner's gone too.'

'And the spare controller for the sky galleon,' said M'Lainte. 'But who –?'

Flydd whirled, eyes glinting. 'Never trust a man who comes back from the dead.'

'You sort-of came back from the dead,' Lilis reminded him. 'Twice.'

He came up and they returned to the room where they had found Klarm.

'A life-renewal spell isn't exactly death.' Flydd raked his cheeks with hooked fingertips. 'Though ... it's the most agonising pain the human body can experience.'

Worse than giving birth to Sulien? Surely he was exaggerating. 'Why would Rulke want those devices?' Karan said stiffly.

'How would I know? He's *your* friend!'

'He was never my friend. Rulke was ... above friendship, if that makes any sense.'

'*It doesn't!* Now the bastard has gone over to the invaders.'

'That's ridiculous. The Charon and the Merdrun have been mortal enemies for aeons.'

'We only have Rulke's lying word for that.'

'You don't know what you're talking about,' Karan said coldly.

Flydd's craggy face went purple. 'You've got a nerve – after we flew five hundred leagues across Lauralin to rescue you.'

'We didn't need rescuing. And your unbelievable negligence has made things disastrously worse.'

Lilis gasped. M'Lainte let her breath out in a hiss.

'Well, if you don't like it here, piss off!' said Flydd.

A reckless urge overtook Karan, to pull down all bridges behind her. 'I will. We're going home, right now! Sulien, get your pack.'

M'Lainte caught Karan's arm in a surprisingly strong grip. 'No one's going anywhere. What did you mean about Rulke?'

Karan fought down the rage. She could not afford to close off options now. 'When Sulien first saw the Merdrun, I lifted the nightmare from her and searched it for clues –'

'I didn't know nightmares could be removed and studied,' said Flydd, calmly now. 'That's a useful gift.'

'And extremely painful; I couldn't do it with the next nightmare. The one where she saw their secret weakness.'

'Go on.'

'Their leader, Gergrig, told his magiz that Rulke was the only person they had ever feared.'

'But when he came out of stasis,' said Flydd, 'and discovered he was the last of his kind, Rulke probably decided to ally with them. They come from the same stock, after all, and blood is thick.'

He turned away. 'There are beds down the hall. Get some sleep, everyone. We're got a lot to do before we leave.'

Sulien picked up her pack and went down the corridor. Lilis and M'Lainte followed. Karan did not move.

'What – about – Llian?'

He sighed. 'The enemy are slaughtering innocent people in their tens of thousands. I can't turn my back on them to look for one man.'

'Then I'll go looking for him myself.'

'I'd prefer you didn't.'

'Why the hell not?' she said furiously.

He hesitated for a long time before saying reluctantly, 'I ... need your help.'

'But you wrote *five* books about the war. You named hundreds of allies.'

'The war ended fourteen years ago, Karan, and half of them were killed during the God-Emperor's ten-year reign of malice.' Flydd stared into infinite distances, his face rigidly controlled, then shook himself and said quietly, 'And of those that survived, many have been rounded up already. The Merdrun will torture everything they know out of them, then kill them. Santhenar's finest gone in a heartbeat, doomed because of my *Histories* – and I can do nothing to save them.'

Karan could read him now. Flydd was overwhelmed by grief, and guilt.

'Now Klarm and M'Lainte have to go after my other folly, the spellcaster,' he went on, 'and it could take a long time to find it – if they come back at all. Lilis has ... her own job to do. My few remaining allies are thousands of miles away, and even in the sky galleon it'll take days to reach them, since I don't have the power to make gates anymore.' Flydd met her eyes, and he was almost begging. 'Right now, Karan, you're all I've got.'

How could she refuse? 'As long as you promise to find Llian, the moment we're done.'

'I'll look for him when I can. But you'll have to send Sulien somewhere safe. It's too dangerous to take her with us.'

Her knees gave. *No, no, no!* 'I did that to her before. I can't do it again.'

To save Sulien from Maigraith, Karan had entrusted her to the Whelm, who had treated her harshly, then betrayed her to the magiz. Had it not been for faithful, tormented Idlis, Sulien would be dead.

'It has to be done,' said Flydd, more kindly.

'What if I'm killed?' said Karan.

'I'll make arrangements for her to be looked after, just in case.'

With Llian gone, and possibly dead, Karan had no choice. But how was she to tell Sulien? She would feel abandoned all over again. She would be shattered.

Karan lay awake, leafing absently through Llian's journal, left behind when he had been dragged through the gate. He would be lost without his precious notes about the Merdrun and their first invasion. They now faced a far worse one, and an enemy so malevolent she could not summon up a smidgeon of hope, because they had no army, no allies and nothing to fight with ...

A hand on her shoulder and she was dragged unwillingly from sleep. It took a dozen heartbeats before she recognised the slim figure beside her.

Karan threw herself backwards across her bunk. 'Maigraith!' she choked.

Maigraith put a finger to her lips. 'Don't wake the child.'

Karan forced herself up in bed, shaking so badly that she had prop herself up. Always, Maigraith exceeded her worst fears. 'How – how did you find us?'

'I'm one of the great powers these days.'

'What do you want?'

'The coming battle will define us all. Prove us, or destroy us.'

'Just as you're planning to destroy my family,' Karan said bitterly.

'You haven't changed at all,' said Maigraith.

'It's only been four days since we fled Shazmak.'

'And 214 grinding years for me.'

'You've weathered them well enough,' Karan lied.

Maigraith had aged slowly, as one with her Charon and Faellem heritage must, yet two centuries had greatly changed her. The muscles of her arms had become stringy, her skin was dotted with age spots, and every year of her unhappy and vengeful life could be read in the lines engraved into her thin face.

'Once set upon a course I follow it to the end,' said Maigraith. 'No matter how bitter.'

'You want revenge on me for escaping to the future.'

Maigraith smiled, a rare and disturbing sight. 'On the contrary, I admire you – you finally showed some spine. More than two hundred years went by before I unravelled the tangle of lies and misdirections your friends set up, and realised that you three were still alive, but I could not discover which future you'd gone to.'

'When did you find out?'

'Half an hour ago, when Flydd called me.'

Karan froze. 'Flydd ... *betrayed* us?' He had called Maigraith here, even knowing she was Karan's deadly enemy?

'He was a scrutator,' said Maigraith. 'He does what needs to be done.'

'And here you are, ready to torture us all over again.'

'Yes, here I am.'

Karan could not go through all that again. Flydd had ordered them to say nothing about Rulke, but damn him!

'After you hear what I tell you,' said Karan, 'you'll never be interested in Sulien again.'

'I never give in,' said Maigraith.

'Rulke was the love of your life.'

Maigraith wrapped her arms around her chest, hugging her thin body.

'He's still alive,' said Karan.

Maigraith's remarkable indigo and carmine eyes flashed, her thin-lipped mouth curved down. 'You've been with Llian the Liar so long, you've become him.'

'When Rulke took that fatal wound in Shazmak, 224 years ago, he had a stasis spell ready and cast it on himself. Later Yalkara reinforced it, then put a slow healing spell on him and hid his body inside the granite statue in Alcifer.'

Maigraith went very still, then reached out and touched Karan's forehead. 'You ... truly believe the lies you're telling.'

'Rulke and Yalkara planned it long ago, in case either of them was mortally injured. It looked as though he had died, but inside he was preserved by the stasis spell, so it and time could heal him.'

'It's – not – credible.' Maigraith wanted to believe it, though. She wanted it desperately.

'When we were in Alcifer, Sulien sensed someone alive in the statue, and freed him. Ask her. Ask Flydd or Lilis or M'Lainte. We all saw Rulke and talked to him.'

Maigraith's stern face cracked, her desperate longing breaking through, and for a second or two she glowed. 'I always felt close to him when I was by his statue.' But the mask reformed, the elderly woman reappeared. 'I've been disappointed too many times,' she said stolidly. 'I can't bear to hope ... How – how was he?'

'Weak. And still troubled by the healed wound we thought had killed him. But otherwise, like the Rulke of old.'

'Did he – ask about me?' Maigraith whispered.

'No.'

'But we swore to one another, *forever!*' Maigraith twisted the heavy gold ring on her finger. 'He would never forget.' She looked up. 'Where is he?'

Karan shrugged. 'Seconds before the Merdrun opened the Crimson Gate, he vanished.'

Maigraith smiled enigmatically. 'He'll come back for me.'

'What about Sulien?' Karan needed assurances.

Maigraith looked over her shoulder at the sleeping child and her hard face softened. '*If* what you say is true, I will renounce all claim on her.'

'Swear it ... on the ring Rulke gave you.'

'Is my word not good enough for you?'

'*Swear it!*'

Maigraith slipped off the heavy gold ring, once Rulke's, which he had shrunk to fit her finger only weeks before his apparent death. She laid it in the middle of the palm of her left hand, covered it with her right and said, 'I swear on this ring, the symbol of my undying love for Rulke, that if he is still alive I renounce all claim on Sulien, forever.'

'What about me? You swore undying revenge on me.'

Maigraith laid her palm on the ring again. 'I will renounce it, too.'

'Just like that?'

'It would no longer be relevant.'

'And Llian?'

'He aroused my hopes with a despicable lie,' she grated. 'Revenge on Llian I will have.'

Karan's fury flared. 'You bitch! You've cost me my home and my friends. You're not touching Llian.'

'I will pay reparation, enough to restore Gothryme, if that's what you want.'

The abandoned manor and estate buildings were probably in ruins, the land overgrown. It would cost a fortune to rebuild and bring it back into production ... but she never wanted to be beholden to Maigraith again.

'I don't want your stolen money.'

'I'm not a thief,' Maigraith said stiffly. 'Everything I have, I've earned.'

'The only reparation I want from you is Llian.' *Assuming he still wants me.*

'And if he's still alive I'll find him – *but not for you.*'

7

DON'T BE SUCH A SOOKY LITTLE BABY

Sulien was woken by whispering in the early hours, and the other woman's voice was so terrifyingly familiar that she almost wet the bed. *Maigraith!*

Sulien lay there, shivering, until Maigraith was gone, then crept across in the dark and got in with Karan. 'What are we going to do, Mummy?'

'You heard?' Karan whispered, drawing her close. 'She's not after you anymore.'

'I don't believe her.'

'It'll be different now. Rulke's all she ever wanted.'

Sulien sniffed. That might be true, but she would never trust Maigraith. Never ever! 'What are we going to do about Daddy?'

After a long pause, Karan said, 'Why would the enemy want him?'

For revenge, just as Maigraith did. Sulien could not say it aloud; that would make it so much worse. She twisted her fear into a knot and thrust it down deep.

'Can you find him, Mummy? Through a mind-link or something?'

'I've hardly ever been able to link to Llian ... But don't worry, darling, I'm working on a plan. We'll get him back –'

Sulien was so annoyed that she wrenched free and stumbled back to her own bed.

'Sulien, what's the matter?' Karan said anxiously.

Sulien pretended to be asleep. Why did grown-ups say such stupid things?

No one could make that kind of promise. The Merdrun tortured their prisoners, then killed them –

She had to bite her fingertips, harder and harder until her teeth broke the skin and she tasted blood, to prevent herself from screaming. Karan had no way of finding Llian, and Flydd was far too busy. And if Maigraith found him she would take a terrible revenge.

It was up to Sulien. She had to find Llian first. And she had two advantages no one else had – she could far-see, and somewhere within her was that lost memory about the enemy's fatal weakness. Could she, dare she use it to bargain for Llian's freedom?

She nearly choked. It was the most desperate idea she'd ever had, and if Karan even heard a whisper of it ... it would be very bad. But Sulien had no choice. If she could not save Llian the enemy would kill him.

But how was she to begin?

A memory popped up, of poor little Uigg, the Merdrun drum boy, and the strange mental connection that had grown between him and herself. Uigg had been so proud, so terrified, so doomed. A tear ran down her cheek.

The connection, the way they had communicated, reminded her of another Merdrun whose mind she had touched.

'Skald!' she whispered.

'What's that, darling?' Karan said sleepily.

'Nothing, Mummy. Go to sleep.'

It was not nothing. When Sulien sensed Skald searching for the amber-wood box at the top of Mistmurk Mountain he had reminded her of someone, and she now realised that it had been Uigg. But why?

Skald wasn't a powerless kid; he was a tough soldier with a gift for the Secret Art. But he was tormented too, and she had a feeling that it was important. Could she use him to find out where the enemy had taken Llian?

It was a desperately dangerous thing to do. Karan would go out of her mind. But since neither Karan nor anyone else could do a thing for Llian, Sulien had to find a way.

In the morning everyone was frantically busy, and Karan wanted Sulien out from under her feet. 'Go and play with Jassika,' she kept saying.

Sulien did not like Jassika, who was loud and rude and bossy, always insulting her own father or making snide remarks about Flydd. She was even rude to Lilis, who was perfectly nice and kind, though she did live in a world of her own.

And Jassika was always rubbing her scarred knuckles and saying, 'I dare you.'

'I dare you to steal a bottle of wine from Flydd.' 'I dare you to go exploring in the wickedest part of Thurkad,' and now, after throwing a rope across to the roof of the crumbling building next door and tying both ends down, 'I dare you to walk the tightrope.'

The rope swayed in the breeze and Sulien felt a spasm of terror. 'No way. I'd fall.' The drop was at least thirty feet. Enough to break bones, if not kill her outright.

'If you do it,' Jassika said slyly, 'I'll ask Klarm to find Llian.'

Sulien was so outraged she could not speak. Did Jassika want her to fall and be badly hurt, or was she just trying to attract attention? 'I – I can't.'

'Don't you care if your father lives or dies?'

The only thing stopping Sulien from slapping Jassika was the certainty that the tall girl would thrash her. She had the air of someone who had been in a lot of fights. 'I don't have to answer to you.'

'Scaredy-cat! I'll show you how easy it is.'

Jassika took off her boots and socks, picked up a long pole, stepped up onto the wall surrounding the roof then, holding the pole horizontally in both hands, put a foot on the rope. She wobbled, steadied herself, stepped on with her other foot and went forwards confidently.

She wobbled again, the pole dipped to the left and she tilted that way, letting out a small, stifled cry. Jassika forced the pole down to the right, regained her balance and took another step, and another and another.

She laughed and looked back at Sulien. 'It's easy, see!'

Maybe it was, for her. Her father had been an acrobat once and, for all Sulien knew, Jassika had been practicing ropewalking for months.

It wasn't so easy out in the middle, though, where the wind, funnelled between the two buildings, was stronger. Sulien could see the strain in Jassika now. Every muscle was tense, and she was constantly using the pole to get her balance back.

She swayed wildly, let out a squawk of terror, almost fell, regained her balance and then – to Sulien's astonishment – Jassika *ran* up the curve of the rope and over the side of the building next door, onto its roof.

She sprang into the air, raising the pole above her head in exultation. 'See how easy it is.' Then she doubled over and threw up on her feet.

'You don't care whether you live or die,' Sulien muttered after Jassika came back, via the stairs. There was vomit between her toes and she did not wipe it off; she did not seem to care about such things.

'That was the best! You've got to try it.'

'No, thanks,' said Sulien.

'You're so unfriendly. Why are you always pushing me away?'

'You're always trying to make me do things I don't want to do.'

'Just have a go! It's so exciting.'

'I can't.'

'Don't be such a sooky little baby.'

Sulien walked away towards the stairs.

'You think you're better than me. You don't like me because my father's a dwarf.'

'You're right!' snapped Sulien. 'I don't like you. But it's got nothing to do with Klarm. I like *him*.'

'Well, your mother doesn't like *you*,' Jassika spat. 'She's sending you away so she can go adventuring with ugly old Flydd.'

'You're a stinking liar!' Sulien screamed. 'I hate you.'

She bolted down to the room she shared with Karan and hid under the bed in the dust and cobwebs. Jassika called, over and again, but Sulien did not come out. Some friend!

She was too loud, too wild and rude, and too much a troublemaker. Sulien could never trust her. But after being stalked by Maigraith, repeatedly hunted by the Merdrun, and betrayed by the Whelm, who could she trust?

She liked Aviel and Wilm, but Aviel was staying here to make a double batch of nivol in a workshop Flydd was setting up for her, while Wilm was going off with Klarm and M'Lainte to some dreadful place called the Sink of Despair, to look for a mysterious device lost long ago.

Was Karan really going to send her away? Sulien did not want to believe it. Besides, the enemy were too strong, and whatever Karan and Flydd tried to do was bound to fail. They would be killed and Sulien would be left all alone.

Jassika's right, she thought, burning with guilt. I mustn't love Daddy enough to try and save him. But she still wasn't game to walk the tightrope, on the unlikely chance that Jassika would convince Klarm to help.

It had to be Skald, then.

When Sulien crept out again, hours later, everyone was so busy making last minute preparations and getting the sky galleon loaded that there was no time to talk to Karan. Sulien and Jassika were kept busy carrying bags and sacks, boxes and small barrels, and buckets of water to fill the sky galleon's twin tanks. Jassika avoided Sulien, for which she was grateful. She had to stop Karan sending her away.

It wasn't going to be easy, especially with the anniversary only days away. The twenty-fourth. Karan was always distracted and jumpy around that day. Tormented.

When all the preparations were done, Flydd and Klarm called Karan aside. 'We'd better make the arrangements. But not here, where little ears might hear.'

Sulien gave them thirty seconds and crept after them, down to a grubby, water-stained kitchen that stank of drains and rotten vegetables. Sulien crouched at the top of the steps, in the shadows, watching and listening.

'I can't take Jass to the Sink of Despair,' said Klarm, 'because there's a good chance I won't come back. But I can't leave her here, either. Thanks to your *Histories*, Xervish, we're all targets now.'

Flydd's jaw tightened but he did not reply.

'And the moment the Merdrun discover we came to the future,' said Karan, 'we'll be targets too. Maybe we already are.'

Of course we are, Sulien thought. That's why they took Daddy.

'The girls have to go somewhere safe,' said Klarm. 'Where no one would think to look for them.'

'There's an old couple I used to know,' said Flydd. 'Rather odd ...' He frowned, and Sulien gained an impression that he did not like them much. 'But reliable, and they live in the middle of nowhere. I won't say the place aloud.'

Mummy, no! But Sulien knew there was no point begging.

'I'm not leaving my daughter with strangers again,' Karan said flatly.

'You can't take her where we're going. It'll be far too dangerous.'

'Why do you need me, anyway?' said Karan.

Flydd sighed. 'Because you know the Merdrun. And their magizes.'

'What if I'm killed? What if Llian is already dead? You said –'

'The arrangements will include provision for the girls' protection and education, and other expenses, until they're of age.'

Sulien pressed her forehead against the wall until it throbbed. How could Karan send her away – *give* her away! – as though she were an unwanted puppy?

Karan covered her face with her hands. 'I – can't – do – it.'

'When you came to the future,' said Klarm, 'why did you chose this particular time?'

'It ... just seemed right.'

'Don't you find it odd that the Merdrun's invasion began only days after you got here?'

'It did seem unlucky.'

'It had nothing to do with luck,' said Klarm. 'I think the summon stone influenced you to end your jump at precisely that moment.'

Why would it do that? Sulien thought.

'Because Sulien saw the Merdrun's fatal weakness,' whispered Karan, sitting down with a thump. 'And they have to eliminate the risk.'

8

WHAT YOU'VE GOT INTO BED WITH

A warm wind whipped across the rooftop, raising dust from the corpse of the dead city and tickling Wilm's nostrils as he hauled barrels of wine, ale and oil up a ramp into the sky galleon. He would have been happy never to see Thurkad again, had Aviel not been staying behind to make more nivol, the only substance that could destroy the summon stone.

She wasn't happy about it but had not complained. Wilm hated it that people walked all over her, just because she was small and young and shy.

As he carried the last barrel up, a small, sloshing one with *black beer* stencilled on the end, a single pink ray climbed the eastern sky, then blushed out to either side like a pair of feathers. Dawn. Time to go.

He turned and there she was, her wind-stirred hair touched by pearly shimmers in the growing light. Aviel had been his dearest friend since he was four and she was two, and he wanted to run and take her in his arms and never let go. Wanted it achingly, but she was complicated and solitary, and shied from physical contact.

Resentment surged. He'd done a lot for her over the years, asking nothing in return, yet she kept withdrawing, and it had got worse since that depraved brute, Unick, abducted and tormented her. The pressure in Wilm's head rose until white specks drifted across his field of view. His fingers clamped around the hilt of his sword and he fought an urge to hack the nearest crate to pieces.

But an impoverished boy with no father spent a lifetime suppressing urges that would do him no good, biting his tongue and bowing to his betters. Besides, Unick was dead. Wilm had killed him months ago to save Aviel and avenge Dajaes, so why was he dwelling on the swine? Because Aviel still had nightmares about that time, and so did he.

'Let's get going,' called Flydd from the bow.

Aviel's big hazel eyes caught the light and she took a step forward, gazing at Wilm yearningly. But yearning for what? He moved towards her then stopped, confused, the small resentment still stinging. She bit her lip and made a small, reaching movement with her arms. He froze, sure that if he went to her, she would push him away again.

Her cheeks turned pink. Her arms dropped and she lowered her head.

'Get aboard, boy!' bellowed Klarm. 'Save the tragic farewells for when you become a man – if you ever do.'

Wilm fought a temptation to boot the little man off the roof.

Aviel rubbed her eyes. 'Goodbye, Wilm. I hope –' Her voice broke. She turned away towards the steps but stopped. Now she was hiding her lumpy right ankle behind her left, even from him.

She had wanted to give him a hug, and he had not realised. Too late now. He climbed the ramp, hurting all over. As soon as he was aboard it was heaved in and lashed against the side, and the sky galleon lifted and headed east. His hands clenched on the rail and he turned, keeping her small figure in sight. She was gazing after him, looking utterly forlorn. Why, why had he held back? Reaching out to him must have been very difficult for her.

Now he could only see the pale hair that framed her heart-shaped face. Then it vanished and so did she, lost in the shadowy ruins. What would become of her, trapped with that manipulative old hag, Maigraith? Who would protect Aviel when Maigraith was away? Would he ever see Aviel again? Given the state of the war, it seemed unlikely.

'You might be a big tall hero while you wiggle your fancy sword,' said Klarm, clunking up beside him, 'but you don't know *anything* about women.'

Wilm's ears burned. Unable to think of anything to say, he kept his mouth shut.

'Happy to give you a few pointers,' Klarm went on, grinning.

Wilm's mother had brought him up to be polite to his elders, though today it took an effort. What had he done to offend the dwarf?

'No, thank you,' he said, contenting himself with a meaningful up-and-down stare.

Klarm snorted. 'That the best you can do? Point out that I'm a short-arse?'

'I wasn't –'

'During the Lyrinx War I was tormented and humiliated by the most terrible people of all – the Council of Scrutators who ran the world. Yet I rose to be one of the greatest of them, through hard work and cunning, and determination to master every aspect of my craft. Now all but two of those scrutators are dead, and I'm still here. And a hundred times more attractive to the ladies than you'll ever be.'

'Only because you buy their favours,' snapped Wilm.

Klarm smirked. 'You'll know otherwise before this mission is over.'

What was he talking about? Klarm went below, wooden foot clunking, leaving Wilm smouldering. Was the dwarf right about him? Was everything he'd achieved due to Akkidul's aid? What *had* he done before he got Mendark's sword?

He and Dajaes had tunnelled into Cumulus Snoat's compound, Pem-Y-Rum, to rescue Llian, though Dajaes had formulated the plan and done all the clever work. Wilm had just been her labourer and, when she was attacked, he had frozen for a few seconds. Long enough for Unick to blast her dead.

Wilm had failed his poor mother, too. He had been far away when the war came to Casyme, and she had died that day. Now he had left Aviel behind. If the Merdrun discovered she was in Thurkad they would kill her like vermin, because she'd made the nivol that had buried the summon stone and prevented them from reopening their invasion gate for two centuries.

He laid his cheek on the brass gunwale. He didn't deserve her, or anything good. He was an utter failure, as his teachers had forecast long ago, and he would soon be dead.

Aching inside, Aviel watched Wilm climb aboard. Why couldn't they get back to being friends again, as they had been most of her life? Now he was going into awful danger and she felt sure she would never see him again.

'Surely you're not crying over that idiot?' said Klarm.

Aviel wiped her eyes. 'I'm not crying!'

'This might take your mind off things you can't change.' He pressed a small wooden box into her hands and folded her fingers around it.

'What is it?'

'Dried hoopis fruit. Do you know it?'

'No,' she said, wondering why he was giving it to her. 'What does it taste like?'

'It's not for eating.' He lowered his voice. 'It has the rarest scent in the world. And, some say, the loveliest. Put it away and keep the lid tightly closed.'

'Thank you.' Aviel was overcome. 'But why are you giving it to *me*?'

'You'll make something beautiful with it. Santhenar could use a little beauty, a little joy.'

After the sky galleon left, she went to her workshop on the top floor. It had once been a beautiful bathroom with a polished travertine counter along one side, and three stone basins spaced at intervals along it, though nothing came out of the taps. She would have to haul all her water up four flights of steps from a well in the basement.

A square bathtub carved from a single slab of pale green marble contained hundreds of dead blowflies, beetles and moths, and the remains of a small, desiccated frog. The poor thing must have hopped in, looking for water, and died there. Trapped, like her.

She went down and filled two wooden pails, lugged them up, scrubbed out the bathtub and tipped in the rest of the water. Then looked around in despair. A grimy window faced south-west to Faidon Forest and the mountains of Bannador beyond. The huge marble floor tiles were scratched and chipped and thick with dirt.

Flydd had obtained the equipment she needed but the glassware was so filthy that she did not see how it could ever be made fit for use. It would take a week to clean everything and set it all up, and she did not have the heart for it right now.

She perched on a stool and put Klarm's little box on the bench. It was a cube about two inches on each side, made from a dark, fine-grained wood. Ebony, perhaps. The lid fitted so tightly that she had to lever it up with the blade of a spatula.

Aviel held her breath as it came open. Inside was a clear bag, the opening folded over and over on itself and clipped down. She undid the clips and found another bag inside the first, also folded and clipped. She unfastened it and took a deep sniff. And closed it hastily.

It was unlike any scent she had ever made. Overpowering. Bewitching. Her head was spinning; she had sniffed way too much.

She folded the bags down carefully, put the clips on and pressed the lid of the box down tightly. Aviel closed her eyes, steeping herself in the scent. She sniffed her fingers; they bore a hint of it too.

Then the backs of her hands prickled; she had smelled hoopis before. Or a perfume containing it. Where, though? It was so faint that, for all her skill at scent making and blending, she could not remember, though it did not give her a good feeling.

～

A young woman came to the rail a couple of yards from Wilm. He turned to say hello but she took a hasty step backwards.

She was very tall, only a few inches below his own height, with teak-brown skin and short, curly hair. Her lips were the colour of a blood plum and she had a small blackberry-shaped birthmark on the right side of her neck. Her shirt and pants were of better quality than his but worn, and neatly patched here and there.

'Hello,' he said, and held out his hand. 'I'm Wilm.'

Her eyes, dark amber, slid away from his and she retreated another half step. What was the matter?

'I'm Ilisial,' she said grudgingly. She pronounced it *Ill–iss-ee-allll*. 'I'm a mech-enchanter ... or will be when I'm finished my training.'

'What's a mech-enchanter?'

'We make and repair the mechanisms that draw power from the fields, for all kinds of devices. Even this sky galleon.'

'And the spellcaster?'

'Don't say the name!' she snapped. 'The enemy have spies everywhere.'

'Sorry. Stupid of me.' The sky galleon was an astounding, absurd creation. 'You can make craft *like this*?'

'Of course not, it's the only one in the world. I don't think anyone but M'Lainte truly understands it. She's a genius ...'

'You must be clever, though, to be taken on as her apprentice.'

'I've made a few little things. Nothing very useful.' Her eyes shone. 'But I can learn so much from her ... and one day I'm going to design my own devices ... but *not for war! Not for killing.*'

'What for, then?' said Wilm, wondering what lay behind her passion.

'To make things better for ordinary people.'

'Why would ordinary people want magic-powered devices? How could they use them, anyway?'

'You're stupid!' she cried, and turned and walked away, head held high.

'I wasn't criticising you,' he said hastily. 'I just wanted to know ...'

She did not look back. *What is it about me?* Wilm thought.

'Need any more proof?' smirked Klarm, strolling across the deck towards him.

It took all Wilm's willpower to restrain himself. *Don't over-react. Klarm could point his finger and blast you to bits.*

'Thanks for the advice,' he said stiffly. 'I want to better myself. Can you tell me why –?'

Klarm snorted. 'One – thing – at – a – time, laddie.'

Wilm crept into the cabin, where M'Lainte stood at the controls. Flydd and Lilis were seated at his table up the back, going through items in a ledger. Wilm edged towards M'Lainte. 'Do – do you mind if I stand here?'

She smiled. 'Why would I?'

'Some people are prickly ...'

'Not me. What do you want?'

'I ... um ... don't know enough to ask.'

'I meant, what do you want from your life?'

'A skill. One that's not to do with war or fighting ... I can't go back to being a despised labourer, at the mercy of –'

'There's nothing wrong with doing an honest day's work, lad.'

'There is when you can barely earn enough to feed yourself,' he said hotly. 'When everyone treats you like a worthless beast of burden. I want more! I want to be valued.'

'You *are* valued. You're a hero ... and a good man, I'm told, brave and loyal and true.'

'What do heroes do once the war is over, M'Lainte?'

'Same as everyone else – they get on with their lives. You want a useful skill? Never stop learning, and constantly ask, How can I do this better? That way, you'll always be useful – to others and yourself.'

'Can I watch you?'

'Of course. Be curious about everything but know your limitations; don't strive for the impossible. You're good with your hands. Work on those skills.'

Wilm sat to one side, watching her hands on the levers. She made dozens of little adjustments every minute, seemingly by instinct, to keep the massive craft flying.

Why had he volunteered to go with Klarm on such an incredibly dangerous mission? The odds were that he wouldn't survive it. If he had stayed with Aviel he would have been some use.

The sky galleon raced east across the long, narrow sea. Thurkad was just a murky shadow behind them now; ahead the water was a grey blur. What would they find at the Sink of Despair, and would they survive it?

If only he hadn't tossed Akkidul to Llian, back in Shazmak. Why hadn't it occurred to Wilm that giving away an enchanted sword would mortally offend it? Had it dragged him and Aviel into the future to punish them? Given the malice it had shown to Llian, anything was possible, and Wilm was forced to an unpleasant conclusion – he could no longer trust it.

The sword might even betray him. Was there any point keeping it? He went to the side of the sky galleon and drew the weapon, thinking that he might be better off tossing it into the water and being done with it.

'What are you doing?' said Klarm. He had followed silently, no small feat with a wooden foot.

'I don't know,' Wilm cried. 'I don't know anything anymore.'

'Put it away.'

Wilm thrust the blade down into the copper sheath until it clicked.

'For all its flaws it's a mighty blade, laddie. Think about all it's done for you, and others.'

'It saved my life on Gwine,' said Wilm. Without it he would not have survived one minute against the Merdrun. 'And it cuts through metal and stone; it made the slave rebellion possible in the first place.'

'And saved your friend, Aviel. Akkidul is self-obsessed, malicious and untrustworthy, but it's also one of the greatest blades ever made on Santhenar, and you'll need it when we run into the enemy.'

'Do you think we will?'

'I know we will. In the meantime, keep it safe.' Klarm lowered his voice. '*Never* let it know what you're really thinking. And above all, *suck up to it*.'

9

HE'S TURNED HIS COAT BEFORE

'The Sink of Despair!' M'Lainte said with a theatrical sweep of her meaty arm. 'Look on it and weep, Wilm.'

The sky galleon had raced east across Lauralin and, on the darkest of nights, Flydd had dropped Lilis at a place called Tullymool, somewhere in northern Tacnah. He did not say what she was to do there. Now the craft was hammering into a ferocious headwind, bucking up and down violently as they curved around the northern flank of the Great Mountains.

The Sink of Despair stretched ahead of them, an oval of sunken land two hundred miles long and a hundred wide. Its flat bed glittered with dried-up salt lakes and it was surrounded on three sides by arid mountains. A number of rivers ran from them into the Sink, but all failed in that cruel desolation. How could anything survive there? How could he?

'That's where we've got to go?' said Wilm. 'To hunt for the, um, secret weapon?'

'Not in the Sink, thankfully. In the hills and mountains to its south.'

From the southern rim of the Sink of Despair an endless network of ridges and ravines ran up to the snowy crest of the range, the lowest of a series of parallel mountain chains that stepped ever upwards, culminating in the monumental arc of the Great Mountains, whose highest peaks stood more than thirty-five thousand feet high, forever sheathed in ice and utterly unclimbable.

Below the sky galleon, everywhere looked the same. Stony ground, bare apart from an occasional withered saltbush, and occasional dune fields which M'Lainte had said were made from windblown dust and salt. Patches of wiry scrub snaked along the bottom of each gully, their only hope of finding water. The place looked miserable.

'How will we ever find the – *it*?' said Wilm. 'It could take years to search all that.'

'We know where the air-dreadnought crashed,' said Klarm, 'because I was one of the scrutators who came looking for survivors. And the secret weapon.'

'If you couldn't find it then, how do you expect to all these years later?'

Klarm glanced at M'Lainte. 'We've worked out a way to scry for it. A method no one had thought of back then.' He consulted his map, pointed, and the sky galleon headed down.

Wilm eyed the bleak landscape with increasing apprehension. There was not a wisp of cloud, the sun scorched his head and the ground radiated heat. It was so dry his lips were cracking. If anything went wrong, it would be easy to die here.

'Getting close,' Klarm called from the bow half an hour later.

He climbed onto the top of the javelard frame, fifteen feet above the deck, and hung on with one hand, pointing left with the other. M'Lainte drifted the sky galleon that way, a few hundred feet above the ground.

He continued to point left, then held up his hand. 'We're next to the wreckage – set down.'

Wilm saw a series of broken bamboo hoops, so weathered that fibres were sticking out, and charred sections of a long, boat-like structure that must have been the main keel and cabin of the air-dreadnought, partly embedded in a glittering salt dune. Shreds of brown fabric, all that remained of the gum-sealed silk airbags, clung to the hoops. The ground was scattered with broken timber and lengths of frayed rope.

And patches of bleached bones. The air-dreadnought had been crewed by twenty-two people, plus the three scrutators and their guards and attendants – more than forty in all. And all had died here when the craft ploughed into the dunes at high speed, or soon after. Judging by the cracked and gnawed bones, the scavengers had fed well.

What must it have been like, watching them creep in and knowing everyone was going to be torn apart and eaten? Wilm's stomach cramped. Were they watching now, waiting for dark?

The sky galleon settled with a crunch and M'Lainte handed the controls over to Flydd. The edge of the Sink of Despair, a few miles north, was a good thousand feet below them. Its far side, a hundred miles away and blurred by the heat haze, was framed by a range of smaller but equally forbidding mountains.

The six guards stood in a huddle at the stern, talking in low voices. Flydd had hired them in Thurkad and they kept to themselves. They did not look happy.

'Keep me informed,' he said, handing M'Lainte a small, buff-coloured farspeaker box. 'When you can – the fields around here can be unreliable.'

'Tell me about it,' she said. 'It took all my concentration to keep us in the air, the last twenty leagues.'

Wilm's entrails knotted. 'You're *leaving* us here?' he said to Flydd.

'The search could take weeks and I've got to get to the east, urgently.'

'Weeks!' Wilm had assumed it would take a few days, at most. 'But ... how will we get out?'

'I'll pick you up when you find it.'

'What if something goes wrong?' His voice cracked. 'What if you can't?'

Flydd, Klarm and M'Lainte exchanged glances.

'Leave us to worry about that,' said M'Lainte. She looked worried too. 'We have a backup plan.'

'Of sorts,' said Klarm.

Wilm swallowed; his dry throat hurt.

Klarm stumped down to the stern, where Sulien and Jassika sat facing away from each other, and tried to embrace his daughter. 'Jassika, I want –'

She pushed him off. 'You're a useless father and I couldn't care less what happens to you. Go away and don't come back!'

Wilm had never met his own father. A wealthy man, he had refused to acknowledge Wilm or give his mother a single copper grint. He must be two centuries dead by now, but Wilm still hated and despised him.

Klarm turned, met Wilm's eye and snarled, 'How dare you judge me, boy?'

'I wasn't!' Wilm spluttered. Why did Klarm hate him, and only him?

'Get the gear over the side.' Klarm turned to M'Lainte. 'We need to find a safe campsite before dark.'

He climbed down. The ground was littered with pieces of salt-crusted shale that crackled and broke and slipped underfoot. He limped off, swaying from side to side.

Wilm helped the guards unload the packs and supplies. He was about to go down when Flydd drew M'Lainte close.

'Keep a watchful eye on Klarm,' he said quietly. 'He's a brilliant man, and as good as anyone I've ever known in a tight spot ... but ...'

'He served the God-Emperor for years,' said M'Lainte, 'and made no apology for it.'

'We weren't at war; no one could call it treachery. But still ...'

'What kind of a man would serve that blood-handed brute?' She gripped Flydd by the shoulder. 'Safe journey, old friend. You'll be in more danger than us, where you're going.'

'We're all targets now. The enemy will do everything possible to kill people like me ...'

'And capture people like me, to compel the use of our talents by torture.' She wiped pudgy hands on her grubby shirt front. 'Oh well – we live, *we die*.'

Wilm did not like what he was hearing. He turned and Klarm was behind him. He'd heard Flydd, too. Klarm scowled malevolently.

'I didn't say a word,' Wilm said quietly.

'But you're thinking it. Judging me again.'

This was so unfair! 'If you care so much what people think,' Wilm snapped, 'maybe you should behave better.'

'I'm a bad enemy, Wilm.' Klarm stumped off.

M'Lainte lowered her heavy body to the ground. The sky galleon lurched into the air and headed east, and only one person looked back. Jassika was staring at her little father as if fearing she would never see him again.

Within minutes the sky galleon had vanished into the heat haze. 'It's late,' Klarm said irritably. 'Come on.'

They humped their gear across a stony ridge and down into the next ravine where, according to Klarm's memories, there had been a spring, though now it was just a patch of damp soil. He sent a pair of guards up to the ridge top to keep watch. Another pair gathered dead scrub for a campfire and the remaining two put up the tents, the guards' tent well separated from the others. Ilisial had gone down the gully, behind a clump of bushes.

Klarm drew M'Lainte aside. Wilm laid flat stones in a ring, piled bark and dead twigs in the middle and larger wood across, and got the campfire going. While he worked, he kept one ear on what Klarm was saying.

'... autonomous spellcaster ... decide what ... human intervention ...'

Wilm could not imagine what an *autonomous spellcaster* was. Nothing good, surely.

'... it had a worrying inner conflict,' Klarm concluded.

M'Lainte's voice rose. 'What idiot decided that was a good idea?'

Wilm did not hear Klarm's reply.

'It must be destroyed,' said M'Lainte. 'And the fragments scattered over a hundred miles so it can never –'

'No, I need it undamaged.'

'If the enemy get hold of it, they could fill one of our old manufactories with slave artisans and make a thousand of them.'

'We've got to have it,' Klarm said quietly. 'It could win us the war. Your job is to render it safe.'

'I'm not sure there's a way.'

Klarm, noticing that Wilm was watching, yelled, 'Dig out the spring, you lazy oaf!'

Klarm drew M'Lainte further up the slope and Wilm heard no more. He found a spade in the pile of gear, dug an oval hole in the moist earth and filled a bucket with seeping, reddish water. It was bitter, with a strong iron taste, and lay heavily in his belly.

He filled a large pot and made a stand in one side of the fire, with flat stones. What did M'Lainte mean by the spellcaster having an inner conflict? How could a persona have one? And why was she so afraid?

Could the sword advise him? Would it even speak truly? He had to try; but first he had to test it. He drew it.

'Akkidul?' he said, 'why did Mendark bury you in the desert?'

Mind your own damned business!

'Did you fail him in some way?'

What do you care? This is the first time you've drawn me in a month.

Wilm had drawn it a number of times but there was no point in arguing.

'Are you angry because I gave you to Llian?'

There's only one reason you'd give me to such an oaf – to insult me.

'Well, you got your revenge. You trapped me and Aviel in the future.'

Akkidul twitched. *So what? I've been trapped in this crappy length of metal for three hundred and eighty-seven years!*

'Not long enough,' muttered Klarm as he went by. 'If you were mine I'd melt you down and turn you into a privy bucket.'

The sword lunged at Klarm's throat, so powerfully that Wilm could barely hold it. Klarm turned a backwards somersault, walked across the campsite on his hands, then tumbled to his feet and strolled away, whistling a cheerful tune.

The sword was shuddering, and it took Wilm three goes to get it into its sheath. He jammed it down hard, so it could not hear, and stalked across to Klarm. 'What did you do that for?'

'Action is character,' said the dwarf. 'Now you know what you've got into bed with.'

And how long before you reveal your *true character?* Wilm thought. *Or have you already done so?*

All things considered, it wasn't a good idea to ask Akkidul about the spell-caster. Wilm wasn't sure he wanted it to know the device existed.

10

DON'T PRETEND YOU CARE!

Sulien huddled in a patch of shade at the stern of the sky galleon, aching inside. Jassika stood a few yards away with her arms crossed across her chest and her fingers clenched, scowling at everyone. Today they were going to be dumped on strangers in the middle of nowhere, and Sulien felt sure she would never see her mother again. This was worse than being sent away with the Whelm. Far worse. Idlis, at least, had always been good to her.

After leaving the Sink of Despair they had crossed a range of mountains and another oval of sunken land, the Desolation Sink, which looked even bleaker. The sky galleon then headed east over endless mountains with not a road or a town in sight, though at least it was green here.

In the mid-morning Flydd landed on a small grassy area at the upper end of a valley indistinguishable from thousands of other valleys. There was forest along the small stream at the bottom and scrub higher up the slopes.

'Where are we?' said Karan.

'Stibnibb,' said Flydd.

'What a miserable hole,' said Jassika. 'We might as well be on the moon.'

Karan looked awful, pale and puffy-eyed. She had slept badly last night, and every night since Llian was taken. 'Why here?' she said to Flydd.

'There's no field, so even if the enemy scry for Sulien, how could they see her?'

'How can the sky galleon fly here, then?'

'Huge banks of a rare kind of crystal – a third of all those ever found. They hold enough power for an hour or two of flying. Depending on conditions ...'

'What if the power runs out while we're flying?'

'We won't need grave diggers.'

Sulien hugged herself more tightly. It didn't help.

Fifty yards away, an ancient, poorly built log cabin huddled between the trees. The gaps between the logs had been chinked with mud but much had fallen out, leaving long cracks that, Sulien imagined, the wind must whistle through in winter. A narrow front veranda was furnished with two wooden chairs, a small table and an easel.

'Wait here,' said Flydd.

He picked up a brown canvas bag, went to the cabin door and knocked. The door opened and he went inside.

'What's he doing?' said Sulien in a dead voice.

Karan put an arm around her. 'It wasn't possible to contact them, darling. Flydd is asking them to take you and Jass.'

'I hope they say no,' said Jassika.

Sulien felt the same. Nothing could be worse than being stuck here, in the mountains of nowhere.

The door opened and Flydd came out, accompanied by a very tall, thin old woman wearing an eye patch over her left eye, and a fat, barefoot old man in a gown that appeared to be made from hessian bags.

'Come down, girls,' said Flydd.

Sulien looked at Jassika, who glared at her and did not move. Sulien swallowed and climbed down, her pack on her back. The man eyed her and Jassika vacantly, then waddled to the easel and began to dab at a painting.

The woman, who wore a man's shirt, loose trousers and knee-length boots, walked around Sulien, inspecting her from all angles. 'Can you chop wood, girl?'

'Yes,' she said in a faint voice. The old woman looked hard and cold and mean. Sulien could not imagine being hugged by her. Or wanting one.

'The woodheap is around the back. Fill the wood box.' She squinted at Jassika, who had put on her most ferocious scowl. 'What are you good for?'

'Nothing,' snapped Jassika.

'That's what I thought. You'll find two buckets at the back door. Go down to the stream and carry water until the tank is full. It'll take ninety trips.'

'Get it yourself!'

'The pantry is locked,' said the woman, glancing at the fat man, 'and I have the only key. If you don't work, you don't eat.'

'I'm not your slave. I'll hunt and fish.'

'Good luck.' The woman turned to Sulien. 'Hurry up.'

'I'll say goodbye to my daughter first,' said Karan.

'You'll ruin her,' said the woman, folding her arms across a chest as flat as a table.

'I'll take the risk.'

Karan climbed down. Her limp was worse than usual and she winced with every step. She folded Sulien in her arms. 'I'm really sorry, darling. I can't take you where we're going. But I'll be back –'

Terror overwhelmed Sulien. 'No, you won't. You'll be killed. And Daddy too!' She let out a sob and, once started, she could not stop.

Karan hugged her more tightly and Sulien could not stand it. She pulled free.

'I'm sorry, I'm sorry!' Karan was shaking, on the verge of collapse.

She took a step towards Sulien, who held up both palms. She had to push her mother away; it was the only way of making the abandonment bearable. 'You're making it worse, Mummy. Just – go!'

Karan let out a cry of anguish and Sulien almost cracked, but she hardened her heart and turned aside.

Flydd, who had gone aboard, cleared his throat.

Karan gave a wrenching shudder. 'Sulien, promise you won't use your mind-seeing gift.'

'What?' said Sulien.

'If you did – if you fore-saw Skald again, for instance – the magiz might be able to hunt you down. Promise?'

'I will if you promise *you* won't do anything dangerous,' said Sulien stiffly.

Karan swallowed. 'I – I don't know what I'll be doing.'

'Daddy's lost and you're going to get killed. I have to look after myself now.'

'Promise you won't mind-see again,' Karan said desperately. 'Please, Sulien!'

'I'm not making promises I can't keep, Mummy.'

Karan came towards her but Sulien backed away. Karan's tremor was worse; she looked ghastly. 'You're only nine. You'll do what you're told.'

Sulien clenched her jaw. 'I'll do what I have to do.' The Merdrun's secret weakness was buried within her and she had to find it. It was the only way out, for everyone.

'Karan, we have to go *now*,' called Flydd.

An awful moan escaped Karan. She wiped her eyes and stumbled towards Jassika, reaching out to her.

'Don't pretend you care!' Jassika spat. 'All my life I've been dumped on strangers. The horrors I've seen. The things they've done!'

'I'm sorry, Jass–'

'No, you're not. You don't give a shit about me.' Jassika walked into the forest, her back very straight, and disappeared.

'She'll be back when she gets hungry,' Flydd said unconvincingly.

'Wood, *now*!' said the tall old woman. Then, to Karan, 'Go, before you ruin her completely.'

'Sulien, please promise –'

'I can't, Mummy.'

Karan lurched to the sky galleon. Her blanched face and look of utter desolation imprinted themselves in Sulien's mind as the sky galleon lifted, creaking and shuddering and, keeping low over the trees, headed away.

She followed a dirt track down to an enormous pile of logs. The wood box, which was the size of a small shed, was empty apart from a rusty axe with a notched blade. No one could cut wood with it.

But escaping the Whelm and the Merdrun last time had been impossible too. Sulien took the axe and knocked on the back door. The woman opened it.

'What?' she snapped.

Sulien did not feel like being polite, but it was ingrained in her. 'The axe is blunt. Do you have a sharpening stone, please?'

The woman's furry grey eyebrows rose. She rifled through cupboards and came back with an oval stone.

'Thank you,' said Aviel.

She sat on a log, put the axe over her knee and began to sharpen it, the way dear old Rachis had done many a time, back in the good old days at Gothryme. Sulien let out another little sob.

'Listen to the edge,' he used to say. 'It'll tell you when it's keen.'

Sulien listened to the edge, her tears falling on the blade. If Karan and Llian were killed, would anyone know she was here? Or care? Would she be stuck here for the rest of her life? Even Jassika's boasting and carping would be welcome now, but there was no sign of her.

She hauled a log out of the pile, rested it on another, and began to chop. And chop.

An hour went by. Her palms were blistered, her arms and back aching. No one came to check on her. Apart from the ringing of her axe against the wood, the place was silent. No birds chittered. There weren't even any blowflies.

The axe grew blunt. She sharpened it again, put on her gloves and split the wood she had chopped, carried it to the wood box and stacked it at the back. Jassika had not returned.

Chop, chop. Every blow was painful now but it was better than thinking about being abandoned; about Karan and Flydd getting killed; about Llian being tortured by the enemy. About being stuck in this terrible place forever.

By the time the job was finished, the sun had set. Sulien had been given nothing to eat and had only taken a couple of drinks from the stream. She loaded an arm with chopped wood and knocked on the back door.

'The wood box is full,' she said to the scrawny old woman. 'I brought some wood for the stove.'

The old woman looked astounded. 'Put it on the hearth, then wash your hands and get your dinner.' Her voice was still hard, though not as cold as before. Sulien wondered if she would ever win her over, or if she wanted to. It might be easier to dislike her.

Dinner was a gluey stew made from anonymous vegetables and mashed grains, with occasional flecks that might have been meat, but Sulien was so hungry that she gulped down the lot, plus a crust of dark brown, gritty bread with a taste of mould. She was still hungry but nothing more was offered.

She washed and dried her bowl and spoon and put them on a shelf made from a crudely split log. Without a word the old woman picked up a battered iron lamp and showed her to a little room out the back. It had a narrow bunk on either side, the rough-sawn planks covered by lumpy, straw-filled mattresses and a couple of ragged blankets each. There were gaps in the walls she could put her hand through, and an enormous population of spiders of every kind and size. The ceiling was strung with their webs, and so was every corner and crevice.

Sulien wasn't afraid of spiders but she wasn't fond of them either. She inspected the bedclothes carefully and got into bed, for it was chilly now and the old woman had taken the lamp. There had been no sign of Jassika all day. Surely she wasn't planning on sleeping in the forest?

Sulien lay on her back, staring at the ceiling until it was fully dark, and mentally following the path of the sky galleon east over the thickly forested mountains. Where was Flydd going? He had not said. He was a brilliant man; he had led the fight that had finally defeated the lyrinx and banished them to Tallallame. Though at the time he'd had great armies at his command, and thousands of allies.

This war could not be more different. Most of Flydd's allies had already been captured or killed, or had disappeared, and Santhenar had no armies anymore. All he had was a handful of friends, far away. He could not hope to stop 190,000 of the greatest fighters of all time ... unless he knew their fatal weakness.

But not even Rulke had been able to find the rest of Sulien's lost nightmare. Was it lost forever? She could not afford to think so. There had to be another way to find it. Uigg the drum boy had also hinted at the enemy's secret, and then there was Skald ...

Lucky I didn't make that promise to Mummy, she thought. I'll start by far-seeing Skald and finding out what he knows.

But not yet. Not until I'm strong enough.

11

IT HAD GONE ROGUE

When Wilm rose at dawn, Klarm and M'Lainte were bent over a scrying dish half filled with quicksilver, in which a blue needle floated on a disc of golden mica.

'That way,' she said, pointing diagonally up the slope. She emptied the dish into a wide-mouthed metal jar, tapped in a few recalcitrant globules of shiny quicksilver and capped it tightly.

'Ilisial,' said Klarm, 'take Wilm and search up the bottom and eastern side of the valley, as far as that rocky knob.' He indicated a grey protrusion, perhaps a mile further up. 'M'Lainte and I will take the western side. The guards will search the next valley east.'

'What does the spellcaster look like?' said Wilm.

'It's disc-shaped, five feet across and a foot through the middle, and made of blue-black metal. It won't be hard to spot.'

'What if we find it?' Wilm had not slept well last night for worrying about the deadly device.

'Back away, making as little sound as possible. Under no circumstances approach it.'

'When you're more than a hundred yards away,' said M'Lainte, 'signal me or Klarm.'

'How?' said Ilisial.

'Make a fire and cover it with green vegetation so it smokes.'

Wilm looked at Ilisial, who seemed to be waiting for him to do something. 'I'll search the bottom of the gully, if you like.'

He had given himself the harder job, since the base of the gully was partly covered in thorny bushes and littered with boulders. He headed up, looking behind every obstacle. Though it was only 6.30 a.m. the sky was cloudless, the sun shining full on him, and it was already hot.

'Too damned slow, boy!' bellowed Klarm half an hour later. 'Stop mucking about!'

He and M'Lainte were a quarter of a mile further up, on the other side of the gully, and Wilm realised that he was wasting time. The spellcaster would stand out in this empty landscape.

They had been told that it was capable of limited flight, assuming there was a field it could draw power from. But the air-dreadnought had crashed sixteen years ago. The spellcaster could be anywhere by now.

The scorching day wore on, every minute hotter than the previous one. Wilm saw nothing but grey lizards and amber-coloured scorpions, which raised their stingers at his approach, and a stubby snake covered in diamond patterns. It stood up on its tail and watched his every movement with swaying head and glittering eyes. He backed away. The sky was empty apart from skeets and other carrion birds riding the updraughts. Waiting for them to die.

'Imbeciles!' he muttered when he came together with Ilisial half an hour later.

'What are you talking about?' she said coolly.

'The people who made the spellcaster.'

She stiffened. 'They were honest crafters, doing their best in a terrible war.'

'It's a killing machine!'

'What would *you* know about it?'

'I know the difference between right and wrong. How can a machine be allowed to choose who lives or dies?'

'You're a common soldier, Wilm. You carry an evil sword – and you kill for *pay.*'

Her contempt was a slap across the face. 'I've *never* been paid for fighting,' he said hotly. 'Not one copper.'

'But you have killed people.'

'Yes,' he said slowly, sure she was building a trap for him.

'How many?'

And there it was. 'I – don't remember. It was in battle. It was chaos. Life or death.'

'So you're a killing machine too.' It was clear that she despised him. 'Tell me, Wilm, as the arbiter of moral values around here, did your victims die instantly? Or did they lie there in agony for hours while you went about your merry way?'

'There's nothing merry about battle,' he said quietly. 'It was the most horrible experience of my life.'

Without any warning, something snapped in her. 'Go away, killer!' she screeched. 'You sicken me!'

She bolted up the slope. Wilm stared after her, shaking. What was that all about? He stumbled across to the gully and continued up it, taking nothing in. Why was she blaming him?

At midday Klarm called them across to a shelf of rock running across the floor of the gully, where a larger seep supported a clump of multi-trunked trees. In their shade, the rock was pleasantly cool to sit on. Ilisial sat as far as possible from Wilm and did not once look his way. She was the only one not sunburned. Klarm looked to be in great pain.

'This is going to take a hundred years,' he muttered, unwrapping his inflamed stump and rubbing a yellow ointment on it. Had he really cut his own foot off, to escape a trap? Wilm could not imagine it.

'Why wasn't the spellcaster near the wreckage?' said Ilisial.

'Should have been,' said Klarm. 'It was supposed to be securely crated up.'

'But?' said Wilm.

'I think the scrutators had it out on deck.'

'Why did the air-dreadnought crash, anyway?'

'Ah!' said M'Lainte, and looked at Klarm.

'I suspect the spellcaster was involved,' said Klarm.

'How?' said Ilisial.

'Perhaps it wanted to escape. I think it damaged the air-dreadnought to make it crash.'

'It hit the dunes at high speed,' said M'Lainte. 'As if the controls had failed ...'

'Or had been taken over,' Klarm said darkly.

'Escape where?' said Wilm. 'There's nothing out here.'

'The weakness of personas is that they're *bound*,' said M'Lainte. 'If a persona forms an amicable bond with the owner of the device it can be reasonably content –'

'Though ultimately, most intelligent things crave freedom,' said Klarm. 'Like Akkidul.'

'How can an enchanted sword be free?' said Wilm. 'It can't move.'

'But it *can* manipulate things to change to a more suitable master. By betraying its current master, for instance.' Klarm looked at Wilm's copper scabbard, meaningfully.

Wilm made sure the sword was pushed all the way down.

'Where would it go?' said Ilisial. 'What does such a device want?'

'Impossible to guess, though ...' M'Lainte glanced at the dwarf.

'Common emotions are anger, bitterness, vengefulness and malice,' said Klarm.

'At the device's owner?' said Wilm.

'Sometimes it's directed at everyone nearby, and they're the most dangerous personas of all.' He rose wearily. 'Wilm, go with M'Lainte. Ilisial, come with me.'

Ilisial beamed at Klarm and they headed up the eastern slope together, talking cheerfully.

'What does she hate me? Wilm said aloud.

'A better question might be, why can't you talk to young women?' said M'Lainte.

'Yes, why?' he said dully.

She clapped him on the shoulder with a meaty hand. 'It's obvious you want something from them, lad.'

Wilm flushed until even the roots of his hair seemed to be burning. 'I've never acted dishonourably to a woman in my life.'

'But with Ilisial earlier, and with Aviel, you radiated anxiety. Just be your normal friendly self and seek nothing in return, and things will change.' She headed up the slope, her eyes scanning the ground, the sky and the top of the ridge.

'Aviel always pushes me away; she scorns the idea of love.'

'She's only sixteen, Wilm! And she's had a hard life.'

'So have I. I don't have a father,' he said bitterly.

'But you had a mother who loved you. Aviel's family used her as a workhorse, then betrayed her.'

'Haven't I proved myself? I've befriended her since she was two.'

'If you keep pushing her for something she's not ready for, it can only drive a wedge between you.'

'How do you know? Have *you* ever loved?'

M'Lainte stopped abruptly.

'I'm sorry,' said Wilm, flushing again, 'that was unforgivably rude.'

She laughed. 'Few things are truly unforgiveable, and I'm not easily offended. Yes, lad, I have loved, long ago. But in the desperate final years of the war I came to love my work more, and to get more satisfaction from it.'

She scanned the slope and continued. What a fascinating woman she was. Wilm could have listened to her all day. 'How did you come to be a mechanician?'

'I was always good with my hands,' she ruminated as they climbed. 'Repairing clocks and wagons, water wheels and other mechanical contrivances, and looking for ways to make them better.

'I fell into mech-magic during the war. The lyrinx were destroying us, Wilm – they were much bigger, three times as strong, and just as clever. Few people ever fought a lyrinx in single combat and survived. And if that wasn't a big enough advantage, some of them, those who could use the Secret Art strongly enough, could fly.

'One night in the pub, more than thirty years ago, when we'd all had too much to drink and were tossing mad ideas around, I said, "What if we could construct an armoped – a mechanical wagon that walked on iron legs and was powered by the fields?" I got quite excited about it.'

M'Lainte wiped her brow with a flowery bandanna and took a sip from a round silver water bottle. 'My drinking companions laughed me down and I thought no more about it, but late that night there was a knock on my door and a small, skinny and rather ugly man stood there. He'd been in the bar earlier, and at first I thought he wanted to go to bed with me.'

She cast an assessing glance at Wilm. Not knowing what to say, he looked straight ahead.

'Which he did,' she continued. 'I wasn't unattractive in those days,' she said self-deprecatingly, 'and the war had taken us far from home and loved ones ... And, viewed through enough glasses of ale, when you can die any day ...'

She smiled at some private memory.

'He was clever, charming, and very good at it. A memorable night. Afterwards we talked for hours about my idea, and I made sketches of the most important components of an armoped – the plate armour, the leg mechanisms and how they were powered, the controller. My lover wasn't a mechanical man, but he had a quick intellect and a strategic outlook, and he talked about how such devices, if they could be made to work, might turn the war our way.

'In the morning he was gone, and so were my sketches. I was annoyed, but I didn't know his name, and in the light of day armopeds seemed ridiculous. I thought no more about them.

'I spent the next few years repairing and improving baggage train wagons, javelards and other devices used in the war, learning to make small devices powered by the field, and generally trying to master my craft and make every new design better and more useful than the one before.

'Then I was posted on a day's notice to a cold, wet, dismal place called Thisp, at the eastern end of the Great Mountains. It's inland from the coastal city of Tiksi, if you know it.'

Wilm shook his head.

'A large building was being built there, for metal-working, and there were mines and foundries nearby. I had no idea what was wanted of me until I entered the place, which they called a manufactory – *the* manufactory, in fact, because it was the first – and my lover from three years ago gave me my orders. I expect you can guess his name.'

'Xervish Flydd?' said Wilm.

'The same. He'd had a chequered history during the war – hence the scars and broken bones – but he'd spent the past years arguing the strategic importance of armopeds, and he had finally gained the consent of the Council of Scrutators, and the gold, for a small manufactory to build an armoped. And he wanted me to be the chief designer.'

'And the rest was history!' said Wilm.

'Far from it. The Council was sceptical, and some scrutators were actively hostile. Flydd was only a junior scrutator and he had to fight for every copper grint. They doled them out grudgingly, only a month in advance of need, and he was under constant threat of having the manufactory closed.

'It took four months to design the armoped, or clanker as they came to be called, and another six months for a team of eighty artisans and artificers to build the first one. We knew quite a bit about drawing power from fields by then – the great mancer Nunar, whom you might have known as Ifoli –'

'I wondered what became of her,' said Wilm. 'After we finished with the summon stone, she went off with Shand on some mysterious project.'

'With his help, long before my time, she worked out the Laws of Power, and how to power small mech-magical devices. But there's tons of iron in a clanker, and to drive its multiple pairs of mechanical legs we needed mechanisms far stronger than anything hitherto imagined.'

They continued up, scanning the terrain to either side.

'Finally the first clanker was complete,' she said, going misty-eyed. 'Nothing remotely like it had even been seen on Santhenar, and with its ten mechanical legs it could go places that would baffle any wheeled contrivance. I felt sure, and Flydd did too, that it was going to win the war for us.'

'And it did!' cried Wilm. 'You must –'

'Sadly,' said M'Lainte, 'it didn't work.'

'But ... What? Why not?'

'It was far too heavy for the power we could draw from the field with any controlling device we could make. The clanker took three steps, ground to a halt and could not be made to go again. Flydd's enemies – and mine, for I'd made quite a few by this time – wet themselves with joy.'

'What did you do?'

'Went back to my drawings. I had to make every part lighter, without sacrificing the armour needed to protect the troops inside from marauding lyrinx. If the clanker was too light it would have been useless. There was only one solution ...'

She plodded up the slope, panting. Wilm sensed that she was waiting for him to speak.

'Um,' he said, 'you had to make a controller that could draw much more power?'

'Precisely! The core of a controller was a crystal called a hedron, and only certain kinds of crystals would do, but few people could tell which ones were good and which were useless. Many thousands of gifted people were tested before we identified the necessary traits. But that was the easiest part.'

'What was the hardest?'

'The crystals we used weren't remotely strong enough. We had to find better ones, and that took years, because we had to test tens of thousands of samples of every conceivable kind of crystal, until we finally discovered ones that would do the job. They were rare, too.'

'But when you found them,' said Wilm, 'it transformed the war.'

'Not immediately. Our first clanker had broken down too many times and the Council wouldn't give Flydd the coin to build more until it had proved itself against the lyrinx. Which it could never so, since they refused to allow it anywhere near a battlefield in case it fell into enemy hands.'

'Stupid fools!'

'The long defeat had made them defensive, limited. But after the disastrous loss of another army, Flydd disobeyed orders and took the clanker out himself, as captain, with myself as its artificer to fix anything that went wrong, and a volunteer crew. He drove into the middle of a squad of lyrinx and killed the lot of them. That's how he got the gold to complete the manufactory and build many more. And make the thousands of clankers that eventually helped to win the war for us.'

'That must have been a wonderful day,' said Wilm.

She stared back down the years. 'Oh, it was, though it took another thirteen desperate and bloody years to defeat the lyrinx. And it was only in the final months that we began to hope for victory ...'

'And now we have to do it again.'

'With hardly any power from the fields. And no army ... and not a single clanker.'

12

WHAT A LITTLE MOUSE YOU ARE

'Just you and me,' said Maigraith, entering Aviel's workshop late on the day that the sky galleon had carried Wilm away.

Aviel did not turn around. She had not met Maigraith, though Aviel had heard her voice as she'd hunted Karan, Llian and Sulien up the tallest tower of Shazmak. From them Aviel knew all about Maigraith, and none of it good, and wanted nothing to do with her.

She scooped a dipper-full of hot water out of the cast iron cauldron perched atop a seven-sided brass brazier, carried it to one of the marble basins, her personal sink of despair, and began scrubbing her stained and crusted glassware.

Thurkad was an ugly place, and even as a girl in the backwater town of Casyme she had known of the city's dark reputation. But Flydd had ordered her to make a double batch of nivol and Maigraith was here to make sure she did.

He had hired two local guards to protect her, but they were cold and contemptuous. They thought Aviel was a stupid little girl, playing with toys while the world was being torn apart. She read them as being like her father – cowards who would run away in a crisis.

She groped for the green glass bead strung on a cord around her neck. It had a little white star inside and had once been part of a necklace, and it was her only memento of the mother who had fled when she was one. The sole reminder of her old life and her family, dead and gone two centuries ago.

She plunged a cleaned flask into the hot water in the rinsing sink, put it upside-down on a cloth to drain, and glanced sideways at Maigraith. She was the most intimidating person Aviel had ever met. Compared to her, Aviel's brutal former master in alchymy, the ill-fated Grand Master Torsion Tule, had been a frolicking puppy.

Had he deserved to die? He had knocked Aviel down and was about to stamp on her face when she'd flicked some Essence of Ague, a mild, disabling scent potion, at him. She had just been defending herself, but a massive dose had gone up his nose and the old man had died a few weeks later. It wasn't clear whether she had killed him, or his own choler had, but she still felt the guilt.

'You don't say much, do you?' said Maigraith.

'No.' Aviel's naturally high voice went squeaky.

'Turn around. How old are you, girl?'

Aviel turned, her wet hands dripping. 'Sixteen.'

'What a little mouse you are.' Maigraith's eyes scoured Aviel. 'You yearn to be loved but, because your family abused and betrayed you, you believe no one could ever care for you. That's why you push people away and immerse yourself in your work. And I dare say your disability makes these feelings worse.'

She walked around Aviel, studying her closely. Aviel flushed and turned to face her, always keeping her lumpy right ankle behind the left.

'Show me,' said Maigraith.

Aviel's cheeks felt scalded. 'Mind your own business!'

'It's not a request.'

Maigraith went down on her knees and drew Aviel's twisted foot forward. Aviel wanted to kick her but that would be pointless; Maigraith had total power over her life. What could not be prevented must be endured, as she had been forced to endure so many ordeals during her brief and mostly unhappy life. She was so fed up with always being at the mercy of others, always being used. She had to take control of her life.

'I won't always be powerless!' Aviel snapped.

'You're threatening *me*?' Maigraith laughed until she choked.

Aviel stood there, burning with mortification, as Maigraith studied her right foot and ankle, compared them to her other, normal foot, then probed the lumpy bones with pointy fingertips. What did she hope to find?

Maigraith, Aviel knew, had been bred to be a triune by Faelamor, one of the towering figures in the Histories. Bred for some wicked purpose, and taught the Secret Art. Later, Maigraith had briefly been lover to Rulke, who had gifted her part of his own incomparable talent for the Art. She was now a mighty mancer, one of the greatest on Santhenar, with powers unimaginable to a little scent potion maker.

Maigraith looked up at Aviel, questioningly.

Fixing the ankle would be small magic to her, and Aviel allowed herself to imagine a life when she could walk, even run, free from pain. But Maigraith did nothing without a purpose, nor gave a gift free of obligation. Though Aviel had been mocked for her disability since before she could walk and longed to have two normal feet like everyone else, enduring and adapting to it had made her what she was today.

'No thanks,' she said.

Maigraith shrugged and stood up. 'Where does the water come from?'

'A well in the basement.'

'You have to carry it all that way? That must be painful.'

Not as painful as being forced to live and work with you!

'The first time I made nivol, I did the final steps in a tent, at ... Rogues Render.' The skin on the back of Aviel's neck crept. 'I don't have to go back there, do I?'

'No.' Maigraith shivered.

It was good to know she was afraid of something. 'But the method requires the Archeus from a ghost vampire.'

'There are other methods, and ingredients that can be substituted.'

'Have you ever made nivol?'

'I never had the need.'

Aviel took a deep breath. She had to make a stand or forever be in Maigraith's thrall. 'If anything goes wrong, it's my life at risk. You will explain every change in the method and justify every substitution.'

Maigraith's unreadable eyes met Aviel's. Was she taken aback at her temerity, or amused at the notion that a mere girl could ever challenge her?

'Very well,' she said, with a small smile.

'What does Flydd want it for, anyway? It didn't work on the summon stone last time.'

'It has to be used from the inside.'

'The *inside*? How is that even possible?'

'You don't need to know.'

Maigraith went out but a hint of her perfume remained, and that hint was hoopis. Aviel put the little ebony box away, sadly. Klarm's gift was tainted now.

Aviel lay on her narrow bed. The timbers were half eaten away by woodworms and every time she moved, streamers of pale wood dust rained down, outlining the shape of the bed on the dark floorboards. The sheets were threadbare and grey, the thin mattress smelled like soldiers' socks and the stained blankets had holes in them. Not even her most cheerful perfumes could conceal the smell.

But Aviel knew all about hovels, because she was a seventh sister and that meant appallingly bad luck for her and everyone around her. After her mother ran away, her father had turned to drink and dicing, and lost all his money. One night when Aviel was eight he had staggered home in drunken despair, dropped his lantern in the hall and most of the house had burned down.

Her six older sisters had been lazy, bullying slatterns, and if not for Aviel's hard work and gift for gardening the family would have starved. She often wondered what had happened to them. Casyme had suffered badly in Cumulus Snoat's war and when Aviel returned the ruined house had been empty. No one had known if her father or sisters were still alive.

Her thoughts turned to the present, and her work. Making another batch of the deadly alchymical fluid did not unduly bother her. It was tricky and dangerous work, but she had done it twice before. And she still had the diamond phial, the only substance that could contain nivol – after Llian used it on the summon stone he had returned the phial, cut from a priceless plum-sized diamond, to her, and no one had asked for it back.

But nivol was an evil substance, and she already gone a troubling distance down the dark path. Why did she yearn for it so? She was a good person, wasn't she? Or had her past deeds corrupted her? Was she sliding down into the pit from which she could never escape?

How Lilis had laughed when Aviel mentioned this fear. 'In the *Register of Wickedness*, which I've read three times,' Lilis had said with a wistful sigh, 'your deeds wouldn't rate a mention.'

It hadn't helped then and it did not help now. Seeking comfort, Aviel took out her books and, as always, felt a little thrill. She might be small and crippled, put upon and without a coin to her name, but she owned three books! Few people on Santhenar had any.

The one she was most fond of was a little volume on the making of perfumes, which she had copied from a great tome, *The Art of Perfumery*. Three years ago, forty-eight pages had seemed enough for a lifetime, but she had quickly filled them with methods and recipes, notes on various scents she had extracted from flowers, herbs, roots and scented timbers, and little sketches of plants that grew in Casyme.

Her second book was a blank journal Lilis had given her. It had two hundred and fifty-six pages and she had counted them lovingly, imagining how much she could write about scent potions in the coming years.

The third book was even more precious, though it scared her. Wrapped in canvas, and inside that in layers of waxed paper, it was thick and square and heavy, for its covers were made of polished rosewood inlaid with camphor laurel and other scented timbers. The leaves had once been cream-coloured parchment, though many of the pages were age-spotted and stained, and some smelled bad.

Scent Potions had been the grimoire of the great master, Radizer, until he blew himself to bits trying to make the Afflatus Effluvium, one of the seven Forbidden Potions in the final section. Shand, who had been Radizer's apprentice hundreds of years before, had taken the unique and terrible book for safekeeping, and had given it to Aviel after she kept borrowing it.

She had made three scent potions from it now – the Eureka Graveolence, one of the Great Potions (all dark and deadly), which she had used to locate the summon stone, next An Essence of Ague, and finally the Balsam of Hereafter, another of the Great Potions, which had allowed Karan to see the way to the future.

Three very dark scent potions. And Aviel had an uncomfortable feeling that Maigraith wanted an even worse one.

YOU'LL SPILL YOUR GUTS

Karan's despair grew with every mile they flew south from Stibnibb. Llian a prisoner and likely killed already. Sulien abandoned to heartless strangers. Aviel and Wilm perhaps never to be seen again.

And today was the anniversary that made everything worse. Though it had happened long ago, whenever she closed her eyes she began to relive that awful scene –

She blocked it and tried to focus on what Flydd was saying, something about 'the fightback.' As if that was possible!

'Fightback with *what*?' she snapped. On her left, beyond the mountains, the sun passed below the horizon of the endless ocean. As far as she knew, no one had a clue about what was on the other side.

'With Nish and Maelys by my side, and Flangers and Klarm –'

'A known traitor!'

'Klarm was never a traitor. He took service with the God-Emperor years after the Lyrinx War ended.'

'He served a monster,' she said coldly. 'Some friend!'

'What's the matter with you today?'

She had never told anyone about it. Karan turned away but saw the attic room again. The mad, twisted sketches. The blood. Shudders racked her.

The sky galleon descended abruptly and Flydd set it down on a mountain slope, foggy and featureless apart from an occasional dead tree sticking up through crusted snow.

He caught her by the shoulder and jerked her around, and his face was hard. 'You with me or against me?'

Forcibly dragged back to the present, Karan could not manage words. She stared at him, shivering.

'Because if you're against me – if you're too afraid to fight – you can get out right now.'

Her blood stopped flowing. He couldn't be serious. But his icy stare did not waver, and she recalled stories Lilis had told her about the scrutators – hard men and women, all of them. Individual lives meant nothing to them; there had been times when they'd sacrificed whole armies, even small nations, to gain an advantage against the enemy.

'You don't think much of me, do you?' she said quietly.

'You were a great heroine, back in your time ...'

'But?'

'You've lost your nerve. You're so afraid of losing the one thing you have left that you're unwilling to try.'

'I haven't given up! I just don't see –'

'How a handful of misfits, long past their glory days, can hope to defeat the greatest army that's ever come out of the void.'

There was no need to reply.

Flydd indicated the side of the sky galleon. 'Off you go, then.'

Karan choked. How could this be happening? 'But ... I have no idea where we are.'

And even if he told her, in this rugged country she would be lucky to make five miles a day. She could live off the land but that took a lot of time. It could take months to find Sulien, if she ever did, but she would never see Llian again. The enemy would have killed him by then.

Flydd was still pointing to the side, utterly implacable.

'I – I'll just get some food and water.'

'You brought nothing but your pack. You leave with nothing but your pack.'

'You heartless bastard.'

'I won't give up a single bean to someone who won't fight.'

Karan fetched her pack and stumbled to the side. Was he bluffing? His face was unreadable. Then she stopped, struck by the realisation that neither would Flydd turn away anyone who could be useful to him. He knew her worth: she was brave, resourceful, and she had survived many desperate situations. And right now he had no one else.

'Nice try,' she said, dropping her pack on the deck. 'But I know the enemy better than anyone, and you need me as much as I need you. All right, I'll fight your hopeless battle – as long as I have your word that you'll help me get Sulien and Llian back, afterwards.' *If there is an afterwards.*

'You have my word.' He managed a smile. 'I'll get the dinner on.'

Karan went to a bench and sat down with a thump. What if she was killed? With Llian possibly dead already, Sulien would be an orphan ... as Karan had been violently orphaned at the age of twelve, twenty-four years ago today.

And it all came flooding back, unstoppable, overwhelming. The staring eyes, the awful smell in that hot attic room, the great gash across –

'Karan, what's the matter?'

Flydd was yelling at her, shaking her. He had been doing so for some time. She was lying on the deck, knees doubled up and arms wrapped tightly about herself, making a dreadful, wailing moan. Trapped in the most awful moment of her childhood and unable to blank it out.

He carried her to his table and sat her down with her back to the cabin wall. She unwrapped her arms but that felt bad, so she hugged herself again. Stared into nowhere. Shuddered.

'Drink this.' He put a porcelain cup, brimming with a clear fluid, in front of her. A rose was painted on the side, blood-red petals and long, curving thorns. She rotated it out of sight.

'What is it?' she said listlessly.

'A liqueur I make, when I can get the right fruit.'

'I don't drink spirits.'

'Drink it!'

Karan did not have the will to refuse. She took a sip. Made from clementines, strong and sweet and tangy. Vapours stung the back of her nose and the spirits burned all the way down.

'All of it.'

She emptied the cup in a series of swigs. He put a large bowl of stew in front of her.

'Not hungry.'

'Eat it or I'll heave you over the side, because this is wasting time I don't have, and right now you're worse than useless.'

This time he meant it. By the time she spooned down the last of the meaty, peppery stew the drink had gone to her head and she was glad of the corner wall behind her, and the table to lean on. Flydd sat opposite and ate his dinner, though he only sipped from his cup. Its decoration was a yellow and iridescent green, striped wasp. Appropriate.

He took the bowls away, washed them and left them to drain, and sat down again. 'Talk!'

'What about?'

'What brought that on.'

His face separated into two; Karan had never had a head for strong drink. She forced the two images to converge. 'None of your business.' Her voice was slurred.

'Anything that affects you this badly *is* my business.'

'I can't talk about it. It's too awful.'

He decanted liqueur into her cup. 'Just a sip this time.'

'Why?'

'To release your inhibitions so you'll spill your guts.'

'You'll despise me.'

Flydd raised his cup, sipped. 'I was a scrutator for twenty years, Karan. A master interrogator, among other things. Whatever you've done, you can't shock me.'

'Bet I can.'

'I've seen every kind of human weakness, wickedness and depravity imaginable.' He looked out into the chilly darkness. 'And some that are truly unimaginable.'

He wouldn't be put off. Karan took another sip, for courage. His face split into two again and she left it that way. She put her cup down, hard; the surface of the table wasn't where she expected. She swayed, caught the curved sides with both hands, shuddered.

'I've never told anyone. Not in twenty-four years.'

He said nothing.

'Not even dear old Rachis knew the truth. It – it's been festering inside me since I was a kid.'

'Time it was out, then.'

'It was the day my mother died. *Killed* herself.'

Karan's head was spinning. She pushed the cup away. Flydd emptied it into his own, dipped a gnarled finger in and licked it. He was not looking at her, and that helped.

'I know she cared about me, but she was sensitive and difficult and angry, and by the time I was five I'd turned away. Daddy's little favourite!' she spat, guilt overwhelming her. 'We cut her out and she got steadily worse. I knew I was being selfish, but she was so hard to love ...

'I've always blamed Mum. I turned a blind eye to Dad's faults: his long absences in Shazmak, the obsession with forbidden mancery that finally got him killed. I told myself that he had to get away from Mum ... Now I'm sure he broke her by rejecting her after I was born. And she got worse after he died.'

'How?'

'A stupid accident up at Carcharon, when I was eight. She spiralled down into despair, then a kind of madness. The family curse.'

Flydd raised half of his continuous eyebrow.

'They were both blendings – Mum was old human with a trace of Faellem, way back, and Dad – his name was Galliad – half old human and half Aachim. That made me a triune, and blendings and triunes are often unstable. He was handsome, charming, couldn't stick at anything. Fatally reckless!'

Karan paused. Flydd was still looking into his cup.

'The year I turned twelve it didn't rain. Summer was a heatwave that went on and on: crops failed; animals starving; money almost gone; unpaid workers hammering on our doors day and night ... then walking out. And on the hottest day of that dreadful year Mum cracked, screaming at me and whacking me with whatever came to hand.

'"It's all your fault Galliad's dead,"' she shrieked. '"He never would have pursued forbidden mancery if you hadn't encouraged him. I wish I'd never had you."'

Karan shuddered and wrapped her arms around herself again.

'I – I suppose I did encourage him. Dad loved to talk about mancery, and I loved hearing about it.'

'You were a little girl, enjoying time with your father. I wish –' Flydd's face went blank and his fists clenched on the table.

Karan didn't pursue it. 'I wanted to be a mancer myself, when I was older. I had the talent for it, back then.'

'What happened to it?' Flydd said sharply.

'I fled to Shazmak after Mum died, and Tensor – the leader of the Aachim, a proud, arrogant fool! – destroyed my gift. Robbed me of the greatest link to my father.'

Flydd's eyebrow became a V. 'Why would he do such a thing?'

'He said my gift was dangerous. He didn't mean dangerous to me,' she said, thumping the table, 'but to him and his stupid plans. Even when he lay dying, I couldn't forgive him.'

'But you *do* have a gift.'

'Just fragments. I'm a sensitive, and I can sometimes make links and do sendings. Malien tried to restore more of my gift a while ago, and a bit came back, but ...'

'What was lost as a child can't truly be restored as an adult.' Flydd gestured to her to go on with her story.

'Mum's hateful words shattered me and I hid up in the loft of the stables, but it was really hot and I fell asleep in the hay. Later she mind-called me, woke me and said she was sorry. She needed me, and she knew I'd heard her, but I didn't answer.

'An hour later she called again – a psychic cry of agony this time. But I couldn't face the abuse, the shrieking, the guilt trips ...

'My rejection must have tipped her over the edge; she didn't call again.' Karan looked up into Flydd's eyes. 'I'm not a monster, Xervish. Just *weak*.'

'Weak?' he murmured. 'I wouldn't say so.'

'If you knew my other secret –'

Karan broke off. She must be drunk, to have mentioned it. He did not ask, and she continued.

'The guilt finally got to me and I crept up to her attic room, under the roof of the old keep. She used to sew there, and paint and draw; it was her refuge. I was sick with dread, because the psychic *sense* of Mum I'd always had was gone. Something bad had happened. Sometimes she did things to hurt herself; I think physical pain eased her emotional torment.

'I thought my heart was going to tear apart, it was beating so wildly. I was afraid to open the door. I could smell blood. Why hadn't I gone to her when she called? If only I had.

'I lifted the latch, shouldered the door open, ran in – and ... and ...'

Karan banged her head on the table. It did not help. Flydd caught her right hand and she gripped his twisted fingers so tightly that he winced.

'Sometimes the sight or smell sends me back,' she said without raising her head. 'The reek in that sweltering room! The floor, covered in wild, tormented sketches – twisted faces, staring eyes, torn mouths.'

Flydd lifted her head and she looked him in the eye. She wasn't seeing double now.

'And blood,' she whispered. 'Gallons of it! Big, skinned-over puddles. Tracked over the floorboards. The rugs. The sketches. Everywhere.'

She reached for Flydd's cup, wanting oblivion, but it was empty.

'There was a long gash in her belly, as if –' Her voice cracked. 'As if Mum had tried to cut out the womb that had nourished such a wicked daughter. It must have taken her a long time to die …

'Her eyes were fixed on me. But no longer accusing me. Saying I was better off without her. There's been times, deep in denial, when I thought I was. I can never forgive myself.'

'You can't save someone who doesn't want to be saved,' said Flydd.

'What if it was a test?'

'No adult should test a child in so cruel a way. Besides, if you'd gone to her that day, she would have tried again another day.'

'How the hell would you know?' she said in a cracked voice.

'In the war I saw hundreds of men and women break, tens of thousands killed. I've seen sickening betrayals and malice that would burn your bones. I've punished thousands of liars, cheats and profiteers, ordered the execution of hundreds of traitors, and as many leaders whose negligence cost us dear. I've seen it all, Karan. I know!'

Maybe he was right. Maybe he did know.

'You'll never heal until you forgive yourself,' he said. 'Is *that* why you cling so desperately to Gothryme, even if it costs you Llian?'

That had never occurred to Karan. 'It's the only thing I have left of Mum.'

'You said she loved you, yet you have no *good* memories of her?' Flydd said sharply. 'I find that impossible to believe.'

Karan scowled at him.

'Dig deeper. Perhaps you blanked the good memories out so you could blame her, and justify neglecting her in favour of your *wonderful* father.'

She rose abruptly. 'Dad wasn't perfect, but he *was* a great father, and I don't have to listen to this.'

She staggered to the hatch, heaved it up, swayed and would have fallen through, head-first, had Flydd not leapt across and caught her.

He pulled her back and sat her down. 'You're sleeping in the cabin tonight.'

Karan did not have the strength to argue. He tossed a cushion and a sleeping pouch into the far corner. She crawled into it, lay on her back and closed her eyes, but that made her head spin, so she turned onto her side and huddled there, trembling.

Could he be right? She did not want to admit it. Had her father's rejection destroyed her mother? He should have been looking after her, not chasing phantoms up in the mountains.

And Karan was more like him than she had realised. She had made Vuula out to be a bad mother when she was just a desperate one.

I failed to love her, she thought. Only ever thought about her in anger and bitterness. Blamed her for the way I became. In denial, seeing my reckless father through ever more rose-coloured glasses.

Yet I was just as reckless. Leaving home after Mum died and making that dangerous trip across the mountains to find the hidden city of Shazmak, and my father's people. Fleeing there six years later and travelling for years, constantly seeking diversion, desperately trying to keep the pain at bay.

I'm still doing it. Sometimes suffocatingly clingy with Llian, other times pushing him away for fear of losing him too. Dominating him and controlling him because I can't bear to give up anything of Gothryme, the only thing I have left from her.

Lying to him, for years and years. Sometimes I think I'm trapped at the emotional age of my twelve-year-old self. Perhaps that's why Llian wants to go his own way. He's had enough.

14

'I WILL NEVER DESPAIR!

Each time Karan woke, Flydd was at his table in the corner of the cabin, hunched over his farspeaker. Listening to reports from Lilis and his other contacts and tearing at his scanty hair.

At three in the morning she roused with a sick headache. It was so long since she'd had a hangover that it took some time to recognise it. The moment she did the memories came back, though less painfully. Confessing had been good for her. *That* secret, at any rate.

She made tea from one of the packets of herbs in the galley. It tasted like wet grass. 'Any news?'

'It's odd,' said Flydd.

She waited.

'The enemy have taken half a dozen cities, and various mines and war-era manufactories, but they haven't done anything with them. And they're not killing and torturing as they've done in the past. They seem to be waiting ...'

'For what?'

'I don't know. Though they're rounding up architects, masons, carpenters and smiths, artists, sculptors and designers, and workers in all manner of other trades.'

'What for?'

Flydd shrugged. 'They're also searching old battlefields where clankers and other weapons of war were abandoned, and hunting down geomancers, artisans and artificers and pilots.' He groaned. 'And I named the best of them in my stupid *Histories*. I've condemned them to slavery ... and whatever comes after.'

'But you sent out a warning four days ago.'

'Only to the people I knew how to contact.'

'What's the plan, then?'

'We're heading to Nifferlin to collect Maelys and Nish –'

'The son of the former God-Emperor?'

'Yes. Nish was a hero of the war and of the long struggle, ten years later, to bring his father down. He's the best man I've got for the coming fight and I can't do without him, or Maelys – if she's in any fit state ...'

'Why wouldn't she be?'

'Her son was stillborn two years ago. And Maelys' little sister died not long after. She's crushed by grief.'

Sulien could well have died at birth, and it was utterly unimaginable. Karan's eyes moistened.

'But they'll be on top of the enemy's list,' said Flydd. 'I hope ...'

He jumped up, ran to the controls and the sky galleon whirled in its own length, scattering snow everywhere, and hurtled into the air.

Hope *what*? That you're not too late?

It was just after sunrise and they were heading down through a walnut forest towards Nifferlin Manor. The ancient trees were widely spaced, the soil a dark chocolate colour, the grass thick and green from plenty of rain. Nothing like Gothryme, then.

Flydd had been on edge ever since speaking to his spies last night, and he had landed well away from the manor, just in case.

Karan stopped in mid-stride. He continued for ten yards, then turned. 'Yes?'

'What keeps you going?' she croaked. 'When there's nothing but bad news?'

He came back. 'My earliest memory – I would have been three or four – is of my father's despair that the lyrinx were going to wipe us out. He was a good, kind man, but his nerves were too close to the surface. He couldn't eat, couldn't work, and one day he didn't wake up. I was only seven, too young to understand, but I swore that despair would *never* control me. That no matter how bad things got, or how hopeless it seemed, I would never stop fighting for the world and the people I loved.'

'And the day I do – *No!*' he cried, shaking his fists. 'The enemy may torture me and try to break me, but until I lie dead before them I will *never* stop fighting. For my father's sake, I will *never* despair.'

He walked on, though not as vigorously as before, and his shoulders were slumped. Yet Karan, treading in his footsteps, found her spirits unaccountably lifted.

'Nifferlin was home to Maelys' huge clan,' he said a few minutes later, 'but the manor was destroyed during the God-Emperor's reign and many of the men, including her father, were killed or died in prison. Most of the clan scattered – only her mother and two aunts, and her little sister, Fyllis, stayed, hiding in the ruins. Maelys and Nish started to rebuild two years ago, after the God-Emperor's death. It's a beautiful place.'

Another pang. No one would have called Gothryme beautiful, but it had been home and Karan was lost without it.

'We'll be just in time for breakfast,' he added. 'I'd walk twenty miles for Maelys' quarter-inch bacon, triple-yolker eggs and crusty bread with bitter marmalade.'

Her stomach rumbled.

As they approached the lower edge of the walnut forest, Flydd stopped abruptly. 'Smoke!' He gestured to her to keep low. 'Not the good kind.'

She slipped behind a mossy trunk. Ahead stretched acres of vines, plentiful with bunches of tiny grapes that would not be ready for harvesting for months. Beyond, the patchwork fields forecast a rich harvest.

But it would never be taken in.

Below the vineyards, the new manor had been reduced to three broken walls at one end, two at the other, and a central pair of chimneys rising from smoking rubble.

Flydd choked. 'I should have flown here the moment the Merdrun found my *Histories*.'

Karan took his spyglass and tried to focus on the ruins, but her hands were shaking too badly. This raised too many bad memories. 'Not much smoke. They must have torched the place hours ago.'

'But did the bastards get what they came for?' Flydd drew his sword and hacked down a walnut sapling. 'And are they still here, somewhere?'

'You any good with that?'

'Used to be. What about you?'

She drew her knife. 'I'm better at throwing knives than fighting with them.'

He headed down, muttering to himself. 'You're a scrawny old bastard who should have been pensioned off years ago. What difference can you make?'

'Wouldn't call you old, exactly.'

'*Younged* myself by a decade or two when I took renewal for a second time, a few years back.'

'You took renewal, *and kept the same appearance*?'

He managed the faintest smile. 'This scrawny body has served me well; this ugly face, too. Even with the ladies, believe it or not.'

'Not,' said Karan.

As they went down, the smell of charred flesh reminded her of past battle-fields, and atrocities she would sooner have stayed buried beyond recovery. They emerged from the vines onto a close-cropped lawn scattered with sheep droppings. Smoke drifted into their faces.

'Your gift telling you anything?' Flydd whispered.

'I'm picking up terror, violence, agony – and grief.'

'Grief suggests someone's still alive. Have the enemy gone?'

'I think so,' Karan said slowly.

The sun broke out from behind the clouds. The lawn was thick and green except near the manor, where it had burned out in a series of lobes. Away to the left, the doors of a stables stood open.

'Front door was this way.' Flydd headed around to the right, across the lawn and onto a driveway gravelled with the half-shells of thousands of black walnuts. They rattled and clicked underfoot. 'No one could sneak up on this place.'

'Merdrun don't have to sneak.'

The sense of grief swelled again, and it reminded Karan of her mother. Every step took an effort now.

Flydd propped, staring at a body sprawled on the front steps. An old woman, tall and lean, with a nose like the bow of a rowboat. The middle of her gown was blood-soaked, and it had run down the steps in banners.

'Haga,' he said softly. 'Maelys' last surviving aunt. A tough, plain-speaking woman.' He touched her neck with the back of his hand. 'Dead for hours.'

Maelys, still grieving for her sister and stillborn child, had now lost her last relative, and her home. If not her life.

He went in through the charred front door opening, sword in hand. Karan followed. There were more bodies inside, two men and a woman, all partly burned.

Flydd bent and checked the faces. 'House staff. I never knew their names.'

He surveyed the mess of rubble, half-burnt timber and furniture, and smashed roof slates. Halfway along, a bed, neatly made including the pillow, was perched on a mound of brickwork. The green quilt was covered in ash and pieces of slate, and charred around the edges. The rest was unburnt.

They searched the hot wreckage but found no more dead.

'They could be buried under the rubble,' said Karan.

'They didn't come to *kill* Nish and Maelys,' said Flydd, 'but to take them.'

There were tracks aplenty on the southern side of the house, where the shaded lawn was softest: deep imprints of many hooves and many pairs of boots, the soles fixed on with big, square nails. And another body.

'Aimee!' Flydd ran. Lying on her face, arms and legs asprawl, was a tiny, bird-like woman, killed by a sword thrust through the back.

He turned her over. 'She was brave and loyal and good and true – and great fun, too. But where's Clech, her man? They were inseparable.'

He knelt beside Aimee, laying a gnarled hand on the top of her head. 'She was one of the team that fought beside me against the God-Emperor,' he said brokenly. 'Why did she have to die? *Why not me?*'

The question had no answer, but Karan attempted one. 'Because no one else can lead the fight-back.'

Flydd planted his fists in the ground and slumped over until his forehead touched the grass.

She studied the tracks. 'They came up across country but left via the entrance road. No need for stealth then. Twenty mounted Merdrun, maybe more.'

'Enough to take a village. They wanted Nish and Maelys badly.' He rose stiffly. 'This is a blow, Karan. I don't know what I can do without them.'

They searched the stables, bakehouse and brew house, and the other outbuildings, but found no one else.

'They must be taking the prisoners to Fadd,' said Flydd. 'It's the only city they hold within a thousand miles.'

'How far?'

'Three day's ride east, the first day down a winding mountain track.'

'Why would they ride? Why not use a gate?'

'It's hard to make gates around here. Fields haven't regenerated yet.'

The grief Karan had sensed earlier swelled painfully and she clutched at the sides of her head. 'Someone's still alive.'

'Where?'

'Can't tell.'

'We've searched everywhere ...' said Flydd, then started. 'Apart from the cellars!'

'If they're under the rubble –'

'No, they're ancient. Up behind the old manor.'

They scrambled up through the vines and Flydd turned right along an overgrown track which ended, a few hundred yards later, at a rectangle of ground, a good sixty yards by forty, scattered with tall weeds, broken stone and slates.

'Must've been an enormous house,' said Karan.

'More than sixty of the clan lived here in the olden days.'

The waves of grief grew stronger; they were almost overwhelming Karan now.

They followed a path downslope, made a U-turn and passed through a broken archway of yellow stone feathered with blue-grey lichen. Flydd opened a wide wooden door in the side of the hill, proceeded down a set of five worn steps, touched a glowglobe to light and held it up. A tunnel with an arched roof ran into the dark. Racks on the left held curved barrel staves and timber. Further on were stacks of used barrels. Full barrels stood on a low platform along the right-hand wall.

'Anyone here?' he called.

Karan heard a sharp intake of breath.

'Xervish?' said a small, choked voice.

A young woman crept out from behind the furthest stack of barrels. She was shorter than Karan and more full-figured, with a round face winged by chin-length char-black hair and eyebrows that might have been brushed on with black ink. She would have been pretty but for the deep purple hollows under her eyes. Her blouse and trews were smoke-stained and torn, there was blood on her right knee and the palm of her left hand, and she carried a wicked carving knife.

'They killed Aunt Haga and Aimee, and took Nish.' The knife shook. Maelys dropped it, stumbled to Flydd and wrapped her arms around him.

'I'm sorry,' he said. 'Haga was a good woman. And Aimee –' His voice cracked. 'How will we do without her?'

Maelys pulled away, wiping her eyes on her sleeve. 'You must be Karan.'

'Yes. I'm sorry for –'

But Maelys had turned away. 'We've got to rescue Nish, today! Once they get down onto the plain it'll be too late.'

'We can't take on twenty seasoned Merdrun warriors.'

'Twenty-four, led by a sus-magiz.'

'Maelys,' Flydd said slowly, 'I need Nish as much as you do ... but it can't be done.'

'Can you hope to defeat the Merdrun without Nish?'

'No, but –'

'He's all I've got left. We've got to find a way.'

When Karan closed her eyes she could see the abyss in front of her. Flydd would mount a suicidal attack on the enemy force, and they would all be killed.

15

HOW CAN IT BE GONE?

They laid the bodies of Haga, Aimee and the servants in shallow graves in the lawn, since there was no time to dig deep ones, and covered the mounds with stone from the collapsed walls.

The sky had clouded over and a gusty wind spat cold raindrops at them. Karan trudged up to the vineyard, leaving Flydd and Maelys to their grief. Was this the way the world she loved would end, house by house and friend by friend, until the Merdrun had destroyed all trace of humanity? She cupped a bunch of tiny grapes, new life in the midst of death, but found no comfort in them.

Maelys came up, wearing a small pack and holding a yellow, egg-shaped object on a fine chain around her neck. She squeezed the object and slipped it down her blouse.

'I'm ready,' she said to Flydd, who had followed. 'How are we going to do it?'

'I have no idea.'

He set such a fast pace up the slope that Karan, whose bad leg was aching, struggled to keep up. Who among her old allies could still be alive? Only Yggur, who was old and weak now, and fading to his longed-for end, and Malien. But Malien had gone to Aachan two years ago with most of Clan Elienor and many thousands of other Aachim. She would never return to Santhenar.

The walnut forest now had a cold and dismal air. Here and there, fallen walnuts from last seasons sprouted vigorously, though few would survive.

'If we can find Clech –' Maelys began.

'He's alive?' said Flydd, brightening.

'He went down to Morrelune two days ago. How am I going to tell him about Aimee?' Maelys stopped, knuckling her eyes. 'I had three wisp-watchers out – Nish got them from Mazurhize – but –'

'What's Mazurhize?' said Karan.

'The ruins of Jal-Nish's underground prison, a few days' walk from here. But the wisp-watchers didn't warn us of danger.'

'That'd be the sus-magiz's doing,' said Flydd.

'A grey-faced, angry fellow with white eyes,' said Maelys. 'We were packing our gear, getting ready to leave at first light, when Aunt Haga –' She stopped again, her eyes leaking tears.

'She'd been poorly, but she heard them on the drive and went out and ordered them begone ... *And they killed her!* Then kicked her aside and cut our servants down inside the front door ...

'The sus-magiz paralysed Nish before he could move, bound him and carried him out, then torched the place. There was nothing Aimee and I could do; we got out a window and ran. But Aimee – you know what she's like – crept after them and I – I couldn't stop her. I should have gone with her.'

'They would have killed you too,' said Flydd.

She slumped. 'I let everyone down. Didn't know what to do. In the olden days –'

'There were twenty-four of them!' He crouched before her, holding her by the shoulders. 'Maelys, think! What would Haga want you to do?'

She found a feeble little smile. '*Family is everything.* She'd want me to get Nish back and destroy our enemies. And make Nifferlin good again.'

Flydd lifted her to her feet and led her to a cluster of round rocks jutting out of the dark soil. 'And we will – though I can't think how.'

Karan sat on another rock, thinking bitter thoughts. He had refused to lift a finger to look for Llian, yet now he was planning an attack that could only be suicide, and she could not get out of it because she had given her word.

'How long until the Merdrun are out of reach?' he said to Maelys.

'A day. The track down the mountains is deadly in the dark; they would have waited at the top 'til dawn. And even in daylight they'll have to lead their mounts down the worst sections.'

'Then if we're to ambush them, we've got to do it before dark. But we haven't a hope by ourselves.'

'Flangers and Chissmoul stopped by three days ago,' said Maelys. She pronounced the name *kiss*-mool. 'Ferrying people into hiding in their air floater.'

'Where are they now?'

'Somewhere north of here.'

He jumped up. 'Come on.'

They went aboard and he sat at the controls, frowning. 'Flangers was one of my best lieutenants in the war,' he said to Karan. 'A brilliant soldier and a good, decent man ... tormented, though.'

Few people who had gone through such a war, and had done what they'd had to do to survive and win, would not be tormented. Karan certainly was. 'And Chissmoul?'

'The best pilot we ever had ... but ... difficult. Highly strung. The bond between pilots and their craft is a powerful one, and she lives to fly. With them and Clech –'

'Maelys said he went down to Morrelune. Would he be coming back on the same track?'

'Part of the way. Maelys, where would Clech be now?'

She took a canvas map from a rack and spread it out on the deck, and they knelt next to it.

'Could be anywhere down here,' said Maelys, pointing. 'Depends how long it took him in Morrelune.'

'I can't fly up and down the road looking for him. The enemy will hear us. I'll try to locate the air-floater.'

He went below and shortly came up again, carrying a wooden box. 'This might do it.'

Inside was a conglomeration of crystals and wires, with a small yellow glass sphere resting in a brown bowl at its centre. He put it on his little table in the rear corner and sat with eyes closed and right hand cupped over the top of the device. Every so often he adjusted one of the little levers, then rotated a toothed wheel. Coloured rays moved across the surface of the glass sphere, blue and grey, then lime green. He traced their paths absently, eyes still closed. The lime green ray turned scarlet.

'North 40 east,' he said softly. His eyes came open but he did not look down.

'How far?' said Maelys.

'It only gives direction.'

Karan was staring at the scarlet ray when it flashed and vanished.

'Ugh!' Flydd clutched his head, then turned slowly and stared at the sphere.

'Was that the enemy, attacking them?' said Maelys.

'I hope not.' He went to the controls and the sky galleon lifted and headed north-east.

'Can you get it back?' Karan carried the contraption across and set it down on the binnacle in front of him.

He touched the glass sphere. 'No. It's gone.'

'*What's* gone?' said Karan, frustrated.

'The air-floater's controller ...'

'How can it be gone?'

'Maybe the Merdrun took it,' said Flydd. 'There are less than a dozen air-floaters in the world, and they would have done everything in their power to locate them.'

'Why so few?' said Karan. 'They're not hard to make.'

'The fields that have regenerated are still weak, so it takes a supremely powerful crystal to make a controller work, and a pilot of rare gifts to operate it. There aren't many of either. And the Merdrun want all of them.'

'Then why can't you see this one anymore?'

'I don't know,' Flydd said grimly.

'If they can find air-floaters via their controllers, can they also find the sky galleon?'

'I desperately hope not.'

Without warning, Sulien's voice burst into Karan's mind.

Mummy, I really hate this place. The old woman never says anything nice. She just orders me about, from sunrise until I'm sent to bed. I'm her slave, Mummy.

And ... and Jassika still hasn't come back. I'm really afraid for her –

Sulien was gone, and Karan could not reach her. *What have I done?* she thought. She turned towards Flydd, then stopped. She knew what he would say.

16

THE RIGHT PERSON FOR THE JOB

Every day was the same here. A cool night lit by thousands of stars, brighter than Wilm had ever seen them, was followed by a blazing red dawn, a cloudless sky then, by mid-morning, baking heat that lasted until sundown. The dark rocks radiated it back at them until he felt like a piece of meat sizzling on a hotplate. From the moment the sun rose he counted the minutes until it would set.

Two days had passed. He was trudging up another ridge, this time with Klarm who had been baiting him mercilessly all afternoon, when grey smoke billowed up to his left.

'It's the signal!' he cried. 'It's been found.'

'Well done, laddie. There's no keeping anything from you.'

Wilm still had no idea why the dwarf had taken such a set against him. He ran down into the gully, slipping on flat pieces of yellow shale, up the other side and over the ridge.

'Stop!' hissed Ilisial, holding up both arms.

Will skidded to a stop. 'Where is it?'

'Down there. M'Lainte said to stay well away.'

She was on her knees beside a solitary mound of grey sand, scraping it away with the blade of a triangular knife. The afternoon shadows were long and Wilm could not make anything out. He went down a few feet, desperate to see the spellcaster.

M'Lainte looked up. 'Ah, Wilm. Come here.'

Ilisial cried out, '*I'm* the apprentice.'

Wilm went down, stepping carefully, and saw a black metal rod, funnel-shaped on the end, protruding from the sand.

'You remember the warnings?' M'Lainte said quietly.

'Yes, but surely Ilisial –'

'You've been blooded, lad, and she hasn't.'

'Blooded?'

'You've shown, in desperate situations, that you have a cool head and a steady hand. That's what I need right now.'

'Not always,' he muttered. 'When Unick –'

'Are you arguing with me?'

'No,' he said hastily.

Ilisial's long face was a storm cloud. 'Killer!' she mouthed.

Why did she despise him? He'd done nothing to her. Or was she *afraid* of him? That was even worse.

'Wilm!' M'Lainte hissed. 'Pay attention.'

'Sorry.'

'Looks as though the spellcaster has been buried here for years. That might mean it's dead –'

'How do you mean, *dead*?'

'Drained of power and unable to draw more. But it might also mean that it felt no need to move until something happened. It's a deadly device, lad, and we need to be careful – and respectful.'

Wilm wasn't sure he knew how to be respectful to a machine.

'Dig the sand away on your side, and I'll do the same here,' said M'Lainte. 'Make no sudden moves. Don't speak unless there's something I need to know.'

They worked in silence. In the distance, Wilm saw the guards climbing the gully, answering the signal. Shortly Klarm crested the ridge, stopped and came down slowly.

'You sure *he's* the right person for the job?' said Klarm.

'Absolutely,' said M'Lainte.

For a moment, Wilm soared. Klarm made a rude noise.

Wilm kept excavating carefully until he had exposed the right side of the spellcaster. It was a metal disc five feet across and a foot and a half deep in the centre, with six stubby arms spaced along metal bands around its equator. Each arm ended in a funnel, black on the outside and an eerie blue within. A cylindrical metal skirt projected down from its circumference for another foot.

M'Lainte had almost cleared the left side now. She carved away the last of the sand, flicked aside a small brown scorpion with her knife and put an ear to the side of the spellcaster.

'Nothing,' she said shortly. 'I think it's safe to move.'

She slung a web of straps under it. As Wilm, Ilisial and two of the guards began to lift it, something went *tick-click* inside.

'Drop it!' hissed M'Lainte. 'Lay flat!'

Wilm, used to obeying orders instantly, let go of his strap and threw himself down, as did the guards. M'Lainte and Klarm did too, but Ilisial was still holding her strap as the spellcaster tilted and hit the ground. It seethed like a boiling kettle, the equatorial bands rotated, *click-click-click*, and one funnel-tipped arm stopped, pointing at Ilisial's face.

'Down!' shrieked M'Lainte.

Without thinking, Wilm swung a leg at Ilisial's ankles and swept her off her feet. Blue fire howled from the funnel, through the space her head had occupied moments before, and blew a dead tree fifty yards away to blazing fragments.

Ilisial fell hard. M'Lainte threw herself at the spellcaster and thumped a protrusion on top with her fist. A metal cover flipped up. She reached inside and wrenched out a dark green crystal. The seething stopped. The spellcaster rocked on its metal skirt, then settled.

'*That's* why I asked Wilm,' M'Lainte said quietly. 'You all right, girl?'

Ilisial lay where she had fallen, rubbing her right wrist; she had broken her fall on it. She shuddered and let out a low, howling sound that raised the hairs on the back of Wilm's neck. Her eyes were vacant.

M'Lainte crawled across and slapped her across the face. Ilisial broke off.

'S-sorry,' she said, rubbing her cheek. 'Took me back ... a bad time.'

The guards were gaping at one another, and Wilm's skin was crawling. He shuddered. Another second and Ilisial's head – he suppressed the ghastly image.

He caught her eye and it burned with hostility. He had just saved her life, yet she looked as though she hated him. What was the matter with her?

'Is it safe now?' he said quietly to M'Lainte.

'Hope so.'

They carried the spellcaster across to some shade, a safe distance above their camp. M'Lainte brushed the dirt off a flat slab of rock and directed them to put the secret weapon down.

The guards set up camp. M'Lainte and Wilm cleaned the sand and dust off the spellcaster. Klarm sat a few yards away, silently observing.

'Got your workbook?' M'Lainte said to Ilisial. 'Sketch everything.'

Ilisial took a square book from her bag, sat cross-legged next to M'Lainte and drew the spellcaster from various angles. Her drawings, labelled in a small, beautifully formed hand, might have been done by a master drafter, and for the first time since Wilm had met her she looked at peace.

Slowly and carefully, M'Lainte began to take the spellcaster apart, laying each piece on a sheet of canvas. Wilm's stomach knotted. What if it was booby-trapped?

Ilisial turned the page and sketched each part, and how it fitted into the device.

'Have you ever done this before?' said Wilm to M'Lainte, fascinated.

'I've never even seen one before.'

'Then how do you know how –?'

'Don't you ever stop jawboning?' said Klarm.

Wilm kept his mouth shut after that. As the light waned, Klarm set up glow-globes on sticks. The guards cooked dinner and made tea, then kindled a small fire at their backs. M'Lainte, totally focused on the perilous job of disassembly, did not even look at her plate.

The evening passed. The guards went to their sleeping pouches and so did Klarm. M'Lainte worked on and Wilm sat by her, not speaking, watching everything she did with eager eyes. Ilisial scowled at him whenever he looked her way. Why, *why*?

'Done,' M'Lainte said when it must have been close to midnight. She laid the last part, a tiny hourglass filled with glittering powder and set in a clockwork mechanism, on the canvas. 'It's safe now. Get to bed.'

Ilisial, who had filled a dozen pages with sketches, went to her tent, snapping the flap closed like a whipcrack.

Will fed the fire behind them; it was cold now. 'It's all right. I want to see everything.'

'I was the same when I was young,' she said approvingly.

'What are you going to do with it?'

'Clean everything up and put it back together.'

'Is that dangerous?'

'Could be.'

She yawned, looked down at the stew of meat and vegetables and mashed grains congealed on her plate, then began to spoon it down, washed down by gulps of cold tea.

'I'll make a fresh brew,' said Wilm.

'That would be nice.'

Her painstaking work continued through the night. Wilm dozed and woke, dozed and woke, and each time M'Lainte was in the same position, utterly focused, reassembling the spellcaster from memory. Finally, as the sun tipped the eastern horizon, it was complete, though to his relief she had not put the dark green crystal back.

'Now I understand it,' she said, rubbing her fingers together. 'I could use a warming mug of tea, Wilm.'

He was heading down to the camp, yawning and stretching cramped muscles, when he heard a faint, rhythmic *thup-thup, thup-thup*.

M'Lainte swore. 'Put the campfire out and get everyone up. Quick, *quick!*'

Wilm hurtled down the slope, skidded to a stop beside the camp, sending stones skidding in all directions, and roared, 'Get up!'

'What's the matter?' Klarm was out so quickly that he must have slept with his wooden foot on.

'I don't know.' Wilm kicked the embers of the campfire apart and stamped on them. 'We heard a *thup-thup, thup-thup* sound.' Everyone was talking at once and he could hear nothing now.

'Quiet!' bellowed Klarm.

M'Lainte had tossed the canvas over the reassembled spellcaster and was crushing out the embers of her fire.

'Get into cover,' said Klarm.

They crept in under the scrub.

He was staring at the eastern sky. The *thup-thup, thup-thup* was louder now. 'Air-floater, and it can only be looking for us.'

'Could Flydd have sent it to pick us up?' asked Ilisial in a small voice.

'I haven't called him yet.'

'But it doesn't have to be the Merdrun. We have air-floaters too.'

'Not coming from that direction. Wilm, that bloody fire is still smoking. Can't you do anything properly?'

Wilm scurried to grind the last ember out under his boot, then slipped back into hiding, gripping the hilt of the black sword.

M'Lainte joined them. The brass curves of Klarm's knoblaggie bulged between his fingers. Four of the guards had drawn their swords and the two archers had loaded their crossbows.

Wilm was about to unsheathe his blade when Klarm said, 'No! Shove it well down.'

Wilm did so.

'Don't use it unless you have to, laddie. We've got to be able to *trust* our weapons.'

The sound of the rotors steadily grew louder, though it was another ten minutes before Wilm could make out the air floater. M'Lainte focused her spyglass on it.

'Merdrun glyph on the airbag.' She handed it to Klarm. 'Do you think they're looking for us?'

'Yes.'

'Have we been betrayed?'

He did not reply.

The air-floater was small, with a long, sleek airbag and a streamlined cabin. *Go past*, Wilm prayed. *Don't see us.*

Memories rose, from his time as a slave on Gwine. The bone-cracking labour, the enemy's casual brutality, sleeping in stinking mud and filth, dragging the dead out each morning ... Every effort to steady his hammering heart failed.

The air-floater cruised by a couple of miles away and several thousand feet below them, tracking along the edge of the Sink of Despair.

'They've missed us,' whispered Ilisial.

'They'll spot the wreckage of the air-dreadnought,' said Klarm. 'It's less than four miles away; they could be here within hours.'

'I'll call Flydd,' said M'Lainte.

'I tried last night. Couldn't reach him. Go back to the spellcaster. If they find us, and we can't escape, destroy it.'

'I'm not sure I know how.'

'Wilm's black sword will cut through anything. Hack the, er ... *core* of the spellcaster – you know what I'm talking about – to bits.'

'Yes,' she said grimly. 'But that could be apocalyptic.'

'Not as bad as the enemy getting it. Your affairs are in order, aren't they?'

'More or less.'

'If they get it, they'll kill the lot of us anyway.'

'Yes. Come on, Wilm.'

He followed her up, keeping to the shrubbery in the bottom of the gully. *I'm going to die*, he thought. *Slaughtered by the enemy or blown to blazing bits by the spellcaster. There's no way out.*

'You got what Klarm said?' said M'Lainte.

'Yes,' he said hoarsely.

'And you're not tempted to run and hide?'

'I – I'm terrified. But we have a job to do.'

'I'm glad you're by my side, Wilm. But it may not come to that.'

As she spoke, the air-floater turned up the slope and hovered.

'They've spotted the wreckage,' said Wilm.

'Yes.'

It settled, and through M'Lainte's spyglass Wilm saw tiny figures moving about. After half an hour the Merdrun reboarded their craft, which began to fly in a spiral.

'Difficult to track us in such hard, stony country,' said M'Lainte. 'We haven't left a lot of traces.'

'Apart from the ashes of our campfires.'

'True,' she said gloomily.

He watched breathlessly, wishing he had made it up with Aviel. She was stuck with Maigraith, who did not have a kind bone in her body. He ached for Aviel, feared for her.

Another ten or fifteen minutes passed, the little air-floater following its widening spiral, then it turned, climbed rapidly and headed back the way it had come.

'I don't understand,' he said.

'It was just a scout. But if they have far-speakers, or other ways of communicating at a distance –'

'They'll soon be back,' Wilm said.

Down below, Ilisial screamed.

17

STUPID OLD BAG!

Ilisial was as rigid as a post, fists clenched by her sides. 'Leave them alone!' she shrilled. 'Leave – them – *Noooooo!*'

Klarm reached up to her. She lashed out, catching him across the side of the head and knocking him sideways, then bolted, moaning and flailing her long arms.

'Stop her!' said M'lainte.

Wilm raced down the slope, intersected Ilisial and caught her by the shoulder. She whirled, punched him in the mouth, then clutched her wrist, the one she had twisted earlier, and stumbled away.

He reached her in a few strides. She head-butted him under the jaw so hard that it knocked him onto his back. She looked out of her mind. She picked up a rock in both hands and raised it above her head; she was going to brain him! Wilm tried to get out of the way, knew he could not.

'No!' bellowed Klarm.

He must have used a Command because she froze, the rock slid from her hands and she fell to her knees, wailing. Wilm got up, spitting out blood, and took a careful step towards her.

M'Lainte panted up. 'Stay back, Wilm.'

She went to Ilisial. 'Before we left Thurkad,' M'Lainte said in a rigidly controlled voice, 'I asked if there was any reason you couldn't go into danger. And you said there wasn't.'

'I – I can't talk about it.'

'You *will* talk about it. Or you'll never work with me again.'

Ilisial remained on her knees, gaze fixed on the ground, racked by shudders. Her mouth opened but nothing came out.

'Speak,' said M'Lainte.

'I – I was a little girl. Five.'

'And?' said M'Lainte when she did not go on.

'Whole family was murdered. At the end of the Lyrinx War,' she said in a halting whisper, as if she could not bear to say it aloud. She directed a hate-filled glare at Wilm.

'Don't look at Wilm. When you were five, he wasn't even born. Look at me.' M'Lainte went to her knees in front of Ilisial.

Wilm knew what went on in war and didn't want to hear her story. He started to back away.

'Stay!' Klarm murmured.

It burst out of Ilisial. 'They were killed by soldiers from our own side. Filthy renegades! I hid. Saw it all. Father was hacked to pieces. Mother was ... I can't say it, I can't say it, *I can't* –'

'You don't have to say it.' M'Lainte took her hand. 'But you do have to get it out.'

'They stabbed her and left her to die while they did – *the same* – to my sisters.'

'I'm so sorry.'

'I was sure they were going to find me too,' Ilisial said shrilly. 'After they left, I was too scared to come out. Three days I hid there, just me and my dead.'

'Why didn't you tell me this in Thurkad?'

'I grew up with nothing. I've worked so hard ... I couldn't bear to give up my only chance. Then *he* comes along, sucking up to you.' She gestured wildly at Wilm. 'A common soldier! A stinking killer, trying to rob me of the one thing I have left.'

Wilm had to defend himself. He took a deep breath but Klarm grabbed his arm, saying quietly, 'Don't move. Don't speak.'

'Wilm has no gift for the Art,' said M'Lainte. 'He could never take your place.'

'You chose him over me,' said Ilisial.

'Not for artisan's work. And he saved your life.'

She scowled.

She can't see a single good thing in me, Wilm thought. This is hopeless.

M'Lainte sighed. 'Ilisial, if I'd asked you to help me disassemble the spellcaster, and you'd had a panic attack, we might all be dead. I can't work with someone who conceals information from me.'

All the fury drained out of Ilisial. 'I'm sorry,' she whispered. 'Please don't cast me out. I'll work day and night.'

M'Lainte sighed. 'I have no quarrel with your work. Swear there's nothing more I need to know, and we'll say no more about it ... as long as there *is* nothing more.'

'There's nothing more, I swear it.'

'Good. And swear you'll treat Wilm like a trusted ally, not –'

'Later!' Klarm was staring after the air-floater. 'We've got to get well away from here.'

'And then?' M'Lainte had slumped to the ground with her eyes closed.

The sleepless night was catching up with Wilm, too. His split lip throbbed and pain ran up the right side of his jaw.

'You'll try to make the spellcaster safe,' said Klarm.

'To what purpose?' said M'Lainte.

'They'll come back for it – and they must not get it.'

'What if it can't be made safe?' said Ilisial.

She slanted a dark look at Wilm. She was going to cause more trouble, he knew it.

'We destroy it,' said Klarm. 'And if we survive, we hide, and pray Flydd can get back to pick us up.'

'What if he can't?' said Wilm.

Klarm did not reply. Ilisial wrapped her arms around herself and rocked back and forth.

'Are there caves around here?' asked M'Lainte.

'Wouldn't have a clue,' said Klarm.

'As we flew in,' said Wilm, 'I saw white and dark layers of rock running across the mountainside. That's where I'd look.'

Klarm jerked a thumb upwards. Four guards picked up the spellcaster in its slings and they headed up, keeping to the hardest ground and trying to avoid leaving any tracks, but when they stopped briefly two hours later Wilm was dismayed to see how little progress they had made.

'How's your leg?' M'Lainte said to Klarm.

'Worn the skin off my stump. Bloody Flydd and his bloody *Histories*! If I ever see the bastard again, I'll spit him and roast him over red-hot pig iron.'

Klarm's skin had a grey tinge and he looked a decade older. M'Lainte was also making hard work of the climb, and even Ilisial, taking her turn on the slings, was labouring.

Wilm was the only one not worn out. He had been used to hard manual work all his life and the time he had spent as a slave for the Merdrun, building a fortress on the Isle of Gwine, had built his endurance. Unfortunately, this freed him to think dire thoughts.

They crossed a line of hills and continued up. High above, the layers of dark and light rock he had seen previously projected out of the slope. There must be seeping moisture too, for he made out patches of scrub and several horizontal bands of blue-leaved trees.

Klarm climbed an outcrop of shiny grey rock and scanned the mountainside with his spyglass. 'Caves, up there.'

He handed the spyglass down but M'Lainte said, 'Keep it.'

'Why?'

'Thought that'd be obvious. I'm holding you back, and I can't go much further. Take the spellcaster and go.'

'Stupid old bag!' Klarm muttered. 'We're not leaving you, even if I have to carry you myself.'

To Wilm's surprise, M'Lainte laughed. 'That's a sight I'd like to see, you old goat!' But the laughing ending in a coughing and wheezing fit that brought tears to her eyes. 'Haven't got the breath for it.'

18

TO WHOM DO YOU OWE YOUR LOYALTY?

In the days after drinking Tataste's life, while Skald worked from dawn until late to master the sus-magiz spells for drawing power from himself, for making gates, and for attack and defence and interrogation, he grew ever more terrified. He kept reliving her emotions and knew he could not conceal them from the magiz much longer. When he cracked, nothing would give Dagog greater pleasure than to suck Skald's life from him.

The thought made his skin crawl. Even doing it to the people of Santhenar, who were so far beneath the Merdrun that they seemed barely human, he now knew to be wrong. But to drink the life of one of their own, his own tormented self, would be an abomination.

He was trying not to think about Tataste's dead children when a memory resurfaced – the enemy girl who had briefly touched his mind when he'd found the amber-wood box. Minds were protected, and not even a magiz could look into someone else's head without the use of a mighty spell, even more perilous to the user than to the target. So how had a young girl done it? She must have a gift for far-seeing and mind-touching. A priceless gift. But why had she come to him?

A messenger entered the spell-casting chamber. Skald was ordered to Durthix's command post, at once. Had the magiz detected forbidden emotions in him? Skald prayed that Durthix would send him into battle. While he was in action and his life was at risk the tormenting inner voices were silent.

'Captain Skald,' Durthix boomed the moment Skald entered the room. 'Shut the door and lock it, and come here.'

Skald locked the door, marched across to the vast table, which had a map spread out on it, and saluted. 'Yes, High Commander?'

For once the big room was empty; Durthix was completely alone. 'I have an urgent job for you. Are you ready to do your duty on a moment's notice?'

'Always, High Commander.'

'Some days ago, the enemy's sky galleon deposited a team of people here.' Durthix's thick finger stabbed a point on the map where an expanse of mountains gave way to a flat oval marked Sink of Despair. 'What do you know about this place?'

'Nothing, High Commander.'

'It's dry, desolate and uninhabited,' said Durthix. 'Scorching in summer, freezing in winter and of no value to anyone, so what are the enemy doing there? You will lead a squad of twelve soldiers there in –' he consulted a water clock on the wall '– thirty minutes.'

'Yes, High Commander. What is our mission?'

Durthix considered him thoughtfully. 'Captain Skald, to whom do you owe your loyalty?'

Was this a trick question? As a sus-magiz, Skald had a new master. But Durthix hadn't called him sus-magiz, he'd called him captain.

'As a soldier, High Commander, I owe my loyalty to my superior officers, and through them to you, and you alone.'

'I'm pleased to hear it, because you lead this mission as a soldier, not as a sus-magiz.'

Skald swallowed. He was caught up in the great rivalry between Durthix and the magiz, and if the magiz won, he, Skald, was doomed.

'Yes, Commander,' he said uneasily. 'You're sending me to fight, rather than to use magic?'

'I'm sending you because you can fight *and* use magic, and both will be needed.'

'What are my duties, High Commander?'

'You will make a gate to the Sink of Despair and search for a secret weapon the enemy lost there long ago.'

'How do you –? Ah! This was written in *Histories of the Lyrinx Wars*.'

'Which you found. How much did you read before you reported it?'

Skald's heart was racing now. To admit reading a word might be a crime. On the other hand, Durthix appreciated initiative. 'A few pages, Commander. And I saw sketches of a number of their devices, as you know.'

Durthix regarded him for a minute. 'Good.'

'Can I ask a question, High Commander?'

'If you're quick.'

'Is it a coincidence, the enemy going to the Sink of Despair?'

'It is not. They were taken there by the wily Xervish Flydd, to a place where one of their air-dreadnoughts crashed long ago and a secret weapon was lost. The team includes their most skilled artisan of magical devices, the mechanician, M'Lainte. You will capture her, *alive and unharmed*, and bring her back. And the secret weapon, if they've found it.'

'Yes, High Commander. And if they haven't?'

'Leave that to me, Captain Skald. You have everything needed?'

'I'm always ready for action, High Commander.'

'Go up to the rooftop. Your troop is waiting. Here is a primed focus –'

'A what?'

'A brand-new device. You're the first to use one. It will allow you to save power by far-seeing your destination much more precisely than you could on your own, since you've never been there.' He passed Skald a long, narrow white crystal, flat on each end, with mirror-silvered sides. 'Tell your squad nothing until you reach the destination. Then they need only know that they are to capture the mechanician, *unharmed*, and bring back the secret weapon. Speak to *no one* about this, Captain. Do you understand me?'

Skald did. *No one* included the magiz. 'Yes, High Commander.'

Skald's gut was tight as he went out and headed for the stairs. What if he ran into Dagog? But as he emerged on the roof and saw the two ranks of six soldiers waiting there, his spirits soared.

A secret weapon so important that the enemy's most skilled artisan had been sent to find it. Such a mission would normally be entrusted to a much more experienced officer. Was it his reward for finding the enemy's *Histories*? He could not fail; he must not!

He went across to his warriors, nine men and three women. All were battle-scarred; it was clear that they were among the best.

'I am Captain Skald Hulni,' he said. 'We are gating to a far-off place. When we emerge, I'll give you your orders.'

They saluted and asked no questions.

As he raised the primed focus to the glyph tattooed on his forehead, Skald felt a moment of self-doubt, almost panic. He had been through many gates, and had created several practice gates since becoming a sus-magiz, but this was his first real gate. What if it failed? His fall would be even swifter than his rise.

He suppressed the fear. He knew what to do, and how to do it. He looked into the heart of the focus, to the destination secreted there, drew power from himself smoothly and created the gate.

It was an oval bubble, a little taller than himself and wider at the bottom, with a rim that glistened like clear mucus. He studied it in awe. So mighty a conduit to have come from so little, from him. And it was perfectly made.

He smiled. 'Go through!'

If any of his troops felt fear, they did not show it. The first soldier pushed through the bubble and disappeared with a hiss of air. The others followed quickly, knowing that it was exhausting to hold a gate open. Skald's muscles were tense with the strain; sweat flooded down his chest and sides.

He glanced to his left and Durthix was watching. What if he, Skald, lost control? No! He forced through the bubble, which clung wetly. Fireworks flared out in all directions; he was hurled forwards, his organs slopping around in his middle, his vision blurring as his eyeballs tried to flatten themselves against the back of his eye sockets.

He was losing the gate! *Hold it!* Skald pressed the focus crystal harder against his forehead, re-visualised the destination and held it tight.

His ears popped, he emerged a yard above the ground, and the gate vanished with an echoing *booooom*. The drenching sweat evaporated instantly in the hot, dry air. He was next to the bleached bamboo hoops of the air-dreadnought. The barren slope, cut with gullies and ridges, extended up, range after range, beyond sight and, according to Durthix's map, all the way to the top of Mount Tirthrax, the greatest peak in all the Three Worlds.

But Skald had no eyes for scenery, no matter how majestic. He scanned the slopes.

A soldier with bristly white hair pointed, 'Up there! Eight of them. No, nine. No, ten; one looks like a child.'

'There's an important old woman,' said Skald. 'Mechanician M'Lainte. She must be taken, *unharmed*.'

'Taken *unharmed*,' they echoed.

'And a device of some sort. A weapon. We must have it.'

The troops acknowledged the order. 'What about the others?' asked the soldier with the white hair.

'They can be killed,' said Skald. 'But if they get away, don't pursue them. All we want is the woman and the weapon. Go!'

Wilm, Ilisial and two of the guards took their turn hauling the spellcaster up a rocky ridge where they would leave no tracks, then everyone stopped for a hasty lunch. No one spoke; they did not have the energy. Wilm, gnawing at a leathery slice of salted buffalo between two slabs of stone-hard bread, could see all the way down to the Sink of Despair.

He looked around and caught Ilisial's hostile eye on him. She turned away at once. No one should have to suffer what she had been through, but why did she blame him? Why did nothing he had done, including saving her life, make any difference? It hurt.

A flash gilded the bamboo hoops of the air dreadnought. Klarm cursed and focused the spyglass. A good few seconds passed before they heard the low thudding *boom* that had accompanied the flash.

'Gate!' hissed Wilm. 'They're after us!'

'Your perspicacity never ceases to amaze,' muttered Klarm.

'How many?' asked M'Lainte.

'Twelve of their finest,' said Klarm, using the spy glass. 'Led by a sus-magiz.' He looked up at the distant bands of rock. 'It'll take us another couple of hours to get to the caves.'

'We can make it.' Wilm swallowed the last of his bread and buffalo meat in a couple of gulps and washed it down with warm, iron-tainted water. 'It could take them hours to find us.'

'Want to bet? Don't move, anyone!'

'Too late,' said M'lainte. 'They've spotted us.'

Klarm cursed. 'Go!'

They scrambled to their feet and headed up, over a ridge and down a dip, from the bottom of which they could no longer see the enemy, though Wilm fancied he could feel the ground shaking under their heavy boots. They were tough and tireless. War had been the focus of their existence for ten thousand years. They would be quick.

An hour passed, and most of another as they hauled the spellcaster up, and ever up. The trees were only four hundred yards above them now, a band of woodland a few hundred feet from top to bottom that extended across the slope for miles, nourished by moisture seeping out from the base of those layers of twisted rock. There were caves, too. He could see their dark mouths here and there.

But caves, unless they extended into an underground labyrinth, would not save them. With twelve Merdrun warriors led by a sus-magiz, the end could not in doubt.

M'Lainte was moving ever more slowly. Her saggy jowls were scarlet, and she was panting but could not seem to draw enough air. Would she make it? Wilm assessed the distance to go, and the pursuit, and knew it would be a near thing.

'Here,' he said, offering her his shoulder. 'We can do it.'

She slumped to her knees. 'No, you'll have to leave me.'

'We're not abandoning –' began Wilm.

'It's not a request, Wilm.'

Leaving her behind would be a betrayal of everything he stood for. Impulsively, he took her hand in his. 'Let me carry you.'

She snorted. You're a good man, Wilm, and if you survive this, you'll go far. But I'm too heavy, and my time is up.'

'M'Lainte, old friend, I'm sorry,' said Klarm. 'What would we have done without –?'

'I know my worth,' she said, 'and when it's over.'

'You've got a knife?'

'Yes, but I'm not the kind of person to employ it on myself.'

'Even facing torture?'

'I should, so my knowledge and talents can't fall into enemy hands. But ... there you go. Oh, you'll need this.' She handed him the green crystal she had taken out of the spellcaster.

Klarm shook her hand, and there were tears in his eyes. 'I dare the choice will come to the rest of us soon enough.' He turned away.

Ilisial was crouched beside M'Lainte, quivering. 'You taught me so much. I'm sorry I let you down.'

'I should have listened to my misgivings. Off you go.' Ilisial headed up. 'Wilm?' M'Lainte said quietly.

'Yes?'

'Would you watch over Ilisial for me? I made a bad mistake with her and I can't put it right.'

'I'll do what I can.' *If she lets me.* He swallowed an enormous lump and turned away. This was so wrong!

They continued up, much faster now. Wilm looked back, his view blurred by tears. M'Lainte was writing in a small book. How could she face capture, torture and death so calmly? He would be wetting himself.

He took a tighter grip on the slings and struggled on. Even his iron fortitude was failing him now. 'How far to go?' It was an effort to raise his head.

'A – hundred – yards,' gasped Klarm, suppressing a howl of agony with every step. How did the little man keep going? 'They've topped the last ridge. We've got to go faster.'

They reached the trees, staggering and gasping. Wilm's fingers and palms, tough though they were, were a mass of burst blisters. 'Which way?'

Klarm could barely stand up. Blood trickled through the padding under his stump and had dried in ribbons on his wooden foot. He scanned the spyglass along the layers of twisted rock, pointed to a cave and said, 'That one looks best.'

'It's the smallest,' said Ilisial.

'Easier to defend, then. And they can only attack straight up a steep slope; there's no coming at it from the sides.'

Wilm continued, stumbling on rubble, up and up and ever up, and finally they got the spellcaster over the lip of the cave and in.

'Take it up the back,' said Klarm. 'In the shadows.'

'They know we have it,' said Ilisial.

'But they don't know what it is, or what it can do.' Klarm sat next to the spell-caster, shuddering. He had been in agony for hours.

M'Lainte must have had second thoughts, for she was on her feet and moving slowly up, but the Merdrun were only a few hundred yards below her. The sus-magiz shouted an order and they stopped while he stared upwards through his glass.

Something snapped in Wilm. 'This is unendurable!'

He ran out and began to skid down the steep, gravelly slope.

'Come back!' bellowed Klarm. 'And that's an order.'

Wilm ignored him. He would sooner die than abandon an old woman. And he probably would die.

He slipped, slid down on his knees, came to his feet at the bottom of the slope, took one giant stride, then Klarm blasted him so hard in the back that Wilm fell and could not move. He was paralysed.

'Go and get him,' said Klarm.

'I can't carry Wilm,' Wilm heard Ilisial reply.

'Then drag him! On his face, if you have to, but get the mutinous little shit up here.'

19

THE FAINT PSYCHIC TRAIL

W hat's that from?' said Maelys from the bow of the sky galleon. Smoke
hung low over the trees a mile ahead.

'Forest fire,' Karan said absently, still agonising about that fleeting mind-call
from Sulien. If she used her gift to probe the enemy about Llian's whereabouts,
they would find her. And then –

'Must've been a fierce one,' said Flydd. They had been searching for hours on
his bearing of north 40 east, the only clue to the air-floater's location. 'It rains
here most of the year.'

He slowed and dropped lower. The sky galleon bucked and dipped in a
strong breeze. The wind-driven fire had burned the trees in a triangle half a mile
long and a few hundred yards at the base, before going out.

'Got a bad feeling,' said Maelys.

Everything had gone bad since Karan brought her family to this accursed
future.

Flydd headed to the origin of the fire, keeping out of range of any attack from
the ground. It began in the centre of a large forest clearing.

'That was an air-floater!' Maelys choked.

Flydd stifled a cry. His knuckles were white on the controls. Flangers and
Chissmoul were also old friends.

As they drew closer, the smoking debris took on the shape of a hull.

'Theirs?' croaked Karan.

'Who else could it be?' Flydd snarled. He set down. 'Maelys, load the javelard and keep watch. Karan, come with me.'

The grass was wet, the ground soft, and misty rain drifted in her face. There was no sign of life as Flydd headed towards the smouldering remains. The airbags, being mainly fabric and cordage, had burned away, and most of the air-floater's hull and cabin. The black, twisted shapes in the middle had once been people.

The smell of charred flesh hurled Karan back to the cave, the red-hot brazier, the stab wound in her belly, and the insane triplets-magiz preparing to kill Llian and Sulien.

She still did not understand how Llian, the world's clumsiest man, and little Sulien had overcome three big, powerful women. Karan's heart lurched, the healed wound burned hot and cold, and she felt an overwhelming urge to run.

'Steady!' Flydd caught her by the upper arm, his hard fingertips gouging into her flesh. 'Stay back. Keep watch.'

Karan fought the panic, as she had so many times before, though it was getting harder, not easier. She scanned the wall of trunks around them, the charred path the fire had made through the forest, the sky. There was no sign of the enemy apart from a pair of dead Merdrun, their uniforms and hair burnt off.

She shuddered, wiped sweat out of her eyes and went after Flydd, who was poking the charcoal and ash with the point of his sword.

'Happened hours ago,' he said.

He stepped carefully into the ashes, probing around him, and headed towards the middle. How could he bear it? She had seen far too much violent death during the Time of the Mirror, and subsequently fighting the Merdrun, and it hit her harder each time. A human being only had so much resilience. Hers had almost run out.

Flydd had seen far more, and far worse, during the war. How did he keep going?

He reached the bodies and bent over, lifting something away with his blade. Three people had huddled together, and another was a few feet away, but all were charred and twisted. He turned aside and Karan picked up a psychic cry of anguish.

'Are Flangers and Chissmoul among the dead?' she said softly.

He turned to her, his gaunt face grey. 'No way of telling.'

He tramped to the bow end, damp ashes falling from his boots with every step, and prodded here and there among the heaps of charcoal. He came back and probed beside the bodies.

'Their passengers were probably old allies. I'm almost out of them.' He inspected Karan for a moment, perhaps wondering if she had what it took. 'We'll search the clearing. Take the western side. I'll do the eastern. Don't trample any evidence.'

Karan scowled at Flydd, but he had already turned away. She made allowances.

Prints in the damp earth had been made by large, heavy boots, the soles nailed in a jagged pattern that raised her hackles. Merdrun, four of them. And a fifth print, smaller and lighter, presumably a battle mancer or sus-magiz.

Flydd came around the bow, studying the ground. She pointed out the prints.

'Flangers and Chissmoul had camped here when the Merdrun attacked,' he said. 'Via a gate, presumably.'

'Can the enemy locate controllers?'

'I hope not. This is bad, Karan. Flight is the only advantage we have, but we won't have it long if they can find our craft and gate to them.'

Again she picked up a faint cry of pain. No, *despair*. Maelys? Karan glanced at the sky galleon but Maelys was out of sight behind the javelard. 'Why did they burn the air-floater?'

'I don't know. But now they have its controller, and our best pilot.'

'We don't know that.' Karan followed the prints.

Why would the enemy burn a precious air-floater? Maybe they hadn't. What if Flangers had, to prevent it falling into enemy hands? And Chissmoul was highly strung, and passionately bonded to her craft. What would its destruction do to her?

'Come on,' said Flydd. 'This could be a trap.'

'Wait!' Near the edge of the clearing Karan saw a small footprint, then a second and a third, gouged into the soft earth as if the person who made them had been running wildly ...

She gestured to Flydd, then followed the small prints into the forest. After a couple of hundred yards they were joined by another set, rather larger. A man's boot prints, but not Merdrun. She looked back; the clearing was lost to sight.

Could it be Chissmoul, bolting in despair when the air-floater blew up, and Flangers running after her? Had he burned their craft after the passengers were slain, to deny it to the enemy?

She curved around a vast, buttressed tree and stumbled over an enemy soldier, on his back with a smear of blood between his eyes and an inch of crossbow bolt sticking out. His uniform was charred in places, his eyebrows and eyelashes burned off.

Flydd came up behind her. The dead look had gone from his eyes but he seemed to be ruthlessly reining in hope. Twenty yards further on they found another enemy, the bolt embedded in the centre of his forehead.

'Masterly shooting, on the run,' said Flydd.

Now Karan understood why Flydd couldn't do without Flangers.

'The tracks end here,' he said. 'Why didn't the others hunt Flangers and Chissmoul down?'

'Too risky against such a skilled archer. The magiz must have called them back to the gate.'

'But did they get the controller?'

Karan followed the faint psychic trail, over a ridge then down into a steep valley, her boot heels gouging into the soft soil as she skidded down. She went around a yard-high waterfall, down again, then stopped.

Under an overhang of yellow sandstone, a long, lean man, his once hand-some face weather-beaten, his hair almost white, rocked a small woman in his arms. She was scrunched into a ball, her head pressed against his chest. Karan's eyes stung. No doubt that this was true, painful love. It had been a long time since she'd felt –

Flydd could contain himself no longer. 'Flangers, you've made my day. My year!'

They were but two, yet Karan was moved. If he could hope again, surely she could too.

Flangers raised a hand. 'They gone?'

'Looks like it.' Flydd skidded down to them. 'They came through a gate?'

'Less than a hundred yards from our air-floater. Six soldiers and a sus-magiz, and they killed our passengers at once. I was gathering firewood and Chissmoul getting water, else they would've had us too. I – I had no choice, Xervish.'

Chissmoul thumped her head against his chest and moaned.

'Fire arrow?' said Flydd.

'Straight into the airbag,' said Flangers. 'It went up like – well, you know what it's like. For a minute or two I was back in the war.' He quivered. 'The blast killed two enemy outright and burned the others, and the sus-magiz. He kept going, though, trying to get the controller.'

'Did he?'

Flangers shook his head. 'I kept a flask of naphtha under the control binnacle, just in case. It went up in a column of flame fifty feet high.'

Another moan, another spasm from Chissmoul. Flangers stroked her hair. She banged her head repeatedly into his chest. 'I hate you!'

'And I love you. I can't do without you, Chissie.' He looked up at Flydd, despairingly.

'I'll – never – fly – again,' she wailed, slamming her head into his breastbone with every word. 'Never, never, *never!*'

'Stop that whining and get up!' snarled Flydd.

She jerked and stopped banging her head but did not look around.

'I've got a job needs doing, but I won't give it to someone I can't rely on.'

Chissmoul and Flangers stood up. All pilots were small, because weight mattered in air floaters, and she barely came up to his shoulders. Her face was creased from being pressed against his coat and her eyes were red. She looked eagerly at Flydd, noticed Karan and lowered her eyes like a shy child.

'What job?' she whispered.

'One that needs the best. You *are* still the best, aren't you?'

She looked up and her eyes flashed. 'I'll never let *you* down, Xervish.'

'I know you won't,' he said more kindly. 'They killed Haga and Aimee, and took Nish.' He looked at Flangers. 'What happened to the other soldiers and the sus-magiz?'

'After I downed two in the forest, he called the last two back and they retreated through the gate. He wasn't happy.'

'The Merdrun don't tolerate failure,' said Karan. 'The survivors will be punished.' She introduced herself.

Flangers' eyes lit up. 'With *you* on our side, anything is possible.'

Flydd choked. 'What about me, and all we've done together these past couple of decades?'

Flangers laughed. 'Never saw you as a man needing to be praised, surr.'

20

I'VE GOT AN IDEA

They boarded the sky galleon and Chissmoul looked hungrily at the controls, but when Flydd showed no signs of handing them over she threw herself down on a bench and scowled. He scowled back at her.

Flangers sat beside Chissmoul and reached for her hand. She punched him. 'Go away! I hate you!'

Hurt shadowed his lined face. He went and stood beside Flydd, who headed south down the spine of the mountains.

'Where are we going?' said Flangers.

'A town where I can hire half a dozen fighters. Then we're going to rescue Nish.' Flydd told him about the attack on Nifferlin Manor, and the plan.

'With rustic guards? Fifty wouldn't be enough.'

'I don't have the time to find more or better. We've got to ambush the enemy today.'

'This is a fraught enterprise, Xervish,' Flangers said quietly.

Karan's stomach clenched.

If Flangers, that vastly experienced soldier, had such reservations, what was the point? What would Sulien do if she, Karan, was killed? Sulien was deep, and could be secretive, and had a strong sense of justice. She would not sit idly by; she would do something dangerous.

'How did they find us?' said Flangers.

'You said the gate opened near the air-floater. They must have detected the controller's power draw – which means every air-floater on Santh is now at risk.'

Flangers did not reply.

Flydd looked across at Karan. 'Get some rest; it'll be hours yet.'

She went below, lay on one of the narrow bunks and pulled her coat over her head, not expecting to sleep, but drifted off at once. She was vaguely aware of the sky galleon landing, and shortly whining into the sky again.

She woke when it landed again, rather heavily. Judging by the light it was well into the afternoon. The sky galleon stood on a wet outcrop of blue-grey slate. Tall spurge trees with fleshy leaves and broad green flower heads surrounded them. Their white sap was both poisonous and corrosive, Karan recalled.

The guards Flydd had hired stood at the bow, laughing at something. There were only four, all were clad in grubby homespun, and the stocky one was toothless. The man next to him was prodding the deck with a rusty sword.

Karan's heart sank further. If they were the best Flydd could hire, even with the promise of massive bonuses, the ambush was doomed.

'Karan, would you come here?' called Flydd.

'Maelys, you know the mountain track,' said Flangers. 'Where's the best place for an ambush?'

On a sheet of paper, Maelys drew a sequence of long, tight hairpin bends down a mountainside, then a river.

'The path is too steep to ride here,' she said. 'Their horse handlers will be leading the mounts. This river is deep and fast, and it can only be crossed via a pair of rope and board suspension bridges half a mile apart.' She pointed them out.

'Wouldn't fancy leading a horse across one of them,' said Flydd.

'I've done it,' said Maelys. 'Hope I never have to do it again.'

'If we strike after they cross the first bridge, and get Nish away across the lower one, we can cut it behind us.'

'There's twenty-four Merdrun,' said Flydd. 'And assuming two of us stay with the sky galleon, we have only seven ambushers.' He eyed the unkempt guards and grimaced.

'We'll have to be quick, and lucky,' said Karan. 'They'll kill Nish rather than let him be rescued.'

'What about a night attack?'

'Too dangerous in the dark,' said Flangers.

'Dusk, then.' Flydd sat back on his haunches. 'Karan?'

She was out of her depth. 'Um ... if we can spook the horses, they'll bolt down the track and across the bridge. With luck, they'll trample a few of the enemy.

'Good, but not enough. Any thoughts, Maelys?'

'Nothing that doesn't risk killing Nish at the same time. If we can't put at least half of them out of action at the very beginning, we haven't got a chance.'

'Wait,' said Karan, looking up at the trees. 'I've got an idea.'

'Ready to go?' said Flydd.

Chissmoul had landed on the far side of the ridge, out of sight from the track and the ambush location. Flydd was tying a pair of blasting charges to one side of each of Karan's sap-filled leather buckets. The four guards finished sharpening their weapons, under Flangers' direction.

'Get airborne the moment you hear fighting,' Flydd said to Maelys and Chissmoul. 'Keep well out of the magiz's spell range.'

The sun was setting behind them as they crept across the ridge. The other side, which ran down to the track, was steep and wooded, with overhanging rocks at the crest. Bare strips down through the trees marked the paths of old landslides.

'Don't leave any footprints on the track,' said Flangers.

The track was also steep here, cutting across the slope and curving around the end of the ridge towards the second bridge, which was out of sight. The outer edge of the track fell steeply to the river twenty feet below. Karan looked over. Below, a landslide had blocked a third of the river, creating a backwater pool. Further out, the current was too fast to swim.

'Can their sus-magiz make a gate here?' said Flangers. 'That's the big unknown.'

'The field is weak in this region,' said Flydd. 'But it might be possible to open a gate to here from somewhere else.' He looked up and down the track, frowning. 'If this goes badly wrong,' he said to Karan, 'and you can call the sky galleon down without risking it, do so. No point us all dying for nothing.'

'Call it down, how?'

He handed her a small silver box, etched with a swirling design on one side, like water going down a plughole. 'Press the centre and you'll be able to speak to Chissmoul. Don't let the enemy get it – the sky-galleon is worth an army to them.'

She pocketed it. 'All right.'

'Stay free,' Flydd said to Flangers. 'And if Nish or I are caught and there's no hope of rescuing us, shoot us down.'

'Xervish?' said Flangers.

'It's an order, soldier. We know too much.'

'Surr!' Flangers stood there for a moment, blank-faced, then shuddered.

Reliving past horrors, Karan thought. 'We'd better win, then,' she said darkly. Talk about lost causes!

The guards got into position, concealed in undergrowth on the slope above the track, and Flydd erased their tracks. Flangers was higher up, between a cluster of boulders. His crossbow was loaded and half a dozen bolts lay on a flat rock beside him.

'Ready?' Flydd said to Karan.

She nodded jerkily.

'I'm relying on you,' said Flydd. 'Maelys –' He hesitated. 'Maelys has been lost since her baby was stillborn, and I have no idea what to do for her.'

'Give her time.' It was all Karan could think of.

'Time is the one thing we don't have. Come on.'

Karan put on gloves and goggles, picked up the leather buckets of milky sap and carried them down to the track. Flydd followed with something long and cylindrical in a bag.

'Don't see how this can work,' he muttered. 'Must be off my head.'

Karan kept her misgivings to herself. She placed the buckets ten yards apart and a couple of yards in from the edge of the track. Flydd cast a glamour to conceal them from view.

'What if the sus-magiz detects your spell?' said Karan.

'I want him to,' said Flydd. 'I've designed it to appear feeble and amateurish, hoping he'll stop to investigate, but not be alarmed.'

Why would he be? The whole ambush was feeble.

'And when he does,' she said, 'you'll set off your charges?'

Flydd grunted and headed up the slope, where he had left his cylindrical device.

'Why can't you blast the sus-magiz and the soldiers down?'

'Even in my heyday I didn't have the power to blast down a squad of soldiers. Few mancers did.'

'What about Nish? If the horses stampede –?'

'He'll have a quick, clean end.'

She stared at him. 'He's your friend.'

'And in the Merdrun's hands his death will be drawn-out and agonising.'

'I've known some hard men –'

'It's my job. Get to your position. They can't be far off.'

'What's *my* job?' It struck her that he hadn't given her one.

'They mustn't know you're here. Don't be seen.'

'Why not?'

'One, you're on their list. Two, Sulien needs her mother. Three, I like to have a secret weapon ... small and dubious though it may be.'

Thanks!

Flydd settled in shrubbery thirty feet up the slope. Karan moved to a suitable spot where she could see the track and pulled her cloak around her. It was cold and misty. Her heart thumped leadenly, her palms were cold and sweaty, and her eyes were leaking. She was way too old for this.

Was there any hope of rescuing Nish? He had been a towering figure in the war against the lyrinx, but at its end he had been imprisoned for ten years by his black-hearted father, Jal-Nish, the self-styled God Emperor. Nish had been freed by Maelys and they, along with Flydd, had led the two-year struggle to defeat Jal-Nish. Then Nish and Maelys had campaigned to clear Karan's and Llian's tainted names.

She had to repay the debt.

After a considerable wait, two columns of five soldiers emerged from the drifting mist at the top of the track. Big men and women, all of them, clad in red leather armour and wearing triple-spiked helms. They moved quietly and were ever watchful.

This isn't going to work, Karan thought. We can't possibly overcome twenty-four Merdrun – and a powerful sus-magiz. We're all going to be killed.

Next came eight horse handlers, each leading a string of four horses down the decline. Five were men and three were women, and all had bruised faces and bent heads. They probably feared that they would be killed at the end of the mission.

They probably would be.

They were followed by a pair of soldiers ahead of a horse carrying a slumped prisoner, and another pair behind.

'Nish,' Flydd said quietly.

He was swathed in a bloodstained grey cloak and his head sagged until it touched the saddle horn. Had he been beaten? He looked completely out of it.

The robed sus-magiz was behind him. Then came a second column of two by five soldiers.

The light was fading now. The leading column was approaching the point where Karan's buckets lay hidden. She glanced to her left. Flydd had removed the cylindrical object from its bag. It looked like a skyrocket attached to a thin stick. He thrust it into the ground and adjusted the angle so it would fly up above the road.

What for? She wiped her sweaty palms, made sure her knife was free in its sheath, and waited.

'Halt!' said the sus-magiz in a screechy voice that made her shudder.

The columns stopped. His face, an unnatural blue-grey, turned this way and that, his white eyes studying the edge of the forest. In the gathering darkness the ambushers would not be easy to see, but he may have had other senses. If he detected them the ambush must fail.

'Weak magic,' said the sus-magiz. 'Probably just a local hedge-wizard, but be on your guard.' As he stepped towards the side of the track, his eyes took on an eerie glow.

Flydd touched the fuse of the skyrocket. A red spark was concealed by his hand, then the rocket hissed up –

And exploded with a monumental *boom* and a red, churning fireball, high above the Merdrun. Waves of heat scorched Karan's cheeks. Shredded bits of rocket rained down on the enemy.

Flydd's charges went off, spraying the contents of the leather buckets across the column and splattering thick white spurge sap across most of the Merdrun. A droplet hit Karan on the forehead and burned like acid. She wiped it off on her sleeve, then spat on her fingers and rubbed the skin, which was already swollen. Her fingers began to sting.

The horses tore the ropes out of their handlers' hands and stampeded through them and the leading column of Merdrun, hurling people in all directions and trampling some of the fallen.

Nish's horse, which was covered in clots of spurge sap, went up on its back legs, screaming and pawing at the air.

Flydd gestured to his four guards and they ran to the attack. Despite their appearance, they were brave enough. Karan assessed the damage. Two of Nish's guards were still on their feet, one clinging to the lead rope of his horse. Four from the rear column were still standing. Another five, drenched in spurge sap, were writhing and clawing at enormously swollen faces or blood-red eyes. Three lay still.

The horses had disappeared around the bend. The uninjured handlers ran after them, though it was likely to be a long chase. Karan could hear hooves rattling on the boards of the suspension bridge.

Three soldiers from the leading column had been trampled and another four knocked over the edge, though the fall, either onto the steep slope or into the backwater pool, might not be enough to put them out of action.

The remaining three were on their feet, one supporting his right arm in a way that indicated his collarbone to be broken, the others apparently unharmed. That left eight enemy able-bodied, plus the sus-magiz, the most dangerous of them all. The odds were still well in their favour.

Thud! An enemy soldier fell, Flangers' crossbow bolt embedded in his forehead. Another crumpled to his knees beside him, shot in the chest.

The right side of the sus-magiz's long and remarkably narrow face was covered in scarlet welts and his right eye was closed. He had copped a spray of spurge sap and must be in agony, but Merdrun knew better than to show pain. His staff was in his hand, his good white eye searching the slope for the crossbowman.

Karan ducked behind a tree. The sus-magiz blasted fire up towards Flangers' hiding place, setting fire to moss on the rocks. Lower down, clumps of turpentine bushes belched black smoke then went up with a roar. Flydd's four guards reached the track, where two were immediately cut down.

Flydd appeared to flicker through the trees to her right. His arms were extended towards the sus-magiz, though Karan could not tell what spell he was trying to cast. The sus-magiz attacked back and Flydd stumbled and went to one knee.

Dark smoke drifted low across the track. Nish's horse went up on its back legs again, screaming in pain, and tore the lead rope out of the soldier's hands. It danced backwards, front legs high in the air, then the ground at the edge of the track crumbled and it went over, carrying Nish with it.

There was an almighty splash as it hit the water. And Nish, tied to the saddle, was going to drown – unless she leapt into the water next to a terrified, wildly thrashing horse.

Mummy, Sulien cried over a mind-link. *What are you doing? Mummy, no!*

21

WHY DO YOU HATE ME SO MUCH?

Ilisial dragged Wilm up the slope, one heave after another, and dumped him inside the mouth of the cave. His whole back felt bruised from Klarm's blast, and broken rock had scored him from his backside to the back of his head. And it had all been for nothing. The Merdrun would take M'Lainte any minute. Wilm groaned.

'Stop whining' said Klarm, 'or you'll suffer the penalty for mutiny in active service.'

Ilisial, who was panting, said, 'You wouldn't … execute him, would you, surr?'

Not that she cared. She shuddered every time she looked at Wilm. And he had promised M'Lainte to watch over her. How was he supposed to do that?

'If we didn't need the moron, I'd seriously consider it.' Klarm laid his spyglass down and removed his wooden foot. The stump was a bloody mess.

Wilm rolled over and looked down at the sus-magiz, who was binding M'Lainte. 'He's a big bastard.'

Sus-magiz were often meagre, but this fellow was as big as any Merdrun soldier and looked just as tough.

'Archers,' said Klarm, 'don't fire until you're sure of the kill. Guards, defend the entrance. Ilisial, see how far back the cave goes and if there's any other way out – or in. Wilm, back here with me.'

'I can fight,' said Wilm. 'I want to do my bit.'

'Which one of us is in charge?' Klarm snarled. 'And which is a disobedient rube who wouldn't know his arse from his armpit?'

Wilm flushed. Everyone was witness to his humiliation.

Klarm re-bandaged his stump and put his wooden foot back on, his face shivering with the pain. He knuckled his cheeks and began to delve inside the spellcaster.

'What do you want me to do?' said Wilm.

'I'll tell you when the time comes. Until then, keep your gob shut. This thing is dangerous enough to work on without your inane chattering.'

'Why do you hate me so much?' Wilm blurted. 'What did I ever do to you?'

Klarm opened his mouth and Wilm braced himself, but Klarm looked away and continued taking parts off the top of the spellcaster. The guards grinned among themselves. Perhaps it helped take their minds off what was to come.

Ilisial came back. 'The cave peters out after sixty feet.'

'No crack or crevice they could squeeze through? Or their sus-magiz blast open?'

'No, surr. It's hard rock top to bottom.'

'Don't call me "surr". Klarm will do fine, *for you*.'

'Thank you, s – Klarm.'

'They're coming,' called the archer on the left.

'Get ready,' said Klarm to the guards. 'At all costs, keep them out for the next five minutes.'

Ilisial said quietly, 'What's going to happen then?'

'If I can get this working, they'll get the shock of their lives.'

'And if you can't?'

'Wilm gets the chance to live up to his great name. Wilm, is Akkidul pressed firmly down?'

Wilm checked. 'Yes.'

'Keep it down unless I give the order. And if I do, if the guards have fallen and we're about to be overrun, draw your blade and bring it down on this point, here, with all your strength.' Klarm indicated a raised square on the top of the spellcaster. 'Then again, crossways. Got it?'

'You trust me to do it, then?'

'Got it?' Klarm repeated.

Wilm checked the height of the ceiling, which was a good twelve feet. Room enough for him to raise the sword. He took a quarter step backwards, so he'd be in the right position. 'Yes.'

'What will happen then?' said Ilisial, a tremor in her voice.

'I rather expect that the spellcaster and the sword will be annihilated,' Klarm said casually.

'What about us?' she whispered.

'Blasted to bits in an instant, along with the enemy. A good result, wouldn't you say?'

'I – I don't want to die, Klarm.'

'Can't say I'm thrilled about the notion either,' said Klarm. 'But it's better than a slow and agonising death at the hands of the enemy. What do you reckon, Wilm? You've seen first-hand what they do to their prisoners.'

'A quick death ... would be better,' said Wilm. How quick, though? And if he did destroy the spellcaster and annihilate everyone in the cave, he would die a killer. Yet if he couldn't do it, he would die a coward. Great choice!

'Quiet,' said Klarm. 'I've got to focus as I've never focussed before.'

He inserted the green crystal and made minute adjustments to wheels and pointers, the angle and arrangements of crystals, and to the clockwork mechanism that turned the little hourglass.

'Now!' someone said in a low voice.

The crossbowmen fired together, wound their cranks and fired again. The four guards stood back, ready to leap into the attack the moment anyone made it up the steep slope below the cave.

Ilisial moaned. Wilm's guts clenched. But over the past months, after facing death many times, he had reached an accommodation of sorts with it. Just live for the moment, knowing each breath could be your last, and do the best job you can.

This time, it didn't help.

Skald's troops raced up the ridge from the air dreadnought crash site and he matched pace with them, exulting in his first solo command, and in the challenge of using his superbly trained body to the fullest. He could do this for an hour without tiring.

The enemy were crawling along. Skald stopped to check with a spy scope. They were but ten, one a hobbling dwarf and the other a baggy old woman, the mechanician he had to capture unharmed. They were holding the rest back. He smiled; he would have them within the hour.

But where was the secret weapon? Ah! Four guards appeared from behind some bushes, carrying it between them on slings. It looked big and heavy, but he felt sure he could lug it to the gate by himself, if he had to.

He slid the 'scope into its loops and put on an extra burst of speed to catch up to his troop. Merdrun captains led from the front.

They were overhauling the enemy rapidly now. They had stopped. No, they were going on, abandoning the old mechanician. What a prize the secret weapon must be, if they were prepared to leave their most valuable artisan behind to save it.

And what contemptible scum they were! The Merdrun would abandon their weak and injured where necessary, for the good of the nation was paramount and individuals existed to serve the nation. But to abandon their greatest mechanician was unbelievable.

He scanned the slope above them. They were making for a cave. Good! It would make it easier to take them. Then Skald had an awful thought. What if they were planning to smash the secret weapon?

'Faster!' he cried. 'Take them before they destroy it. I'll secure the mechanician.'

His troops sprinted up the slope, went around the old woman and on. Skald ran up to her. She was fat and unfit and utterly exhausted, and he felt no respect for her. How could she let herself go like this? No Merdrun ever would.

'I am Captain Skald Hulni,' he said, 'and you are my prisoner.'

She rose, trembling a little, and wiped her doughy face. 'Mechanician M'Lainte. Are you going to kill me?'

'My orders are to bring you back, unharmed.'

He bound her wrists behind her back, using knots that could only be undone with a knife. His first thought was to leave her here and run up to the attack, but what if she had a suicide poison secreted on her somewhere?

'We go up,' he said. 'Move.'

'Can't! I'm done.'

Skald lifted M'Lainte to her feet and heaved her over his shoulder. A heavy burden, even for him, but his orders were to protect her at all costs. He carried her up towards the cave.

The enemy had chosen their refuge well. The entrance was at the top of a steep slope covered in broken rock that would be tricky to climb, and the cave could not be reached from the sides. His troops were attacking furiously but already two lay dead, killed by a pair of crossbow archers partly concealed inside the entrance.

'Take the secret weapon!' Skald bellowed.

He was torn between the need to bring M'Lainte back and the dishonour of not leading his soldiers in the attack. Honour won; he had to take a risk on her. He left her behind a boulder, thirty yards below the entrance, and scrambled up.

A Merdrun warrior came hurtling up the slope. Two bolts hit his chest plate but did not penetrate far enough to stop him. He reached the opening, sprang and drove both boot heels into the chest of the archer on the right. He collapsed, struggling to breathe.

The soldier landed on the lip of the cave and was going for the second archer when a bolt went through his open mouth. He lost control of his limbs, fell and slid backwards down the slope.

But five more were coming now, and another three behind them. The archers had not taken down as many as Klarm had hoped. Two Merdrun stormed the entrance and the guards were no match for them. The leading warrior swung low, hacking one of the guards off at the knees. Blood sprayed across the cave and all over Wilm. Ilisial screamed and went into another panic attack. The Merdrun shouldered the guard aside as he fell and skewered the fellow next to him.

The second archer and a third guard had fallen now, and only the last man, standing square in the narrow entrance, was holding the rest of the enemy out.

'Ready, Wilm?' said Klarm. 'But don't draw yet. Ilisial, turn away.'

She did not move. She was on the floor, thrashing and moaning.

Wilm's heart was thumping so wildly that it hurt. Klarm was making the final adjustments to the spellcaster, fingers moving so fast that they were just a blur. Now he was putting everything back in place.

'Go, damn you!' he muttered as the last of the guards fell.

But the spellcaster did not even quiver. It was all over and they were going to die.

'Wilm, draw your sword –'

As Wilm raised the black blade, the spellcaster rose from the floor for a couple of feet, its funnel-tipped arms slowly rotating, its mechanical innards whining.

'Wilm, stop!' yelled Klarm. 'Hold the enemy off.'

Wilm was already swinging the blade down. He turned it above the spellcaster, spun on the sole of one boot, leapt forwards, and a charging Merdrun ran straight onto the blade.

'Down, down!' yelled Klarm.

Wilm dropped to the floor of the cave beside Ilisial, who had recovered enough to cover her head with her arms.

Klarm snapped a Command, 'Haggergrind, attack my enemies!'

The spellcaster shot forwards and blasted jagged blue fire at the two Merdrun in the entrance. One fell forwards, his leather armour ablaze. The other went backwards down the slope. The spellcaster attacked the remaining three soldiers one by one, blasting them down unerringly.

'Back, Haggergrind!' cried Klarm.

It rotated in its own length, as if inspecting whomever had the temerity to give it orders, rotated again, then drifted out of the cave and hovered above the bloody scene. Wilm eyed it, askance. If it chose to target him, he would die most unpleasantly.

'Haggergrind,' said Klarm, 'don't go near the sus-magiz!'

The sus-magiz had stopped halfway up the slope, but when the spellcaster killed the last of his soldiers he raced down to where he had left M'Lainte.

Was he trying to lure the spellcaster through? What a victory that would be.

It hung motionless in mid-air a couple of yards below the cave mouth, tilted towards the sus-magiz as if watching him.

'Stay, Haggergrind!' roared Klarm.

He hobbled after it, leapt out of the cave and landed spread-eagled on top. The spellcaster dipped under the impact but continued to hover, though Wilm could not imagine what Klarm hoped to do – unless he planned to kill M'Lainte rather than allow her to be taken.

Wilm could not bear to watch.

Skald crouched low on the slope, watching the secret weapon in uneasy awe. His orders were to bring it back, but neither his martial skills nor the sus-magiz magic he had learned so far equipped him to do so. If he approached it he would die, and the mechanician would be lost as well.

Yet leaving without it, uninjured when all his troops lay dead, felt so wrong. Would it be seen as cowardice under fire? No, he would not become his father!

If he could take the mechanician back he would not have totally failed, and he had learned vital information about the secret weapon. He ran down towards the boulder he had left her behind. Durthix could send a stronger force for the device. The three survivors could not carry it far.

'Come,' he said to her.

Skald conjured the gate that would lead back to the rooftop of Durthix's command centre. It was far more exhausting than the gate that had brought him here, and he understood why a sus-magiz sometimes needed to drink lives. The yearning rose but he crushed it down. Focus! Complete the gate.

As it materialised, the ridiculous little dwarf hobbled to the entrance of the cave, sprang and landed on top of the hovering secret weapon. Was he planning a rescue?

Skald must not lose the mechanician. He dragged her to the gate.

One of the arms of the secret weapon rotated towards him. He thrust M'Lainte through and dived after her, but as the gate began to carry them away, the secret weapon blasted.

Reality went wild, the gate whirling and spinning, shrinking and expanding and shrinking again. Blistering rays seared past him, going in all directions then looping and sizzling back, burning him, blinding him, his knowledge of the destination slipping away.

The sus-magiz shoved M'Lainte through the gate and backed into it, still watching Klarm.

'Be damned!' cried Klarm.

He thumped the top of the spellcaster and a jagged bolt of fire leapt out at the gate, which glowed like a miniature sun. The heat scorched Wilm's face. Rays roared out of the gate in all directions, then it collapsed in on itself and vanished. He could not tell if the sus-magiz had escaped with M'Lainte, or if they had both been killed.

Klarm, his hair and beard smoking, let out a whoop and turned the spellcaster up the range, leaving Wilm staring after him, surrounded by corpses.

'You stinking traitor!' Wilm bellowed.

The spellcaster slowed, and he thought Klarm was going to come racing back to blast him to gobbets, then it continued up the slope and out of sight.

On the floor of the cave Ilisial kicked and thrashed and screamed herself hoarse.

22

AM I A BEAUTIFUL WOMAN?

The moment Maigraith heard that Rulke was alive, she had abandoned her two-century-long project to recreate the line of the Charon, though it had been replaced by an even more desperate obsession – getting him back. Now she oscillated between frantic activity and listless despair.

'He swore to me,' she kept saying. 'Forever!'

Aviel, who was lugging two pails of water past Maigraith's salon to the workshop, stopped. She was seated at a long black table with her back to the door, staring into a pentagonal mirror propped up on the table before her.

'*Forever*,' she repeated. 'And Rulke is an honourable man; he would not lightly go back on his word ... yet for all that, he *is* a man. Will he still want me? My mastery of the Secret Art must almost be the equal of his now. And yet ... and yet ...'

She turned her head this way and that, illuminating one side of her face, then the other, with the flickering yellow light of a candle, followed by the harsh white of a glowing globe. Clearly, neither pleased her.

'Aviel!' she said peremptorily. 'Come here.'

Aviel started, slopping water into her boots. No good could come of this. She put down her pails and crept in. 'Yes?'

'Look at me. What do you see?'

Aviel did not want to say it. 'Um ... what do you want me to see?'

'Am I a beautiful woman?'

'What's beauty, anyway? Ask a hundred people ...'

Those scarifying eyes pinned Aviel. 'You know what I mean. Tell me the *absolute* truth, or it will go badly for you.'

'Y-you were never beautiful.' Aviel was shaking. 'But ... you aren't *unattractive* ... for the age you look.'

'What age is that?' Maigraith said coldly.

'Um ... you might pass ... might pass for a woman ...' she gulped, 'of sixty.' Aviel was putting the best possible face on it. Sixty-five was closer to the mark.

'Sixty!'

'You asked for the truth.'

'But ... *sixty*.' Maigraith sank her head into her hands. 'Rulke is a lusty man. Exceedingly lusty ...' She smiled at a memory. 'And women are drawn to him. You've seen him, haven't you?'

'Yes,' said Aviel.

'How old did he seem?'

Another loaded question. 'He'd been ill, and he was in a lot of pain. He was haggard, at first.'

'But after he'd eaten and rested, did he look *my age*?' Her voice went hoarse.

Aviel fought to control her face, to not give the answer away, but by the way the colour drained from Maigraith's face Aviel had failed dismally.

'The absolute truth, girl!'

'He looked like a man in his forties,' Aviel said truthfully. 'Strong and powerful, and handsome.'

'Late forties or early forties?' Maigraith said relentlessly.

'Mid.'

Maigraith sagged; she looked seventy now. 'He might come to me because of his oath,' she whispered, 'but he won't stay with a barren old hag. I've got to face it; no oath can bind two people down the centuries.'

'You're not an old hag,' said Aviel. Why was she being nice to a woman who had never had a kind word to say to her? 'Besides, if Rulke really meant his oath he wouldn't care what you looked like.'

'Easy for you to say, since you're young and beautiful.'

'I'm not –' Aviel began.

Maigraith cut her off with a slashing gesture. 'Enough!' She backhanded the mirror, which fell face-down on the table. 'Rulke's the last of the Charon. Saving his people from extinction has been his reason for being all his adult life, and I'm way beyond childbearing ...' She peered at Maelys, thoughtfully. 'Or am I?'

'I don't know what you're talking about.'

'The old writings mention certain remedies – rejuvenating spells and potions – that can make a man or a woman young again.'

'The great Magister, Mendark, is said to have used the life renewal spell thirteen times,' said Aviel.

'Renewal is a lottery. There's no way of knowing what body you'll end up with, or what face. No point making myself younger if I end up even more hagridden. I have to be *me* – but far younger.'

'What about a love potion? There are love scent potions in Radizer's grimoire.'

'Would you use such a potion to make a man love you?'

Aviel did not answer. Even if she had been interested in love, the idea was absurd.

'I'm not looking for the *appearance* of love,' Maigraith said softly. 'That would be lying to myself as well as to him. Any love that has to be compelled or deceived is no love at all. Nor do I want my youth back – I never want to revisit that awful time again. All I want is my middle years, and to create, with Rulke, the children he needs to save his people. Is that too much to ask?'

'I don't see how it could be a *bad* thing,' Aviel said carefully.

'But how is it to be done?'

'The other day I overheard Flydd and Klarm talking about the Magister's spell vault –'

'What about it?' Maigraith said eagerly.

'Flydd asked Klarm if he had a key.'

'Mendark was Magister for a thousand years, and he collected everything known or rumoured about the Secret Art. Every spell, every kind of power, and samples of all manner of arcane devices, though the spell vault was said to have been sacked and destroyed long before I became Numinator. The lying scrutators must have hidden it from me.'

～

'Come,' Maigraith said imperiously, two days later.

It was late in the evening of a wet and windy day. Aviel looked up from the stench she was extracting from foul earth dug from a slaughter-yard of long ago, and she kept imagining the poor beasts being prodded to their deaths, their wild eyes and their panic. She capped her flasks and washed her hands, for once glad to leave her workshop. Nivol, how she hated it!

'Where are we going?'

'To find the spell vault.'

'Why do you need me?'

It was a mystery why Maigraith, who had been a loner most of her life, spent so much time with Aviel.

'Maybe I enjoy your company.'

Aviel snorted and followed her down several streets to a large public building built from red and blue marble. It must once have been imposing, but the six columns at the entrance were broken, it had been gutted by fire and was now in a ruinous state, and the central hall and the public chambers at the front were choked with rubble. They clambered over it to reach a rear staircase that ran down.

In a basement crammed with furniture grand enough for a stateroom but eaten away by woodworm, Maigraith opened a narrow door, rotted at the bottom, and went along a narrow but lengthy passage. There were boot marks in the dust on the floor. Small feet; probably Flydd's. The passage ended in the lower basement of an adjacent building, almost magically clean of dust. Seven doors led out, all closed.

Maigraith moved her fingers in the air and a translucent white globe formed and floated there. She spun it this way and that, studying it with her head cocked to one side. The globe turned opaque, became as clear as glass, and a blue dot appeared on the far side. She sighted through the globe at the dot, which was pointing towards the third door on the left.

It was locked but she opened it with a touch and they went through, down a set of eleven steps, the white limestone worn down in the centre of each tread, then along and down again. More basements and cellars followed, more doors were scried out with her globe, more staircases descended, until they must have been a hundred feet below street level. Aviel's bad ankle was throbbing now and, because she favoured the good one, her left knee and hip were aching.

The air grew thicker and more stale with each level they descended, and smelled ever more strongly of damp and mould and other things, bordering on the offensive, that not even her sensitive nose could identify. Aviel stopped; she did not want to go any further.

'Why are you shivering?' Maigraith turned to study her by the glow from the yellow crystal.

The little hairs on the back of Aviel neck stood up. 'What happened down here?'

'What does it matter? It was long ago.'

'I need to know.'

'Good people were betrayed, tortured for knowledge they did not have and, when they could not provide answers, cruelly put to death.'

'Who did it?'

'It would have been at the Magister's orders.'

'Magister Mendark? What a monster he was!'

'So quick to judge! Until you've been in a desperate situation, with everything depending on you –'

'I *have* been in desperate situations with everything depending on me,' Aviel snapped, 'and I didn't kill innocent people to get out of them.'

Maigraith bared her teeth. Age had yellowed them. 'About time you showed some spine, girl. You don't get anywhere in this life by being docile.'

'When you're small and young and poor and crippled and friendless, you have to be docile to survive.' Aviel added quietly, trying to empathise, 'I read that you were oppressed and tormented and manipulated by Faelamor –'

'Do you really want to remind me of the worst time of my life, *down here*?' Maigraith grated.

'I thought that, having suffered so much yourself, you might feel compassion for other suffering creatures.'

'Suffering is character-building. It made me what I am today.'

'As long as you survive. Many people don't.'

'Life isn't fair. You either survive or you perish ... and in the end we all perish. Enough chatter!'

They were in a large round chamber shaped like a squashed sphere. No doors led from it save the one they had come through, up five steps. Seepage ran down the walls. The floor was covered in an inch-thick accumulation of dust that the damp had turned to mould-streaked mud. Here and there were accumulations of small bones from rats or other little creatures. Aviel was so tense that it was hard to breathe.

'Flydd came here,' said Maigraith, 'and the dwarf. Why are there no prints?'

'They concealed the way they went?' said Aviel.

'It'd have to be a mighty concealment if *I* can find no evidence of it.'

'If the spell vault is that important –'

'Have I been *led* the wrong way. Can I see truly here? Can anyone? I wonder ...'

Holding the globe high, she climbed the steps and, before Aviel realised what was happening, Maigraith went through, closed the door behind her and the lock clicked. The darkness was absolute.

Aviel fought an urge to scramble up the steps and pound on the door. Why had Maigraith locked her in? Was she going to come back?

If she did not, how long before the rats gathered? Aviel would not see them coming, but they would have no trouble finding her.

23

THERE IS NO DARK PATH

Locked in! It roused memories of being trapped deep under mad Basunez's ruined tower, Carcharon, when that vicious drunkard, Unick, had planned to feed Aviel to the summon stone.

She felt panic building, a scream rising, and she had to fight it or she would never stop. She stumbled in a circle, arms out, trying to orient herself.

Crack! Pain speared through her left knee. She had whacked it on the edge of the steps. It broke through the panic and she sat on the third step, rubbing her kneecap.

Maigraith must be testing her, but for what? Aviel's only gift was for making scent potions. Could it have to do with her acute sense of smell?

She closed her eyes, not that it made any difference in the pitch darkness, and allowed the odours of the room to wash over her: nose-tickling dust and mould, a hint of decay from the rodent bones, her own cold, clean sweat, and a lingering trace of the new perfume Maigraith had been wearing since she first saw her rival. It was soft as rose petals, but with flinty undernotes.

And something else, so tenuous that, when Aviel thought about it, she couldn't smell it at all. She went to the centre of the room and stood there, breathing carefully.

Lamp oil? No. Nor was it wax, tallow, lard or any other kind of animal fat. It had more of a mineral smell ...

Grease! But why here?

It must be lubricating a mechanism. For what?

Something scuttled across the floor and she almost wet herself. She clenched and walked around, bent double. She could not detect any grease down here; the other smells were too strong. She climbed the steps, put her back to the door and went up on tiptoes.

There it was again, and it had to be coming from above. Aviel tried to remember what the ceiling had looked like, from a brief glimpse in the light of the yellow crystal. It curved up at the sides but was flat in the middle, like the shape made by pressing on an inflated balloon. Was something hidden up there?

Though she was tempted to pound on the door, she gathered all her self-control and knocked twice.

Maigraith opened the door. 'Well?' she said flatly.

Aviel smiled to herself. It was good to be underestimated. 'There's a mechanism. Up high.'

Maigraith stood beside her on the top step and reached up with her right hand. Light streamed from each fingertip, harshly illuminating the ceiling, and the slanting shadows picked out a circular indentation at its centre. 'That's it!'

'How you going to get up there?'

Maigraith swept her finger-beams back and forth, though her eyes were closed as if she were thinking. 'I'm not.'

She tried several opening spells, one after another, though not to any effect.

Then she whispered, 'Descend!' and with a creaking and a groaning the circular indentation separated from the ceiling and corkscrewed its way down. It now formed the base of a rusty staircase, so narrow that Aviel wondered how anyone bigger than Maigraith could have climbed it. The base of the stair stopped a few inches above the floor.

'Go up,' said Maigraith.

Aviel did not move. 'There might be booby traps.'

'That's why you're going first.'

She crept up the treads, the whole stair quivering, and through the hole at the top. Maigraith came after and directed her down a passage revealed to the left. With every step Aviel expected a trap to snap closed on her shins, or her head.

After a hundred yards they encountered a solid brass door with a curving band of symbols across the top.

'W-what do they say?' said Aviel.

Maigraith grimaced. 'Better you don't know.'

She unsealed it and shoved Aviel through into a five-sided chamber whose roof was held up by a series of slender grey columns, their sides carved with a variety of spiders, scorpions and other arachnids, all with fangs or stingers erected. A warning? Or a statement? It was a very obvious one.

'The Magister's spell vault,' sighed Maigraith. 'Many have sought it in vain.'

Aviel's knees had gone weak. She supported herself on a long table strewn with dusty parchments, maps and books, some open, others in stacks. Bookcases lined three sides of the room. The fourth side had floor to ceiling pigeonholes, many containing scrolls or rolled papers. Everything was covered in thick dust or furry mould; the vault must have been closed for a very long time.

Maigraith lit lamps mounted on brackets on the walls, took one lamp down and carried it back and forth. 'What a mess! No wonder Mendark failed.'

'Only after a thousand years,' said Aviel, then wondered why she was defending so dark and dubious a man.

'His folly showed the Merdrun the way to Santhenar in the first place. Get to work!'

'What am I supposed to be doing?'

'Finding scent potion methods, of course.'

Did Maigraith think the rejuvenation magic was a scent potion? Aviel turned over books and unrolled several scrolls. 'How?'

'Sniff them out. Why do you think I brought you?'

No scent would have lasted that long. 'I assumed it was to torment me.'

Aviel took down a lamp and wandered the spell vault, turning over parchments, opening papyrus scrolls and reading the spines of books, those she could read. Many were in languages unknown to her, others in hands so convoluted that she had to decipher each word.

'Is there a catalogue?'

'Mendark didn't have a well-ordered mind.'

But Tallia had. She had been Mendark's assistant, then Magister after he was killed, and Aviel had known her well. At the age of thirteen she had done Tallia a great service and it had not been forgotten.

Tallia's ledger was in the first place she looked, in a tall cupboard on the left side of the door. Aviel wiped the dust and mould off a bowl-shaped reading chair, its cracked leather as wrinkled as an old man's face, sat down with her legs dangling over the side and turned the pages. The books and scrolls weren't listed by category, only by name, and soon the letters began to blur before her eyes. It had been a long day ...

Something heavy landed on her lap, jerking her awake. 'What?' she cried, looking around frantically.

'Scent potions,' said Maigraith.

The book in Aviel's lap, bound in green and grey lizard-skin, was so battered that she could not read the title. If, indeed, it had ever had one, for the title page had been torn out. There was no author name, either. She turned to the list of scent potions and a shiver passed down her spine. The first was *To Liquefy the Bones of an Enemy*, and the others were just as dire.

'I don't want to know any more dark potions,' she said.

'Why ever not?'

'There are more than enough in Radizer's grimoire. I couldn't master them all in a lifetime – even supposed I wanted to.'

'But you're a scent potioneer. Why wouldn't you want to master them all, good or bad?'

'I never wanted to make them. I was forced into it. I just want to be a perfumer.'

'Too bad,' said Maigraith. 'Santhenar needs you to master the art.'

'I'm afraid.'

'Of what?'

Aviel hesitated. 'I – I'm drawn to the dark potions, and if I take one step too many down that path, I'll be lost.'

'What a load of rubbish! There is no dark path of the Secret Art; only dark people.'

Aviel noticed that Maigraith carried a small, rose-coloured volume with intricately worked silver corners. 'What's that?'

Maigraith slipped it into a pocket. 'Never you mind.'

Had she found the magic to make her young and fertile again? If it was a potion or scent-potion, she would force Aviel to make it. And Aviel felt sure that giving Maigraith what she wanted would be a bad thing – for both of them.

As Maigraith departed, Aviel slid the unnamed book of dark scent potions down between a cupboard and the wall. She had enough troubles without it.

24

BLOOD DARKENED THE WATER

Karan froze, straining to link to Sulien, but her warning cry was not repeated. How had she sensed that Karan was about to do something desperately rash? There was no way of knowing.

Keeping within the drifting smoke, she scurried across the track and looked down. Nish's horse was on its side in the backwater, still kicking. Further out, three soldiers, knocked over the side in the stampede, thrashed desperately. The Merdrun came from a barren rock in the void and, clearly, did not know how to swim. With any luck the current would carry them away. A fourth soldier, a broad-shouldered woman with bristly black hair, was draped over a boulder, dead.

Nish, bundled in the cloak and tied to the saddle, was head and shoulders underwater, and if she could not free him in the next minute or two, he would drown. But the horse was terrified and kicking wildly, and a hoof blow could break bones, or crush her chest or her skull.

She hesitated. Llian might already be dead.

His head thrust up against the cloak, and again. He was alive and desperate; she had no choice. Karan picked the safest part of the backwater, ahead of the horse, and jumped, praying that the water was more than a few feet deep. If it wasn't, she might break an ankle when she hit bottom.

The cloudy water went over her head, and it was icy. She swung her arms down to slow her plunge, her feet struck a cobbled bottom and she pushed up to the surface. The horse was slowly rotating and drifting out towards the current. It must have broken a leg, for it could not right itself.

She swam behind its back, where it was safest. Karan was a good swimmer, but she was fully dressed and wearing boots, and it was hard work. Nish's hands were tied and his ankles had been roped together under the horse's belly. It would not be easy to free him.

Someone up on the track was screaming. Was there any point trying to save Nish? If the Merdrun won, as seemed almost certain, they would both be better off dead.

Sulien needs you! She pulled the cloak away and ducked under. Nish's eyes were open but staring fixedly. Had he drowned? No, his chest was heaving.

His wrists were bound to the saddle horn. Karan drew her knife and hacked at the ropes, which proved to be exceedingly tough. The horse kicked wildly, she took a strip of skin off his left wrist and his blood darkened the water. She sawed by feel and the ropes parted.

Freeing his feet would be far more dangerous. She filled her lungs and went under again, feeling her way down Nish's leg to the ankle; she could not see anything now. As she sawed the rope, the horse kicked with three legs and she lost her grip. It was above her now and its frantic movements were pushing them towards the racing current. Once in it, there would be no getting out.

Karan located the rope again, but Nish had stopped moving. He'd been under water for two or three minutes. Was he still holding his breath, or had he drowned? She was also running out of air. She had to free him on this breath, or fail.

She hacked desperately at the rope, it parted, and he slid free. She sheathed the knife, caught him by the shirt and kicked for the surface. Nish lolled, apparently lifeless, though there was a faint bubbling in his throat. She drew back a fist and thumped him below the ribs, thrusting her fist in and up. He coughed up water, explosively, then his chest expanded as the air rushed in.

But they were only a couple of yards from the current, and the horse was closer. It was doomed.

'Swim!' she hissed. 'Or we're dead!'

Karan turned onto her back and swam towards the shore, towing him. He made some ineffectual swimming motions, no use at all. Karan felt the tug of the current and swam harder, ignoring the pain in her bad leg.

The soldiers who had fallen into the water were gone, taken by the river. The horse drifted out, whinnying piteously. The current caught it and it was whirled away, out of sight. Nothing could survive the rapids further down; she prayed that its end was quick.

It took a minute to go ten yards. She reached the shore and, her leg tormenting her now, hauled Nish up into a concavity in the steep slope, where he would not be visible from above. It would not hide him from a search, though. She crouched and checked him over.

He was a short, stocky man about her own age, with thinning hair and blotchy welts on his face and neck where spurge sap had soaked through the cloak. Fist-shaped bruises showed where they had worked him over, and he was very cold.

There was nothing she could do; the cold was creeping into her as well. 'I'm Karan,' she whispered, her teeth chattering. 'You all right?'

'Give me a minute. Is Maelys –' He choked.

'In the sky galleon with Chissmoul. Flydd and Flangers attacked, though it seems hopeless.'

'I need a weapon.'

Karan slipped down to the dead soldier on the rock, drew her curved sword from its sheath and gave it to him.

'Stay out of sight,' she said. 'I'll find out how it's going.'

As she was about to move, an enemy soldier was outlined against the darkening sky above her, looking down. Had he seen her? The shadows were deep down here now. She held her breath as he walked along the edge, then turned away.

She climbed the slope, which was so steep that she had to use vines to haul herself up. The exercise was not enough to warm her, and her sodden clothes weighed her down.

The track was littered with bodies, including all four of Flydd's guards and two horse handlers. Only four enemy were still on their feet – three soldiers, two men and one woman, and the sus-magiz. The rest had been blinded or otherwise disabled by the spurge sap, trampled in the stampede or killed in action. One soldier had a blade embedded in his chest; the remainder lacked obvious wounds. Shot by Flangers, Karan assumed.

The sus-magiz, whose face was enormously swollen, loomed over a small man on his knees on the track. His hands were bound behind him. Flydd! One of the soldiers raised a curved sword as if to behead him, and Karan choked. The sus-magiz shouted at the fellow, in a language she did not know, and he backed away.

The sus-magiz kicked Flydd in the side. He toppled over.

Was there any hope of rescuing him? Possibly, if Flangers was still free, though she could not imagine how.

But he had orders to shoot Flydd if he were captured. Flangers was a good soldier, tormented by things he'd had to do in the previous war, and an honourable man. Would he obey Flydd's order? Probably.

There came a cry of triumph from some distance up the slope. Blue light burst from a crystal in the head of the sus-magiz's staff and he raised it above his head, illuminating the steeply sloping track.

A fourth soldier appeared from the forest, driving a stumbling Flangers before him. There was blood on his face and down his front.

Karan could not count on Nish, which meant it was five against one. She was a fair shot with a crossbow and if she could find Flangers' weapon she might take down two Merdrun, possibly three. But not all five.

All depended on what they did now. If they made camp and attended their injuries, there was a tiny chance. She crept up to a bend in the track, out of sight, then across into the forest and back down to the attack point.

A fifth soldier appeared, plodding up the track from the direction of the lower bridge. The left side of his face was ballooned out grotesquely. The sus-magiz bellowed at him, though the only word Karan understood was 'horses.' The soldier held out empty hands. *Gone!*

The sus-magiz turned and said, to another soldier, 'Nish?'

He pointed over the side and drew a finger across his throat. The sus-magiz let forth a torrent of abuse, held up a skinny arm and slowly closed his fist. The soldier fell to his knees, choking. He withered visibly and slid sideways, dead.

Karan shuddered. Had the sus-magiz drunk that man's life? It seemed so, for the sus-magiz looked bulkier than before. He issued orders and two soldiers began to heave the dead over the edge. She counted sixteen bodies: Flydd's four guards, two horse handlers and ten of the enemy. Plus the four who had been hurled into the river in the stampede. That left ten enemy soldiers, though she could only see nine.

The sus-magiz walked along the injured, inspecting them in the light from his staff, then reached down to one and she sensed a vast flow of power. The sus-magiz drank the soldier's life, and the lives of three more who had been badly injured, and their shrunken corpses were also dumped in the river. His skin was now a ruddy colour, a faint red nimbus surrounded him, and his white eyes glowed like twin lamps. He was so charged with power that his long, narrow feet barely seemed to touch the ground.

But what did he want all that power for?

Five soldiers remained, three with lesser wounds or burns, the other two unharmed. They piled logs and branches in heaps twenty yards apart along the track, then two soldiers climbed down the bank, carrying water skins.

Nish! They would be bound to find him. But minutes passed and there was no shout of triumph. Had he dragged himself away? Or slid back into the water and drowned?

In her wet clothes, Karan was getting colder by the second, but she dared not move. The water carriers returned. The sus-magiz ignited the wood piles with his staff and they blazed ten feet high, though none of the warmth reached her. Nish must be freezing by now, and he had already been in a bad way ...

The soldiers prepared food and put water on to boil. The sus-magiz drew markings on the muddy track midway between the two fires and began to chant and make intricate movements with his hands.

What was he up to? The Merdrun did not tolerate failure and he had lost his captive, the horses and their handlers, and most of his troops. Flydd was an important prisoner, though without knowing the strength of the ambushers the sus-magiz might be loath to continue on foot.

He needed a gate, but the field was weak in this region and, even where it was strong, making gates took a lot of power. Had he drunk those lives to make one, or to call on an ally in Fadd to direct a gate here? How could Karan stop him?

She slipped up to the rocks Flangers had hidden behind and groped around in the dim light. His crossbow lay where he'd dropped it when he was attacked but she could only find one bolt – the one he'd been loading as they took him.

She crept down. The wavering firelight was tricky for accurate shooting, though if she could get close enough she might kill the sus-magiz and prevent the gate. But the soldiers would take her in seconds. She had to call the sky galleon down.

How long since the attack began? No more than fifteen minutes, though it felt like hours. Taking out the little silver box, she pressed the swirling markings and whispered, 'Maelys?'

'Nish?' Maelys said as if she were speaking in Karan's ear.

'He's free ... somewhere. Most of the enemy are dead, and all our guards, but they've got Flydd and Flangers.'

In the background, Chissmoul let out a cry of despair.

'I think the sus-magiz is trying for a gate,' Karan added. 'Or calling for one. You've got to stop him.'

Chissmoul gave another wail. 'Chissmoul, no, wait –' hissed Maelys. Then they were gone and Karan could not get them back.

A distant, mechanical shriek echoed back and forth and the sky galleon, lit from within, howled across the sky. The Merdrun yelled and pointed. The sus-magiz took a swift look but continued with his spell.

Flydd and Flangers, their wrists bound, had been dumped on the track near the uphill fire, guarded by two soldiers. Karan had no way to rescue them.

The sky galleon reappeared and came hurtling up the track towards the fires, twenty feet above the ground. The sus-magiz scrabbled in his pouch, raised a pink rod and shouted a Command. The sky galleon lurched and angled toward the forest.

Karan caught her breath. It was going to crash!

Chissmoul must have regained control because it hurtled upwards at an angle to the track, smashing small branches out of the treetops and leaving a tornado of shredded bark and leaves in its wake. The sus-magiz shouted his Command again, and again the sky galleon lurched, then wobbled across the sky like a drunken bee.

'I can see how this is going to end,' Nish said from behind her.

Karan started. 'How?' she croaked.

'Chissmoul has no defence against magic,' he said in a slow, exhausted voice. 'Either the sus-magiz will break her mind and seize control of the sky galleon ...'

'Or?'

'Or if she knows she's going to lose everything that matters to her ... she'll slam it into the track at full speed, and annihilate the Merdrun, and herself.'

'And Maelys, Flydd and Flangers,' said Karan, shocked numb.

'It's all or nothing with Chissmoul, and when she thinks it's nothing, life is unbearable. I've seen it before. In the past Flangers has kept her together, but without him ...'

'What do we do?'

'Kill the sus-magiz. You any good with that?'

He meant the crossbow. 'Middling,' said Karan.

Nish took it. 'I was a good shot, once. Though ... never mind.'

He sounded on the edge of collapse. 'There's only the one bolt,' she said.

'I'd better make it count, then. Come on.'

As the struggle between Chissmoul and the sus-magiz continued, the manoeuvres of the sky galleon grew ever wilder. Many times, Karan thought it was going to crash into trees or mountainside. It skimmed the jumbled rocks at the top of the slope, setting small boulders loose. One crashed down towards them, slammed into a tree with a ground-shaking thud and broke into pieces.

'Shoot him, quick!' she whispered.

Nish was shivering fitfully. He supported the crossbow on a branch and aimed. 'By the bloated look of the bastard he's drunk quite a few lives.'

'At least five.'

'He'll be difficult to kill, then.'

Karan's speaking device came to life. 'No!' Chissmoul shrieked. 'I can't take it. I won't!'

The sky galleon whirled, hurtled up into the sky, looped over and plummeted down towards the two campfires and the sus-magiz between them. His right fist was clenched around the raised rod in triumph. Clearly, he hadn't realised what she was going to do.

'Now!' Karan hissed.

The crossbow went *snap* and blood sprayed from the top of the sus-magiz's head. He crumpled to his knees, dropping the crystal. Nish swore.

'What's the matter?' said Karan. 'You got him, didn't you?'

'Bolt only grazed his skull,' Nish said sourly. He dropped the now-useless crossbow.

Would Chissmoul realise she had control back? It seemed that she was going to slam the sky galleon into the ground at full speed, but she levelled out, just missed the sus-magiz and struck the soldiers a glancing blow. One was hurled twenty feet up into the forest, missing the trees and landing in front of Karan with a heavy thud, his blade still in hand.

He wasn't badly hurt, and he swung at her, blindingly fast. Karan hurled herself backwards, tripped and fell. The soldier was reaching forward to thrust into her middle when Nish jammed the curved blade through a gap in his armour. He toppled and she rolled aside, the blade sliding into the ground beside her. The soldier fell sideways, dead.

'Thanks,' she said to Nish.

He attempted a smile. 'Least I could do.'

The other soldiers had also been tossed off the track, but some or all might have survived. It was far from over.

The sus-magiz was on his knees and had found the pink crystal. Blood ran in curtains down both sides of his head and across his bloated face, but he wore a look of savage triumph. He thrust the crystal high and spoke a different spell.

A few yards ahead of him the air began to shimmer in a man-high oval. The gate was forming, and nothing could be done about it. The sky galleon had disappeared.

25

YOU MISERABLE GRUB!

The gate vanished, flinging Skald down onto a hard surface. His uniform was ablaze; he rolled over and over to put it out. Sight returned. He was on the roof of Durthix's command centre, but where was the mechanician? Had he lost her? Failed?

No, she was twenty feet away, her trews covered in licking flames. He scurried across and put them out, crushed out a smouldering patch on his sleeve and sprang up.

And froze, because Durthix stood to one side, massive arms crossed across his chest. Had he known Skald was coming back? He must have, and another man was with him, a meagre fellow with claw-like hands and an offensive smell. The magiz would have sensed the gate before it opened.

'You'd better have a good explanation for your flagrant disobedience, Sus-magiz Skald,' Dagog said coldly.

Skald quailed inwardly but managed to keep it off his face. He was caught in a power struggle and either man would sacrifice him in an instant, if it became necessary.

'He went as my captain, not your sus-magiz,' said Durthix.

'When I appoint a sus-magiz,' said Dagog, 'all military commissions are revoked.'

'Unless I say otherwise. Which I did.'

'Why was I not told?'

'You didn't need to know.'

Dagog shook in fury but said no more, though Skald knew he would pay later. The magiz's malice was legendary.

'Your report, *Captain* Skald,' said Durthix. He gestured to a pair of guards, who bound M'Lainte's hands and led her away. 'Make it brief.'

'The targets were fleeing up the mountain with the secret weapon,' said Skald. 'I secured the mechanician and my troops attacked the other nine. They were in a cave at the top of a steep scree slope, with no approach from the sides. We killed their six guards ...'

'And you lost all twelve, Captain?'

Merdrun never made excuses. 'Yes.' He glanced towards Dagog, uncertain about saying more.

'You may speak freely,' said Durthix.

Dagog's eyes glittered with fury, not just because Skald had looked to Durthix first, but because he had given permission to speak in front of the magiz. Skald would pay for that insult.

He described the secret weapon. 'It flew out of the cave, hovered and blasted the rest of my troops down.'

'Why didn't you take it, *as ordered*?'

'Because he's a stinking coward, like his father,' said Dagog.

'Well?' said Durthix.

'I had no defence against its blasts. Had I'd approached it, it would have killed me. And the mechanician, and everything I'd learned about the secret weapon, would have been lost. I reopened my gate and pushed her in but one of the enemy, a dwarf –'

'Klarm,' said Durthix. 'A former scrutator and a dangerous man. Greatly skilled in mancery.'

Skald committed the name to memory. 'Klarm directed the secret weapon to blast at the gate, striking it. It took all my strength to bring us back.'

He bent his head. It was a big failure, though not a total one.

'Useless fool!' said the magiz. 'You are confined to your quarters, Sus-magiz Skald, until further notice.'

Skald should have obeyed instantly but he was caught between two masters. His eyes flicked to Durthix for confirmation, and the magiz saw that too.

Durthix held up his hand. 'I'm not happy, Captain. You lost twelve of my most experienced soldiers, and all you brought back was the mechanician.'

'And without a scratch on him,' sneered the magiz. 'Like father like son.'

No greater insult could be made to Skald. 'I – am – not – a – coward!' he said passionately. 'Give me another chance, High Commander. We must act quickly before the enemy's sky galleon returns for the secret weapon. I'll find a way to bring it back, I swear on –'

'On your *father's* honour?' said Durthix coldly.

'No,' Skald said desperately. 'I – I swear on – *your* honour.'

There was a deadly silence. He had gone way too far.

'You dare swear on your *high commander's* honour?' Durthix said softly.

No backing out now. 'Yes, High Commander.'

'You do realise that if you fail such a mighty oath your entire family – grandparents, parents, siblings, uncles, aunts, cousins, nieces and nephews – will be dishonoured, and must be obliterated?'

Merdrun oaths were sacred, and many and varied, and each had its cruel and ingenious penalty for oath-breaking. Skald had spoken without thought or consideration, but the oath could not be taken back. His entire family erased, because of his folly! Terror almost unmanned him, but he could not show it.

'I will not fail!' he said in a ringing voice.

Durthix studied him for a full minute. 'After making two gates across such a distance, in quick succession, you must be drained to the dregs,' he said finally. 'Write down and sketch everything you learned about the secret weapon and give it to me, then go to your quarters.'

Skald was so exhausted that he could barely think straight, but he spent two hours writing and sketching, then handed his papers to the high commander. Durthix merely grunted. Skald saluted and went out, knowing Dagog would soon come for him, and dreading what he would do.

Skald bathed, ate, dozed for an hour then, unable to sleep, went to the practice area and duelled furiously until every stiff black hair on his body had its own quivering droplet of sweat. Dagog did not come, and the longer he delayed the more afraid Skald grew. Had Durthix decided that a mere captain was not worth deepening the rift between himself and his magiz?

Durthix had hundreds of junior officers. Sus-magizes were rarer, but there were dozens of them, and new ones could be made at need. Magizes, however, were exceedingly difficult to replace and it could take months for a new one to settle into his or her position. Months they did not have.

Late that night, after Skald, desperate for sleep, had relaxed enough to doze off in his chair, the magiz came.

'Sus-magiz!' Dagog snarled.

Skald cried out, tried to leap to his feet and fell out of his chair.

'You miserable grub!' said Dagog, standing over him. 'Get up!'

Skald scrambled to his feet, expecting Dagog to drink his life on the spot.

'When I made you sus-magiz you swore an oath,' hissed Dagog. 'As a sus-magiz your loyalty is to me, and me alone.'

'High Commander Durthix said that when I am acting as captain my loyalty is to him,' said Skald. 'Who am I to argue with the High Commander, who has authority over *every* Merdrun?'

'For now!' the magiz said direly. 'I fear you're no use to me, worm. And you know what that means.'

A dishonourable death was Skald's deepest fear, but he had to face the threat with courage. He must not show emotion. 'I am a loyal Merdrun, Magiz. If I ... can best serve by giving my life to be drunk ... it must be so.'

No one would ever know how much those words cost him, but nothing else would do. If he showed a hint of fear Dagog would end him. And Durthix would thank him for it, since Skald would have proven his utter unworthiness.

The magiz looked even more put out. 'Damn you, Sus-magiz! If it were up to me ...' He hooked his claw-like fingers. 'But,' he smiled evilly, 'Durthix has accepted your oath – upon his honour.'

'Accepted?' Skald croaked.

'You are going back to the Sink of Despair for the secret weapon. Return without it and your life, and your family's lives, will be mine.'

His smile dripping with malice, Dagog stamped a small, stinking foot, and vanished.

Why had Skald begged for this mission, when going back was an almost certain death sentence? How could he hope to capture a weapon that could blast him to bits from twenty yards away?

He had to find a way. For his family, his own honour, and the honour of the high commander he admired and respected. Desperate action would also shut off the howling inner voices, and the unmanning emotions that now had their claws in his innards and would never let go.

If he were killed, at least it would put an end to them.

26

WE COULD BE HERE FOR WEEKS

'You treacherous swine!' Wilm roared as Klarm rode the spellcaster up the mountainside. 'I hope it does for you.'

Klarm did not look back.

Wilm went inside. Ilisial lay in the rear of the cave, doubled up, though she had stopped screaming. He approached her warily, because he was covered in blood and it might set off another panic attack.

'Ilisial,' he said quietly. 'It's over.'

She continued to stare at the back of the cave. 'Klarm?'

'Flew away on the spellcaster.'

'Where?'

'Don't know.'

She sat up. 'He's taken his pack. Why would he do that?'

'I overheard Flydd talking to M'Lainte about Klarm,' said Wilm. 'Flydd wasn't sure he could be trusted.'

'He was always nice to me,' said Ilisial, as though that proved anything.

Because you're an attractive young woman and he's a filthy old roué! 'The gate had closed; he didn't have to run away like a stinking traitor.'

'Klarm would never run away.'

There was no point arguing. 'We can't stay here,' said Wilm. 'The bodies will attract every predator within miles.'

Ilisial shuddered. Four of their guards lay in bloody ruin in the cave mouth, plus two Merdrun. The other twelve bodies littered the slope below and none had died easily.

'I thought I'd just be helping M'Lainte fix devices,' she said in a tiny voice. 'I never imagined we'd see any enemy.'

'I'll be reliving today in my nightmares for years. Come on.'

'Can't.'

'We can't stay here,' said Wilm.

'You'll have to blindfold me.'

Ilisial was far more fragile than he had thought. What had possessed her to volunteer for such a dangerous mission? And if the enemy came back, as Wilm was sure they would, how could he protect her?

He dragged the corpses to the entrance and let them fall. It was not something he would ever forget, because the ruined bodies were still warm. Half an hour ago they had been living, breathing people and, whether allies or enemies, each must have had their all-too-human hopes and fears and dreams. Now they were corpses with severed limbs, maimed faces or opened bellies, they reeked of blood and piss and shit, and soon every carrion feeder within miles would be gorging on them.

When this was over, assuming Wilm survived, he would take an oath of non-violence. Become a carpenter, perhaps. Or a gardener. A creator, not a destroyer.

He washed his hands with a pannikin of water, collected all the food and water they could carry, one of the crossbows and M'Lainte's spy scope, and stowed everything into their packs.

He tore an unstained shirt into rags and went to Ilisial. 'Close your eyes and I'll blindfold you.'

She recoiled. 'You stink of blood.'

And you of cowardice! But there was no point saying it. She could not cope, and that was that. He put the rags into her hand and backed away. She sniffed them, tied three blindfolds across her eyes, one after another, poked smaller strips up her nostrils, shuddered and got up.

'Take my hand,' said Wilm. 'I'll lead you out.'

She backed away, the dangling strips of cloth quivering. 'I can't touch you. I – I'll hold your pack.'

As they went out and headed up the slope, she was shaking so wildly that she was pulling him off balance. He made allowances. Again.

'You can look now,' he said when the cave was no longer visible. 'Which way do you want to go?'

Ilisial took off the blindfolds and removed her nose plugs. Her eyes were vacant. 'Makes no difference,' she said listlessly. 'We're going to die.'

'We've got enough food for weeks.' He trained the spyglass along the side of the mountain, looking for another cave.

'They'll come back.'

'An hour ago we thought we were done for, and we're still alive.'

But there was no consoling her; she had lost hope. They trudged across the slope, in the shade of the band of trees, heading for a distant, triangular cave.

It turned out to be small and narrow; Wilm had to bend his head to enter. But it went in a long way, following a flaw in the rock, and seepage had formed a tub-sized pool twenty yards back. While Ilisial waited outside, he bathed, washed his bloody clothes and put on clean ones, and she finally stopped shuddering when he came near.

'Why would Klarm betray us?' she said that afternoon, returning to the inexplicable question. 'What could he gain that would be worth having?'

They were on either side of the entrance. Down into the trees, a crinkle-horned goat was tearing at a thorny shrub, a hornless kid at its side. Even in this desolation, life was everywhere. It lifted his spirits a little.

'Why does anyone do anything?' said Wilm.

'But he was one of the heroes of the war.'

'And afterwards he became one of the God-Emperor's lieutenants.'

'He ended up fighting on the right side at the end.'

'Maybe Klarm believes the Merdrun are going to win, and he wants to earn their gratitude.'

'Why don't you like him, Wilm?'

'I've never done anything to him, yet he treats me like scum. I'll see if I can contact Flydd.'

Wilm unpacked the farspeaker and called, the way he had seen Klarm use it. 'Mister Flydd? Xervish?'

'Who the hell is this?' said Flydd, loud and clearly.

'It's Wilm.'

'What do you want?'

'To tell you what's happed ...'

'I assume it hasn't gone well.'

There was no point dragging it out. 'We found it.'

'But?'

Wilm told him about the air-floater and the attackers coming through a gate, and how Klarm had fled. 'That was half a day ago and we haven't seen him since. Flydd, surr,' Wilm said tentatively, 'do you think he's betrayed us?'

'Why would you think that?' Flydd growled.

'I overheard you warning M'Lainte about him.'

'Next time, keep your ears out of other people's business.' He sighed heavily. 'I don't know what to think.'

'What do you want us to do now?' said Wilm.

'How much food do you have?'

'Plenty.'

'And water?'

'We know where to find it.'

'You might have a bit of a wait. We're half a continent away and up to our necks in trouble.'

'What's gone wrong, surr?'

'Everything!' said Flydd. 'Though *nothing* compares to you losing M'Lainte. We can't do without her.'

Now Wilm felt personally responsible. 'I went down to get her, but Klarm –' The farspeaker went dead.

THE BITCH MUST HAVE ENSORCELLED HIM!

'He's got a *woman!*'

Maigraith's shriek of outrage echoed through the building. Aviel heard it clearly from her workshop, where she was reaching the end of her interminable work on nivol. Flydd needed much more than she had made last time and the key steps had taken three times as long.

Who's got a woman? Rulke, of course.

After days of searching, using a variety of spells, Maigraith had located him in the obvious place, his long-abandoned city of Alcifer. She had invented a tiny, undetectable spy portal, directed several of them to the parts of Alcifer he frequented most, and had been spying on him day and night ever since. Feasting her eyes on him, laughing and weeping and making plans for the future. And brooding about her aged face and scrawny figure.

Aviel had never seen Maigraith so emotional, so unlike her cold, controlling herself. She was like a schoolgirl in love. A schoolgirl who looked sixty-five – both ridiculous and pathetic.

If Rulke had found someone else, she would not stand for it, but what would she do? It was bound to involve the dark and perilous spells Maigraith had found in the spell vault. More importantly, what would she require of Aviel?

She climbed off her stool and kneaded her ankle. With all the standing, and constantly carrying buckets of water up four flights of stairs, it never stopped aching. Perhaps she would be better off having her bad foot amputated and getting a wooden one, like Klarm. She imagined the knife hacking through skin and flesh, the saw rasping through bone, leaving behind flecks of bloody sawdust and smears of marrow, and flinched. Be happy with what you have, fool!

Maigraith was seated at her table, staring into a pulsing circular spy portal, no larger than a finger ring, suspended in the air before her. She was banging her clenched fists against her head, and the pentagonal mirror she had spent the past week staring into lay on the floor, smashed to fragments.

'Something the matter?' Aviel said from the doorway.

Maigraith sprang up, her eyes blazing and thin mouth twisted in bitterness. She grabbed Aviel's wrist and hauled her, hopping and dragging her twisted foot, across the room.

'Sit!' She forced Aviel into the chair. 'Look!' Maigraith shoved Aviel's face towards the spy portal.

Rulke, bare-chested and hair tangled as if he had come from his bath, was leaning back at one end of a long sofa, smiling. What a specimen of manhood he was; muscular; powerful; vastly competent. Thoughtful at times. Generous, Aviel had been told. Her eyes rested on the pair of purple scars curving across his side. Vulnerable, too, and for a second she felt the lure of him.

She reminded herself that he was a very dangerous man with a dark reputation. A man Maigraith considered her own.

Rulke leaned forwards and spoke to someone. Aviel did not hear what he said; the spy portal did not transmit sound. Maigraith seethed, reached over Aviel's shoulder to move the spy portal, and a striking woman sprang into view at the other end of the sofa.

She looked about thirty, with flawless creamy skin and remarkable – no, unbelievable – hair. Each thread shimmered in reds and greens and blues as she moved, as if it had been drawn from polished black opal. Aviel had never seen anything like it.

The woman was no taller than Maigraith but extremely curvaceous. A short blouse of grey silk exposed a slender waist; knee-length pants of the same material clung to broad hips and full thighs. Her slim calves and small feet were bare, and she was laughing at whatever Rulke had said.

'The scheming trollop!' Maigraith exploded, almost choking on her bile. 'Prancing around half-naked, flaunting herself. How dare she try to steal my man!'

Aviel thought that was a bit rich, since Rulke probably assumed Maigraith to be a hundred years dead – if he thought about her at all.

'The bitch must have ensorcelled him! Of himself, Rulke would never go back on his word.'

'Did he swear to take no woman but you for the rest of his life?' Aviel said mildly.

Maigraith caught Aviel's blouse in her left fist and raised the right as if to strike her. 'We swore to each other, *forever!*'

'They may just be friends.'

'No woman can ever be *just friends* with Rulke. They always want more, and she isn't having him.'

'It looks very much as if she *does* have him,' Aviel said, to provoke her.

'When she's gone, the ensorcellment will break and he'll be mine again.'

Aviel shivered. 'What do you mean, *when she's gone?*'

'Never you mind. How's the nivol going?'

'I've done as much as I can do without the Archeus. When you get it, I can complete the work in a few days.'

Maigraith grunted. 'Good, because I've got another job for you, and it's urgent.'

'What?'

'A rejuvenation potion. It'll take me back to the age of thirty … thirty-five at most.'

'Does it work? And is it safe?'

'That's for me to worry about. Your job is to make it.'

'You know how to make potions. Why don't –?'

'It's a *scent* potion. My nose isn't keen enough.'

Maigraith handed over two leaves of thick, rose-coloured paper, likely torn from the small book she had found in the spell vault.

Aviel read it. 'There are dozens of ingredients. I'll need to find a lot of different scents, odours, stenches and reeks.'

Maigraith wrinkled her nose. 'It's not hard to find stenches and reeks in this festering place. Give me a list.'

'I have to collect each source material and *personally* extract the scent or odour, before I can blend the potion. The method has to be followed exactly, or …'

'Your guards will escort you to the sources of the scents and reeks you require. You will begin in the morning.'

∾

The following evening Aviel was still in her workshop, extracting the scent from a barrel of offensively rotten onions, when Maigraith returned bearing a large lead crystal flask containing an oily, yellow-green fluid that wisped up at the wired-on stopper as if to force it out. In an instant, Aviel was hurled back more than two centuries to Rogues Render –

She was trapped in a rendering vat with Lumillal, an all-powerful ghost vampire intent on stealing her life force to bolster his own, and he was reaching out to her.

Your life force is very rich, he said, drooling strands of glowing plasm. *It might even be enough to bring me back to life as a real vampire.*

Aviel felt an agonising pain in the top of her head and the cast iron vat glowed like a yellow searchlight.

I'm taking my freedom now!

He lunged at her with open hands, ripped bundles of her life force from her and wound them furiously. The strength drained out of her; she staggered and nearly fell. The tip of the sword grounded on the bottom of the vat then jerked back in her hand so hard that she was forced upright. Her back struck the side of the vat and the blade in her hand rose of its own volition.

You can't touch me, Lumillal said mockingly.

'Get a grip!' said Maigraith, setting the flask on the bench and shaking Aviel, and Rogues Render was gone.

The yellow-green fluid attacked the stopper again, forcing it up against the wires. She was shaking so badly she had to sit down. Maigraith snapped a command and the fluid went still.

'Archeus of Eidolon,' she said, head tilted to one side. 'A necromantic fluid of vast potential and a thousand uses.'

'All dark,' said Aviel, scrunching herself up and trying not to think of Rogues Render or Lumillal, though she would not be able to escape the memories when she used the Archeus. 'Where did you get it? No, don't tell me.'

'You can get anything in Thurkad if you know who to ask.'

The days dragged by. Aviel carried out the final steps on nivol during the daylight hours; she was not game to work on it at night. In the evenings, with considerable reluctance, she prepared the first scents and reeks for the rejuvenation potion.

Maigraith was deluded in thinking she could get Rulke back. Even if the potion did succeed in making her younger and restoring her fertility, Aviel could not imagine it working on Rulke. Anyone who had come back from the dead, two centuries later, must have moved on.

Though Maigraith knew the stage Aviel was up to, and that it would take more than a month to complete the rejuvenation scent potion, she was constantly demanding progress reports, sometimes two and three times in an hour.

The rest of her time she spent her days, and probably her nights, obsessively watching Rulke and the unknown woman through one spy portal or another. Every day Maigraith looked older and more haunted, and in the brief moments when she wasn't spying, she was scowling at her face in the largest shard of the broken mirror, and wailing.

'It's over. I've lost him. I want to die.'

It was pitiful, but Aviel was unmoved. Maigraith had destroyed too many lives. And she had never given a damn about anyone else.

One morning Aviel reached her workshop at sunrise, feeling unusually tired, and the grimoire, which she always kept closed, lay open in the final section, the Forbidden Potions. The scent potion she saw there was one of the blackest of all – a potion to turn a clever person into a drooling imbecile. She stared at it, shivering. Surely not even Maigraith would do such a thing?

Yes, she would. Maigraith was looking for ways to get rid of her rival, permanently.

When the batch of nivol was complete Aviel decanted it into the diamond phial with exquisite care and twisted in the stopper. Maigraith took the phial without a word of thanks, sealed it in a small lead cylinder with a ruby set in each end, that in a slightly larger cylinder made of brass and encircled with a pair of silver rings, and that in an unadorned cylinder turned from a piece of red-and-black-streaked ironwood. She cast a series of spells on it, slipped it in a pocket and returned to her spy portal.

'I thought you'd be off to destroy the summon stone,' said Aviel, who was looking forward to Maigraith being away.

'What's done with it is none of your affair,' said Maigraith, not looking up.

In the morning she was gone. She returned the evening of the following day and handed back the empty diamond phial. The team she had led to destroy the summon stone had found it almost drained, as if the enemy had drawn most of its power. Maigraith had dissolved it with nivol to make sure it could not vanish and regenerate in another place.

'That's that, then,' said Aviel. 'I'll never have to worry about it again.' It felt as if all her work had been to no purpose.

She washed the diamond phial out seventeen times, to be absolutely sure the last dram of nivol was gone, packed it away and went back to the rejuvenation potion.

And Maigraith to her spying.

That evening, Aviel crept in and peered over Maigraith's shoulder. The curvaceous woman wore a clinging, powder-blue gown and was brushing her opaline hair. Her fingernails and toenails had the same shimmering play of colours. Aviel did not think it was painted on, though how could her nails be made of *real* opal? Even more improbably, how could her hair be opal?

'Who is she?' Aviel wondered.

'The bitch's name is Lirriam,' Maigraith said bitterly, 'and I don't think she comes from Santhenar. But how did she get here?'

Aviel remembered something about Rulke that Maigraith did not know. In Alcifer, after they had freed Rulke from the statue and the stasis spell, he had extracted the first part of Sulien's lost nightmare.

A child of a lesser race can defeat us if her mighty gift is allowed to develop –

Then Rulke had spun around, staring into nowhere, as if he had seen or heard something they had not.

'Incarnate?' he had whispered. '*Incarnate!*'

And he had vanished.

Not even Flydd had known what Incarnate meant, though when Maigraith finally located Rulke in Alcifer he had been alone. Lirriam had not turned up until days later. How had he found her? Or had she found him? If she did not come from Santhenar, where was she from and how had she got here? More importantly, what did she want?

The following morning Aviel woke late and exhausted, though she had gone to bed early and slept soundly. It was a struggle to keep her eyes open ... and why did her dreams smell of hoopis?

She checked the little box Klarm had given her, but it had not been opened. The only other place she had smelled hoopis was in the perfume Maigraith wore when she was at her lowest –

Aviel rose hastily, but the moment she stood up her ankle began to ache, as if she had been standing up for hours. An unpleasant suspicion stirred. Had Maigraith cast an enchantment on her when she slept, to compel her to do something Maigraith could not do herself? Perhaps to make a scent potion so dark that Aviel would never agree to it?

A scent potion to rid Maigraith of her rival! And she had to do it secretly; Rulke must never find out.

But if she was compelling Aviel to make such a dreadful scent potion, would it corrupt her too?

She could not allow herself to be dragged down into the dark. She had to break Maigraith's power over her, *forever*. But how was she to do that without going further down the dark path she yearned for, yet feared?

28

A GRASPING TROLLOP

Aviel locked her door that night, and it was still locked in the morning, but again she woke exhausted and with her ankle aching.

Then, that afternoon, she realised that more than an hour had passed with no memory of what she had done in that time, though her workshop had a faint smell like rotting meat that she recognised at once – the stench of the stinkhorn fungus. It was a common ingredient in dark scent potions, though she had never used it.

Dare she confront Maigraith? No, she might use a more powerful spell next time, one to permanently rob Aviel of will. She was just a tool to Maigraith, one to be thrown away when it was no further use.

But she had to know what was going on. Secretly, in times when she knew Maigraith would be away for hours, Aviel began to craft a memory-restoring scent potion.

'Where is the strumpet from?' Maigraith was muttering, the next time Aviel passed her salon.

She always called Lirriam a strumpet or trollop or man-stealing bitch, though Aviel had seen no evidence that she and Rulke were more than friends. Maigraith had to demean her rival to make her easier to destroy, in the same way that the Merdrun thought of all other peoples as subhuman.

'What does he see in the fat cow?' spat Maigraith.

Aviel wasn't having that. 'Lirriam isn't fat! She's voluptuous. Bounteous. Any man –'

Maigraith exploded. 'What would you know about it, you virginal little runt?'

Aviel suppressed the retort, *Hag!* 'Every time you demean Lirriam,' she said pointedly, 'you also demean the man you love.'

For a moment she thought Maigraith was going to slap her.

After an inner struggle, she said stiffly, 'I accept the rebuke. But clearly, she's a grasping trollop, out for what she can get. She cares nothing for the noble purpose of Rulke's life. Where did she come from, anyway?'

Aviel shrugged. 'Why don't you go to Alcifer and find out?'

'I dare not risk Rulke –'

Aviel could guess why Maigraith had stopped. She dared not risk Rulke seeing her as a haggard old woman. Perhaps she feared that, even if the rejuvenation potion made her young and fertile again, he would always see her as she was now.

Colour rose up her thin face and she cried, 'I'll kill the bitch! How dare she rob me of what is mine?'

'Got to get back to your rejuvenation potion,' Aviel said hastily, and fled.

Her own memory potion was ready for blending, the numbered scent phials concealed among more than a hundred others in her racks. She wasn't game to label them with their names; if Maigraith compared the names of the new scents to the methods in Radizer's grimoire she would soon deduce the name of the potion.

Aviel checked down the corridor. Maigraith was not in sight. Aviel began to blend the twelve individual scents into a tiny bottle, mixing in the scents one by one, and each time shaking the bottle the prescribed number of times. She capped the bottle, turned it up and down seven times, removed the cap and took a deep sniff.

The first memory hit her so fast that she barely had time to cap the bottle again.

Maigraith at Aviel's door. Unlocking it in the early hours, touching her on the forehead and whispering a compulsion.

Come. Remember nothing of what we are about to do. Afterwards, never speak of it.

The compulsion began to fog her memories. She took another sniff, which cleared the fog, closed her fist around the bottle and sat down to relive the night.

In Aviel's workshop, Maigraith had handed her part of a papyrus scroll. 'Make this!'

'What is it?' It was bound to be dark, otherwise why the secrecy?

Maigraith pressed a fingertip to Aviel's forehead and she felt a dull ache there. 'Make it!'

She wanted to disobey but had no will of her own.

The top and bottom of the scroll had been torn off. All she saw was a list of scents, odours, reeks and stenches, nineteen of them. Many were horrible, with the smells of stinking corpse flower, cat vomit and rotting toad being the worst.

'I don't have any of these,' she said. 'I'll have to find and extract the lot.'

Maigraith looked down at the papyrus. 'We'll start with the easiest: blood of a two-century-old virgin.'

'How is that even possible –?'

Maigraith picked up a small tube and, before Aviel could move, thrust the point of a knife into her bare upper arm and pressed the tube to the flow until it was half full of blood. Maigraith sniffed the tube, capped it and put it in a rack. 'Next!'

Aviel was too shocked to speak. She stood there, feeling faint as the blood ran down her upper arm and dripped off her elbow.

'You *are* a virgin?' said Maigraith.

'Of course I am,' Aviel whispered. 'But I'm only sixteen ...'

'Surely I don't have to spell it out.'

Aviel pressed her hand over the wound, which was far more painful than it should have been.

'Oh, give it here!' said Maigraith.

She wiped the blood away, pushed the two sides of the wound together and pressed the flap down. Her lips moved as she subvocalised a healing charm and the wound slowly sealed itself, leaving a red-brown scab. But the pain grew steadily worse until Aviel's head spun; she could barely stand up.

'Got to lie down,' she slurred.

'Not until you extract the scent of two-century-old virgin's blood.'

'I can't!'

Maigraith slapped her across the face, bringing tears to Aviel's eyes. 'Get it done. The smell of fresh blood doesn't last.'

The blow carried her back to her childhood, an unloved, unlucky seventh sister, taunted and picked-on by her six big slatterns of sisters until, in what still seemed like a miracle, Shand had rescued her, perhaps to alleviate his own feelings of guilt, and changed her life forever.

The memory helped and she went to her bench. It took an hour and a half to extract and preserve the subtle scent of her own fresh blood, by which time she was so drained that she could barely stand up.

'Bed!' said Maigraith. 'Remember nothing. Say nothing.'

She stroked her fingers across Aviel's eyes and pushed her towards the door. Aviel stumbled out, her surroundings blurring, and the next thing she knew was the rising sun lighting up her shabby room in reds and golds.

She came back to the present, in her workshop, her fist still clenched around the memory-recovery potion. Dare she use it again, to find out what Maigraith had done to her next? Not now, it was too risky. Small steps.

Her upper arm gave a painful throb. She pulled up her sleeve and the scab was gone, leaving a small, unobtrusive scar. Better get to work.

Over the next three days Aviel used the memory potion as often as she dared, and relived making the stinks and odours for Maigraith's dark potion. Most were unpleasant and hard to get rid of – the reek of the Golden Stinkbug clung to her fingers and she had to scrub away the outer layers of skin to get rid of it. But when she looked through her racks of phials it was not there, nor were any of the other scents Maigraith had forced her to make. Had she already blended the scent potion? Had Maigraith used it?

Aviel did not think so, because Maigraith was watching Rulke and Lirriam as obsessively as ever. Was she hoping to catch them in bed together, to justify the use of this dire potion? Aviel had not been able to identify it; it was not in Radizer's grimoire. Could it be from the unnamed, lizard-skin grimoire she had left in the spell vault? She had no way of going back to find out.

The recovered memories had brought Aviel up to last night, and extraction of the final, disgusting reek, the gorge-heaving stench of a long-dead skeet.

Tonight, Aviel felt sure, Maigraith would compel her to blend the potion. She stumbled through the rest of the day, so tired that she could not think anything through, gulped down a bowl of cold turnip soup, scrubbed her stinging hands again, sniffed them, grimaced and, though it was only 7 p.m., fell into bed.

Maigraith woke her half an hour later. 'What's the matter with you?'

'Exhausted,' said Aviel. 'Feel as though I haven't slept for a week.'

'Pathetic!' said Maigraith. 'When I was your age – never mind. I have a charm that will let you go without sleep –'

'I prefer the real thing.' Aviel closed her eyes, and Maigraith took the hint and went away.

But Aviel could not sleep now; she was too exhausted and anxious. What was

Maigraith going to do with the scent potion? Was it to attack Lirriam – or could it be to restore Rulke's feelings to the moment he had sworn to her, forever?

Aviel took a double dose of the memory-restoring potion, hoping it would allow her to remember what Maigraith compelled her to do later tonight, and fell into a troubled slumber.

Before midnight Maigraith shook her awake, so vigorously that Aviel whacked her ear on the end of the bed. 'Get up!'

Her voice quivered with suppressed fury. Or was it excitement? She cast the compulsion on Aviel, then the charm of forgetting.

But the memory-recovery potion had cleared Aviel's head and she knew what was happening to her now. She perched on a stool, barefoot and quivering, while Maigraith took nineteen scent phials out of their individual loops in a leather pouch and lined them up along the bench. Each was named in her small, neat hand.

She handed Aviel a length of papyrus torn from the bottom of the previous scroll. It was the method for blending the nineteen scents.

'What's the scent potion for?' Aviel asked yet again.

'Doesn't matter.'

'My potions always work better if I know what they're for.'

'Superstitious nonsense! Put the scents in order. Check and double-check the labels.'

Aviel picked up the first phial and started to remove the cap.

'No need to check what's inside,' said Maigraith. 'I labelled them when you made them.'

'Don't tell me how to do my job,' Aviel said coldly. She removed the cap, took a tiny sniff, her head jerked backwards and her eyes stung. 'Burning brimstone,' she said, and checked the label to confirm it.

Maigraith said nothing. Perhaps she approved when the 'little mouse' stood up to her. Aviel checked every scent as if she were making the most important potion in the world, and with every foul and offensive odour her stomach muscles clenched tighter and her bad ankle throbbed all the more, because her sense of the potion grew ever more dire.

She re-read the blending method. Dare she make a deliberate mistake, to ruin the potion? No, Maigraith missed nothing; she would notice instantly. Besides, an ill-made potion might have the opposite effect to that intended. Or be disastrous in some other way. Or Maigraith might decide to test it on Aviel first.

In any case, it was not in it to her to ruin her work, any more than a sculptor could smash the nose off her finest sculpture. Whatever the purpose of the potion, good or ill, she would make it perfectly.

Aviel blended the nineteen scents, carefully and precisely, capped the bottle and inverted it seven times, just to be sure, then removed the cap to take a careful sniff.

'No!' cried Maigraith. 'Cap it tight and give it to me.'

Aviel did what she was told. Maigraith closed her fingers around the bottle and, for the first time in many days, she smiled. It was not a pleasant smile.

'Go back to bed,' she said quietly. She pressed a forefinger to the centre of Aviel's forehead. 'Remember nothing. And if a stray memory does come back, give no hint of what you and I have done here, *ever.*'

29

NOT QUICKLY ENOUGH TO SAVE HER

The shimmer of the sus-magiz's slowly forming gate brightened. Once it opened, the troops waiting on the other side would take them in seconds. The pain in Karan's left hip was so bad that it was a struggle to stay upright; tears were running down her face. She pressed her forehead against the rough bark of a tree and closed her eyes. Hrux was the only thing that could get her through this.

But only the Whelm's best healers knew how to make hrux, and they had allied with the enemy. No hrux ever again. Be strong; you can do it.

By herself? Nish was unconscious, Flydd and Flangers were prisoners, and the sky galleon had vanished. Karan called via the silver box but Maelys did not reply. The sky galleon had probably crashed on the other side of the mountain, since Chissmoul was overcome by suicidal despair.

Karan took the curved Merdrun sword, which was too long and heavy for her to use comfortably, and left Nish where he had fallen. He might live or he might die; there was nothing more she could do for him.

She hobbled from tree to tree in the gloom, an itch between her shoulder blades. If any of the soldiers Chissmoul had knocked over the edge had survived, and came after her, it would all be over. Unless – could she free Flydd or Flangers? Better be quick; the shadowy figures on the other side of the gate were becoming more real by the minute. Why was it taking so long?

And how could the sus-magiz make one *here*, where the field was so weak? Perhaps, with the power from drinking all those lives, a gate could be *forced* open.

She crawled to where Flydd and Flangers lay and cut Flangers' bonds. His eyes focused on her but he did not move. The sus-magiz must have paralysed him.

She freed Flydd, who did not stir either. She dragged both men into the woods. A bolt was tucked into Flangers' belt; he must have put it there before he was captured. She took it and crept up to where Nish had dropped the crossbow.

Karan loaded it and headed down towards the gate, which was crackling and sparking, lighting up its surroundings in luminous blue. It was almost open, though the sus-magiz was on his knees, throwing up. It had taken all he had.

Shoot him and there's no gate. Shoot him and it's over!

But it was not easy for her to shoot a man in the back, even an enemy.

This is war, fool! Just do it.

A nailed boot scraped on stone behind her. Another soldier. Only twenty feet away. Sword in hand. Karan started, her finger jerked and for a dreadful moment she thought her only bolt would end up embedded in a tree.

A bright red spurge sap welt, the shape and size of a maple leaf, covered most of his left cheek. It was raised half an inch above the rest of his cheek and the skin, split in a number of places, oozed blood. He must be in agony, but he came at her, raising the blade. By the time she trained the crossbow on him he was only ten feet away.

Twang. The bolt went into the base of his throat and she saw the shock in his eyes, but he was already leaping towards her, the weapon swinging with enough force to take her head off.

No time to move and nowhere to go; all she could do was drop, and pray. The blade sang over her head. He landed a yard in front of her, stumbled, and his driving knees caught her in the middle, knocking the breath out of her and dumping her on her back. Momentum kept him going another few steps. His boots trampled her belly and chest and just missed her face, then he fell.

Karan was too winded to move. The crossbow was gone, she knew not where. A thud behind her as he hit the ground; a gasp and a thick, liquid gurgle; a strong smell of blood. She rolled over slowly, her trampled guts throbbing. It felt like something had torn inside.

He was kicking and clawing at the ground, trying to force himself up. He had also lost his weapon. It was on the ground a few feet from him but she dared not go for it.

He came to his hands and knees and took up the sword. With awful, gurgling gasps, he forced himself upright. Blood trickled from his mouth and down his chin. He was going to die, but not quickly enough. He took a wobbly step towards her, and another, and she hurt too much to get up. There was nothing she could do, no way she could escape him.

Fool! Use your knife!

She hurled it, aiming for his heart, but he stumbled and the tip struck sparks off the bolt embedded in his throat, and snapped. He clutched at the wound but kept coming, swaying like a wind-blasted tree.

Karan rolled aside, rolled again, and it hurt; it really hurt. But he was in a bad way too and a couple of seconds passed before he turned from his mechanical path. She rolled again, came up against the base of a tree and had nowhere to go.

The soldier attempted to pull the bolt out of his throat, choked, and blood sprayed from his mouth; from the wound too. He staggered and thrust at Karan. She shrank down into the leaf mould and the sword embedded itself in the trunk a couple of inches above her head. He lost his grip and the sword vibrated up and down, *thrum*.

He forced two fingers into the wound, heaved the bolt out and sucked at the air. A cluster of bubbles formed there, like red frog spawn. His eyes went blank, his knees gave, and he fell beside her.

Karan crawled away and felt around for her broken knife but could not find it. Behind her the throat wound sucked and bubbled for a while, then stopped.

She reached the edge of the steep track and saw that the sus-magiz was on his feet again. Blood had crusted in his hair and down both sides of his sap-burned face; vomit clung to the front of his robes. He was shrivelled and shrunken now. The prodigious power required to create and open a gate here had taken more from him than he could spare.

But it looked like a real gate now, and the moment it opened, all would end.

Karan fumbled out the silver box, pressed the swirls and hissed, 'Maelys, where the blazes are you? They're about to come through!'

Karan did not expect an answer, but shortly she heard Maelys speaking urgently. Chissmoul let out a mad cry. *Slap!*

'Is Nish –?' Maelys whispered.

'He's alive,' said Karan. 'And Flangers and Flydd.'

Chissmoul was moaning. 'He's *alive*, you stupid bitch!' snarled Maelys, and slapped her again.

'But if you can't stop the gate *in the next two minutes*, we'll all be dead,' said Karan.

Chissmoul howled, then Karan made out the whine of the sky galleon, growing ever louder. The sus-magiz looked up sharply, raised his shrivelled arms and cried out in a great voice.

Karan crept out of the forest and onto the track, the better to see. The sky galleon flashed into view, diving towards the fires.

Through the silver box Karan heard Maelys shriek, 'Chissmoul, no!'

Karan caught a fleeting glimpse of her, wrestling with Chissmoul at the controls. The sky galleon rolled on its side, just missing the gate, and soared up again, a cavity in its keel glowing like a furnace.

The sus-magiz drew more power from himself, pointed at the gate and it snapped open with a reverberating clap, like nearby thunder. Fog billowed out in all directions, and through it appeared a Merdrun officer, looking around warily.

'Gate's open!' hissed Karan. 'They're coming through.'

The officer ran to the blood-covered sus-magiz, who was doubled up on the track, heaving. The officer yelled into the fogged-out gate. A pair of red-armoured soldiers came through and many more pairs were behind them. They stopped in formation, awaiting orders from the sus-magiz, who seemed unable to speak.

Crash-crack!

It came from the top of the ridge, a quarter of a mile up the slope. Chissmoul must have driven the armoured bow of the sky galleon into the overhanging rocks there. The sky galleon whined, there was another almighty crash and crack. Karan heard boulders fall, then a great roaring. They had dislodged the mass of broken rock on the upper slope and it was forming a landslide.

Karan heaved Flangers and Flydd behind the biggest tree and crouched between them with her arms over her head, praying the trunk was solid enough.

High above, broken rock thundered down the slope, following the path cleared by one of the previous landslides, and carrying earth and stone and shattered wood with it.

Nish! He lay unconscious in the forest, but it was too late to go after him.

The officer looked up, clearly wondering what the racket was. It was too dark to see anything up there now.

But he was quick! 'Landslide!' he bellowed. 'Out of the way!'

Some of the soldiers went left, others right. The troops behind them turned to run back through the fog-belching gate but collided with the ranks marching through, and they had nowhere to go.

A churning river of rock, earth and wood hurtled down the path through the forest, exploded across the track ten feet deep and carried the fires, and most of the soldiers, into the river.

The officer was hammered through the gate by a boulder the size of a covered wagon. The centre of the landslide poured in after, obliterating the Merdrun who were coming through, and jamming in the gate.

It shuddered, cracked and boomed. Lighting flashed out in all directions. Then, with a cataclysmic roar and a shockwave that almost embedded Karan in the tree trunk, the gate vanished, leaving a crater a yard deep and about five yards across, glowing an eerie blue at the bottom. The fires were gone apart from a few scatters of red embers.

Her knees gave out and she settled onto her rump, unable to get up. If a single Merdrun had survived it was all over.

The sky galleon reappeared, moving slowly and erratically. Was Chissmoul injured? It wobbled along the line of the track, twenty feet up. Maelys was holding Chissmoul up at the controls, one arm around her. The sky galleon dropped sharply, skidded along the rock-littered track towards the brink and stopped with several yards of the bow hanging over.

Maelys let Chissmoul fall and scrambled over the side. 'Karan?'

'Up – here!'

Maelys ran up to her, her face a ghastly blue in the light from the crater. 'Are the enemy all dead?'

'Wouldn't bet on it.'

'You all right?'

The pain in Karan's belly was part of a symphony now, played by every part of her. 'No.'

Maelys looked down at Flydd, who was moving his right arm as if testing it. Flangers was still under the paralysis spell. 'Where's Nish?'

Karan pointed up into the forest. 'Wasn't time to get to him.'

Maelys ran that way. Nish had not been in the direct path of the landslide, but rock and shattered wood had been hurled into the forest to either side. If he'd been unlucky ...

Flydd was on his knees now and had his hands on either side of Flangers' head, whispering. A healing spell, perhaps.

Flangers shivered and opened his eyes, blankly. Flydd rapped him on the forehead. Flangers took a shuddering breath and sat up.

'You all right?' said Flydd.

'Apart from the metal spike though my head.'

Flydd looked at Karan, then down at the track and the tilted sky galleon, lit by that eerie blue glow. 'You did all that?'

'Nish helped, and Chissmoul and Maelys.'

'But without you saving the day in every possible way –'

'It'll keep. Check on the enemy,' said Karan.

Maelys appeared, supporting Nish. Karan staggered after them, fighting pain so bad that she thought her guts must be full of blood. The side of the sky galleon might as well have been a mountain on the moon, for she had no hope of climbing it.

She slumped on the track. 'Just have a little lie down.'

'Not here!' Flydd said brusquely.

He lifted her and went to put her over his shoulder. Karan screamed.

'Flangers?'

Flangers had just taken Karan under the arms when a harsh voice gasped, 'Drop her. Hands in the air.'

The sus-magiz was supported by two soldiers who had survived the landslide. He pointed his iron staff at Flydd, and a cruciform crystal in its head glowed the same blue as the crater.

Flangers let Karan down and slowly raised his hands. 'If there's anything in your box of tricks, Xervish, now would be a great time to pull it out,' he said out of the corner of his mouth.

'It's empty,' said Flydd.

'Bind the prisoners,' said the sus-magiz.

He was a bloody, blistered, withered ruin, but exultant now. Taking Flydd and the sky galleon, in addition to the other prisoners, might win the war for the Merdrun. *After all we've done!* Karan thought bitterly.

The track was scattered with the weapons of the dead, but all were out of reach. She lay in the mud in her wet clothes, shivering convulsively, while a soldier with charred hair bound Flydd, Flangers, Nish and Maelys, then herself. The other soldier, who had a turned eye blotched with red, kept watch. She tested her bonds. Immovable.

'Get them aboard,' said the sus-magiz. 'Bind the pilot. Take no chances!'

The soldier with the charred hair was prodding Flydd and Flangers up the ladder when Karan heard hooves pounding on the wooden deck of the lower suspension bridge.

The sus-magiz cocked his head, then bared broken teeth. 'That'll be Gomlax; he went after the horses.'

He raised his staff but was so drained that the blue light from the crystal only illuminated a few yards around him. Above, the overcast had cleared, though only the brightest of stars could be seen.

'Only the most desperate of men would ride a horse over a suspension bridge,' Flydd said quietly.

'At a gallop, in near darkness?' said Flangers. 'I'd call him suicidal.'

The horse rounded the bend. It was enormous and so was its rider, a vast dark shape in the dim light. He came up the track at a full gallop, risking everything on the rough surface.

'Gomlax!' yelled the sus-magiz, raising his staff and stepping out into the road. 'Stop! There's a great pit here.'

The rider swerved around a fallen rock and kept going.

'Under the hull!' rapped Flangers, shouldering Flydd in under the sloping side of the sky galleon and heaving Karan after him.

'That's not Gomlax!' said the sus-magiz. 'Take him down.'

Karan hit the ground hard and pain howled through her. She opened her eyes and saw a miracle – the horseman riding down the two soldiers, one after another, and the horse trampling them.

He stood up in his stirrups, a giant of a man, and galloped towards the sus-magiz, raising a blade a couple of yards long. The sus-magiz thrust out his staff. The rider swung savagely, his blade skidded along the staff in a shower of sparks and lifted the sus-magiz's head six feet off his shoulders.

It was over. Really over this time. They had won. Karan could not take it in.

The horse stopped, breathing hard. The rider stood there for a moment, eyeing the headless sus-magiz, who was still standing there. The rider pushed him over, then his shoulders slumped. He dismounted, cut their bonds and dropped the sword.

'Clech!' cried Flydd, getting up. 'How did you know ...?'

'Maelys found me a while back, coming up the road,' rumbled Clech.

'She told you about Nifferlin ... about Aimee?'

Clech's broad face seemed to crack. 'What am I going to do without her, Xervish?'

Flydd embraced the giant. 'I don't know. I ... just don't know.' He looked around. 'Let's get out of this shithole. Clech, Karan saved us today, again and again. But she's hurt inside. Would you carry her aboard?'

Clech bent over Karan. 'I'm so sorry about Aimee,' she said.

'Thank you,' he whispered. 'This might hurt.'

He lifted her effortlessly, carried her up into the sky galleon and below, and laid her on one of the bunks. Flangers was bent over Chissmoul, who was on her back, eyes staring upwards, jaw clenched, bloody foam around her mouth.

'What is it?' said Flydd, who had followed.

'Some kind of a fit,' said Flangers. 'It's happened before.'

'Probably precipitated by the sus-magiz's sorcery. Take her below.' He looked down at Karan. 'What happened to you?'

It hurt to breathe, and hurt more to speak. 'Soldier trampled me. Tore something inside. Stabbed in the belly – couple of months ago. Nearly died.'

Flydd looked grave. 'Lie still. I'll get to you the very moment I can.' He went up to the controls.

Maelys rose from Nish, wiping blood off her hands with a rag, and called up. 'She doesn't look good, Xervish.' Maelys felt Karan's forehead, then her hands. 'She's freezing.'

'Get those wet clothes off her.'

Flydd lifted the sky galleon into the air and headed away through the darkness. Karan did not know where he was going and did not care. The pain grew ever worse; she could not think about anything else.

Maelys took off Karan's wet clothes and wrapped her in blankets. It was a long time before the sky galleon settled and Flydd came. He pulled her blankets away and probed her middle with gnarled fingers. Karan was too ill to feel embarrassed.

'So many scars,' he said. 'What a life you've lived.'

That from a man whose face and hands were little but scars.

'Deep bruising here and here,' he said, feeling along her left ribs. She winced. 'Must've been a big fellow, the boot nails have left their mark.'

'He was stumbling, falling with my bolt in his throat.'

'And that killed him?' He was still probing her; perhaps he was just talking to distract her.

'Eventually.'

She closed her eyes but the image of the dying soldier, the bloody foam rising and falling from the wound with every sucking breath, remained. She would see his face in her nightmares tonight, and many nights to come.

Flydd was feeling her belly, across and back, across and back. 'That hurt?'

'Not much.'

He touched the long scar and she cried out.

'What's this from?'

'Knifed by a mad magiz, one of mind-linked triplets. Should have died ... a great healer dragged me back.'

He felt along her right ribs, one by one, and up over her breast to the collar bone.

Pain shrieked through her. 'Aah!'

Flydd pulled the covers over her and got up painfully. 'Three broken ribs, two digging in. I'll have to move them back in place or they could pierce the lung. It'll be painful.'

'Get on with it, then.'

Flydd gave her a mouthful of a sweet liquor with an underlying stinging heat, and the fumes rose up her nose and overcame her. But even deep under, she could feel the pain.

30

I KNOW WHAT SIDE I'M ON

Ilisial had lain down at the rear of the cave and refused to get up. Wilm, who now had to keep watch for the enemy day and night, was so exhausted he could barely keep his eyes open.

In the middle of the following night he was pacing outside the entrance, thinking that they were going to die here, forgotten by the world, when a pale-yellow light flickered further up the range. He rubbed his eyes, looked again. It wasn't fire, and sometimes it brightened in regular pulses before dying out, then starting up again a minute or two later.

Found you, you treacherous bastard!

Every time he thought about Klarm's betrayal, and what it could mean for Santhenar, Wilm's fury rose. What a contemptible worm he was.

'Ilisial?' he said softly, keeping his distance. He never knew what would set off one of her panic attacks. 'I've found him.'

'Who?' she said listlessly.

'Klarm,' he said in a neutral voice. She refused to believe anything bad about the dwarf, and any hint of Wilm's feelings about him was likely to result in her abusing Wilm again.

She sat up, beaming. 'I miss him so much.'

Great! Just great!

After three hours of climbing he saw that the flickering light came from a cave with a broad, low mouth, a ledge to either side and a projecting shelf of rock above it. The moon was sinking behind the mountains on their left when Wilm edged across to the cave mouth and peered in. Klarm was up the back, staring at the partly disassembled spellcaster.

'What do *you* want?' he snarled.

'What are you up to?' said Wilm, biting down on the word, *traitor*.

'I was worried about you, Klarm,' Ilisial said softly.

He smiled at her. 'You don't get second chances with devices like these, my dear. If you get control, you have to ride it all the way to the end.'

'But why didn't you come back?'

'Spellcaster had a tantrum and stopped working, and it's too heavy to carry.'

'You might have come down and told us,' Wilm muttered.

'All that way on my bleeding stump? What'd Flydd say?'

'How did you know –?'

'I'm well aware that you're his *informer*.'

Was that what he believed? Was it why Klarm was so hostile?

'I'm not an informer,' Wilm said stiffly. 'But I did do my duty. I hope you can say the same.'

'What's that supposed to mean?' snapped Klarm. 'Oh, I get it. Wilm the hero, who sees deeper and further than ordinary men, thinks I've turned my coat.'

'Again!'

'What would know about it, you obnoxious little turd? You weren't there.'

'I know what side *I'm* on,' Wilm said recklessly.

'You're so arrogant and stupid that I'm not even going to talk to you. Go away!'

'I'm not going anywhere until you tell me what you're really up to.'

'Get out!' roared Klarm, standing up on one foot and his bare stump. 'Before I throw you out.'

'Go on then, *short-arse*.'

Klarm put on his wooden foot, then came across, slowly and, Wilm thought, warily, and stopped. Then Wilm made the mistake of laughing.

'Wilm, Klarm, no!' cried Ilisial.

Klarm clenched a fist around his knoblaggie and Wilm was blasted out of the cave. He slid down for a good thirty feet, sharp slates tearing through his shirt and pants and scratching down his back, which was still bruised and scored from last time. His left shoulder slammed into a boulder and he rotated around it and cracked his head on another rock.

He rolled over and tried to get up, but the pain in his shoulder was excruciating.

'Wilm?' called Ilisial. She actually sounded concerned, which was novel. 'Are you all right?'

He stifled a groan. 'Think I've dislocated my shoulder.'

'Stay there, I'm coming down.'

'Leave the judgemental bastard,' said Klarm. 'It'll do him good.'

Ilisial skidded down to Wilm, heaved him to his feet, roughly and angrily, then recoiled. 'There's blood all down your back.'

'Don't panic,' he muttered. 'It's only *mine*.'

She thumped him. 'Put your arm around my shoulder – and shut up.'

He put his left arm in through his shirt to support it, and his right arm over her shoulder. With a series of heaves, each more painful than the last, Ilisial got him up to the cave.

'Idiots!' she muttered, though Wilm was pleased to see that she was more like her old self.

'What'd you say?' said Klarm, glowering.

She glowered back. 'What's the matter with you two? We're supposed to be on the same side.'

'I know what side I'm on,' said Wilm. 'Not sure about him.'

'Bugger off then,' said Klarm.

'Stop it!' she screamed. 'Wilm, I believe Klarm.'

'What's there to believe? He won't tell us anything.'

'I *know* he's on our side.'

'No, you don't,' said Klarm. 'You don't know anything, Lassie.'

'Don't call me Lassie, you stupid old fool!' she snapped. 'Apologise and shake hands.'

'Never!' said Klarm.

'Damned if I will,' said Wilm.

Ilisial stamped on his wooden foot, so hard that it must have jarred Klarm's stump. 'Next time it'll be your good foot.'

'All right! Anything to get you off my back. Wilm, I apologise for telling you the truth about yourself so bluntly.' Klarm held out his hand. 'I know you'd prefer to hear a lie.'

Wilm ignored it, fuming.

'Wilm?' Ilisial said in a dangerous voice, 'Do you want me to fix your dislocated shoulder, or will I leave it to Klarm?'

Klarm grinned menacingly.

'Klarm,' said Wilm, 'I'm sorry I'll always think of you as a stinking turncoat.'

Ilisial growled.

'Best we can do, my dear,' said Klarm with his most disarming smile.

The uneasy truce lasted another day and a half. Klarm spent all his waking hours working on the spellcaster, and sometimes he called Ilisial and they debated the efficacy of one modification or another. Wilm realised that he had badly underestimated her. And how could it be otherwise? M'Lainte was brilliant and it stood to reason that her apprentice would also be the best.

'I think I've got it now,' said Klarm after she had explained a complicated part of the spellcaster's mechanism, pointing out details on the sketches in her notebook. 'Would you and Wilm mind going out for an hour or two while I finish it off?'

'Aha!' cried Wilm, his suspicions rising again.

'Give it a rest,' Ilisial said wearily. 'It's dangerous; Klarm doesn't want us all to be killed.'

Dangerous for whom? Wilm nodded curtly and went out.

'Get well away!' said Klarm. 'Just in case.'

Ilisial emerged, looking strained. She brushed past Wilm in a way that said clearly, *Leave me alone!* and sat at the furthest end of the ledge, in the shade, staring out.

He climbed a third of a mile to an outcrop of pink and white, contorted rock with a good view west, south and east, and stared moodily at the arid range that formed the far side of the Sink of Despair. Beyond, he knew from Flydd's great map, was the long, narrow desert of Kalar, then the Wahn Barre or Crow Mountains, about which he knew nothing.

North again stood the rain-drenched plateau, one of many rising out of a large expanse of rainforest, known as Mistmurk Mountain. There Flydd had foolishly written his *Histories of the Lyrinx War* that had told the enemy so much about mech-magery.

And Ilisial, as an apprentice to the greatest mechanician of all, already understood such devices better than all but a handful of people. How had she known it was the right path for her?

Wilm sighed and turned towards the north-west. Out there, hundreds of leagues away beyond the drylands of Carendor, was the Sea of Perion. In the Time of the Mirror, and for an age before that, it had been the Dry Sea, a sun-baked abyss more than ten thousand feet deep. A salt-scalded wilderness beside which the Sink of Despair was a garden.

Until, on what was to be the last day of the Lyrinx War, the Aachim had blasted away the Trihorn Falls, reopening the channel that had been blocked thousands of years before and allowing the ocean to pour in. In a decade the Dry Sea had flooded again, and it had transformed the dry lands all around.

He looked down. Ilisial was still on the ledge, looking up, but the moment she saw him she turned away. He was about to head down to the cave when a blot of darkness formed outside its entrance and a thread of white lightning, so bright that it hurt his eyes, streaked up from it.

Ilisial shrieked and sprang up. Terror clamped around Wilm's heart and for a second he could not move, then he ran, knowing he was going to be too late.

31

THE ECSTASY WAS ON HIM NOW

Two days after his return from the Sink of Despair Skald was ordered to the rooftop again, where six soldiers were waiting, and Durthix. Dagog scowled in the background.

'We've located the secret weapon,' said Durthix, 'in a cave high on the mountainside.'

'How was it found, High Commander?' said Skald.

'You don't need to know. Your orders are to bring back the secret weapon and kill the three enemy.'

'Yes, High Commander, though ...'

'Is there a problem?'

'This will require my third and fourth long-distance gates in two days, High Commander. And such gates are very draining.'

'Are you saying you're not up to the job? After begging for it, and swearing on *my* honour?'

'Not at all,' Skald said hastily. 'I'm worried that I may be short on power to make the return gate.'

Durthix handed him a primed crystal. 'This focus has been improved. It's more accurate and will take less out of you. However, at need, you may replenish yourself by drinking lives.' Durthix's mouth turned down. Most Merdrun considered that act, necessary though it might occasionally be, as dishonourable.

'What if there aren't any enemy lives available?'

Dagog came forwards, panting and licking his lips.

'Do whatever is needful to recover the secret weapon and bring it back undamaged, Captain,' said Durthix.

That was clear enough. 'Yes, High Commander.'

'If you succeed, your previous failure will be forgotten.'

'And the price of failure?' said Dagog.

'If Skald fails,' said Durthix, 'the price of his oath will be paid. I'll leave that to you.'

That was also clear – the magiz would drink Skald's life, if he had survived, and the lives of all his relatives. He licked his lips again; he ached for Skald to fail.

Skald looked into the primed focus and saw the destination – a wide-mouthed cave high on a mountainside – as clearly as if it had only been fifty yards away. He conjured the gate.

Because he had not fully recovered his inner power it was much harder this time. It took most of his reserves to direct the gate hundreds of leagues south, to the cave. But if it proved sufficiently accurate they would take the enemy by surprise, kill them and seize the secret weapon in under a minute.

Bang!

As Wilm started to run, the blot of darkness outside the mouth of Klarm's cave flowered into a gate. Ten yards away, at the end of the ledge, Ilisial crumpled.

Six soldiers in red battle armour stormed from the gate, followed by the big sus-magiz who had taken M'Lainte. They had come for the spellcaster. Had Klarm called them here? How else could they have gated to the cave so precisely?

A yellow beam zipped from the cave, and again. Wilm dashed across the lookout, jumped a gap, cruelly jarring his sore shoulder, and began to scramble down the ridge. The enemy would probably kill him out of hand, but it wasn't in him to hold back.

Because the moment they laid eyes on Ilisial, they would kill her.

Skald opened the gate and the broad cave mouth was two strides in front of him. Perfect! If they could be in and out in a minute, he should be able to hold the gate open, which would save a lot of power.

He stormed in. The dwarf was at the rear of the cave, crouched behind the secret weapon. The other two enemy were not here.

The dwarf raised his hand and something round and brassy glinted there. A searing yellow flash, a shattering blast, and gravel and grit stung Skald's face and arms. Part of the roof fell on the soldiers behind him, then he felt a thump in his side, *crack*. A flying rock had broken the primed crystal in his pouch. When his sight returned the dwarf was gone, and as Skald turned, the gate folded in on itself and disappeared.

He cursed; it would not be easy to reopen it. He wiped blood out of his eyes and from his lower lip. Had the dwarf escaped via a gate? No, he must have scuttled through that crevice up the back. Skald blasted after him but did not think he had hit.

He took stock. Five of his six soldiers were down. Two had been killed by the rockfall, two were badly injured and another was on his knees, face scorched and eyes bleeding. He had been right in front of the dwarf's blast. The sixth soldier was unharmed.

But the secret weapon was unguarded. 'Watch that crack in the back of the cave,' said Skald.

The uninjured soldier stood before it, blade extended. Skald checked outside. The tall youth was scrambling down from a lookout far up the rocky ridge, though it would take him several minutes to get here. The young woman lay unconscious ten yards away. He would deal with her once the secret weapon was his.

The *spellcaster*. Their interrogation of the old mechanician had taught them much about it, including that it was malicious and predictable, and how to disable it. Gingerly, remembering how it had killed the last of his previous force in under a minute, Skald approached it. It did not quiver. Had the dwarf deactivated it – or was it luring him in?

Sweat drenched him as he took slow steps towards the device, and his heart was beating painfully fast. As a soldier, he expected to die in battle and had no fear of it, but this was different. The spellcaster had killed his troops with fiery, mutilating blasts and he did not want to go in so terrible a way.

He felt the fear all the way down to his bowels.

Another step. Another. He could hear a faint ticking inside it now, as if it were counting down to something. Or waiting for the perfect moment. The soldier guarding the rear of the cave glanced over his shoulder and Skald could see the terror in his eyes.

Skald almost choked. He fought an urge to turn and run. *No! I am not my father!*

He sprang, flipped up the top hatch and plucked out the green crystal M'Lainte had told them about. The spellcaster was safe now. Relief hit him so hard that his knees went weak. He pocketed the crystal, heaved the spellcaster up and lugged it to the cave entrance, staggering under the weight.

But as soon as he attempted to conjure the gate, Skald knew that, without the primed focus, he did not have the power for it. The previous gate had drained too much from him. He needed much more power and there was only one place to get it, dishonourable though it was.

But failing his oath could not be countenanced. He cast the emotion-protecting charm on himself, reached out towards the blinded soldier, spoke the life-drinking spell and established the psychic link, and used it to drain the life force out of the doomed man.

Power exploded in him; his veins throbbed and his nerves stung. It was glorious!

The guard watching the back of the cave whirled, staring in horror. No wonder soldiers hated and feared all who could use that dreadful spell. But the blinded soldier did not have much life in him; not nearly enough for such a long-distance gate.

Skald reached towards the next injured soldier, a woman who had suffered two broken legs, though the moment he looked into her eyes he knew she wasn't going to go easily.

'Curse you!' she shrieked. 'May you rot from the inside before you die a coward's death, *like your father*, and be buried in a traitor's grave!'

The abuse brought up memories and emotions Skald had sworn never to experience again, and he lost focus and had to begin anew. She could not stop him, but she had shaken him, and he drew her life in desperate gulps, wasting half of it. The other injured soldier, whose chest had been crushed, died easily but his life force yielded little of value. Some people were like that.

Skald still lacked the power to reopen the gate, and the tall youth was racing down, recklessly leaping from rock to rock. He carried a black sword whose magical aura stirred a great unease in Skald, for he had been taught about it in training. A similar youth, with a similar black sword, had led the slave's rebellion during the Merdrun's ill-fated invasion two centuries ago, and with the sword's aid that youth had fought Gergrig, their leader and greatest warrior, to a standstill. Shortly after, one of the freed slaves had killed him. The shame had tainted every Merdrun since.

Skald dared not take the risk; a lucky blow from the black sword could mean the loss of the spellcaster. He leapt into the cave, pointed at the uninjured soldier and cast the life-drinking spell.

'Captain, no!' shrieked the soldier.

'I need your life more than you do,' said Skald, and laughed, for the ecstasy was on him now.

The betrayed soldier cursed him too, for as long as his breath lasted, but it was not long. Skald sucked his life dry and cast the husk aside. He had the power now, more than he needed. He raised his right hand and a fiery, crackling nimbus sprang into existence around him. As he went out of the cave the spider webs above, and the leaves and twigs underfoot, burst into flame.

He recreated the gate and was about to carry the spellcaster through when he remembered his orders to kill all three enemy. The young woman lay crumpled at the end of the ledge; the explosive opening of the gate had knocked her out. He could have cut her throat, but the lust for lives burned in his veins now. Why not have hers as well?

But as Skald cast the life-drinking spell at her, the emotion-protecting charm, which he had only made strong enough for one life-drinking, faded and he was hammered by the emotions of his four victims.

May you rot from the inside before you die a coward's death! Their collective agony was so powerful that he lost purpose for a moment. What had he done?

With sheer will he blocked the disabling emotions and cast the life-drinking spell anew. The young woman convulsed and her life force had just started coming across the link when, with a roar of fury, the youth with the enchanted sword leapt down onto the ledge and hurled himself at Skald. Skald ducked the blow and his spell snapped. The youth slammed into Skald's fiery nimbus and was driven back, his clothes smouldering.

But it did not stop him; even when his shirt caught fire the youth kept attacking, thrusting and hacking savagely with the black sword, which greatly amplified his speed and skill and power. With it he might even be Skald's match, and Skald could not take the chance.

He drove the youth backwards with a flurry of blows, heaved up the spellcaster and backed into the gate with it. The youth came at him again but the gate knotted a fist around Skald's middle and heaved, carrying him and the spellcaster away.

But he had failed to complete half of his orders. Was taking the spellcaster enough to save him – or had he condemned himself and his entire family?

The bastard Merdrun was gone with the spellcaster. Ilisial lay still, her eyes open, and the sight so reminded Wilm of Dajaes, his first and only lover, that tears ran down his cheeks.

He tore off his burning shirt, beat out his smouldering hair, poured a pannikin of water over his burned chest and left shoulder, and crouched beside her. Was she still alive? If he had failed her as well, it would break him.

He thought he could feel a pulse in Ilisial's throat, but what if the sus-magiz had partly drunk her life? What would that do to her? Would she be better off dead?

He was utterly out of his depth. Wilm stumbled into the cave. The air had an acrid odour that he had sometimes smelled after a lightning strike. 'Klarm! *Klarm!*'

Wilm expected to find him dead, but he was not there, just his wooden foot, heaps of broken rock, and the bodies of the six Merdrun. Four were withered, their lives drunk.

A groan, a scuffling sound, and Klarm crawled out of a hole at the rear of the cave.

'I thought they'd killed you,' said Wilm.

'Don't sound so disappointed.' Klarm put on his wooden foot, grimacing. 'They would have, if I hadn't brought the roof down and crawled around the corner.'

'Why didn't you use the spellcaster against them?' Wilm's suspicions rose again.

'The cursed thing had gone dead. Sulking, I expect. Where's the far-speaker? I've got to tell Flydd –'

'Klarm, that sus-magiz tried to drink Ilisial's life. If I'd been a couple of seconds slower ...' Wilm related what he had seen on the way down.

Klarm knelt beside Ilisial, felt her heart and throat, then rolled his knoblaggie across her brow, and back. Her eyelids fluttered, she came to and jerked upright, eyes wide and staring, mouth opening as if to scream her lungs out, body rigid.

'You're safe,' said Klarm. 'Wilm, hold her.'

Wonderingly and gingerly, Wilm put his arms around Ilisial. She gave a half scream.

Klarm touched her with the knoblaggie again. 'You're safe,' he repeated. 'Wilm risked his life to save you. He's the better man, Ilisial.' From the look in Klarm's eyes, it pained him to say it.

Ilisial sighed, her iron-hard muscles relaxed, and she subsided against Wilm, weeping. Her face was pressed against his blistered chest but the pain seemed worth it.

He looked up at Klarm. 'Did he start to dr–?'

Klarm held up a hand, mimed, *Not now.*

'How did you know what I did?' Wilm said quietly to Klarm.

Klarm shrugged. 'I was a scrutator. I read people.'

'He got away with the spellcaster. How do you read that?'

Klarm did not reply. He showed no emotion at all.

'They'll take it to a manufactory,' said Wilm, 'and build a thousand like it.'

Klarm took the farspeaker up to the other end of the ledge and, after a series of attempts, spoke in a low voice for a minute or two. He packed it away and came back. 'Flydd's not happy. And he can't come for us.'

'Why not?' said Wilm.

'Bigger problems. We'll have to make our own way home.'

'But we're hundreds of miles from anywhere, in one of the most barren places on Santhenar.'

Ilisial pulled away and wiped her swollen eyes. She looked haunted, desolate, lost.

'If we go down to the Sink of Despair and walk west,' said Wilm, 'there are towns we could reach in a few weeks. We've got food enough.'

'My stump isn't up to two leagues, much less a hundred,' said Klarm.

'Then what's the plan?'

'Sleep. I'll think on it.'

Wilm put salve on his burns and bedded down, fretting. Klarm did not seem upset at the loss of the spellcaster. Was that why he had hidden? Had he wanted it to be taken, to ingratiate himself with the Merdrun? But if so, why hadn't he gone through the gate with them?

Because he had more betrayals to engineer? Nothing made sense about him.

~

Skald staggered out of the gate in Guffeons, his knees shaking under the weight of the spellcaster. Blood ran into his eyes and he could not wipe it away. The power was draining from him almost as quickly as he had stolen it from its owners. He locked his knees, went forwards stiff-legged and put the device down in front of Durthix and the magiz.

Dagog blanched and leaped backwards. Durthix, trained to never show fear, suppressed a shiver.

'This is the secret weapon I swore, upon my high commander's honour, to bring back,' said Skald.

'You have done well, Captain,' said Durthix.

'Has he?' snarled Dagog. 'He may have kept to his oath, Durthix, but yet again he returns with all his troops lost, leaving no witnesses to what he did or how he did it.'

'We have the spellcaster. It's enough.'

'What about the three enemy he was ordered to kill?'

Durthix looked to Skald, who could barely stand up. 'Are they dead, Captain?'

'No,' Skald whispered.

'What, *none of them*?' said Dagog.

'None of them.'

Dagog smiled. 'There will be consequences for this failure. Won't there, High Commander?'

'It will be taken into account,' said Durthix.

32

YOU WILL TELL NO ONE

Several days after Skald returned with the spellcaster, Durthix called him to another private meeting.

'What do you know about thapters, Captain?'

'They were mighty flying and fighting craft,' said Skald, who now spent all his free time reading about the enemy's magical devices, 'developed from abandoned Aachim constructs. Which, in turn, were based on the original construct designed and built by Rulke during the Time of the Mirror. But all failed when the fields died fourteen years ago, and most were taken to pieces for their metal. Parts of one were used to create the enemy's sky galleon.'

Durthix grunted. 'A thapter lies intact in the desert near the southern end of the Sea of Perion, and –'

'You want me to recover it,' Skald said eagerly.

He regretted his rash words the instant he spoke, for Durthix scowled. Skald had made the error of presuming.

'Clearly you think more highly of yourself than I do, *Junior* Captain,' he said coldly. 'Perhaps your lofty ambitions even stretch as highly as *my* position.'

'Never,' said Skald truthfully, his voice trembling.

'Are your emotions getting the better of you, Junior Captain?' Durthix said like a whipcrack.

This was getting dangerous. 'No, High Commander.' Skald exerted iron self-control. 'It was just excessive zeal.'

Durthix curled his black-bearded lip. 'Your ambitions lie in another direction, don't they? You want to be *magiz*.'

'That's entirely beyond my imagination, High Commander,' lied Skald. 'It will be many years before I've mastered all the skills to even become a senior sus-magiz.'

'If you live that long.'

'If I live that long,' Skald echoed, his heart sinking. Had he made an enemy of Durthix too?

'A squad led by a *senior* officer has been sent to find and guard the thapter while a team of skilled slave artisans repairs it. If it cannot be repaired, it will be destroyed so the enemy can't use it.'

'Are they likely to, after all this time?'

'Xervish Flydd is also after the thapter.'

'How do you know? Do you have a spy in his inner circle?'

'If I did, I would hardly tell a junior captain about it.'

'Your pardon, High Commander.'

'As it happens, I know Flydd is after the thapter because I instructed one of my spies to hint that we want it.'

'But why – *ahh*! Bait for a trap.'

'Flydd must not get it.' Durthix considered Skald thoughtfully, then said, 'that's why I'm sending you.'

'Thank you, High Commander,' said Skald, maintaining even more rigid control over his emotions.

'You are permitted to ask the nature of your mission,' Durthix said wryly.

'Am I to assume that it's Top Secret?'

'No one save you and I can know why you're there.'

'You're concerned that Flydd has spies and informers in our midst?'

'Precisely. You will even keep it from your magiz.'

'Umm ...'

'Can you swear to this, Captain, on your sacred rue-har? Because if you can't ...'

If he could not, or if Durthix came to doubt his word, Skald would not leave this room alive. The thapter mission was that critical.

'I can and I will,' said Skald, meeting and holding the High Commander's gaze.

After Skald swore on his rue-har, Durthix continued. 'The thapter is of great importance, but it is not the most important matter.' He paused, looking at Skald meaningfully.

Skald could not see what Durthix was getting at or why he wanted Skald to be there.

'Xervish Flydd,' said Durthix. 'A meagre little man; you could crumple him up in one hand. But a fine swordsman, I'm told, a great mancer, an even greater leader, and very probably the wiliest opponent we have ever faced, apart from Rulke himself. Flydd sees farther than other leaders and is known for swift, unpredictable and decisive action. He's assembling a team, many of whom distinguished themselves in past wars and conflicts, and he must be stopped.'

'You want me to capture him?' said Skald, awed at the magnitude of the task.

'No, Captain Skald, I want you to assassinate him.'

Skald shivered; he could not help it. 'Why me, High Commander?'

'You don't feel you're fit to be entrusted with so vital a mission?'

Skald chose his words with particular care. 'If you require me to assassinate this prodigious thorn in our side I will do my best, but at the present time I don't know enough about the thapter site, the people you have sent there, or Flydd and his allies, to judge whether I can hope to complete the job. Or whether it's way beyond my capabilities.'

It was a long speech to Durthix, who mostly heard, 'Yes, High Commander' or, 'No, High Commander.' Had it harmed Skald? Made him seem wishy-washy?

'All right,' said Durthix. 'I will entrust the task to you.'

'How many troops will I be leading, High Commander?'

'None.'

'I'm going alone?'

'I wish I could send a battalion, to make sure of the mongrel. But I'm constrained on all fronts.'

Durthix walked to the window, looking out at the grimy, smoke-stained buildings of Guffeons. He seemed to be worrying at something. Skald remained at attention, and shortly Durthix came back.

'Your oath also holds with what I'm about to tell you,' he said in a low voice. 'In every particular.'

'Yes, High Commander.'

'I'm sending you by yourself because we're desperately short of power. We drained the summon stone preparing Skyrock and the stone will never replenish, because the enemy have destroyed it.'

'We can draw from the fields of Santhenar, though.'

'They're barely enough to meet our daily needs. But to prepare for the Day of All Days we need all the magical power we can find. We'll have to draw on every field within range to its limits, and even that won't be enough. But –' Durthix shook his head. 'Not your problem.

'That's why, though I would dearly love to send a hundred troops to eliminate Flydd, I can only spare the power for a one-man gate. I've reserved enough for you to gate there and back, but that's all. Do you understand, Captain?'

Skald's thoughts were a fever of possibilities. The Day of All Days. How he wanted to help bring it about. 'Yes, High Commander. Though as a sus-magiz I can draw on a different source of power.'

'Drinking lives.' Durthix's mouth twisted down. 'Ordering it is one of my darkest duties. But if that were the only obstacle ...'

'What other obstacles are there, High Commander?'

'Life-drinking is addictive, Captain. Have you not felt it?'

Was there a right answer and a wrong one? Unable to tell, and because Durthix had confided such vital secrets to him, and also because the high commander was skilled at picking a lie, Skald settled for the simple truth.

'Yes, I have, High Commander. And it troubles me. Once I begin the process of drinking a life it becomes so exhilarating, so ecstatic, that I might not have the strength to stop.'

'Thank you for your honest admission, Captain. Life-drinking corrupts the very soul. You have seen it in our magiz, I'm sure?'

Again Skald hesitated; Dagog might consider the truth as a betrayal. Was this why Durthix had gone against his magiz? 'Yes, High Commander.'

'No one in the grip of that addiction can be trusted to put the True Purpose first. If it comes to the choice, that person will feed their addiction before anything else. So, *no!*'

'High Commander?'

'I do *not* wish you to drink any more lives, for fear of losing you to the addiction. Whether your attack on Flydd succeeds or fails, you may only drink a life if there is no other way to escape.'

If it fails, thought Skald, I will surely be dead. But it was warming to know that Durthix cared. No, he didn't *care* about Skald. *One for All!* He *valued* Skald for the contribution he could make to the True Purpose.

'When do I leave, High Commander?'

'Tomorrow. Go to your barracks; prepare yourself. This is the most important mission of your life.'

'Thank you, High Commander.'

Skald went out, duelled in the practice yard for four hours, sharpened his sword and knife, ate and went to his bed – a canvas stretcher in an empty corner of the vast barracks – early.

And again the magiz woke him in the dead of night.

'Are you plotting against me, Sus-magiz?'

Skald instinctively shrank away, and Dagog smiled. His lips were plump and blood-red – he had been drinking lives again – and his crooked teeth were sharp.

'No, Magiz!'

'You spent a long time with the commander yesterday. In a locked room.'

Skald sat up. He wanted to rise and dominate the much smaller man with physical size, but that could be fatal. 'Yes, Magiz.'

'Do you forget that, by your oath as a sus-magiz, your ultimate loyalty is to me?'

Another question with no right answer. The tension built up to the snapping point. Skald wanted to punch the wizened little man's head in, then drink *his* life.

'Try it,' whispered Dagog. 'Please, do.'

He was trembling with eagerness. Or was he deep in the thrall of his addiction? Either way, it was a deadly moment. If Skald cracked, the magiz would have him. Or if Dagog's desperate need to feed his addiction overwhelmed him, he would lovingly, sickeningly take Skald's life ... and there was nothing he could do to prevent it. The magiz's power was ten times greater than the power of a lowly sus-magiz.

No, a hundred times.

33

A HATEFUL ALIEN DEVICE

Karan roused sluggishly, rubbing her crusted eyes. She was on a narrow bunk, downstairs in the sky galleon. She tried to sit up but it was too much of an effort. Her head throbbed, her ribs and belly hurt, and her heart was racing. Just being awake was exhausting.

And Nish's rescue felt oddly remote, as if it had happened ages ago. Though, given the horrors of that hour, this was no bad thing. She pushed herself upright, inch by inch. Maelys sat a few yards away, gazing fixedly at something in her lap.

'How long have I been asleep?' said Karan.

'Five days,' Maelys replied without looking up.

'*What!* But no one sleeps for –'

'You were in a bad way, bleeding inside. Xervish had to put you out so he could work on you. It ... it was touch and go ...'

'He saved my life?' The pain in Karan's belly turned icy. She had nearly died, without ever realising? 'What about Nish?'

'He's all right,' Maelys said indifferently. 'You can't kill *good old Nish.*'

Previously, she had been desperate to rescue him. What had happened between them? Why was she so hostile?

'And Flangers?'

Still Maelys did not look up, and Karan felt a twinge of unease. 'In a lot of pain, not that you'd know it. He's such an old soldier.'

'Have you known him long?'

'Four years. Flydd and I found him and Yggur in the Numinator's special prison, a tower made from ice in the frozen south. After escaping, we fought together against the God-Emperor. Flangers is a good man. Chissmoul doesn't deserve him ...'

'How is she?'

'When she's flying, as now, she's in a state of bliss,' Maelys spat. 'But if the little bitch thinks she may never fly again, she makes sure everyone feels her pain.'

Her rage was so corrosive, so undermining of all they had achieved during the rescue, that Karan had to get away. She dressed slowly, every movement an effort, and got up, hanging onto a rail for support. She looked down at the object in Maelys' hand – and felt a sickening jolt.

'*Where did you get that?* That's not – It can't be –'

The Mirror of Aachan looked much as it had when Karan had carried it long ago, and she never wanted to see the cursed thing again.

'It's changed,' said Maelys, a trifle vacantly. 'Yalkara cleansed it before she gave it to me.'

'How?' said Karan suspiciously.

'She passed it through chthonic fire. The mirror was completely erased, she said. And if anyone would know ...'

Yes, Yalkara ought to know, but to Karan it would always be a deceitful alien device, and never to be trusted.

'It was a gift for my unborn son, her grandson-to-be that she wouldn't live to see.' Maelys' dark eyes grew wet. 'He was stillborn, the worst day of my life. Losing him destroyed me, Karan. And three days later my little sister, Fyllis, was gone as well.'

She put her head between her knees and wept, silently.

Karan knelt beside her. 'I'm sorry. I can't imagine – that must be unbearable.'

'My son was perfect in every way, yet he was born dead. Why?' Maelys cried. 'He so reminded me of his father, Emberr – the first man I loved.' She looked up the steps towards Nish, who was leaning on the side of the sky galleon talking to Flydd, and lowered her voice. 'I now think he was the only man I've *truly* loved.'

Karan got up and walked away. How would Nish feel if he knew? Maybe he did; maybe that was what was wrong between them.

'I *did* love Nish ... for a while,' Maelys added. 'We were good for each other. But it was too soon.'

'Llian and I, we've had our troubles,' said Karan, turning back. 'Massive troubles, but –' If they survived, everything had to change, and most of all, herself. But how could she ever tell him what she'd done?

'Nish thinks I should *get over it*,' Maelys said bitterly. 'But the baby wasn't his. Maybe he was secretly glad it died.'

Karan's cheeks flamed. 'You shouldn't be telling me this.'

'Who else can I talk to? All my family are dead.'

'I'm happy to listen,' Karan said carefully, 'but you need to –'

'Long before we met, Nish fathered a child with a young woman called Ullii, but someone who wanted to use her special gift killed the unborn child with sorcery. Does Nish ever think about his child, or grieve for it? *Or does he think a dead baby doesn't matter?*' she said shrilly.

'Why don't you ask him? He might be tormented by the loss.'

'I can't talk to him. It hurts more every day. I can't think about anything else.'

Llian, Llian, where are you? Karan slumped on her bunk, her eyes flooding. She had abandoned Sulien into the care of cold strangers, and Sulien was probably going to do something reckless to find him.

'I'm sorry.' Maelys knelt beside Karan. 'I'm so selfish, after all you've done for us. And you've lost so much.'

'I still have Sulien, the best thing in my life,' said Karan. 'And Llian might not – might not –' She changed the subject. 'Why don't you ask someone to be a mediator?'

'Who?' cried Maelys. 'Chissmoul?' A peal of hysterical laughter. 'Flangers? He isn't that kind of man.'

'That still leaves Flydd.'

Maelys flushed. 'Nish is his closest friend, now. Don't mention it again.'

She turned back to the Mirror of Aachan with such yearning, as if what she saw there was her only comfort now, and Karan felt profoundly disturbed.

But it wasn't her problem; Llian was, and Flydd had given his word to look for him. Nonetheless, Karan was knotted inside as she went to his little table. He was hunched over the farspeaker, his maps and notes spread on the floor around him.

'Xervish?' she said tentatively. *No, get straight to it, he owes you.* 'I did all you asked of me ... and now I'm holding you to your promise.'

At his flash of irritation, her anger, never far below the surface these days, flared. 'Assuming you're a man of your word.'

'I don't forget my promises,' he said coldly, 'and I don't appreciate –'

'You were a bloody scrutator! I assumed you were used to plain speaking. But if I've hurt your *feelings* –'

His face hardened, the scars standing out lividly, then he sighed and indicated the seat on the other side of the farspeaker. She sat, her guts throbbing.

'I've made a search for Llian, the best I can with the devices I have, and asked all my spies to keep an ear out. No one has heard a whisper.'

'You said you'd *go looking* for him.'

'I said I'd *look* for him *when I could*. And I have. How can I *go looking* for a man who could be anywhere in the world? Besides, I've had bad news from my spies, lots of it.'

'What bad news?'

'I'll tell everyone when I finish this.' He looked down at his notes, clearly wanting her to go away.

'If you can't look for Llian now, when? We're at war; there'll always be an excuse –'

'It's not an excuse, it's a *reason*. And since we are at war, with thousands of people dying daily, I'd need a damn good reason to abandon them to look for one man *who's probably dead.*'

It was a punch in the gut that left her breathless. No argument would sway him now, but she felt an urge to strike out, to assuage her own agony by hurting him.

'I won't be so quick to save your hide next time, you hideous little creep!'

'Nor I yours.'

'Gratitude isn't your strong suit, is it?'

'Nor is appreciation of the bigger picture yours,' he said pointedly.

'Go to hell!'

He smiled thinly. 'I'm glad we understand each other so well. Now piss off. I've got another eleven spies to try and contact, and I'm not expecting any of them to have good news.'

Nish came down the steps, followed by a great hill of a man, as tall as Rulke but broader in the shoulder. His dark face was vaguely familiar, though Karan had no idea where she could have met him.

Maelys must have seen her confusion for she said quietly, 'It's Clech.'

Fragments of memory bobbed to the surface. Karan had been on the verge of collapse when he had stormed up the track, rode down the last two Merdrun and savagely beheaded their sus-magiz. A quiet, gentle, loyal man,

Nish had said. A former fisherman with a lantern jaw and deep wrinkles around his eyes.

Clech shook her hand, gravely. 'Thank you for all you did for my friends.'

'I'm so sorry about Aimee.' Again she saw that tiny, fine-boned, brave woman, face-down on the lawn. She had been no threat. Why had the enemy killed her?

'I should have been there.' The muscles in his face went slack, the skin sagging. He screwed his eyes closed, his shoulders heaving. 'We finished the mongrels, at least.'

'We did what we could.'

'Aimee was my life and I will have no other mate,' he said. 'Nothing to live for now. Plenty to die for.'

He went up and she followed, needing fresh air. Clech headed forwards, his hands gripping the bow shields so tightly that Karan would not have been surprised to see indentations in the metal.

Half an hour later Flydd called them together. 'I've spoken to everyone I can contact, and no one had good news. I'll start with the worst, from Wilm. The enemy sus-magiz, Skald, who captured M'Lainte, gated back to the Sink of Despair the following day with another squad, and took the spellcaster. This is a disaster.'

'Where did he take it?' said Nish.

'No way of knowing ... though Lilis tells me the Merdrun have cleared the land and are building a gigantic camp next to a towering rock pinnacle called Skyrock, in the Ramparts of Tacnah. At the western end of the Great Mountains,' he said, indicating it on the map. 'There's a monster node beneath Skyrock.'

'What use is it, in the middle of nowhere?' said Nish.

'None of my spies lived long enough to tell me.'

'That all?'

'Aviel made the double batch of nivol, and Maigraith took a team to the summon stone to destroy it, but found it almost drained.'

'Why isn't that good news?' said Maelys.

'The Merdrun had drawn most of the power out of it,' said Flydd. 'She dissolved it with nivol in case it regenerated and scattered the remaining sludge over a wide area.'

'I assume they used the power to make their gates to Skyrock?'

'Yes. They've sent thousands of labourers there already, and many skilled slaves. Architects, designers, masons, carpenters and so forth.'

'What are they building?'

'No idea. And in another troubling piece of news, Tiaan Liise-Mar was abducted this morning.'

'She was a pilot, wasn't she?' said Karan.

'Yes, though before that she was a brilliant artisan and geomancer,' said Flydd. 'With Malien, she helped to create the first thapter –'

'Which is?'

'A flying construct. Tiaan played a vital role in the Lyrinx War, though, *fool that she was*, her conscience got the better of her and she destroyed all the nodes at the end of it – which is why we're in such a dire situation now.'

'Have they taken any other former pilots?'

'Another eight,' said Flydd. 'There never were many; it's a rare talent. And quite a few were killed in the war – or when Tiaan destroyed the nodes. She didn't think of that when she was being so high and mighty.'

'Ancient history,' Nish said hastily. 'What are we going to do?'

'I'll tell you when I know. We're flying to a place I won't name – a refuge for people with rare skills – to hire a few of them. I'm also after a force of archers and swordsmen.'

'What for?' said Nish.

'When you need to know, I'll tell you.'

Karan, too tired to wonder what he was up to, went below. Though she had only been up for a few hours, she needed more sleep, days of it.

Karan woke abruptly when Flydd came pelting into the camp, followed by three men she had not seen before, ten archers carrying crossbows, and a dozen guards with swords.

'Sky galleon!' he yelled. 'On the double!'

They scrambled aboard. Flydd gave instructions to Chissmoul, who lifted the sky galleon with a stomach-heaving jerk and streaked south. The three men were thapter artisans; Flydd did not introduce them. The archers gathered at the left side of the stern and the swordsmen at the right side, talking among themselves.

Flydd called Nish, Flangers, Maelys, Karan and Clech down below. 'Gather round. Keep your voices low. Tell no one. Not even Chissmoul.'

'What's the matter?' said Nish.

'I know why the Merdrun abducted Tiaan. They want a thapter desperately.'

'But they were all destroyed when she exploded the nodes,' said Nish.

'Except the one she and Malien were flying,' said Flydd. 'They had enough power stored in a crystal to bring it down safely.'

Nish frowned. 'Where was that? I don't remember.'

'In the desert eighty leagues south-west of Ashmode. Four hundred leagues from here.'

'Ashmode!' Nish went still, eyes staring into nowhere.

'Sorry,' said Flydd, and to Karan's astonishment the hard man put an arm around Nish.

'That afternoon in Ashmode, after she destroyed the nodes and my father came with Gatherer and Reaper, was the worst day of my life.'

Maelys' face hardened. She turned away.

'One of my worst, too,' said Flydd.

Nish shook himself. 'Ah, well, fourteen years ago.'

'We saw Irisis again, at the end. And retribution was delivered.'

'The destiny of the dead.' Nish managed a faraway smile. 'But the thapter will have been robbed of everything useful long ago.'

Flydd shook his grizzled head. 'The desert dwellers saw it as a sacred object fallen from the heavens, and protected it. But with the fields regenerating it might be repaired and flown again. We've got to stop the enemy getting it.'

34

WHAT IS THIS ABOMINATION?

The gate ejected Llian into a gloomy, cavernous space partly filled with huge curved objects like metal eggs and snail shells. He skidded across a hard floor, raising billows of dust, and fell over. The gate flashed dark green and disappeared.

The stump of his little finger, though excruciatingly painful, was not bleeding. The red-hot edge of the gate had cauterised the stump. He sat in the dust, cradling his maimed left hand in his free hand and wanting his finger back.

And wishing, uselessly, that he could return to the age of twelve and defy Mendark, even if it meant he never went to the College of the Histories. Just to grow up with his mother and father and sisters.

But all were long dead and he had to come to terms with it, in the unlikely event that he ever got out of here alive. He felt sure he had been abducted by the Merdrun. What he could not work out was why.

The dusty air was warm and stale. Llian sensed that he was well below ground. The floor was a quarter of an inch deep in fine, soft dust, surely the accumulation of centuries. The dim light was the same in every direction and showed no tracks but his own. The floor was vibrating ever so slightly, as if a gigantic mechanism was slowly ticking over. He could feel it through the seat of his pants.

He reached out to touch the nearest object, a dusty metal curve like the pointy end of an egg but twice his height. Pain speared through the stump and he froze, hand in the air. Someone was watching him.

Llian turned slowly, straining to see. The enemy's interrogation methods were cruel and inventive, and they had plenty of reasons to torture him.

During their previous invasion, at the climax of the battle on the Isle of Gwine, he had helped to destroy their most powerful magiz, the mind-linked triplets Jaguly, Unbuly and Empuly. And not long afterwards Llian had been the one to cast nivol onto the summon stone, the source of most of the Merdrun's magical power, allowing Yggur and Shand to trap the stone in a force cage and cut off its connection to the field.

Oh yes, the Merdrun wanted him badly, but if they had brought him here they would be torturing him right now. He reached out to the curved surface again, stroked his fingers across impossibly smooth black metal, and *knew*.

'Rulke!' he yelled. 'Where are you?'

White light appeared a long way away, outlining a number of flat, corrugated coils that resembled monstrous metal ammonites, and casting long streaks between them that steadily brightened. After a minute or two Rulke appeared, right hand upraised, holding a luminous stone the size of a lemon. His left hand was pressed to his side, over the scar left by the wound that should have killed him, and he was moving slowly and painfully. He came up to Llian, puffs of dust rising with every footstep, and dimmed the stone to a glimmer.

'Why did you bring me here?' Llian snapped. His stump was excruciatingly painful.

'I need you.'

'What for?'

'I've got to do something urgently, and I can't do it by myself.'

'I'm sure Flydd would have helped you.'

'I don't know him. How could I trust him?'

'Why did you disappear like that? What's going on?'

'I ... don't know. Come with me.'

His uncertainty was disturbing. Rulke had always been so strong and commanding, and he'd always had a plan. Waking from the stasis spell, in a future where both the world and the Secret Art had been radically transformed, must have unnerved him.

He headed back the way he had come. Llian followed. After several minutes they passed through a curved iron door, which Rulke closed behind him, and entered a cubic chamber lit by yellow light coming through diamond-shaped holes in the high ceiling.

A large, lumpy object at the far end was covered in a grey sheet, though there was no dust here. A long table against the left-hand wall was scattered with books with metal covers: some copper, some brass, one tin and one silver. A plan drawing, on orange leather marked with deep blue ink, showed the parts of a complicated mechanical contrivance. At the back stood three vaguely familiar devices that, Llian assumed, Rulke had stolen from the sky galleon. A smaller table to the right held only a slim volume bound in worn red leather. There was no dust here.

Rulke turned and his face grew hard. 'I also brought you here because you owe me.'

Pain stabbed through Llian's stump. 'What for?'

'As I lay dying in Shazmak, tormented by the knowledge that my people would soon be extinct, I did you a very great honour. I gave you the key to my secret papers, here in Alcifer, and asked you to tell my tale. And you swore you would.'

Llian swallowed painfully.

'*But you did not!*' Rulke thundered. 'Ten years went by, yet you did nothing. When you finally came to Alcifer it was by accident, because a gate brought you here.'

How did he know so much? 'I – I couldn't tell your tale,' stammered Llian. 'I was under a ban from the College.'

'What for?'

Llian felt his cheeks glowing. 'For breaking one of our greatest commandments and meddling in the Histories. Chroniclers and tellers must remain aloof, but I interfered, more than once. My taunts drove Tensor to attack you and we all thought he'd killed you.'

'You're a reckless man, Llian, but a *small* man for all that,' Rulke sneered. 'You willingly broke the chroniclers' commandments, yet you were too *afraid* to work while under a ban? How tiny your courage is. How feeble; how *limited*.'

Llian hated making excuses but he had to make Rulke understand. 'I was on my last chance. If I broke the ban, the college would have made it permanent.'

'You could have defied them. What were they going to do?'

Llian could think of nothing to say. He had never forgotten his oath to Rulke. He had often thought about the papers and daydreamed about using them – not just to fulfil his oath, but to write another Great Tale. Had he done so, it would have raised him above every other teller who had ever lived, and he'd craved that, but he'd been too afraid of the college's power over his life. He had kept putting Rulke's tale off, expecting the ban would be lifted.

'I'm sorry,' he said feebly. 'I let –'

'No excuses, Llian!'

Rulke stormed across to the table, picked up the slender red volume, came back and slapped Llian hard across the face with it, the left cheek and then the right. Tears of pain formed in his eyes.

'What,' roared Rulke, brandishing it, 'is this *abomination*?'

He reversed the cover, which said in black, *Tale of Rulke*, by Thandiwe Moorn. And underneath, in larger letters in gold leaf, *The 24th Great Tale*.

'Where did you get that?' said Llian.

'Am I to believe that you *contracted out* the story of my people to your former lover,' Rulke said icily, 'and this insulting *little* story is the result? Did you set out to deliberately undermine me? To make the lives and deeds of myself and my people, the greatest of all the human species, seem *ordinary*?'

'No, I didn't,' Llian choked. 'Thandiwe stole your papers soon after I found them. Before I could translate any of them.'

Rulke's dark eyes narrowed. 'How did she get into Alcifer?'

'She stole the little silver key you gave me and rode here, pell-mell, to find your papers – she was desperate to have her own Great Tale.'

'And you didn't stop her? Even for you, Llian, that's worse than feeble. It's pathetic!'

'When she stole your papers, she was with Maigraith, who –'

Rulke stiffened. 'What was she doing here?'

'Hunting me and Karan,' said Llian.

'Why?'

'Long story.'

'Shorten it.'

'Maigraith wanted your son, Julken, to be mated to Sulien once they came of age.'

'I have a child?' Rulke whispered. '*A son*?' He stumbled to a five-legged stool and sat down.

'You had two sons. Maigraith had non-identical twins by you,' said Llian. 'Julken and Illiel. Illiel took after Maigraith's Faellem side, Julken after you. In looks, at least.'

'I – don't understand. Why did she want him to be paired with Sulien?'

'She was crushed by your death, and the extinction, as she believed, of the Charon, and she wanted to do something about it. *Who else can a triune's son mate with but a triune's daughter?* she said to Karan when they were both heavily pregnant. *From our loins spring a new people, a new species, perhaps with more of the strengths and fewer of the weakness than those that engendered us. Let us agree to pair them now.'*

'Monstrous!' said Rulke. 'And Karan rightly refused.'

'But Maigraith was obsessed and kept at her. When Sulien was nine, Maigraith pressured us to allow Sulien to live with her and Julken. She wanted them to grow up together. We refused, of course, but it didn't end there –'

'Where was my other son? Where was Illiel?'

'Maigraith didn't want him.'

'*What?*' Rulke bellowed.

'She sent him to live with the Faellem side of the family, somewhere in the forests of Mirrilladell.'

Rulke's jaw tightened. He stalked across the chamber and back, picked up the five-legged stool and raised it high as if to smash something with it, but winced and clutched at his side and sat again. 'Go on with your story about Thandiwe.'

'When she got here, Maigraith compelled Thandiwe to help her trap Karan –'

'Same long story?'

'I'll make it brief. Thandiwe was choking Karan, on Maigraith's orders, and the reward was to be your papers. I warned Thandiwe that what she was doing would destroy her chances of ever gaining a Great Tale, but she –'

'Really?' said Rulke more calmly. 'What did you tell her?'

Llian quoted from his perfect teller's memory. '*If you steal the tale or kill for it, in your own mind that's what your real identity will be when you tell your tale to the masters: not a teller, but a thief or a murderer. You can't be both. In reaching for the prize, you will have put it forever beyond your reach.'*

'But she got her so-called Great Tale,' Rulke said icily. 'How did that travesty come about?'

'The College of the Histories had become corrupt, and I didn't count on the hunger of the masters to gain another Great Tale, to their own honour and glory. Thandiwe's tale was in no way worthy of the honour, and she told it poorly, but –'

Rulke heaved Llian into the air by his shirtfront. 'You were *there?*' His eyes radiated shards, and he picked up the *Tale of Rulke* in his free hand and whacked Llian across the ear with it. 'You *heard* this miserable tale told?'

'Yes,' Llian squeaked.

Rulke held him out at arm's length, effortlessly. 'Correct me if I'm wrong,' he said in a deadly voice, 'but I understood that a tale could only become a Great Tale by the unanimous acclamation of the masters.'

The pit yawned before Llian's feet and he had no way to avoid it. 'That's – right.'

'And you, being a master of the college, had the right to vote.'

'I ... umm ... abstained.'

Rulke might have been turned to his granite statue, so hard and still did he go, then he dropped Llian. He wanted to run into the dark and hide.

'You *knew* Thandiwe's tale was unworthy to be a Great Tale,' Rulke said, very softly.

'Yes.'

'In fact, an utter travesty that insulted and diminished me and my people.'

Llian's cheeks were burning. 'Yes.'

'You could have voted it down ... but by abstaining, you collaborated to make it a Great Tale.'

'You don't understand.'

'I'm trying to.'

'Thandiwe could have destroyed me.'

'How?'

'When Maigraith captured Karan in Alcifer, the only way I could save her was by telling Maigraith an untrue tale –'

'A lie!'

'Yes,' Llian whispered. 'I invented a story ... about your identical twin brother, Kalke ...'

Yggur's dark eyebrows rose; his thick lips started to form a smile, but he did not complete it. 'Kalke! You live dangerously, Chronicler.'

'I don't understand.'

'Had Maigraith known the word she would have slain you on the spot.'

Llian tried to speak but his mouth was too dry. He swallowed. 'Why?' he croaked.

'In the Charon tongue, Kalke means *gullible fool*.' Rulke shook his head. 'You're a treasure beyond price, Llian. Go on.'

'I told her Kalke had been badly injured in a raid on the Merdrun long ago and still lay hidden in the void, under a stasis spell.'

'A stasis spell! How did you know about such things?'

'I ... collect knowledge.'

'So you can abuse it. Continue.'

'Maigraith was desperate to find Kalke and left Alcifer at once, but later

Thandiwe found out about my untrue tale. If I'd voted the *Tale of Rulke* down she would have told the masters and destroyed my career.'

'Then the name the future knows you by, Llian the Liar, is well deserved.'

Llian could not speak. He nodded jerkily, the shame burning him.

Rulke shook his head in disgust. 'You wouldn't describe yourself as bound by unwavering moral principles, would you, Llian?'

'I'm flawed ... like everyone else.'

'More flawed than most.' Rulke looked down. 'What happened to your little finger?'

'The edge of your gate cut it off. Can you –?'

'Get it back and reattach it?'

Llian wanted it back, more than he could have imagined. 'Yes.'

'I could ... assuming I gave a damn.'

Had it been anyone else, Llian would have begged. But that would only lower him further in Rulke's eyes. 'And you don't.'

Rulke didn't bother to reply.

'What do you want me for?' said Llian. 'To rewrite your tale?'

'Do you really think I'd give you the chance to betray me again?'

35

GOT A DEATH WISH, CHRONICLER?

Rulke sat at the large table, shoved the books and the chart aside, and stared at the three devices he had stolen from the sky galleon.

'Then what do you want me to do?' said Llian after a long interval.

'Shut your mouth.'

The stub of Llian's little finger throbbed with every heartbeat. He perched on a stool and watched as Rulke began to take the devices apart. His hands, matching the rest of him, were huge, his fingers long and thick, but he worked with remarkable dexterity.

He was an astounding craftsman. After escaping from the Nightland he had single-handedly built his flying construct, presumably here in Alcifer. Maigraith had taken his body to Aachan with it, and later the Aachim had used what was left as a model for their own constructs, though theirs were mere land transports, incapable of either flying or making gates.

'Come here,' said Rulke. 'Hold this upright.'

Llian took the crystal Rulke was holding. It was blue, with three glowing specks of a deeper blue inside, and disturbingly warm.

'Hold it *still!*' said Rulke.

When working on a manuscript, Llian's calligraphy, taught by his scribe father as a child and practiced to this day, was perfect. His mother, who had been an illuminator, had also taught him her art and his hand was rock-steady when working on an illustration. Yet whenever he tried to do ordinary things, from fixing a leaking tap to digging carrots in the garden, he was embarrassingly clumsy. Karan had refused to let him chop the firewood for fear he'd cut his foot off. He forced his hands to stillness.

Rulke fitted a cap carved from pale yellow soapstone to the top of the crystal, frowned, took it off and carved small pieces of the soft rock off the inside of the cap with a scalpel. He worked swiftly and when he put the cap on it fitted perfectly.

'What are you making?' Curiosity was Llian's consuming weakness.

'None of your business.'

Rulke stopped and turned to Llian, studying him minutely, then smiled. It was not a kind smile.

'Yes?' said Llian.

'How come you and Karan only had the one child?'

Llian swallowed. 'That's a very personal question.'

'Indulge me. You know how much issue matters to us.'

The Charon were blessed with extremely long life, but after they escaped from the void to Aachan, and some had subsequently come to Santhenar, they had been cursed by such low fertility that they had almost died out. Rulke might well be the last of his kind.

'Triunes are normally sterile. Karan only got pregnant because of the little black pill you gave her.'

Rulke stared at him, opened his mouth and closed it again.

'What?' said Llian.

'I compounded it to permanently reverse the block that prevents triunes from having children. And it enhances fertility in other ways. Karan could have had as many children as she wanted ...' He eyed Llian, speculatively.

'We tried! It didn't work.'

'Then the failure must be in you,' said Rulke with a hint of malice. 'I could concoct a pill to make a man of you, if I cared to. Though perhaps Karan prefers things the way they are.'

Llian flushed. Rulke was really enjoying this. 'No, thanks!'

The hours passed. As Rulke came and went, returning with complicated devices of unknown purpose, Llian brooded.

Sulien's birth had been long, agonising and traumatic for both mother and baby. Had it not been for Idlis the Whelm, Sulien and Karan would probably have died.

Even so, Karan had wanted another child, even two, and so had Llian, though after trying for a couple of years she'd told him that her triune's sterility had come back. She had sensed the change in herself and it was permanent. Though Llian had not doubted her, he had wanted to keep trying in case a miracle happened, but from that moment she had kept him at bay. Made him feel even more of a eunuch.

Had she lied to him? If so, why? Because he was such a disappointment that she could not bear to have any more children with him? The thought was crushing.

Well, perhaps it was for the best. If it was now over between them, as it seemed, at least only one child would be affected ...

Rulke took each of his devices to pieces and, late in the day, began to assemble a new device from the myriad of parts. It was a foot tall and half as wide, and a large yellow crystal, its upper end cut away to form a hollow the shape of an eggcup, was fixed on top. The base was made from a pair of circular metal discs, the lower one resting on the table.

The upper disc, which rotated on a rod, was fixed half an inch above the lower and marked around the rim with the thirty-two points of the compass. The eggcup crystal was attached to the base by a metal elbow joint so it could be rotated to any direction, and pointed anywhere between the horizontal and the vertical.

'Are you making a scrying device?' he said, not expecting an answer.

'Not exactly.'

Rulke raked his fingers through his black hair, leaned back on his stool, then winced and clutched his side. The blood withdrew from his dark face.

'You all right?' said Llian.

Rulke's forehead was spotted with sweat. 'Every movement pulls on the scar tissue. It'll take weeks of exercise before I'm my old self again.'

'Is that why you're hiding here?' said Llian.

'For a man whose trade is words,' said Rulke, 'that's a remarkably ill-judged turn of phrase.'

'Sorry, I meant –'

'I know what you meant.'

'You're the only man the Merdrun ever feared,' said Llian. 'If they discover you're alive, and ... not yourself –'

'They'll find a way through my defences.'

'Then why are you sitting here on your flabby arse –?'

Rulke rose and his right hand caught Llian around the throat. 'Got a death wish, Chronicler?'

Another spasm struck him, he took three wobbling steps to his stool and sat down. 'What I'm looking for – matters more than life itself.'

Llian rubbed his throat, which was bruised from Rulke's grip. 'Before you vanished the other day you cried, *Incarnate!* What was that about?'

Rulke did not speak.

Llian replayed the scene in his mind's eye. 'You weren't afraid. You seemed full of wonder – *or hope.*'

Rulke stared at him, unblinking, and Llian felt it was safe to go on. 'After thousands of years, and all you've seen and done, what could arouse your hope? What matters more to you than the coming Merdrun attack – more than life itself?'

A faint smile played on Rulke's full lips.

'The hope that you're not the last of your species after all,' Llian concluded.

Rulke's breath hissed between his teeth. 'Sometimes I forget that inside the crooked, lying buffoon lurks a man with a keen understanding of people, and what motivates them.'

'Are you going to tell me what you're looking for?'

'And rob you of the pleasure of working it out for yourself?'

'I've no way of guessing what *Incarnate* means.'

After a lengthy pause, Rulke said, 'Back in the deeps of time, when my people were newly exiled into the void and desperate to escape it, it was the name of a forbidden object ... a Waystone.'

'And that is?'

'Something crystallised from the tears of a tortured wyverin.'

Llian stared at him.

'A legendary magical beast resembling a two-legged dragon,' Rulke added. 'But the wyverin's body was reshaped by a banished clan of Charon sorcerers –'

'Why were they banished?'

'For using forbidden mancery and defying many edicts to desist.'

'Why did they reshape the beast?'

'So it would be in continual agony, and produce more tears. It takes a vast quantity of wyverin tears to crystallise out a Waystone. And a Waystone – or rather *the* Waystone, for as far as I know there was only ever one – allows its owner to make a portal from anywhere to anywhere, *without leaving a trace.*'

'Why is that forbidden?'

'I should have thought that'd be obvious.'

'Humour me,' said Llian. Then, realising he'd been over-bold for someone in such a precarious position, 'If you wouldn't mind.'

'It's extremely difficult to make gates or portals ...'

'And some places won't allow gates to open,' said Llian, thinking about the various ones he'd seen, and had been through.

'Normally, gates can't be disguised or hidden,' said Rulke, 'Because they connect places whose very natures are different. They open with a bang, strong winds rush through them, often fog condenses, and they glow or flare or are surrounded by bright, crackling, deadly discharges.'

Llian touched the scab on his stump.

Again, that faraway look appeared on Rulke's face. 'But a portal made by the Waystone is small, silent and unobtrusive. A scoundrel who had it could commit any crime – secretly enter a guarded vault and steal its contents, for instance – and escape without leaving a trace. Or commit murder, assassination, sabotage, molestation, abduction or any other villainy in secret, and get away with it. The great virtue, and great flaw, of the Waystone is that any sentient creature capable of wielding the Secret Art can use it. No one would be safe and no treasure could be protected.'

'If there was only ever one Waystone, how come you recognised it?'

'I was shown a chip off it when I was very young. The chip had no power to make gates, but it had a unique magical signature.'

Llian wondered if Rulke was telling the whole truth. Probably not. 'What happened to the Waystone?'

'The tormented wyverin caught the clan of sorcerers who made it, and ate them. It was thought to have consumed the Waystone as well but ... evidently not.'

'And you hope the person who has it is Charon, from a branch thought extinct long ago? Is your device designed to find the Waystone?'

'No, it's a beacon for the bearer, if he or she chooses to follow it.'

Llian's hair stood on end. 'What if the bearer isn't Charon? There are thousands of deadly species in the void, and they all want out.'

Rulke stared Llian down. 'Free, or chained?'

'What?'

'I didn't bring you here to be my friend, Llian, or to give me dumb advice; I brought you here to punish you. And because I sometimes need an extra pair of hands. Should you prove useful, I might, *possibly*, abate the savage punishment I've planned.'

Llian's mind raced. He'd presumed far too much. Rulke was utterly ruthless when he needed to be.

'You can be an extra pair of hands while chained to the floor. Or remain free – and keep your opinions to yourself.'

But how could Llian allow Rulke to open this Pandora's Box? 'Are you sure you've thought this through? What if the Waystone –?'

Rulke pointed at Llian and, with a rattle and a clank, a set of rusty iron manacles, so cold they stuck to the skin, locked about his shins. They were fixed to a heavy chain, ten feet long, bolted to the floor.

Rulke turned the circular base of his device in minute increments. Llian tried to adjust the left manacle but tore a patch of skin off. He winced.

'I'll keep my mouth shut. You can take the chains off.'

Rulke made a slashing movement with his left hand, *Shut up!* The chain jerked, pulling Llian over backwards and dragging him across the floor.

He carried the rattling chains to his stool and climbed on it. Rulke scowled and raised a fist, and for an awful second Llian thought he was going to be blasted into the far wall. Rulke pointed a finger at the beacon, which rotated on its base, the points of the compass inching around. He seemed to be holding his breath. Llian did too.

The eggcup-shaped crystal at the top glowed yellow. Rulke waved a hand at the wall globes, which faded to a dim twilight. The device began to rotate backwards and forwards, making a small rasping sound. The crystal glowed brightly, highlighting his large nose, heavy brows and jutting chin. The light passing through his beard turned the individual hairs dark red.

He adjusted the hinged joint to point the device lower and rotated the base again, but the crystal failed to light. He angled it higher, turned it a fraction and the crystal emitted a yellow flash, like lightning.

He turned Llian's way, and even after the twilight returned Rulke's eyes had an indigo afterglow. His breathing was breathing quick and shallow, his body racked by shivers of anticipation.

'It *is* a Waystone,' he whispered. 'And a woman has it, possibly a lost Charon. I'm not alone.' He leapt off his stool, threw his arms around Llian and embraced him, crushingly. '*I'm – not – alone!*'

Rulke's passion was moving. What could be worse than being the last of one's kind?

Being duped into thinking that another Charon existed and was, perhaps, also searching for one of her kind! 'What if you're wrong?' said Llian.

'In the unlikely event that I ever want your opinion, Chronicler, I'll ask for it.'

'But you said the Waystone was created by a criminal clan of sorcerers. What if their descendants are looking for a new world to plunder? With the Waystone, they need have no fear of the Merdrun or anyone else.'

Rulke scowled and set off the beacon. Llian did not see any change, though in his inner ear a note vibrated at the lower edge of hearing, throbbed up through the register to an ear-piercing howl, stopped and began again. He rubbed his manacle-seared shins and thought through the possibilities.

'What if it isn't the Waystone at all?'

Rulke did not deign to answer, though he looked even more annoyed.

'You first detected its fingerprint just before the Crimson Gate opened. But what if there is no Waystone?'

Rulke looked up sharply, his eyes smouldering. Llian felt a quiver of fear but ploughed on. This had to be said.

'The Merdrun read our Histories and Great Tales two centuries ago, so they know your weaknesses. What if they created a semblance of the Waystone to trap you?'

'Humbug!' Rulke walked away.

Then Llian pushed him too far, and knew it the moment the words left his mouth. 'The Rulke I knew of old was arrogant and ruthless, but deep down he always acted for a noble purpose. But you seem ... diminished. I – I'm sorry, Rulke, but I have to say it. I think your mind was damaged while you were under the stasis spell.'

'You're meddling in the Histories again, Chronicler,' Rulke said with icy calm. 'Trying to push me into a course of action. Or away from one. Isn't that why you were banned?'

'Yes, but –'

'No *buts*.'

Rulke unfasted Llian's chain, jerked him into the air by the scruff of the neck and carried him along one dark corridor after another.

'What are you doing?' Llian said, quietly now.

'Know what usually happens to crowing bantam cocks?' Rulke asked grimly.

At Gothryme, their heads were chopped off and they ended up in the pot.

He carried Llian up several long sets of metal steps, the treads shaking under his weight. Llian could not break free.

'If you keep struggling, Chronicler, I might decide to drop you.' Rulke snapped two fingers and azure lights came on, above and far below. Llian gasped. He was suspended above a hundred-foot drop. 'And when you hit the floor, you'll burst like the rotten egg you are.'

Llian froze. Rulke carried him across a narrow platform, opened a door and went into a small, plain room whose curved walls, floor and domed ceiling were entirely made of moss-green metal. There was a small metal table and chair on one side, a long but narrow window partly covered by a metal blind, and an open door, through which he saw a smaller room with a metal bunk.

'I made it ready before you came. Knowing you as I do, I knew I'd need it.'

'What is it?' Llian's voice, normally fully under his control, trembled.

'Your new home. There's food for a week or so, and water for a couple of months. And provision – very basic – for your other necessary needs. I expect your rehabilitation will take that long.'

'You're imprisoning me for *months*?'

'You insulted and maligned me, Llian. Even though you knew what a vengeful man I am. And you question *my* judgement, *my* mental stability!'

'But what am I supposed to do?'

'Work on your tales. Bang your head on the wall. Contemplate your suicidal stupidity, it's all the same to me.'

'But I don't have my notes or my journal.' Llian prayed that Karan was looking after them, for they contained months of work on his tale of The Gates of Good and Evil.

'There's paper, pen and ink. I'm sure *Llian the Liar* can find a way to occupy the time.'

Rulke dropped him and, as Llian came to hands and knees, booted him across the room. 'The window is unbreakable, as is the door lock. The air ducts are too small to crawl through and all else is solid metal. I'll bring food every week or two,' he said with a malicious grin. 'Assuming my *damaged mind* can remember to.'

Llian got up, rubbing his backside. The door closed and locked; he didn't bother to test it.

He sat at the table, picked up the sheaf of paper and put it down again. And smiled.

Another copy of the complete Histories of the Charon was hidden somewhere in Alcifer and he was going to find it. And then he would pursue and craft the greatest tale of all, the *Tale of the Charon*, of which Thandiwe's *Tale of Rulke* was little more than a chapter.

The story of the Charon stretched back to the earliest of human times, long before any recorded old human history. And, clearly, it meant everything to Rulke, especially after his close shave with death and the near extinction of his people. And who better to tell it than Llian?

But how could he possibly convince Rulke to trust him? Llian would have to do him an almighty service, and that wasn't going to be easy from here.

36

HE TOOK THE BAIT

With desperate self-control, Skald avoided any emotional reaction that would provoke his enemy.

'Presently, Magiz,' he said quietly, hunching his massive shoulders to make himself less physically threatening, 'I am forced to serve two masters. From time to time Commander Durthix requires my services as a captain, and has made it clear that, as a captain, my previous oath to him forever binds me. I also know that, whenever I am acting under your orders, my oath to you is paramount.'

'And if you're acting as both a captain and a sus-magiz?' said Dagog, his voice dripping with malice. 'Who then do you serve?'

No right answer! 'I can't say, Magiz.'

Dagog smiled. 'I thought as much. But you're mine, Sus-magiz, and one way or another, I'll have you.'

Skald needed to be fresh for the most vital mission of his life, but after Dagog had gone he found it impossible to sleep. Was the magiz losing control, the addiction taking him? If it was, this was bad for the Merdrun and the True Purpose, and something needed to be done.

But such matters, troubling though they were, were way beyond his responsibilities. Skald returned to the practice yard, where he found another captain unable to sleep, and they sparred furiously for hours, practicing all their strokes.

The familiar exercises, and the real physical danger of sparring with sharp weapons, would normally have driven his worries away. But not this time.

'I trust you are well rested?' said Durthix when Skald reported to him that afternoon, at the appointed minute.

'Enough,' lied Skald.

'At this address,' he showed Skald a scrap of paper, 'a senior sus-magiz will prepare and open a gate for you.'

Skald memorised the address. 'Open *for me*, Commander?'

'To have a hope of assassinating Flydd you will need all your strength, and you cannot be drained from creating the gate. Besides, it may be necessary to overcome certain defences around the destination, enemy wards far beyond your ability to break. The senior sus-magiz knows nothing about your mission. She will simply open and direct the gate as required, break any protective wards at the destination without leaving a sign, and close the gate the moment you've gone through. Do you have any questions?'

'Yes, High Commander. How many people will be there?'

'My team charged with repairing and recovering the thapter numbers twenty-four: eighteen guards, a sergeant and a captain, and four of our artisans, watching everything the slaves do to repair the thapter. There are nine of them. Eight are former artisans and artificers who were familiar with thapters, and the ninth is a former thapter pilot.'

'What about Flydd?'

'He took the bait. His sky galleon is only hours from the thapter site.'

'Do our people know he's coming?'

Durthix hesitated. 'No.'

Why not? 'Are you going to warn them?'

'A Merdrun force is always prepared to fight off an attack.'

Skald was not sure he liked the sound of that. Yet, if no one else knew about the assassination attempt, there was no way Flydd could be warned in advance.

'I don't know how many people he has,' Durthix added, 'but it will be a strong force. Your gate will take you to a gully a couple of miles from the thapter, so the small sound of the gate's opening won't be audible. You will recon the area and devise your assassination plan. Nothing more can be planned in advance. That's why *you* were chosen, Captain Skald – for your initiative. Get ready; you'll go when we know Flydd's attack is close. It wouldn't do for you to arrive first and be slain by our guards.'

Skald saluted Durthix, and went, still troubled.

~

After he had gone Dagog emerged from his hiding place. 'I don't like this, Durthix. There's much about Skald that troubles me.'

'He's done well so far.'

'His mouth says one thing but I'm sure his mind is saying another. I suspect him of being *emotional!*'

'When we were solely a warrior race in the void,' said Durthix, 'all a soldier needed was superb training, absolute endurance and instant obedience. But now we're in reach of the goal that has eluded us these past ten thousand years, different abilities are required. We all must adapt, Magiz. Even you.'

'I'm aware of it!' Dagog snapped.

'Now who's being emotional?'

'I don't like him. Let him make one small slip and I'll have him.'

Durthix did not conceal his revulsion. 'Be careful it's not you who makes the slip, Magiz. Besides, it's almost certain that Skald will fail and be killed, which will punish him for his previous failures and solve the problem. There is, however, a small possibility that he'll succeed in assassinating Flydd, and this is worth any risk.'

Dagog grunted, which Durthix took for agreement, or at least, not disagreement.

'We stand on the precipice, Magiz,' Durthix went on. 'On the one hand, the True Purpose we've fought towards for all our aeons in the void – the goal that will complete our transformation and gain us our long-delayed revenge. On the other hand, should we fail, utter ruin. Nothing can stand in our way, *including you.* You will master your addiction, or you will no longer be magiz.'

The threat was a deadly one, for there was no resigning from the position. A redundant magiz was a dead magiz.

'At so critical a time?' said Dagog. 'There's no one to replace me.'

'All the more reason, if you truly care about our True Purpose as much as I do,' Durthix said softly, 'to master your addiction to drinking lives before it masters you.'

~

In the walled yard, Skald stood at the point marked while a senior sus-magiz, a stocky, taciturn woman called Zilzey, took various measurements and pointed three tripod-mounted devices, each separated by a number of yards, at his chest.

'Is all this really necessary?' he grumbled, the stress momentarily overcoming his good sense.

'You're a very *junior* sus-magiz,' said Zilzey.

He took the rebuke in silence.

'Any error of aim or opening could reveal the gate, and you,' she went on. 'In which case you will fail and die.'

'Thank you for correcting me,' said Skald. He did not need any more enemies.

'Ready?' she said.

'Ready.'

Three beams of pale-yellow light touched his chest. Zilzey adjusted them slightly until they converged in a circle, struck the iron shoe of her staff on the cobblestones, and he was gated into darkness.

He fell a foot onto hard ground, knees bent to take the impact in silence. The night was hot here; he smelled desert herbs, a hint of wood smoke and dry, baked earth, refreshing scents after the humid stench of Guffeons. Zilzey's precisely targeted little gate had brought him to the destination in almost perfect silence. It was a marvel beyond his understanding, though one he was determined to master ... if he survived.

First, he had to avoid the Merdrun's outer guards, who would kill anyone who came near.

Skald used all his skills, and some subtle sus-magiz magic, to avoid being detected as he wormed his way across the stony ground to a small, rock-crested knoll. From its top he should have a clear view of the site.

The thapter, which had lain on its side for the past fourteen years, was a quarter of a mile away, near the crest of a low hill. It had been righted and was lit by a variety of glowing lanterns on poles. The sparse vegetation had been cleared and burned, leaving a mound of ash and red coals. At the base of the hill a small creek, presumably dry at this time of year, had also been cleared for a couple of hundred yards.

Sections of the thapter's metal skin had been removed and three slave artisans were bent over it, watched by two Merdrun. The rest of the skilled slaves must be inside. A ring of Merdrun guards, thirty yards out from the thapter, were led by a sergeant and watched by a captain.

The other six guards must be patrolling further out, and if Skald had not known they were there he might never have located them. After finding the last he lowered his head and merged into his surroundings as only a skilled Merdrun could. He would not move until Flydd attacked. Hopefully, in the chaos of battle, Skald could creep in and cut him down.

The minutes stretched into an hour. And two. Three. Four.

Where was Flydd? Durthix had said that Skald would not be sent until the attack was imminent. What was causing the delay? Had the plot been discovered? He wiped sweat out of his eyes and studied the stars. Only half an hour until dawn. Assassinating Flydd would be far more difficult in daylight. Realistically, almost impossible.

Metal clanged on metal, then he made out a faint humming. With exquisite care he checked on the thapter again. The slave artisans were replacing sections of its metal skin. They had completed the repairs and must be testing its mechanisms and controls.

If all was working perfectly, they would direct the slave pilot to fly it to a safe place, and what a prize it would be. With a working thapter the Merdrun could quickly collect other thapter and construct parts and, in one of the enemy's manufactories they now controlled, make more of them. With a fleet of thapters they would soon put an end to the resistance.

But if it was gone Flydd would have no reason to land. An opportunity lost, because the man who cut him down would be honoured, and success here would make it harder for the magiz to bring Skald down. Heroes mattered, and heroes risen from the ranks were an inspiration to everyone. However, if he returned without killing Flydd, Skald would be more vulnerable. The failure, through no fault of his own, would remain on his record for ever.

A scream echoed through the night. Had Flydd attacked? How could his force get into position without Skald realising they were here? Only if it was concealed by a mighty illusion. And if Flydd's archers detected him, he would die from a bolt to the back of the head without ever knowing he had been hit.

37

TRYING TO LOOK LIKE ALL THE OTHER DEAD

Three Merdrun guards in the inner ring fell to enemy archers firing from the darkness. Then another two fell and, though they had only taken flesh wounds, both were writhing on the ground, unable to get up. Poisoned bolts! The scum! And Skald's orders were to do nothing. It felt so wrong.

Flydd must have landed the sky galleon miles away and sent his archers in, concealed by a mighty glamour, because when Skald looked behind him to the places they must be firing from, he saw nothing. They had found and killed the outer ring of six guards without a sound – skilled warriors indeed.

Two more Merdrun fell; of the twelve inner guards, six were down, plus the sergeant. Two of the four Merdrun supervising the repairs had also been killed. The other two butchered the slave artisans and the pilot and doused the lights, but a minute later the area was lit by a brilliant white flare that hung in the air several hundred feet up. Three more guards fell, then the enemy swordsmen stormed in.

A Merdrun fighter was normally the equal of two enemy, but the odds were too great. The three remaining soldiers turned the site into a killing field, but they were quickly cut down, and their captain last of all.

This wasn't right. Merdrun were supposed to *win*.

Why, since Durthix had known about the coming attack, hadn't he sent a greater force? Why hadn't the captain set some guards even further out, well hidden?

An unpleasant thought surfaced. Had the squad been sent to the thapter to lure Flydd out into the open? Did Durthix intend them to be sacrificed? Surely not.

The attackers were led by a short, stocky man that Skald recognised, because he had studied sketches of all the key enemy, as Cryl-Nish Hlar, known as Nish, a hero of the Lyrinx War. Astonishing! A runt like him would never have been admitted to the Merdrun army.

And where was Flydd?

A white flare burst in the sky, eastwards. 'Nish's signal,' said Flydd. 'He's taken the thapter.'

Maelys, who, despite her previous hard words, had been biting her knuckles since Nish left, let out a great *huff*.

'Chiss–' began Flydd.

Chissmoul, who had been beside herself since Flangers left with the attack force, hurled the sky galleon into the air, raced to the thapter site and landed so fast and hard that the craft skidded in a half circle, raising eye-stinging clouds of dust. Flydd gave her his most ferocious scowl.

'Flangers?' she wailed.

'Here!' He appeared out of the dust, unharmed.

As it settled, scatters of bodies were revealed: many red-armoured Merdrun, half of Nish's grey-clad swordsmen and, near the thapter, the enemy artisans and all their skilled slaves, who had presumably been killed to prevent Flydd rescuing them. Karan looked away; she had seen enough violence to give her nightmares for many lifetimes.

And yet, she could not help thinking that the victory had been a little too easy.

'Get started on the checks,' Flydd said to his three artisans, 'and make it snappy. The enemy may send a relief squad.'

Nish, unharmed save for a gash on his left forearm, issued orders. The bodies around the thapter were dragged further away and he set out his guards. Flydd's artisans began to inspect the thapter, double-checking every mechanism. He followed them around but kept coming out to study the sky and the landscape.

His anxiety rubbed off on Karan, who expected an enemy gate to form at any moment. The Merdrun had two defeats to avenge now.

After midday Flydd's chief artisan, a bow-legged, bent-backed southerner of indeterminate age, climbed out. Flydd was in the shade behind the thapter, staring east.

'It's ready, surr.'

'You've double-checked every mechanism?'

'I know thapters like the back of my hand.'

Flydd allowed himself a small smile. 'Finally, something goes right.'

He roused Chissmoul, who was curled in a dark corner of the sky galleon, beside Flangers. A good soldier never missed the opportunity to catch up on sleep, and there had been little last night.

'Get up. You've got flying to do. Your very own thapter.'

Chissmoul unfolded herself and a smile of pure joy lit her face. 'You mean it, Xervish?'

'How often do I say things I don't mean?' he growled. 'Make sure all is working as it should, then take it up.'

She reached out to wake Flangers.

'Just you,' said Flydd. 'Let him sleep.'

Chissmoul ran barefoot to the thapter, and scrambled up and in. The mechanisms whined, it shuddered and shook, and dust boiled up from underneath. It rose vertically and hovered, then rotated in place for a couple of minutes.

The whine grew to a roar, then it rocketed away across the desert, raising clouds of dust. It raced back, past the campfire and on, climbed and looped the loop and hurtled down again, only to slow and land sedately beside Flydd.

Flangers, who had woken the moment Chissmoul left his side, was on his feet, grinning like a prize-winning schoolboy. He went across to Flydd, who had been listening to reports via his farspeaker and was now writing on a square piece of paper. Flydd signed at the bottom, folded the paper in on all sides to form an envelope, sealed it and handed it to Flangers.

'What's this?' said Flangers.

'Your commissions and your orders.'

'Commissions, surr?'

'You are given charge of the thapter, and Chissmoul will pilot it. Head north to Roros. Yulla Zaeff, the former Governor, has hidden many talented people and amassed a great war chest. When you get there, open your sealed orders and do whatever she requires while you await my further orders.'

'Where will you be?'

'Wherever the war takes me, Lieutenant. I'm heading to Stassor, then north-west to Faranda, to seek the aid of the Aachim. Though I don't hold out great hope of getting it.'

Flangers gathered his gear and climbed in. Chissmoul did not come down to say farewell; Karan supposed that she begrudged leaving her precious flier, even briefly. What a strange, nervy woman she was.

She waved joyfully from the hatch and pulled it down. Nothing happened for a minute, then the thapter rocketed into the air, buzzed the campfire, climbed to a great height, the sun striking brassy reflections off it, and turned north.

The sky galleon raced in, skidding sideways across the stony ground, and a small, scrawny, ugly fellow descended. Skald caught his breath, for there was no mistaking the great enemy. Flydd gave orders and headed for the thapter, accompanied by a group of artisans and two women, one with long red hair and the other, who could not have been more than five feet tall, with short black hair.

Nish ordered the bodies near the thapter dragged further out. Skald, who had been trying to think of a plan since the attack began, now saw his chance, but he had to move at once. Dawn was no more than fifteen minutes away and every minute of growing light would make the job more difficult, and success less likely.

He wormed his way down towards the cleared area, which was still partly obscured by dust, then to a place where two dead Merdrun lay together. The nearest corpse was drenched in blood; a bolt embedded in his groin must have severed an artery.

No one was looking Skald's way. He rolled against the corpse, allowing the soldier's blood to cover his chest armour and right side, then smeared blood in his hair and down one side of his face, and gashed his left arm with his own knife, for realism. He crawled away – three bodies where there had formerly been two would look suspicious; a body lying by itself would not – sprawled on his belly with his eyes narrowed to slits, trying to look like all the other dead, and waited.

The dust settled. The sun rose and within minutes the area was buzzing with flies. What did they feed on when there were no bodies? They were crawling all over him, especially along the gash on his left arm and on the blood he'd smeared on his face, biting him and making him itch everywhere they touched. They swarmed around his eyes and even up his nose. It took all his self-control, and all the stoicism developed over a lifetime of training, to ignore them. He must not move, must not even twitch.

Flydd emerged from the thapter and went aboard the sky galleon without coming anywhere near Skald. Some minutes later he led a tall, white-haired lieutenant and the two women down to the dry creek, where a campfire burned, and they ate and drank.

The sun was hot now. Skald badly needed a drink, but he had to ignore hunger and thirst. If his chance came, it would be fleeting. He would leap to his feet, run and hack Flydd's ugly head from his narrow shoulders from behind. Or, if Flydd was coming Skald's way, drive the heavy sword blade clean through his ribs and out his back.

Then bolt and try to make a gate on the run, though that would almost certainly fail, because Skald dared not do any of the preliminary steps beforehand. It would drain him at a time when he needed all his strength, and such powerful mancery might be detected.

Another hour went by, and he began to smell the bodies. They would decay quickly in this heat and, if the enemy decided to move them further away, he must be discovered.

Guards went from body to body, collecting the weapons. Skald forced himself to lie still as his sword, a key part of his honour, was taken. Curse them! He wanted to draw the long knife hidden in his left boot and kill the lot of them, but the loss must be endured.

The sun rose higher. The enemy dead were taken aboard the sky galleon. The Merdrun, presumably, would be left for the scavengers. Flydd headed down to the campfire, returned sipping from a yellow china mug and went into the thapter again.

Skald's mouth and throat were paper-dry now. He had expected Flydd to be here when he arrived, and to attack him in darkness. The intervening eight hours, five of them lying in direct sunlight, had dehydrated him and he was weakening, but he dared not touch the pannikin on his left hip. The slightest movement could give him away.

Xervish Flydd climbed out of the thapter, smiling and wiping his hands on a rag. He thought he'd succeeded. *Not yet, you hideous little runt!*

He was still too far away. Nish and the white-haired lieutenant were at the rear of the thapter, but both were watchful, and Skald recognised, by the way the lieutenant's gaze constantly swept the area, a professional like himself.

Skald would only have seconds to leap to his feet, run to Flydd and cut him down. Any longer and the crossbow-armed sentries would shoot him. His best hope of succeeding was if Flydd was less than five or six yards away.

But still the chance did not come. Flydd walked between the thapter and the sky galleon several times, but Skald was a good thirty yards away from both.

Higher the sun rose. There were even more flies now, and their biting and stinging, and the itchy trails their feet left all over him, were almost unbearable.

Endure! For the True Purpose!

Now Flydd was shaking hands with Flangers and a small woman Skald had not seen before, and she climbed aboard the thapter. She must be a pilot, and they were about to fly it away. It was a bitter moment and he felt his uselessness keenly. How he longed to thwart them, to seize the precious thapter for himself and compel the pilot to fly it, and himself, home in triumph.

Everyone moved back, and after several minutes of testing the mechanisms the thapter lifted slowly, circled the area, set down again and the lieutenant went aboard, carrying what Skald took to be sealed orders. The thapter climbed high into the sky and headed north. Now Flydd would leave as well. Skald closed his eyes in despair.

All this, for nothing.

A bright yellow flash high above. The thapter's mechanism stuttered and it dropped as if it had momentarily lost the field, but climbed again. It levelled out, there came a dazzling blue-white flash, a whipcrack echoed across the sky, then it fell.

'What the blazes is Chissmoul doing?' cried Flydd. 'Pull up, pull up!'

The thapter did not pull up. Karan watched in helpless horror as it fell faster and faster, slammed into the top of a rocky hill a couple of miles away, hurling shattered stone everywhere, and burned furiously.

The awful silence lasted minutes. She kept thinking that if she just closed her eyes and opened them again it might not have happened. But the evidence was all too clear, the fire so hot that it must have melted the rock into which the thapter had embedded itself.

'Two great friends,' choked Flydd. 'Two of my best gone, for nothing.' He reeled around in a circle.

Nish steadied him, clung to him. 'But ... everything was checked and double-checked.'

'The Merdrun must have booby-trapped it,' Maelys whispered.

'They butchered the artisans so we couldn't question them,' he said in a dead voice. 'They must have a sus-magiz nearby, and when the thapter was high enough he blocked the power controller from afar.'

'But the thapter was invaluable to them,' said Flydd dazedly. 'I don't understand ...'

Nish put an arm across his shoulders. 'To kill you, Xervish. They must have hoped you'd go aboard, and it was worth losing the thapter to have you dead.'

Karan scanned the landscape and focused on another hill, a mile to the left. 'He's been watching from there, I'd say.'

Flydd was running towards the sky galleon when a round green glow blossomed near the top of the hill, and faded. 'A gate opening and closing. He's gone.'

'The utter, utter swine!' said Nish. 'What do we do now?'

Flydd looked to have aged fifty years. The scars stood out lividly on his gaunt face and his eyes had a mad look. He stumbled across to the chief artisan, who was huddled with his two assistants. 'Get your gear. And plenty of water.'

'Surr?' said the hunchbacked old fellow, anxiously.

'Now!'

They ran for their packs and gathered water bags.

'Ashmode is eighty leagues that way.' Flydd pointed north-east. 'Get going.'

The chief artisan stood his ground. 'We haven't been paid.'

Flydd's face went a ruddy purple. 'You said you knew thapters backwards. You lied! You said you'd double-checked every part. Another lie! I have no room in my army for liars, or incompetents.'

'Wasn't my fault,' the chief artisan whined. 'Slorper checked the flight mechanism.' He gestured to the smaller of his two assistants, a skinny fellow with an odd-shaped head, pointed at the top but massive in the jaw, like an egg standing on its base.

'Well, Slorper?' said Flydd.

'I checked it as best I could, surr,' Slorper said thickly. 'But ... I've never seen one before. *And I told him so*,' he added with a flash of fury.

Flydd raised his staff, and for a moment Karan thought he was going to blast the chief artisan to shreds. Then he pointed north-east and said, with icy calm, 'If you're still in sight in five minutes, you three will suffer the cruellest death listed in the scrutators' torture manual.'

They ran, their water bags wobbling.

'Would you?' Maelys said quietly when they were out of sight.

'What good would it do?' said Flydd, his shoulders sagging. 'Why do I bother?'

Everyone had their breaking point. Was this Flydd's? But if he gave up, the war was lost.

'We have to fight on, Xervish,' she said. 'We're the world's only hope now.'

'I was tempted to take the thapter,' Flydd said in a dead voice. 'Very tempted. It's – it was – faster than the sky galleon. I wish I had.'

'Don't say it!' cried Nish. 'I won't hear it.'

'This has gone on too long – the bloodshed, the ruin of everything good, the loss of so many innocent lives, so many old friends. The awful responsibility. My shoulders aren't broad enough, Nish. I – I just want an end to it.'

Flydd seemed a broken man, and if he was, all they could do was run for their lives. But that would be condemning Sulien, and Llian, and everyone else Karan cared about. The Merdrun did not suffer an enemy to live.

She could not let it happen. She had to drag him out of his funk, and words would not do it.

She stalked up to Flydd and struck him across the face, knocking him sideways. 'Stop whining and pull yourself together! We've got a job to do.' Instantly, she wanted to run. It took all her self-control to stand there and face his rage. *'Whatever it takes, Flydd!'*

He felt his cheek, where her finger marks stood out lividly. His right hand clenched around his staff. 'When I was a scrutator you would have died for that.'

'Then act like one! Be the man Flangers would expect you to be. And avenge his death in the only way that would matter to him, by defeating the enemy.'

'No one else can do it, Xervish,' Nish said quietly. 'Only you.'

Flydd took a long, shuddering breath. 'All right.' He raised his staff. *'All right!'*

He looked them in the eye, one by one. 'A while ago you asked what we were going to do, Nish. We're doing what we've always done.' Flydd's voice strengthened. 'What you did when Chief Scrutator Ghoor held every one of us, save you, captive at Fiz Gorgo and began to make a fatal example of us. Even though there were hundreds against you, and Ullii was hunting you to cut out your heart, you never gave in.

'You saved us that day, just as Karan's implacable determination saved us on the mountain pass. We will fight the enemy to the last breath and the last drop of blood. If they want Santhenar they'll have to kill us all, for we will *never* give in while one of us can stand and fight.'

Flydd looked at them, one by one. 'Will we?'

Nish raised his blade, and Maelys and Clech their fists, and Karan hers. They had to win, because she knew better than anyone what the enemy would do to them if *they* won.

'Never!' she said.

As Karan turned away, Flydd hissed in her ear, 'If you ever strike me again, you're a dead woman.'

38

—————

I DON'T NEED YOUR HELP

W e'll head down to where the air-dreadnought crashed,' said Klarm at dawn.

Wilm was already up, eating cold, days-old stew. It was starting to taste bad, but he'd had much worse as a slave. It could take weeks to get out of here and they had no food to waste. 'What for?'

'Got an idea.'

Wilm didn't bother to ask. Klarm was even more prickly before he'd eaten.

'It must be seven or eight miles from here,' said Wilm as they set off. 'Best part of a day's walk, at your pace.'

'Feel free to run ahead, boyo. Two's company.'

'Not when you're like this,' said Ilisial.

'I'll get the camp set up,' said Wilm. It would be a pleasure to get away from the dwarf.

It was pleasantly warm, the sun just peeping between the teeth of the eastern mountains. He strode down the track they'd made going up and down to a drinking water seep. Behind him Klarm said something Wilm did not catch and Ilisial laughed.

He walked faster, wanting to be alone to think about the war. In brief farspeaker calls, Flydd had listed the latest disasters, but had not said what he was up to. Nor had he provided any news about Karan or Aviel, or what had happened to Llian.

Wilm admired the Teller more than any man he had ever met, because Llian's selfless help and inspiration had made Wilm the man he was today. And saved his life, too. If Llian, surely the world's most incompetent fighter, hadn't carried Mendark's sword through incredible danger to help Wilm escape from the Merdrun's slave camp, he would have died there.

And what about Aviel, stuck with that malevolent bitch, Maigraith? Wilm never stopped thinking about Aviel. Why had he volunteered for this disastrous mission? Why hadn't he stayed with her, where he belonged?

He set up camp at the seep nearest to the wreckage of the air-dreadnought. It was nearly dark by the time Ilisial and Klarm appeared, and the agonising trek had reduced him to a shadow of his former self. Wilm ran up to them.

'I'll carry you the rest of the way, surr,' he said quietly.

'You'd enjoy showing off your strength, your young body, your two good legs, wouldn't you?' snarled Klarm.

'I'm just trying to help.'

'Ilisial has already offered, and I don't need her help either. I'm not going all soft and helpless now.'

'At least let me take your pack.'

'Bugger off! I've carried it this far; I'll take it the rest of the way.'

Wilm accompanied them down. Klarm sat next to the seep, which Wilm had dug out to form a yard-wide pool, now lined with stones, and began to remove his wooden foot.

'Can I do anything?' said Ilisial.

'Heat some water.'

'The pot's boiling on the campfire,' said Wilm.

Klarm favoured him with a sour smile. Ilisial carried hot water up to Klarm, who was unwinding the bandages from his stump in the gloom and shuddering.

She came down again, anxiously. 'I'm worried. His stump looks infected. Do you know anything about healing?'

Klarm let out a howl of agony, swiftly cut off. Ilisial jumped up.

'Leave me alone!' yelled Klarm. 'Water's a bit hot, that's all.'

Ilisial sat down again, twisting her fingers together.

'I've looked after quite a few battle wounds –' Wilm broke off, fearing that it would set her off again, but she merely looked away. 'But if he won't let us near –'

'What do we do if he gets really ill? We can't carry him a hundred leagues to safety.' She looked towards the campfire. 'That stew ready?'

'Yes, I made it hours ago.'

'I'll take some up to him.'

A few minutes later she came back, the bowl untouched.

'Said he wasn't hungry. I've never known him to refuse a meal before.'

What if he died? Wilm did not like Klarm, but had to admire the way he kept going, no matter what. And without him, how would they ever get out of here?

He remained in his sleeping pouch the following day, and again refused food, though he did accept mugs of tea. The day after that he was up at dawn with his wooden foot on.

'Are you better?' Ilisial said anxiously.

'Worked a bit of a healing on my stump. It'll be all right now we're not on the march ...'

He sat on a rock, staring at the bamboo hoops.

'You've got a plan,' said Ilisial. 'Care to share it with us?'

'I'm not even getting *my* hopes up yet.'

He took a mug of tea in each hand and went up the long, crusted mound of wind-blown dust and salt to the charred hull. Wilm followed tentatively.

'What's wrong with what we're seeing here?' said Klarm.

'There's not nearly enough wreckage for an air-dreadnought,' said Ilisial. 'Only one hull, for starters – it had three.'

'Where's the other two?' said Wilm.

Her long face grew animated. She was the one with the answers now, and it really mattered to her. 'If it hit the ground at high speed, tilted to one side, the triple hulls would have come apart.' She walked away, studying the ground.

'The scars where the left-hand keel hit the ground have been filled in with wind-blown sand,' she said, 'but you can still make them out.' She indicated a long gouge with clusters of bones on one side. 'The impact hurled some people over the side.

'It bounced and struck again, here.' Another gouge. 'The other two hulls broke off, cut through the salt crust and buried themselves in the soft earth of the mound. The remaining hull hit that boulder and disintegrated, then caught fire.'

'What about the cabins?' said Klarm, who had followed.

'Nothing to them. Just silk or canvas, bamboo and cord, to keep the weight down.' She pointed to the rags and hoops fifty yards away.

'And the airbags?'

'Tore free. If they weren't punctured, they would have risen for miles. They might have drifted right across Lauralin and out over the Great Ocean.' She walked along the charred hull and came back. 'What are we doing here, Klarm?'

'Isn't it obvious,' said Klarm infuriatingly. 'Get the spade, Wilm, and start digging out the other hulls.'

'That's going to take days,' said Wilm. 'Weeks, maybe.'

'You got an appointment somewhere else?'

Wilm began to dig into the mound. Under the crust the windblown salt and dust was soft and powdery, but it was hard to make progress because the sides of the hole kept falling in. 'I need a shovel for this kind of work.'

'There's flat metal lying around,' said Klarm. 'Ilisial can make you one.'

'It'll take a day, at least,' said Ilisial.

Klarm raised an eyebrow.

'I'll get started.'

The shovel tripled Wilm's earth moving, and late the following day the blade, thrust deep, thudded into something hard. He excavated around it.

'The side of the middle hull,' said Klarm. 'Keep going.'

'What are you looking for?'

'Whatever's inside it.'

Ilisial made herself a shovel and some trowels, and after another two days they had exposed the tops of both hulls.

'Bad smell here?' said Wilm.

'What kind of bad?' said Klarm.

'Dead animal.'

Wilm prised up boards. It was not an animal. The passengers and crew inside during the crash had been killed on impact, or had suffocated soon after, and had been mummified.

Moving the brittle bodies was grim work, and afterwards it took ages to clear out the inside of the hull and reach the storerooms. Wilm was uncomfortably aware that their food was dwindling. What on earth was Klarm up to, and how could he imagine that it would help?

The pantry had once contained food for more than forty people, but it was all gone – spoiled or eaten by small, burrowing creatures. The middle hull, which was wider, was much the same. Another three days passed with no hint of what Klarm was looking for. Wilm felt sure it wasn't there.

Then, as they broke the lock on the central storeroom and dug it out, Ilisial's spade struck metal.

'Carefully now,' said Klarm. 'Use your trowels.'

Ilisial had made several, and they scraped away the soft earth to reveal a large steel cylinder, several feet across and about five feet high, with a brass tube and stopcock rising from the top.

'I see,' said Ilisial.

'I don't,' said Wilm.

'Floater gas,' said Klarm. 'All airbags leak, and air-dreadnoughts carried tanks of floater gas to replenish them.'

'Not even M'Lainte could get this wreck back in the air.'

'But we might make a crude air-floater out of it,' said Klarm.

'The rotor mechanisms were destroyed,' said Ilisial. 'And I don't have the tools to replace them.'

'All we need is an airbag, enough floater gas to lift our weight, and a basket,' said Klarm. 'If we pick the right wind it'll carry us for hundreds of miles.'

'How are you going to make an airbag?' said Wilm.

'All air-dreadnoughts carried spare cloth and gum and ropes, laddie. Keep digging.'

39

LEAVE THEM FOR THE MAGGOTS

Suddenly there were shouts, gasps and cries of horror. Skald had no idea what was wrong; whatever was happening was out of his field of vision. A woman wailed; a man groaned. A whistling sound grew ever louder until it was cut off by a distant, ground-shaking thump.

He risked a brief glance. Everyone had their backs to him, looking north to a hill, at the top of which flames burned crimson. The thapter had fallen from a great height. It had been destroyed, denied to the enemy, and Flydd's trusted lieutenant and best pilot were dead. It was a wonderful moment, and Skald savoured the allowable emotions.

But had it robbed him of the chance to assassinate Flydd? He might still get the chance.

Flydd had a brief, deadly altercation with the artisans who had checked the thapter, then ordered them away. Unbelievable! For such incompetence, Skald would have flayed the skin off them, impaled each man on a stake and left them to the predators. The people of Santhenar were soft; no wonder they had been beaten so easily.

Flydd looked shattered, and Skald's hopes rested on what he did now. If he boarded the sky galleon from the other side, an opportunity would never come. If he came around this side, there was a chance. No one was looking Skald's way, and he inched his right hand down to the knife in his boot.

Almost everyone had boarded now. Only Flydd, Nish and the two women remained on the ground. Skald recognised them from sketches in Durthix's enemies' gallery. The curvy, black-haired young woman was Maelys, a hero of the struggle to bring down the God-Emperor. She did not matter.

But the older woman, who walked with a limp and had wavy red hair halfway down her back, made the blood throb in Skald's temples. Karan Fyrn! She had been one of the chief culprits in the Merdrun's disastrous loss on the Isle of Gwine two centuries ago.

Karan, he now knew, had found a way to bring her family and two other people to the future, and six days ago she had helped to rescue Nish and annihilate two squads of Merdrun and an experienced sus-magiz. She was at the top of the Merdrun's vengeance list, along with her man, Llian, and their daughter, Sulien, though the daughter, being unusually gifted, was wanted alive.

If he could kill Karan and Flydd, Skald would have made up for the stain on his family's line, and even if he was killed, as was probable, he would die a hero.

～

'Get aboard,' said Flydd. 'We'll bury our dead somewhere pleasant, far from here.'

'What about the enemy?' said Nish.

'Leave them for the maggots.'

After Nish gave the orders, Flydd took him, Karan, Clech and Maelys aside. 'An urgent message came through earlier. The enemy have abandoned Fadd and Guffeons, and several other captured cities.'

'I don't believe it,' said Nish. 'Unless it's a ploy.'

'Maybe it is, but for what?'

Nish and Clech followed the guards aboard. Maelys, who was in the shade under the stern of the sky galleon, was gazing into the Mirror of Aachan again. Karan found this even more disturbing here, though it did seem to comfort her.

Flydd took Karan aside and they walked along next to the sky galleon. 'Have you linked to Sulien lately?'

She shook her head. 'When I try, all I get is a *sense* of her, and a feeling.'

'And that is?'

'She's very unhappy.'

'Well, at least she's safe. Stibnibb is hard to reach – there's virtually no field there.'

'She's not *that* safe.'

'Why do you say that?'

'Sulien has linked to me a few times since I left her there ... so presumably the enemy could reach her.'

'Only if they knew where she was – and only you and I know that.'

And Sulien, Karan thought. *And she as good as told me she was going to mind-look for Llian.*

Karan stopped, stepped around a puddle of congealed blood, shivered and moved on.

'I can't bear the stink of these scum any longer,' Flydd said abruptly. 'Come on.'

But as they turned back, Karan was struck by an overwhelming rage, close by –

≈

Flydd and Karan were pacing along the nearer side of the sky galleon, talking quietly, and neither of the guards on the sky galleon were looking Skald's way. His luck had turned at last. Another few steps and he would have his chance.

Flydd, said to be a fine swordsman, was the greater danger. Skald would take him first. As soon as they turned, Skald would cut Flydd's throat from behind, stab Karan in the back, then run in under the sky galleon where he could not be seen from above and, if his luck held, gate home in triumph.

His mouth was so dry that it itched, and he knew dehydration would slow him. As he tensed to spring up, they stopped, twenty yards away, facing him. He could not risk it. In his current condition, lying prone in heavy leather armour, it would take four seconds to gain his feet and sprint that distance, plenty of time for Flydd to blast him down or draw his sword. Not even Skald, armed only with a knife, could hope to take down a skilled swordsman face to face.

Just another few yards. If they came within eight yards, even ten, he would attack.

They came on, but then Karan stopped, peering at the hull of the sky galleon. They took a few more steps and stopped again, twelve yards away. Skald suppressed a groan of frustration. Still too far.

'I can't bear the stink of these scum any longer,' Flydd said abruptly, and turned back. 'Come on.'

It was Skald's best chance. He leapt to his feet, transferred his knife to his right hand, and sprinted. Four more giant strides and they were dead. Three. Two –

Karan whirled and, in a blindingly fast reflex, drew her knife and hurled it at Skald.

He was about to sidestep when his leading boot landed on a puddle of congealed blood, skidded and he fell forwards. He turned it into a lunging dive at Flydd, intending to gut him or, if he fell short, slash across the femoral artery.

But Karan's knife found a gap in Skald's armour and sank deep into the muscle behind his right collarbone, next to his shoulder. It must have hit a nerve because his right arm went dead, though his fingers remained clenched around his own knife.

Flydd sprang sideways but not quickly enough. Skald's blade carved across his left hip, opening it to the bone, and Flydd staggered backwards and went down, blood pouring out of him. Skald cursed; it wasn't a fatal wound. He hit the ground two yards away on his forearms and the knife jarred out of his dead hand and skidded away. Up on the sky galleon, people were shouting.

'Guards, *here!*' Karan shrieked.

Skald tried desperately to get to Flydd's sword, but the injury and the dead right arm slowed him.

Karan yanked it out of its scabbard and stood over Flydd. 'Try it!' she grated, holding the weapon out in both hands.

Clearly, she was unskilled, and had they been alone Skald would have quickly disarmed and killed her, then finished off Flydd. But two men, one a giant, were scrambling down the ladder, and a third man, on the sky galleon, was bringing a crossbow to bear. Skald had failed.

He had to avoid the dishonour of being captured. He rolled under the overhanging deck of the sky galleon, scrabbled his way around the stern and crashed into Maelys, driving her backwards against the hull and knocking something out of her hand.

A small metal mirror with a powerful magical aura. It rang on the stony ground and he saw on it, momentarily, a big, broad-shouldered young woman.

Maelys was dazed and no threat to him. Skald put his back to the hull and frantically conjured a gate.

As the guards came running, and Karan appeared around the stern with Flydd's sword, and bloody murder in her eye, Skald snarled, 'I'll be back for you!' and vanished.

But the gate, made in such desperation and without time to visualise the destination, only carried him a couple of miles. It opened in mid-air with pyrotechnics that must have been visible for leagues, dumped him on the ground from ten feet up, and vanished with a boom.

~

Karan was too late. Skald opened a tiny gate, dived through it and it closed behind him.

She looked down at the Mirror, which showed the face of a strong-jawed, big-nosed woman with shoulder-length black hair. Karan picked it up, shuddering at the memories it raised, thrust it into Maelys' pocket and helped her up. Pain stabbed across Karan's ribs and she winced.

Flydd staggered around the stern, one hand pressed to the gash across his hip. His pants leg was saturated in blood. 'He gone?'

'Yes.'

'You hurt?'

'Pulled a muscle throwing the knife.'

Nish hurtled around the stern, along with a pair of guards. As Clech came the other way, blue and red light flared a mile or two to the east.

'That's his gate!' Nish bellowed. 'Come on.'

Clech ripped off his shirt, which was the size of a tablecloth, wadded it up and held it against Flydd's hip. 'Press down, hard.'

Flydd did so. Clech picked him up and ran. Karan followed, wincing with every step.

Clech had seated Flydd at the controls and was holding him upright. Nish bound the wadded-up shirt on with several turns of rope.

Flydd, who looked as though he was about to faint, took off and the sky galleon raced towards the place where the gate had opened.

'There he is!' yelled Nish from the bow. 'Bastard's trying to make another gate. Quick, quick!'

~

Skald landed heavily, twisting his left ankle, and cursed the pain and the weakness. Karan's knife was still embedded in his shoulder and he wasn't game to pull it out in case it had nicked a vein. The sky galleon would be here in minutes and he only had room for one thought – he must not be captured!

How had Karan, a small woman carrying old injuries, bested him? He could not fathom it. There was something vaguely familiar about her, too. What was it? Not the sketch of her he had seen in Durthix's gallery, something else, though Skald could not bring it to mind.

He was desperate for water now but dared not stop to gulp a mouthful. He had to make another gate, a long distance one this time, though he did not see how he was going to manage it.

He went through the steps and created the magical structure of the gate, but did not have the power to open it. What if he waited until the sky galleon landed, then drank the life of the first person he saw? No, the victim had to be close. Besides, the process wasn't that quick; drinking lives wasn't a defensive weapon.

Nor could he tear the knife from his shoulder and hurl it at Flydd. Accurate knife throwing required years of practice and Skald's right arm was still partly numb.

The only honourable option was suicide, by disembowelling himself with Karan's knife. It was an agonising way to die but better than the ignominy of capture.

Skald was pressing the knife to his belly when another possibility occurred to him, one so desperate that he was sure no other sus-magiz had ever thought of it. Could he gain the power for a gate by drinking from his own life?

Was it even possible? He had to try, because the sky galleon was closing in. But he had just begun the life-drinking spell when a desperate danger occurred to him.

Drinking a life was so exhilarating that, previously, Skald had not been able to stop until the victim was drained to a husk. What if he did that to himself? What an irony that would be. Dagog would laugh until he choked.

But what choice did Skald have? He continued the spell. It began to draw from his own life-force, the blood burned like hot metal in his veins and he sensed, as he always did, that no magic was beyond him.

Then agony seared through his liver and kidneys and other internal organs, as if they were being torn open to extract the power inside. His head began to throb mercilessly. Power surged into his arms, but his legs grew so weak that they could not hold him up. The muscles felt withered, flabby and wasted.

He slumped to the ground, full of power at one end, drained at the other. His head was such a mass of pain that he could barely remember the steps to opening a gate. And the sky galleon was only seconds away.

'There's the mongrel!' a lookout yelled.

The craft altered course and raced up. Flydd was taking no chances this time. It looked as though he was planning to drop the sky galleon onto Skald and squash him to paste. And Skald could do nothing about it. He could not move.

As the life-drinking spell continued, the agony grew worse, as if he were being liquefied inside. Blood was running from his mouth and nose and dribbling from his backside.

'I want him alive,' said Flydd.

The sky galleon crunched into the ground only a few yards away and the giant sprang down, followed by Nish and three soldiers. As they pounded towards him, Skald folded the power he had drawn from himself into a bundle and used it to complete the gate-opening spell.

It tore him out of space and time, carried him away and dumped him, with a boom and a roar, onto the long chart table in Durthix's command centre. A whirlwind picked up the maps and papers and hurled them in all directions.

Skald lay, bleeding from his shoulder and from every orifice, in the middle of a large canvas map of Lauralin. Durthix came running up, with Dagog.

'Whatever he's done to himself,' said Durthix, 'fix it.'

Dagog identified and cancelled the life-drinking spell, though Skald's pain did not ease.

'Well?' said Durthix.

'Thapter destroyed,' croaked Skald. 'Not my doing.'

'And Flydd?'

'Sorely wounded, but he'll survive. I did my best ... but I failed.'

Durthix and the magiz exchanged glances, then Durthix said the heart-stopping words, 'Do it, Dagog.'

40

HOW COULD SHE STOP MAIGRAITH?

Aviel went to her bed exhausted and desperate for sleep, but it would not come. Her mind was buzzing, for this time her memory of the last few hours had not been lost. Her blending of Maigraith's scent potion was as clear as the diamond phial.

What did she plan to do with it? It must be for some fell purpose, otherwise why the secrecy?

Aviel crept towards the salon from which Maigraith did her spying. The door was open, though it was dark inside. Aviel made out a round lens of light floating above the table, one of Maigraith's spy portals. It was obscured now and then as she bent to glare through it at her rival.

She began to work on a spell, using complicated hand movements with a kidney-shaped stone Aviel could not see clearly. Slowly a small green shape grew in the air, like a coiled tube.

Maigraith took hold of the nearer end and pulled, gently stretching the entrance of the tube into a funnel. It looked like a tiny gate, though the other end was dark. Not the dark of midnight, though. It was completely black, like a hole to nowhere.

Aviel crept closer, her heart thudding.

A glimmer surrounding the spy portal revealed Maigraith unscrewing the cap of the scent potion bottle, though she left it sitting on top.

Very wise. Whatever wicked potion you compelled me to make, you don't want to accidentally smell it.

Maigraith peered through the spy portal as if to check something, then moved it a few yards to the left and went back began to work on the funnel gate. Aviel knew that even tiny gates, if opened close together, could interfere violently.

Maigraith checked the spy portal again and let out a hiss. Aviel crept closer so she could see through it, over Maigraith's shoulder. Lirriam was soaping herself in a circular bath and her lips were moving. Was she talking to herself? No, she must be singing.

She was a striking woman, her neat, heart-shaped face framed by that astounding, opaline hair. She was full-figured and curvy and young, while Maigraith was wrinkled and stringy and far past her prime. The hairs on the back of Aviel's neck rose and she had an awful premonition.

She edged sideways until she could see the half-made gate more clearly. Was Maigraith intending to ambush Lirriam in her bath?

It must be so, and Aviel could not allow her work to be so abused, though the thought of taking Maigraith on was absurd. What could the potion be?

Aviel ran through her memories once more, mentally lining up all nineteen phials and recalling each scent, and how she had blended them. The ingredients were disturbing, the combinations more so, but she could not work out what it was. Radizer's grimoire contained 187 scent potions, but this particular combination wasn't one of them.

Maigraith continued crafting the tiny funnel gate, and frequently checking on Lirriam through the spy portal. She was still singing in her bath.

'Yesss,' Maigraith said.

The intense black of her little gate slowly changed to a deep, velvety purple. She lifted the cap off the bottle. An air current stirred Aviel's hair; the gate was opening.

As Maigraith was about to tip the scent potion into the air stream, Aviel launched herself at her. Maigraith started at the noise and her left arm knocked the little gate sideways towards the spy portal.

The portal and gate touched with an almighty *thud*, a reverberation that seemed to come from a long way away, and everything in the room blurred as if ripples had passed through the solid wood and masonry, and even Aviel's own body. Her flesh was shivering back and forth on her bones, her cheeks inflating and deflating, and an unseen force drew on her eyes as if to pull them from their sockets.

Maigraith was shaking all over, her joints click-clacking, her knees knocking against the underside of the table. The spy portal was gone, while the funnel gate had grown to the size of a bucket. It wasn't a passage to Lirriam's bathing room, though; perhaps Alcifer's defences had driven it away.

Through the gate Aviel saw a succession of landscapes: pasture, then forest, mountains, sea and more mountains. With another reverberating thud the view locked onto the top of a large rooftop garden, where a party was going on. No, a wedding.

Dozens of well-dressed people, young and old, were gathered around an open space on which a young couple were dancing. The woman wore a long, pale green silk gown with flowers embroidered around the hem and sleeves, and the same arrangement of flowers in her chestnut hair. Aviel sighed, for the woman was tall and slender and very beautiful, and her man, whose uniform consisted of dark blue coat and trousers with a thin yellow stripe down the sides, was exceedingly handsome.

The gate burst open before them and they sprang apart. The young woman took two steps towards the gate, staring at it.

Someone called her back. 'Cally, no! What if it's the enemy?'

The groom, who wore a ceremonial sword, drew it and turned to pull his bride aside.

Maigraith let out a cry of dismay and tried to cap the little potion bottle, but she was shaking so violently that she dropped it and it broke. The scent potion was drawn in streaks across the table, atomised and blasted through the gate into Cally's face.

She sniffed, wrinkled her nose and wiped her face. She looked puzzled, then upset. The groom drew a folded cloth from his pocket and handed it to her, absently, his eyes still on the gate. She wiped her face again and again, gagged at the smell, then threw up.

Her pretty attendants came forward with damp cloths, then froze, staring at her. Someone gasped; someone else cried out in shock. The groom turned.

'Cally?' he said, then dropped his ceremonial sword and reeled backwards, his mouth open.

Her attendants were backing away, their faces twisted in horror and disgust. Cally's face was swelling, gross purple nodules and fleshy protrusions forming all over it, and on her throat and upper chest and arms. They were even visible under her gown now. Her once pretty mouth gaped, so warped that she could no longer close it, while a massive wen completely covered her left eye.

She cried out and reached out to her groom with disfigured hands, but he could not look at her. Everyone seemed repulsed.

Maigraith moaned and muttered one spell after another, evidently seeking a counterspell that could reverse the damage. None had any effect.

The guests cowered at the edges of the roof garden, as far as they could get from Calluly, as if to avoid the contagion. She stumbled to the wedding table, picked up a silver lover's cup and examined her face in it.

She screamed, but only once, then regained control and looked contemptuously around at the groom, and her cowering relatives and friends. Maigraith was still frantically speaking counter-spells, but Calluly was unchanged. Could the effects of a scent potion be broken by anything other than a counter-potion?

Calluly straightened her back and squared her shoulders, and walked slowly to the fallen sword. She picked it up and reversed it, and, as Aviel watched in mounting horror, put the tip under her ribs and with a swift jerk, drove it upwards as far as it would go.

She stood there for a good thirty seconds, the blood flooding down her gown, then collapsed. Even then, the groom hung back in fear.

Maigraith gave a great cry, fell forwards and her head thudded into the table. The gate winked out of existence.

Aviel was stricken, unable to move. Why had she interfered? In trying to prevent one death she had precipitated another – and it had been done with *her* scent potion.

She crept forwards, half-hoping Maigraith was dead, though that did not seem likely. She might regain consciousness any second, and she must never know that Aviel had been here.

A glimmer leaking from Maigraith's fingers revealed that her long face had gone lumpy on the left-hand side. She must have inhaled some of the spilled scent potion. Was it poetic justice that, in seeking to destroy her young rival's looks, Maigraith had ruined what remained of her own?

For the rest of the night, Aviel kept reliving the awful moment: the beautiful bride, at the happiest moment of her life, turned into the outward semblance of a monster. And it was partly her doing.

She had to make amends. She could not let Maigraith use and manipulate her, ever again.

Maigraith had to be stopped, even if Aviel had to turn down the dark path to do it.

41

WE'VE GOT 48 DAYS TO SAVE HUMANITY

Flydd was on his back on the deck of the sky galleon with his trews down. Maelys knelt beside him, threading a needle, the size of a small harpoon, threaded with cord the thickness of an anchor rope.

'If he'd been half a second quicker, we'd both be dead,' said Flydd. 'And I didn't even realise he was there. How did you react so quickly, Karan?'

Karan felt cold, sweaty, dizzy, and her ribs hurt with every movement. 'I – I sensed his rage. By the time he came to his feet I was going for my knife. I've – always had fast reflexes.'

Nish and Flydd exchanged glances. 'Lucky you were beside Xervish,' said Nish. 'If it'd been me, the assassin would have killed us both.'

Only a few minutes had passed between the attack, the escape through a small gate that only carried the assassin a couple of miles, then that second, desperate gate, but blood had already soaked through the folded shirt tied around Flydd's deeply gashed hip.

Maelys removed the shirt and cleaned the wound, which started to bleed again. 'This is going to hurt.'

Flydd nodded stiffly and she began to sew the lips of the eight-inch gash together. Karan, who could see his hip bone, looked away.

'So that was Skald,' said Nish. 'A bold, determined man. Though ...'

'What?' grunted Flydd as the thick black thread was drawn through leathery skin and stringy flesh.

'He looked oddly withered as he went through his second gate. And he was bleeding from the mouth and the arse. His trews were soaked in fresh blood.'

'He must have partly drunk his own life to get the power for the gate. Such desperate ingenuity. What's he going to do next?'

'With any luck the swine won't survive it.'

Karan wasn't so sanguine.

After the surviving fighters had been paid a hefty bonus and returned to where they had been hired, and the bodies buried, Flydd took the controls again. In a grim mood and a lot of pain he headed north-east, passing over the beautiful marble-built town of Ashmode on the shore of the Sea of Perion.

Karan had nearly died there, thirteen years of her life ago, after escaping with Shand from the devastation Yggur and Tensor had separately wrought on Thurkad. Shand had helped her to regain her health and her sanity, and had supported her on their desperate trek across the Dry Sea to Katazza, to free Llian, who had been kidnapped by Tensor. She often wondered what had happened to Shand. He had lived an exceptionally long life, but he must be long dead now.

Flydd did not cross the sea, but passed over the Carendor Desert, which had turned green since the Dry Sea filled, and beyond it brown, sun-baked Kalar, which remained desert. More than a day later he turned right through a gap in the mountains and headed east and down towards the edge of the Sea of Seas, the great ocean that, for all anyone knew, covered the rest of the globe. A huge, molten red sun hovered just above the mountains behind them.

'Hell of a lot of smoke,' said Karan, who was standing at the bow, her hair streaming out for a yard behind her in the wind. Taking pleasure in little things, since every big thing in her life was out of control.

Nish came up beside her. 'That's Maksmord. Is the city on fire?'

'Not just the city. Farmland's burning as far as I can see.'

'Xervish?' called Nish.

Flydd locked the controls and came forwards, wincing with every step. 'Why would they capture a city, then burn it? Doesn't make sense.'

As the sun went down, he landed the sky galleon on the peak with a view in all directions and set to with his farspeaker. Clech made a campfire and Nish prepared food. Maelys sat by the fire, gazing into the Mirror. What could she be seeing on it, that had kept her entranced for so long? And was it real? The Mirror had never shown truth in the past.

Shortly Flydd said, 'Lilis reports that the enemy are abandoning all their captured cities. They've made a series of enormous gates, at an unfathomable cost in power, and the whole Merdrun nation – including their civilians – are going through to Skyrock. She hasn't been able to find out why.'

'But there's nothing *at* Skyrock,' said Karan, 'and it's high country, too cold for crops. How can they feed hundreds of thousands, and all their slaves? How can they house so many?'

Flydd shrugged. 'They're building furiously. And they've occupied several of our old mines and manufactories, nearby.'

'Why would they go there, anyway?' said Nish.

'I told you – the greatest known node of power lies under Skyrock.' Flydd paced, staring east at the smoke. 'I can't bear to think what they've done to Maksmord.'

Nish offered him a steaming bowl of chowder that Clech the fisherman had made from smoked eel heads. 'Take the weight off your feet.'

Flydd took the bowl. 'Sitting hurts too much.' He sniffed the contents, grimaced and took a piece of hard brown bread. 'Don't feel like eating.'

'It's a sad day when you knock back a bowl of eel-head chowder,' said Clech with a rare smile. 'Hand it over.'

Flydd passed it to him and gnawed at the bread, but abruptly tossed it into the fire. 'The first slaves they took to Skyrock were miners and stonemasons. Lilis says they're cutting the pinnacle down to form a tower and carving out chambers inside it.'

'What are they building?' said Karan.

'I suspect ... it's a gigantic device ...'

Shivers passed up and down her back. 'What for?'

'I assume it's a weapon. To subjugate Santhenar. Or ... get rid of us.'

'Why would they want to?' said Maelys.

'They've lost 40,000 troops, from an army of 190,000, and in a war of attrition they could lose that many again every year. In five years, they'd be wiped out.'

'So the only solution is to wipe us out first.'

'Hence this Skyrock device. And one of Lilis's spies heard it has to be ready by the sixty-fifth day. Counting from the day of the invasion.'

'And today is ...?' said Maelys, looking up from the Mirror for the first time.

'Day 17. We've got 48 days to save humanity.'

~

Maksmord was a ruined city.

Built largely of timber, it had burned like tar paper when the Merdrun set their cunning fires on a hot, windy day, then abandoned it. Only the stone-built city centre had survived, scorched and smoke-stained and covered in knee-deep drifts of hot ash.

'Eighty thousand people lived here,' said Flydd.

'And now?' said Karan.

'Only one.'

He set the sky galleon down on the sole surviving wharf. All the others had burned, and this one creaked and quivered under the weight. He climbed down and Karan followed, glad to be able to stretch her legs, even in so grim a place.

'And here he is,' said Flydd.

A wandering pedlar was approaching, a man once tall and muscular but fallen on hard times. His back was bent under the weight of his load, his clothes were grey with ash and full of burn holes, and he had the drawn look of a man who had not eaten well in weeks.

'Madder,' said Flydd, limping to him and extending a hand.

Madder held out his right arm, ruefully. It terminated in a red, infected stump.

'Come up, we can feed you, at least,' said Flydd, clasping his shoulder. 'And I know a healing charm or two.'

Madder took off his packs and went awkwardly up the ladder. Flydd introduced Karan, Nish, Maelys and Clech, offered Madder a seat and gave him a drink and a hearty slice of pickled buffalo organs and onion pie. Madder wolfed it down and wiped gravy off his mouth onto his sleeve. 'Best meal I've had in a month.'

Nish put a larger slice on his plate. Madder prised out a buffalo eyeball the size of a lemon and moved it to one side of his plate.

'They left us *nothing*,' he said, between gulps of pie and slurps of cold tea. 'Collected all the food and supplies. Drove hundreds of wagon loads through their mighty gates. Enough to do them and their slaves for a month or two, I'd reckon.'

Forty-eight days, to be precise, Karan thought. And what happens then?

'Then they torched the rest,' Madder continued. 'Granaries, warehouses, manufactories, the mansions of the rich and the shanty towns along the river. And all the crops that would burn for miles around.'

'What about the people?' said Flydd, offering Madder a mug of red ale.

'First thing the bastards did was round up everyone with building skills. Masons, metal workers, carpenters, architects and even artists –'

'Why artists?'

Madder shrugged. 'And they killed everyone who had been an officer in the Lyrinx War, on the spot.'

'To deprive us of everyone with experience in war.'

'The word passed around quick. A lot got away. I don't know where.'

'Can you find out? I need an army – though I don't know how I'm going to feed one.'

'Do my best,' said Madder, slicing the buffalo eyeball in half and swallowing one piece with a sigh of appreciation.

The other half seemed to be staring at Karan. She felt a touch of nausea.

'What about ordinary folk?' said Flydd.

'They took the big, strong men and women. Whatever they're building, they need a lot of slave labourers. Everyone else fled, but they're leaderless and desperate, and hungry.'

'And with the crops burned, they'll stay that way,' Flydd said grimly.

'There's another thing, surr,' said Madder. 'Don't know if it means anything. But they took all the silver they could find. And the silversmiths.'

'What's odd about that?'

'They didn't bother with the gold. Just the silver.'

'Maybe it's precious to them.'

'I never saw them wearing silver, men or women.'

'Silver and silversmiths,' said Flydd. 'How peculiar.'

He worked a healing charm on Madder's stump. In the morning the infection was almost gone, and he went on his way. They flew north-east to the next big city, Gosport, then north again to Guffeons and Twissel, spending a day or two in each place while Flydd located and spoke with his spies, and surveyed the scene for himself.

It was the same everywhere. Ruined cities and the crops burned for many miles around. Former military officers, and other people who could pose a danger, killed. The strong and the skilled shackled and sent through a mighty gate, presumably to Skyrock.

And every scrap of silver collected.

'It'll be different in Roros,' Flydd said. 'It's the biggest and strongest city on Santhenar, and Yulla has always been well prepared. Even the God Emperor had to make a deal with her.'

'Wouldn't get my hopes up,' muttered Nish. 'The enemy attacked Roros with sixty thousand troops.'

'And didn't make much progress; it was too cunningly defended ...'

'What's the matter?' said Karan when Flydd did not go on.

'I haven't heard from Yulla in the past week ... But it can be hard to contact her.' He bit his lip. 'We'll be there in the morning. Everything will be all right.'

I hope so, Karan thought gloomily. *Though I very much doubt it.*

Down the back of the cabin, Maelys was gazing into the Mirror of Aachan as if it was the only good thing left in her life – though Karan could not help thinking that the Mirror was an addiction Maelys could not break.

42

THEIR ONE TRUE WEAKNESS

*S*top *it, you wicked little boy! Better you die a coward's death, like your cursed father, than say such things.*

Sulien jerked upright on her hard bunk. A woman was screaming at Skald. No, he was remembering something from long ago. Something shameful.

Help me! He sounded desperate for comfort. *Please. I don't want to be like this.*

Sulien must have touched his mind while he was asleep, and if ever she was to discover news of Llian, now was her chance ... but Karan had begged her not to use her mind-seeing gift again.

Besides, if Sulien could sense Skald, he might be able to sense her. Had he sent these awful memories to gain her sympathy and lure her in?

She blocked him, put her boots on and went out the back door in her night-gown, intending to walk down to the stream and sit on a rock by the water. She always found the sound of running water soothing.

It was a cool night, quiet and still, with the moon in its first quarter, mostly showing the dark face that was an ill omen.

'What do *you* want?' said Jassika, who was perched on Sulien's favourite rock.

Sulien jumped. 'Where have you been all this time?'

'In a cave. Up a tree. Wherever.'

'For two and half weeks?'

Jassika shrugged. As Sulien's eyes adjusted, she saw that Jassika's clothes were torn and dirty, her hair tangled, and she smelled. But she did not seem so unhappy.

Sulien sat on a smaller rock. 'What do you live on?'

'Fish and small animals, and wood grubs and roots. Every day I try something different. It's exciting.'

Never knowing if she was going to get a meal the next day? Or be a meal for some beast hunting in these endless mountains? Sulien squirmed. 'Don't you get lonely?'

'I've been lonely all my life. It's easier being lonely alone than it is in company.'

'I'll never understand you.'

Jassika snorted. 'I watch you working all the hours of the day, and wonder why. The old hag has made a slave out of you. Run away with me. We'll have fun together.'

'I'm earning my keep,' Sulien said primly.

'Flydd paid for our keep, with Klarm's money.' She mostly called her father by his name, rather than Father or Daddy. 'The ugly old witch has to feed you whether you work or do nothing. What do you do for fun?'

'I read in bed, until my rush light burns out.'

Jassika got down from her rock and splashed towards Sulien. 'I sometimes watch you through a crack in the wall. What do you read? Doesn't look like it's much fun.'

'Um, instructional scrolls. The old woman writes them.'

'What about?'

'Doesn't matter.'

'What about?' Jassika said loudly.

'*How to ferment cabbage in a pig's stomach*. And *How to preserve fish by putrefaction*. And, um ... *How to make toilet wipes from cutty grass*.'

'Ouch! What about the fat old fool?'

'He paints pictures of grains of sand.'

'All day and every day?'

'Yes, but he's not very good. They just look like crumbs.'

'Is he insane?'

'How would I know?'

'What are you doing out at this time of night, anyway?'

'I – I sensed Skald again.' Sulien told her about it.

'If he's tormented, it's because he's done something really nasty.'

'It was when he was a little boy, and he's still in pain. I ... I felt for him.'

'You're so stupid!' Jassika said furiously.

'Why?'

'Everyone's in pain. And you can't fix anyone else's pain – though I can't imagine why you'd want to. Karan was right. Block him out.'

'Um ...' said Sulien.

'What's the matter now?'

Should she tell Jassika about her plan? Sulien had to tell someone. She lowered her voice and leaned closer. 'The very first time I saw the Merdrun, in a dream – no, a nightmare – I also saw their one fatal weakness.'

'What was it?' Jassika said eagerly.

'I don't know. Their magiz attacked me and the secret got lost – but I know it's still buried in my mind.'

'And you think, if you spy on Skald, you might find it again.'

'Yes.'

'How do you know it's their fatal weakness?'

'Their leader, Gergrig, said so. That's why they were trying to kill me, before we came to the future.'

'I didn't know that,' said Jassika in a breathy voice, as if Sulien had finally done something interesting. 'Tell me about it.'

Sulien told the story. By the time she'd finished, the moon had set.

'Wow!' said Jassika, sighing. 'You're so brave.'

'I was just trying to survive.'

'I wish I had adventures. Nothing ever happens in my life except Klarm goes away and dumps me with people who don't give a damn about me ... *or worse.*'

Sulien did not want to think about *or worse*. 'Is that why you walk tightropes? And live in trees? For the excitement?'

'I'm sick of being told what to do. No one ever asks what I want.'

After a long silence, Sulien said, 'I touched another enemy's mind a few months back. A kid ...'

She told Jassika about the drum boy, Uigg, Gergrig's son. 'The poor little boy was tormented too. If I can find out what's the matter with Skald it might be a clue to the enemy's weakness.'

Jassika sat next to Sulien on her rock. Up close, she was very smelly. 'You've got to find out,' she said quietly.

'But I told Mummy I wouldn't go anywhere near Skald's mind again.'

'We're losing the war, idiot! You've got to break your word.'

'That's easy for you to say.'

'You're so selfish!'

'And you stink!' cried Sulien, nettled. 'Don't you ever wash?'

'Don't you tell me what to do!' Jassika jumped up and stalked off into the forest.

Sulien was shaking with cold as she got back into bed. How dare Jassika! She didn't care what happened to Sulien as long as there was plenty of excitement along the way.

But she could not stop thinking about it. Was it her duty to find the enemy's weakness, as Flydd had seemed to think? Or was Karan right?

To get into Skald's mind, Sulien would have to relax the barriers that protected herself, and that was scary. Back in the past, the sus-magizes had attacked her mind. It had been awful.

Besides, if Karan was right, Skald might be able to find her, even here. Don't get close to him. Don't reveal your true self to anyone who might take advantage, or use it against you. *You can't trust anyone.*

Including Jassika. She wasn't pressuring Sulien to spy on Skald to find out the enemy's weakness. Jassika did it because she loved taking risks. Sulien had to push her away.

43

YOU KNOW BEST, OF COURSE

A vast dark brown pall covered half the sky and stretched east over the ocean for at least a hundred leagues. A week had passed since the assassination attempt on Flydd, and the Merdrun gating to Skyrock, and Roros was still burning.

Day 24, Karan thought. Forty-one days to stop the Merdrun from cleansing Santhenar.

But most of Flydd's old allies had been killed or taken to Skyrock, and the rest were in hiding. Unless a miracle awaited them in Roros, the war was lost – and Karan did not believe in miracles.

Flydd's scarred hands clutched the bow rail, claw-like. The gashed hip had healed but he had lost more weight and looked like a skinned rat.

'Yulla has never let us down,' he said. 'Even in the worst days of the war, and the dark times under the God Emperor, she always came through.'

'But she's old and ailing,' said Nish. 'We've got to prepare for the worst.'

'Nish, old friend, I've got to keep hoping. You know why.'

'The black dog has been stalking me lately, too.'

'All my adult life,' Flydd said with a shiver. 'But we're old adversaries and I know how to keep it at bay. It's not depression I'm worried about, it's despair. If I once give way to it, you might as well cut my throat and heave me over the side, because I'll drag everyone down with me.'

'We still have Rulke,' said Nish. 'And Maigraith. Two of the greatest figures in the Histories.'

Flydd laughed hollowly. 'That would be the Rulke who, the moment he heard about the Merdrun, nicked three of my most important devices, pissed off and hid like the cowardly swine he is. And the Maigraith who, as the Numinator, did nothing to aid Santhenar *in the entire 160 years of the war with the lyrinx*. Try again, Nish.'

'Give Rulke time. He wasn't fully healed.'

'He had 224 years under the stasis spell! If that couldn't heal him, nothing will. And need I remind you that he was known, for most of his life, as the Great Betrayer?'

'Karan had faith in him.'

'Until he buggered off. Then dragged Llian, all but his little finger, through that gate.'

'What?' cried Karan, who had not been paying attention. She stood up, staring at him. '*Rulke* took Llian?'

'Who else could it have been?'

'I assumed it was the enemy.'

'Why would they waste a gate on Llian, of all people? It was Rulke, it had his fingerprint.'

'Then why didn't you say so three weeks ago?' Karan shrilled.

'I didn't realise it until recently.'

'If I'd known you were holding out on me, I might have been a bit slower to save your bony backside. Twice!'

'I'm sorry, but it doesn't change anything. I don't know how to contact Rulke.'

'It changes *everything*. I thought the enemy had him ... had tortured and killed him. You've got to take me to him. You gave your word.'

'I can't.'

'It's all *take* with you,' she snarled, struggling to restrain herself. 'I've done everything you asked of me. I keep risking my life to save yours, and you won't even do this little thing for me.'

'I have no idea where Rulke is.'

'Wait! Why don't you try Alcifer,' she said with deepest sarcasm. 'His *home*.'

'Why would he hide in the obvious place?'

'Because he loves Alcifer, and he knows its defences.'

'Well, in the time it took to find him, the war might be lost.'

Flydd was not going to budge. Karan stalked away. Would Llian be safe there?

He had a way of antagonising people, and he'd had some notable disagreements with Rulke in the past. But still ... Better in his hands than the enemy's.

As they approached Roros, the scale of the ruin grew ever more apparent, and it was worse than any of the other cities. Fields, orchards and forests had been burned for a good ten miles around the city. There would be no summer harvest in southern Crandor this year.

'The Merdrun made a special effort here,' said Nish, studying the charred ruins through Flydd's spy glass. The city was almost gone, just a few stone buildings surviving, battered islands swamped by seas of rubble and ash. 'Until three weeks ago, a million people lived in Roros. Now it'd be lucky to house ten thousand.'

'Last I heard, the Governor's Guard and the city militia had fought the enemy to a standstill,' said Flydd. 'Twenty thousand Merdrun died taking a third of the city – half of all their dead in the invasion.'

'But they made Roros pay.'

'How they made them pay.' Flydd looked close to the despair he so feared.

'Yulla's mistake was thinking they wanted to capture the city and plunder its wealth,' said Nish, 'and she prepared the defences well. But on a hot, windy day at the end of the dry season, if your enemy is determined to raze the city ...'

'I'm not giving up hope,' Flydd said doggedly. 'She raised a fortune for my war chest and sent hundreds of people into hiding. Former army officers, great artisans and mancers, all kinds of people I need for the conflict.'

'Be very careful. The enemy's assassins will try again.'

'Then we've got to be quick.'

The sky galleon raced across the wasted city towards a six-sided compound surrounded by three massive sets of solid stone walls, with bare killing grounds between them where attackers who broke through could be shot down by hidden defenders. Inside the inner wall, lawns ran for several hundred yards, bare except for a number of defensive towers and shooting platforms.

And at the centre, a gigantic hexagonal citadel, surrounded by six smaller buildings linked to it by broad flagstone paths.

'The Governor's Compound and Palace,' said Flydd.

In the Time of the Mirror it had been one of the Eleven Wonders. But the triple walls, each built from solid stone more than ten yards thick, had been battered down and breached in three places. The emerald lawn was scarred by deep gouges and littered with hurled boulders, while charred patches marked where burning barrels of oil had been catapulted in.

Of the Inner Wonders, only the hexagonal palace remained. Everything else had been burned or smashed down to the foundations. Outside the western breach in the inner wall thousands of bodies had been heaped up and incinerated, and the ghastly mountain was still smoking. The smell of charred, foul flesh was so overpowering that Karan did not think she would ever be rid of it – her clothes and hair were already steeped in it.

'Xervish,' said Maelys, 'there's no point going on. We've got to think of ourselves now.'

The face Flydd turned to her was the face of a stranger, almost a madman, twisted in a rictus of grief or despair. But he shuddered and regained control.

'We fight on,' he said in a blank voice. 'We *never* give in.'

He set the sky galleon down on a star-shaped area of paving outside the main doors of the palace. It was littered with boulders too, and fragments of smashed gargoyle and carved wood. As they climbed down, the tropical heat washed over them. Thunderclouds were building out to sea –the wet season would start any day now. A week too late.

At the vast front doors, he lifted the door knocker, a massive brass sculpture shaped like the head and long curving horns of a mountain goat, and let it fall.

It symbolised unshakeable defiance, and the sound must have rung through the entire palace, but the three people who came out looked defeated. All had the dark skin and purple-brown eyes of Crandor. An obese old woman, moving painfully on swollen feet, a slender, black-haired young man no taller than Nish, and a strikingly beautiful young woman.

'Yulla,' Flydd said heartily, shaking the old woman's hand, then the hand of the young man. 'Renly, good to see you again.'

'The only times we see you is when you want something,' Yulla said sourly. Then she smiled. 'But at least this time we all want the one thing.'

She introduced Maelys, Nish and Clech to Renly. Karan stepped out from behind Flydd and Yulla frowned.

'Karan Elienor Melluselde Fyrn,' said Flydd, 'this is my old sparring partner and former Governor, Yulla Zaeff.'

They shook hands. Yulla's hand was dry and cold, despite the sweaty heat, and as soft as dough. Flydd introduced her to Governor Renly, whose hand was warm and hard. Behind them the young woman was staring at Karan.

'And Persia bel Soon,' said Flydd. He pronounced her name Per-*see*-ar.

He was gazing at her as if she meant something to him, but she would not meet his eyes. Why not?

'I've read the *Tale of the Mirror*,' Persia said to Karan. 'The true tale, not the scrutators' bowdlerised version. I heard you'd contrived to come to the future.' Her voice was soft and deep and melodious.

Karan started. 'Back in my era, Tallia bel Soon, the Magister after Mendark, was a dear friend. Can you possibly be related?'

'She was my great-grandmother, four times back,' said Persia. 'She died long before my time, of course, but you have an honoured place in our family Histories.' To Karan's astonishment, Persia hugged her.

'Without Tallia and Zanser, a truly great healer, I would not be here today,' said Karan. 'She loved children but feared that she had left it too late to have any.'

'She bore twins. I can tell you about them, later on. Come inside.'

'They'd better hear it here,' Yulla said darkly.

'Hear what?' said Flydd.

'Xervish, I have to say it plainly. I've nothing for you. And no one.'

Flydd staggered and clutched at his healing hip. Maelys steadied him.

'But you said – I expected –'

'The key to happiness is always to *hope*, and never to *expect*,' said Persia softly.

'I had a mighty war chest for you,' said Yulla. 'Plus a room full of magical books and devices, many of them unique. And more than three hundred and thirty men and women: senior officers from the war, masters of all the branches of the Secret Art, mechanicians, artisans and so on. All hidden in the crypts under the Old Palace.'

Flydd looked towards the smoke-stained pile of rubble to the right. 'Go on,' he said grimly.

'The Governor's Guard kept the enemy out for sixteen days, but they kept coming. On the seventeenth day they set fire to Roros in thirty different places and nothing could save it. Everyone except us and the palace guards fled with whatever they could carry. The Merdrun let them go.'

'They knew what they wanted, and they were determined to get it,' said Renly.

'We made them pay dearly,' said Yulla. 'But the Governor's Guard was down to a thousand, and the enemy sent six thousand against them ...'

'They broke my mancers' wards one by one, and everyone outside the Hexagonal Palace was killed. We went down to the secret chamber deep below the palace, our mancers secured the doors with more wards, and we waited for them to break in and kill us.'

'But they never came,' said Persia. 'The enemy weren't interested in us.'

'They must have known about the people hidden in the crypts, because they targeted the Old Palace with ballistae. Smashed the roof in and lobbed in dozens of barrels of naphtha.'

'And burned everyone to death?' whispered Maelys, her dark eyes round in horror.

She must be remembering the night the enemy burned Nifferlin Manor. The smell here was an ever-present reminder.

'They were down deep,' said Renly. 'Safe from the fire. But ... it burned so fiercely that it sucked all the air out of the crypt. After the enemy left, we broke in, but it was too late. All three hundred and thirty of them had suffocated.'

'Roros's finest, gone just like that.' Yulla sagged. 'I'm sorry, Xervish, old friend. I can't do this anymore.'

'Let's get you inside,' said Flydd, holding her up with an effort, for she must have been twice his weight. 'That's all that matters now.'

She pushed him away and stood upright. 'I'll finish my sorry tale. They took the books and magical devices. The war chest too, though I think only to deprive you of it. They don't seem interested in plunder, apart from silver –'

'And they want that for some fell purpose,' said Persia.

'They could have killed us too, but they didn't bother. They opened a monster gate to Skyrock and the whole army, and all their captives, passed through.'

They went in. Yulla lay on a slab of green, veined marble and closed her eyes. Flydd held a grim council of war with Renly and Persia.

'We're praying for a good wet season and a bountiful autumn harvest,' said Renly, 'otherwise there'll be mass starvation by winter.'

'If what the Merdrun appear to be planning in forty-one days comes to pass,' said Nish direly, 'there may be no need for a harvest.'

'I'm not giving in,' Flydd said unconvincingly. 'This is just a setback.'

But Karan knew it was a fatal blow, and even Flydd must see it. All they could do now was run and hide.

'But how can I raise an army with no war chest,' said Flydd, 'and hardly any experienced officers?'

'Skyrock is guarded by 150,000 troops,' said Nish, 'and they're rapidly building defensive positions. You'd need three times that number to attack them successfully.'

'And even if you could raise, train and supply such a mighty army, which would take months,' said Renly, 'how would you get them to Skyrock? We don't have the power to send a squad of soldiers through a gate, much less an army.'

'You're proposing we should give in.'

'No, I'm saying you have to find another way to attack Skyrock. A clever way that no one will think of.'

'If I had any cleverness left, we wouldn't be in this position.'

'It's over, you old fool!' cried Karan. 'So keep your damned promise! Pick up Sulien and take us to Llian. Leave us in Alcifer where you found us. Then you can do whatever you bloody well want.'

'If I give up now,' said Flydd, 'it will nullify my life and everything I believe in. I'm going to Faranda, to seek the aid of the only power left on Santhenar – the Aachim. And you're coming with me.'

'They won't help you.'

'I know the Aachim of today a damned sight better than you do.'

Karan sank onto a seat and put her head in her hands. 'I wonder if you do.'

44

SHE MIGHT STILL KILL THEM

Maigraith disappeared for three days, then entered Aviel's room at sunrise and shook her awake as though nothing had happened. As though the despicable scent potion she had compelled Aviel to make had not led to the death of an innocent young woman.

'Up! Work to do.'

'I finished all my work while you were gone,' said Aviel, rubbing her eyes. For the first time in weeks she'd had enough sleep.

'Except the rejuvenation potion.'

'The first of my scent blendings has to mature for another ten days. And even once it's done, *and* the second blending, I can't do the final blending until the moon is in its first quarter. That's more than three weeks –'

'I know when it is!'

Aviel glanced at Maigraith's face, careful not to arouse suspicion in someone who was already paranoid. She looked haunted, though Aviel did not think it was remorse. Maigraith seemed devoid of a conscience. It must be because she had failed to destroy her rival.

The gross deformities from the potion were gone but the counterspells had not quite restored her face to normal. The left side was unnaturally smooth and did not move when she spoke. She looked lopsided.

Good! You didn't get away with it, you malicious old hag!

'Get up!' Maigraith repeated.

'Go away and let me get dressed in peace.'

Maigraith dragged her out of bed and Aviel's bad ankle turned under her, bringing tears to her eyes. Maigraith watched while she washed her face and hands, took off her nightgown and dressed. She felt hideously uncomfortable, but what could not be changed must be endured. *For now.*

'How did your scent potion go?' she said casually, as though it had just occurred to her.

'Imperfectly.' Maigraith gave her a sharp glance. 'I need an antidote.'

'I can't devise one without knowing what the potion does,' Aviel lied.

'I have the method. All you have to do is make it.'

'If the process was mechanical you could train a parrot to do it,' Aviel snapped, knowing she was taking a risk but needing, for her own sake, to put on a show of defiance. 'What's the scent potion for?'

'How dare you question me?' Maigraith cried, raising her hand to strike Aviel.

After a childhood full of blows, Aviel was skilled at evading them and delivering blows of her own to her father and sisters, who had all been bigger and stronger. She ducked and swung her right hand in a ferocious backhander against Maigraith's left cheek.

Maigraith fell backwards onto the bed. Aviel wrung her aching hand; Maigraith's cheek was almost as hard as stone. Was that from the scent potion, or the spell she had used to try and reverse its effects?

She sat up, and the look on her face was malevolent. Aviel had to take control, or die.

'You will never touch me again,' she said, raising her throbbing hand. 'Understood?'

For a full minute, as they stared into each other's eyes, she thought that Maigraith was going to blast her dead. Perhaps Maigraith thought it, too, then the tension drained out of her.

'Understood,' she said with a twisted little smile. 'Come.'

As Aviel followed Maigraith to the workshop, she finally understood her. She had been created and brought up by Faelamor, her entire existence moulded to Faelamor's fell purpose, and Maigraith had not broken free until she was well over a hundred. Even now, two centuries later, she compensated by dominating everyone she met. But she felt only contempt for those she dominated. The only people she respected were those who stood up to her.

She might still kill them, Aviel thought wryly, but she did respect them.

Maigraith gave her the recipe for the counter-potion and Aviel spent the next few days working on it with her customary care yet, at every step, praying it would fail. Why should Maigraith get what she wanted?

Maigraith did not leave the workshop whilever Aviel was working. Maigraith checked every ingredient, measurement and process, and locked away the constituent scents at the end of each day. But when the scent potion was finally blended, and she had sniffed the specified amount, her face looked the same.

'You've made it wrong,' she said furiously.

'You double-checked everything I did.'

Maigraith sniffed the antidote three times, taking a greater dose each time, but her left cheek remained as rigid as ever.

'Make it again.'

Aviel re-read the method, checked all the scents and blended the scent potion anew. It did not work either and she could guess why – because she had willed it to fail. When using the Secret Art, the intentions of the maker mattered.

Aviel's expression must have given her away because Maigraith gave her a deeply suspicious look. She turned away, sweat prickling the back of her neck.

Don't gloat, fool!

Maigraith was at her spy portal again, though the face Aviel saw out of the corner of an eye as she passed was not Rulke's, but a far younger man.

'Who's that?' she said, not expecting Maigraith to answer.

'Skald, of course. The young battle mancer who found Flydd's *Histories*.'

'Why, *of course*?'

'He's famous now. Don't you know *anything* about the war?'

'How could I? My gaoler doesn't see fit to tell me anything.'

'The mouse snaps her tiny teeth in vain,' sneered Maigraith. 'Skald is brave, enterprising and fiercely determined. He could be just the man I need.'

'And our enemy!'

'He's not *my* enemy.'

'You sound as though you admire him.'

'I admire anyone with the courage to overcome their cruel upbringing.'

'Except me.'

'Except you, mouse.'

Aviel went closer, peering through the spy portal. 'There's a hint of Rulke about him. Is that why –?'

Maigraith closed the portal, irritably. 'Haven't you got work to do?'

Aviel returned to her workshop, thoughtfully. What was Maigraith up to *now*, and why was she being so defensive?

Aviel turned over in bed and drew her knees up under her chin, but tonight no position was comfortable. She had to free herself from Maigraith's thrall, yet could only do so by using a dark scent-potion on her. But would that be a step too far?

A week ago, she would not even have considered it. And what if it made things worse, as Karan had when she had attacked Maigraith not long after Sulien first saw the Merdrun?

Desperate to protect her daughter, Karan had dosed Maigraith with the addictive Whelm pain-killing drug *hrux*, but Maigraith had proved unusually sensitive and it had driven her out of her wits for many days. The attack had led to a rift between Karan and her old friend, Shand, Maigraith's grandfather, and afterwards she had pursued Karan, Sulien and Llian relentlessly.

What kind of scent potion, anyway? Aviel lit her lamp and flipped through the pages of Radizer's *Grimoire* to the first of the Great Potions. It was unlikely that Maigraith would be affected by any of the lesser potions.

Murderer's Mephitis.

Aviel recoiled so violently that she struck her head on the wall. She slammed the grimoire shut and thrust it away from her. Was she seriously considering *murdering* Maigraith?

Of course not, she was just exploring options.

Because she was stuck here with Maigraith, who never gave up. She would go after Lirriam again and, if Aviel did nothing, she would be complicit in her death too. No matter how Aviel looked at her situation, she always came back to the same place. Maigraith had to be stopped and she, Aviel, had to do it.

She rolled onto her stomach, closed her eyes and steadfastly refused to think about scent potions. There must be something good happening in the world. She conjured up her last image of Wilm, the way he had moved and spoke just before he boarded the sky galleon, the scent of him, his courage and kindness. Her eyes misted. How she missed him ...

Her face grew hot as she remembered how he had turned away, and she contemplated the awful thought that he had given up on her. That he had gone off to fight, and probably to die, believing that she did not care about him. Her eyes stung. She cared more about him than anyone, but it was so very hard to escape an upbringing where her whole family had used and betrayed her.

She picked up the grimoire and opened it from the back. The final six leaves were blank, and as age-spotted and stained as the rest of the book.

As she was turning the first of these pages, which had a rat-shaped brown blotch at the bottom as if dark beer had once been spilled there, she noticed faint squiggles in the body of the blotch. Could they be writing?

Aviel held it up to her lamp, which did not help. She held the leaf above the lamp and the heat slowly revealed faint words there, in the same hand as the rest of the book. Radizer's hand. He had written down a scent potion in invisible ink.

A potion to rob a mancer of his or her gift for the Secret Art.

Was this the answer? The words were already fading. She warmed the page and read the description again. The scent potion did not appear to be dangerous. It merely blocked (or removed or destroyed – the text was not clear) the victim's ability to use the Art. And what could be the harm in turning Maigraith into an ordinary person?

If Aviel did, and if Maigraith could no longer work magic, she would have to accept that she had no future with Rulke. It would do her good!

Dare I?

Aviel warmed the leaf again and re-read the method and the list of fourteen scents needed to blend the scent potion. She had most of them, and the three she lacked (the reek from the rotting head of a catfish, the smell of well-aged urine – she could get that from the former guards' pissoir – and the pungency of gently heated horseradish) were easily come by ...

Worms wriggled across her scalp. This was a dire potion and making it would be taking a decisive step down the dark path. Aviel could justify destroying Maigraith's gift for magic as a form of self-defence, or a necessary evil ... yet evil it undoubtedly was.

The lesser of two evils, surely.

Three days later, working only when she knew Maigraith was away, the gift-blocking scent potion was complete. Now all she had to do was wait for a chance to use it. Aviel stoppered the phial tightly, put it in her pocket and went on with her slow, meticulous work on the rejuvenation potion, the most complicated and difficult one she had ever made. She had to act normally, because Maigraith was famously paranoid.

That afternoon her chance came. Maigraith was at her spy portal, muttering imprecations. As Aviel peered over her shoulder, Lirriam drew Rulke close and stood up on tiptoes to kiss him on the mouth. An odd little shiver passed through Aviel. He smiled and left the room.

'You harlot!' Maigraith shrieked. 'You man-stealing bitch! You're dead!'

She conjured another of those funnel gates, reached into the cedar box beside her chair for a round, crystal bottle, and set it on the table. It contained half a pint of a thick, red-brown, oily liquid, tendrils of which oozed sluggishly up from the surface as if trying to escape the bottle. It wasn't anything Aviel had made, or had ever seen before, but Maigraith was more than capable of making all manner of potions and poisons.

Do it now, while she's distracted!

Maigraith's eyes were fixed on her rival. Aviel's heart was thudding leadenly as she uncapped her phial and drew the prescribed amount of the gift-blocking potion, four drops, up into an eye dropper. No! Use less, in case she's over-sensitive. As Maigraith began twisting out the tight stopper of her bottle, Aviel released two drops of scent potion onto the collar of her gown.

'If you value your life, keep back,' Maigraith said irritably, without looking around.

Aviel stepped backwards, holding the eyedropper behind her in fingers slick with sweat. If Maigraith realised what she had done she would not live one minute past the completion of the rejuvenation scent potion.

'What's that smell?' said Maigraith.

'Mice,' Aviel lied. Her potion smelled like a mouse-infested cupboard.

Maigraith held her crystal bottle at arm's length and, very carefully, twisted the stopper back and forth to free it. The contents must be deadly.

Suddenly her hands shook and she set the crystal bottle down, hard. 'What ...?' she mumbled.

She reached for the bottle again but knocked it over and a small quantity of the eager red-brown fluid oozed out from around the stopper. Maigraith froze, staring at it, then pushed her chair backwards.

'Wha ...? Wha ...?'

The spy portal and the funnel gate vanished. Aviel slipped the eye dropper into its case, put it in her pocket with the stoppered phial, and hastily stood the crystal bottle up.

Maigraith rose jerkily to her feet, turned halfway around, then her aged face cracked. 'It's ... *gone!*' she screamed.

She fell to her knees, writhing and shrieking. Aviel dragged her out of the salon and down to her sleeping room, then pushed her onto the bed. Maigraith fell like a stone and lay still, her mouth open in a scream that went on and on.

Aviel returned to the salon, wearing two pairs of gloves and plugs up her nostrils, and cleaned Maigraith's red-brown fluid off the table, using wet rags that she dropped in a bucket. The rags began to fizz and char. She put the crystal bottle in the bucket, carried it out and down a side road to a dried-up well, and dropped it in, plus the gloves. Afterwards she washed her hands five times, just to be sure, and flushed her own potion down the sink.

When she checked on Maigraith an hour later she was still screaming.

What have I done? thought Aviel. Have I driven her insane? Is she going to die?

Am I as big a monster as she is?

45

I WILL NEVER DRINK A LIFE AGAIN

After failing to assassinate Flydd, Skald had expected the magiz to drink his life. And Dagog had been preparing to, right there in the command tent, when Durthix changed his mind and ordered that Skald be spared.

Dagog's rage was apocalyptic, and for a long, desperate interval Skald thought the magiz was going to defy Durthix and drink his life anyway. He probably would have, had Durthix not gestured to his guards, who formed a circle of blades around Skald.

'He failed!' snarled Dagog.

'Brilliantly, heroically, self-sacrificingly,' said Durthix. 'No one has ever demonstrated *One for All* more compellingly, Magiz, and he's worth far more to us alive.'

Skald had subsequently spent six days in the healing station. Yet, as he began to recover, he wondered why Durthix had bothered. Why not let him die a hero? Or a failure, if that was how Skald was regarded, given that Flydd was still alive.

But Skald had been attended night and day by the Merdrun's best healers, and the magiz had resentfully cast spell after spell, trying undo the damage Skald had done to himself in his desperate escape. Durthix had visited twice, the second time bringing a copy of Flydd's *Histories of the Lyrinx War* for Skald to study. Why? What did Durthix want from him?

The healing station was a long yellow tent with a canvas floor and a high roof held up by a central line of poles, painted blue and marked with the Merdrun glyph in black at the top. Stretchers were spaced along each side, each holding a gravely ill soldier. It was draughty and cold, and reeked of septic wounds and a variety of poultices.

It was also noisy, though most of the noise came from outside. The distant click of thousands of hammers on thousands of chisels, the bellowing of overseers, the crash and crack of falling stone, the perfectly synchronised footsteps of squads of marching troops.

Inside the tent it was almost silent. Merdrun learned as children to ignore pain, and only excruciating agony could induce a soldier to cry out. Though Skald was in agony during his initially brief lucid moments, and tormented by nightmarish hallucinations, he had more to prove than any of his fellow patients. He endured the tearing pain in his guts with no more than an occasional stifled moan.

At the end of the sixth day he was able to don his uniform and stand up shakily by his stretcher to wait for the high commander. When Durthix finally came, Skald was shivering and his toes were like sticks of ice in his boots. He could not remember being cold on Santhenar before. Truly, he was a miserable shadow of the soldier he had once been.

'You have cost us dear,' said Durthix. 'You had better be worth it, Captain.'

'I'm not,' said Skald. 'I failed.'

All the self-confidence had been burned out of him, and all ambition. His guts felt torn to pieces and his jelly knees wanted to fold under him. A soldier's strength was valued above all other qualities save courage, and Skald's weakness made him contemptible in his own eyes. Almost worthless.

'Are you questioning my decision to save you, Captain Skald?'

'No,' he whispered, sounding timid and unworthy. 'No, High Commander!' he said, too forcefully, and had to support himself one of the side poles of the tent. His head spun and he was forced to gasp the shameful words, 'High Commander, may I sit down?'

Durthix's thick upper lip curled, but he brought a folding chair.

Skald sat down hard, still holding the pole for fear of falling on his face. His teeth chattered. 'W-why is it so cold?'

'You were gated to Skyrock in a coma. This place is 8,000 feet up.' Durthix inspected Skald dispassionately. 'I'm told you will never again be fit for active duty.'

Skald almost howled, but managed to choke the ruinous emotions off.

'Are – are you dismissing me from the army?' he said desperately.

'The means you used to escape capture was an act of genius. You did something that has never been attempted before – and pulled it off. At great cost to yourself, but also with an unexpected benefit.'

Skald felt strong enough to let go of the tent pole. 'A *benefit*, High Commander?'

'By partially drinking your own life, and successfully using that power to create a gate, you amplified your gift for mancery. You offer us new possibilities, Captain.'

'Thank you, High Commander,' said Skald. 'What –?'

'Later! In the meantime, you will be given work suited to your capabilities.'

As Skald went to the door, Durthix said something that, to the best of Skald's knowledge, he had never said before. 'Well done, Captain.'

That was not the magiz's opinion. He made it clear, on his daily visits to the healing tent, that he loathed Skald more than ever. And Dagog's addiction seemed to be getting worse. His face was as purple and bloated as a blood-engorged leech; he must be drinking the lives of slaves every day now.

The worse he became, the more sickened Skald grew with himself, for he now knew exactly what Tataste and his other victims had gone through, and each time he relived their deaths his flesh crawled as if maggots had hatched under the skin.

I will not become him, he thought, over and over. *I will never drink a life again.*

Yet the temptation was always there now. The yearning to feel that ecstasy, and know that nothing was beyond him, was all that got him through the pain. It was harder than ever to hide his emotions, and ever more necessary that he suppress them utterly. They would be the death of him if he did not.

Yet not all was dark. In between hallucinations he had dreamed that a woman was gazing at him as if she actually cared about him, and that was novel. In all his life, no one had ever cared about him as a person.

And once or twice his mind had been touched, fleetingly, by a young enemy girl, almost as unhappy as he was. She seemed familiar; had she come to him before? He could not remember.

Who was she, and how could she reach him at all?

~

When Skald reported for duty the following morning he was sent to an even larger tent, one of hundreds in a cramped tent city next to the officer's compound, to report to the chief provisioner.

These tents were so large that he could see nothing beyond them. Only the deep blue, cloudless sky, the gritty grey soil underfoot and the crisp, cold air told him that he was far from stinking, sweaty Guffeons.

The provisioner's tent was forty yards long and half that wide. It contained eighty-eight tall folding tables, each with a uniformed Merdrun standing at it, and stacks containing hundreds of crates of papers, scrolls and ledgers.

'I'm to be a *clerk*?' he said, unable to conceal his dismay.

'Someone has to supply the bold adventurers,' said Provisioner Tiligg, a narrow-shouldered little man wearing hemispherical eyeglasses and frayed green slippers on odd-shaped feet.

Slippers! Skald felt nothing but contempt for the man. His own army boots were so polished that he could see his char-black beard shadow on them.

'Food and water,' Tiligg continued, 'firewood and tents and stretchers, and everything else an army requires, all must be ordered, shipped, checked, protected from theft, vermin and spoilage at every stage, and delivered when needed. Without our work, there is no army and no True Purpose.'

'I understand,' said Skald.

But Tiligg was determined to educate this arrogant upstart. 'Building stone must be quarried, ores mined and smelted and the metals purified, forests felled, cut into timber and delivered to manufactories and workshops. And a hundred thousand slave artisans and labourers must be fed and watered, guarded and supervised to complete thousands of tasks, each of which must be done exactly to schedule. Schedules that *humble clerks* like yourself must devise and enact.'

Skald wanted to tear the man's slippers off and stop his grey-lipped mouth with them, but Tiligg was vastly higher in rank, so he listened in silence, then went to the table assigned to him and began to check his crate of manifests against the entries in the official ledgers.

First, sacks of grain of various types and qualities: sacks ordered, delivered, spoiled or eaten by vermin, consumed or, in all too many cases, disappeared, presumably stolen by the slaves. Later, bags of dried peas of various kinds and grades, sacks of sweet potatoes and dozens of other kinds of root vegetables, onions, garlics, herbs and spices ...

The work was surprisingly exhausting and there was no end to it, because his crate was refilled with new documents faster than he could empty it. And there was none of the easy camaraderie of a captain with his troops, here. The chief provisioner discouraged any interaction that was not work-related.

Besides, sus-magizes were feared for their magic, their capriciousness and their life-drinking, and only a fool would befriend one. None of the other clerks would meet his eye.

⁓

After several days of brain-numbing work, Skald was summoned to the black command tent, which stood a quarter of a mile away inside the officers' compound. This compound also contained of dozens of large tents, laid out with geometric precision. It was surrounded by a palisade of split logs and had a gate and gatehouse at the northern end.

Durthix, half a dozen other senior officers and Dagog stood around a large table spread with maps and plans, some of which still bore the ineradicable stains of Skald's blood. No one acknowledged him and he took an unobtrusive spot to the side, where he could hang onto one of the tent poles if necessary.

'It's worse than we thought,' said Durthix. 'Superintendent Furnix was crushed to death, the fool, along with Chief Architect Hunsor.'

'Another slave rebellion?' said the magiz.

Durthix bared his big, square teeth. 'Not after the way I dealt with the last one. Furnix took Hunsor down to inspect the tunnels below Skyrock, but part of the roof collapsed, killing them both. I suspect sabotage.'

'By the miners?'

'By Hunsor. The Aachim was a bitter man who could not come to terms with his enslavement. But the work must go on. We cannot fall behind by as much as a day.'

'What work?' said Skald. Everyone stared at him and he added, 'I don't know anything about it – or Skyrock, for that matter.'

'Skyrock was a towering stone pinnacle at the western end of the Great Mountains.' Durthix indicated a large painting hung on the side wall of the tent behind him.

A mass of pale rock rose high in the sky to three peaks and was surrounded by radiating dikes of similar rock, each standing several yards above the surrounding countryside. The pinnacle was centred in a shallow, bowl-shaped valley some miles across, and the ground was grey, littered with stones and sparsely covered in wiry tussocks. A snowy range was visible in the far distance.

Durthix continued. 'And we came to Santhenar to build this.'

A second painting depicted a tall tower made of interwoven spirals of blue and white, carved stone, on top of which stood a smaller tower made of iron with a large, crystal-driven mechanism at its top. A vast, broad tunnel, a shimmering blue, carved through the base of the tower. 'It will allow us to fulfil our True Purpose.'

'It's ... enormous,' said Skald.

'And way beyond our capabilities, which is why we abducted Hunsor, the greatest living Aachim architect, and compelled him to design the tower according to our ancient plan. But so vast a structure, over a thousand feet high, would have taken many years to build. The only way it could be done in time was to cut Skyrock down and hollow it out. And now the fool is dead!'

'Hunsor's design is complete,' said General Chaxee, a one-armed old woman with a stubble of white hair and a red eye patch over her right eye. She had distinguished herself in many battles of earlier times and was Durthix's Sixth in Command. 'And the slave architects and designers are doing all the detailed work. All we need is someone to manage them, according to Hunsor's plan.'

'Then appoint a Superintendent of Works and get it done,' said the magiz.

'I've lost half my officers in a few weeks,' said Durthix. 'I can't spare anyone.'

'What about the one who'll never be fit for active duty again?'

Dagog was looking at Skald, who quailed. This was why he had been ordered here. But any position Dagog recommended Skald for would be designed to ruin him.

Durthix swung around, staring at Skald and tapping his fingers on the table. 'Superintendent of Works is a very senior position.'

'I don't have the experience,' said Skald.

'You're a man of great initiative; you'll work it out. Brief him, Chaxee.'

Dagog gave Skald a triumphant glare as he went out, and the others followed, leaving just Skald and Chaxee in the black command tent.

'General Chaxee?' he began. 'I don't –'

'Shut up and listen.'

Her eye patch slipped, revealing radiating white scars around the empty eye socket. The skin inside it was mottled in shades of grey and red. She did not bother to adjust it and his admiration grew. Her disfigurement was a badge of honour.

'You will not repeat what I am about to tell you, to *anyone*,' she added.

'No, General.'

'The great martyr, Anubelux, our eleventh magiz, was the first to recognise our darkness of the soul, and that we would have to heal ourselves before we could go home.'

'Heal ourselves of what, General?'

'Our corruption. Our original sin, if you like.'

He could not take his eyes away from her eye socket. 'I don't understand.'

'At the dawn of our Histories, when Stermin separated us from our fellows like sacrificial goats and ordered us through the Crimson Gate, it corrupted us, and we've grown more corrupt with every succeeding generation. You know what I'm talking about.'

'Yes,' he said quietly. War for the sake of war. Killing their enemies for the sake of killing. The magiz's life-drinking for the pleasure of it. He shivered. This was close to heresy.

'That's why Anubelux created the True Purpose – to cleanse us before we go home and make a new start. And she set out how it was to be done in words and paintings, safely hidden until invasion day.' She indicated the second painting. 'This tower is a vital symbolic object. Do you know why?'

'No, General.'

'It's the antithesis of the Crimson Gate that ruined us, the gate which we've been forced to recreate over and again in our practice wars against other worlds, and even against Santhenar. The tower must be beautiful, harmonious and perfect in every way – but we know nothing about beauty or harmony. Until now the only things that mattered to us were war – and winning.'

Skald's guts spasmed. 'I'm just a soldier and a junior sus-magiz. What do I know of –?'

'You don't need to know. We abducted the most brilliant architects, designers, stone carvers and artists on Santhenar, and put them to work following Anubelux's notes and drawings. The detailed designs are now done. As Superintendent of Works, your job is to ensure the plans for the tower and tunnel are followed down to the smallest decorations and symbols, and every deadline is met.'

'I will do my best.'

'Your best isn't good enough,' said Chaxee. 'Follow me!'

46

A SUMP FOR TOXIC MAGICAL WASTE

Chaxee led Skald out past the guards at the gates of the officers' compound. On the other side of a broad, gravelled road that ran up the hill to Skald's right, and down towards Skyrock, was another compound, with split-log palisade walls twenty feet high.

'Slaves' compound,' said Chaxee. 'For 100,000 slaves.' She pointed up the road towards an expanse covered in thousands of smaller tents. 'Army camp, 150,000 troops.' And far beyond that to another, much smaller camp. 'The Whelm who have sworn to Durthix. 4,000.'

She rotated to indicate another high camp to the left of the road. 'The rest of the Merdrun nation.'

She turned left and headed down the road. The ground to either side had been stripped of all vegetation and levelled. Ahead, a circular compound, perhaps a mile across, was surrounded by a partly built stone wall. Where the road intersected it, ten enormous gateposts had been sunk into the ground, equally spaced across an opening two hundred yards wide, and workers were attaching yards-long hinges to each side of each post.

'Why such an enormous gateway?' said Skald.

'When you need to know, you'll be told.'

Inside the compound the radiating dikes had been cut away and the ground levelled, and the area immediately inside the wall was being paved with slabs of coloured rock laid to an intricate design. The rest of the compound was bare ground littered with piles of cut and broken stone, stacks of timber and lengths of metal. The racket of hammer on chisel, and the crash and crack of falling stone, grew ever louder as they approached the pinnacle.

At the centre of the compound stood what remained of the sky-piercing pinnacle of Skyrock. It must originally have been two thousand feet high, but the top half had been cut away to leave a flat surface on which, Skald assumed, the iron tower was to be erected.

The upper third of the pinnacle had then been carved into spirals clad in either blue or white stone, enclosing a massive central cylinder of rock into which windows had been cut here and there. The middle third was encircled by bamboo scaffolding socketed into the rock and thousands of slave masons worked on three platforms there, more than six hundred feet above the ground. The workers on the lowest platform were cutting the pinnacle to shape with hammers and chisels, the ones on the platform above them polished the stone, and the workers on the upper platform fixed the blue and white cladding to the spirals.

From the lower platform, cut rock thundered down on all sides, forming mounds around the base of the pinnacle. A roofed tunnel allowed safe access to the interior, and the gigantic opening that was to run through the base of Skyrock. Even unfinished, the tower was awe-inspiring.

But the amount of work still to be done, and now Skald's responsibility, was terrifying. What was it all for? Only Durthix and the magiz knew what the True Purpose really entailed.

'I have to do all that ...?' Skald began.

'It's one of your *two* jobs as Superintendent of Works,' said Chaxee. 'Complete the tower, inside and out, and the tunnel through it.'

'But there must be tens of thousands ... How can I possibly ...?'

'Every supervisor knows what they have to do, and when,' she said impatiently. 'Your job is to ensure that they get it all done in time.'

As he eyed the small, labouring figures on the scaffolding, a mason slipped from the lower platform, fell for about five seconds, and slammed into one of the piles of rubble. Skald winced.

'Hundreds of slaves have been killed already,' she said dispassionately, 'and many of our supervisors. And many more will die before the Day of All Days.'

'Dangerous work.'

'Sometimes the slaves jump, and sometimes they nudge their supervisors off. Or drop rock on their heads. Be careful where you stand, Superintendent.'

Skald turned away and saw, halfway across the far side of the compound, a black stone building shaped like a perfect cube. 'What's that for?'

'You are not permitted to know.'

Nearby was a large rectangular pit, like an inverted pyramid, with a spike at its centre. He did not bother to ask about it.

'And that?' He indicated a hazy hole in the ground away to his left, near the partly built compound wall. Tendrils of a greenish miasma rose from it.

'An old quarry. Now used as a sump for toxic magical waste.'

'I didn't know there was such a thing.'

'All magic produces uncanny waste, though normally you can't see it. But we're using such vast amounts of magical power here that the waste builds up, and it's extremely dangerous.'

'Can't it be dumped further away?'

'It's tricky to handle, and not even the magiz knows much about it. If it touches living things, or even inanimate objects – well, you can worry about that at a later date.'

'It's part of my responsibility too?'

'You wanted the job, Superintendent.'

No, I didn't!

She looked back at Skyrock. 'The tower must also be untainted by any dark source of power. You know what I mean.'

'Drinking lives,' breathed Skald.

'You, who have been dragged from the pyre after drinking your own life, know more than any man how dark that power is. It's not why the magiz proposed you,' she grimaced, 'but it *is* why you were accepted.' She paused. 'That, and your determination to succeed at any cost. You're unique among us, Skald. That's why you were chosen for this honour ... and this burden.'

Chaxee's one eye burned into Skald, but he could not think of anything to say.

'Unfortunately, you also have a taste for the Despicable Spell. You must resist it, lest you taint that which you seek to make perfect.'

The Despicable Spell – life-drinking. 'What's my second responsibility?'

'We need power desperately, far more than the field here can provide. Where are we to get it?'

'I don't know.'

'Have you read *Histories of the Lyrinx War*?'

'Parts. Durthix gave me –'

'Read it all, study it, understand it. It's the enemy's greatest folly, and finding it may turn out to be your greatest triumph. For instance, a chapter in the second last book describes Flydd's attempt to block the draw of power from a node, but it failed, and all the node's power was released in a cataclysm that destroyed it.'

'I'm ... not sure why you're telling me this, General.'

'The greatest node yet discovered lies beneath Skyrock,' said Chaxee. 'And if we can tap it, we'll have all the power we need – pure, untainted power. Your second task is more important than ever after yesterday's fiasco.'

'Is that what Furnix was doing when he was killed?'

'He should never have gone down the mine tunnels. When the roof fell on him and Hunsor, *or was magicked down on them*, it set our True Purpose back by many days, time that will be very difficult to make up. But the node is our only credible source of power, so it must be done.'

And Skald had to make it happen, though on such a tight schedule even making up one lost day would be difficult. Making up many days was hardly possible, in which case the True Purpose must fail. And he would be blamed.

'Are there power sources that *aren't* credible?'

'Just one. Alcifer.'

Fear thrilled through Skald. Excitement too. His discovery of the strange beacon originating from Alcifer had gained him the opportunity to become sus-magiz in the first place. 'Rulke's ancient city.'

'Where he now lies in hiding, recuperating from his injuries.'

'He was a great and terrible foe.'

'But he's a shadow of what he once was,' said Chaxee.

'And the non-credible possibility?'

'It's said that within Alcifer, whose defences have, unfortunately, proved impenetrable, there is a great Source.'

'Another node?' said Skald.

'An entirely different kind of power. But even if it's true, there's no way to get to it. The Charon have long been our enemies and Rulke has tailored Alcifer's defences against us.'

She paused, then said, 'One final thing, the most critical of all. Both your tasks must be complete and ready for use by Founder's Day.'

Skald's heart sank. 'The tower complete, *and* supplied with enough power?'

'Yes,' she said grimly.

He sensed an undercurrent of despair. Chaxee knew it could not be done but could not admit it, so she was shifting responsibility to him.

'Why that day?'

'A rare conjunction of the heavenly bodies offers the chance to reach our goal. But that window is only open for eight hours – and the conjunction does not occur again for 287 years.'

Unlike Charon, Merdrun were not long-lived. If Skald failed, the True Purpose would also fail, and his people, and many generations to come, would suffer.

'And in 287 years,' she continued remorselessly, 'anything could happen to prevent our descendants reaching the goal that has driven us ever since we were forced to pass through the Crimson Gate. Now do you understand why it must be done?'

'I will do everything in my power –' Skald said desperately.

'Not good enough!' Chaxee said in a harsh croak. 'You will swear, *by our sacred Founder's Stone*, that you will complete the tower and tunnel, and ensure sufficient power is available, by midday of the day before Founder's Day.'

'How can I swear when I don't know what the tower is for, or what devices and mechanisms are required?'

'The magiz has designed the necessary mechanisms, and a team of artisans and artificers, led by the slave mechanician, M'Lainte, is building them. That's all you need to know. Swear!'

Was Dagog watching in secret? How he would be enjoying this. 'How can I swear to the impossible?'

'I have revealed one of our most vital secrets to you – the date of the Day of All Days. If you cannot swear, I will disgrace you on a pretext, have you killed to protect the secret, and someone else will be appointed.'

Skald looked at her, numbly. There was no possibility that everything could be done in time. Yet it had to be done, for the sake of the Merdrun nation.

'I swear by our sacred Founder's Stone,' he said grimly, 'that all will be built, powered and ready for use by midday of the day before Founder's Day.'

And when he failed, as he must, his fate would be unimaginable.

47

A WONDER YOU DIDN'T LET ME DIE

An inner voice said to Aviel, 'You're just as bad as Maigraith.'

But another voice whispered, 'Let her die. It'd be a mercy for her. And a reprieve for everyone else.'

Aviel's gift-blocking potion had left Maigraith comatose and barely breathing, her heart only beating a few times a minute. She looked dead, save that the unmarred half of her face was twisted in an agony so brutal that Aviel could not bear to look at it.

It should have been easy to go out and close the door. If she had, in this hot weather, without food or water Maigraith would probably have slipped away without ever regaining consciousness.

It was the best thing to do ...

But the grief got to Aviel. The other emotions she had seen time and again in Maigraith – the sneering mockery, the hatred, obsessive rage, jealousy, bitterness, and most of all the cold indifference to the suffering or fate of anyone else – told Aviel to let her go. Yet Maigraith's aching grief at the loss of her magical gift brought them together, because Aviel would feel the same way if she had been robbed of her own small gift.

So here she was, holding Maigraith's slack mouth open while she trickled honeyed water down her throat with an eyedropper. It took ages and Aviel felt the need to do it at least every three hours, night and day.

Until the sixth morning, when Maigraith's eyes quivered open, the twisted half of her face relaxed and her right hand rose and sent the eyedropper flying, to shatter on the floor.

'Mooning over me now?' she said in a cracked voice. 'Got a bad conscience, mouse?'

Aviel had not expected thanks, but still ... 'You took ill after you opened the bottle,' she lied. 'You've been unconscious for many days.'

'A wonder you didn't let me die.'

'I thought about it.'

Maigraith eyed her suspiciously. 'I would have told you to, if I'd been able to speak. My gift was gone ... But now it's back, and as strong as ever.' She smiled twistedly.

Because Aviel had relented, fool that she was, and only given half the specified dose. *And now it was all going to start again.*

'But you couldn't do it,' Maigraith sneered. 'You *are* a mouse, a terrified little rodent.'

'I'll know better next time.'

'There won't be a next time. Where's my trull toxicant?'

'The poison in the crystal bottle? I chucked it down a well.'

Maigraith's eyes flashed and she tried to get up, but did not have the strength. 'That took ten days to make.'

Aviel did not bother to answer.

'No matter. I've had a much better idea.'

Maigraith pushed herself upright. She now looked much as she had before Aviel dosed her, though a little older, and the tip of her nose had a droop. She really resembled a hag now. Aviel took a small, spiteful pleasure from it.

'I'll get back to work on your rejuvenation potion, then.'

'Hurry up. I'm going to need it soon.'

'It'll be a couple of weeks, yet.'

Maigraith gave her a cold stare. 'That's not good enough.'

'It can't be hurried – assuming you want it to work properly.'

As Aviel headed back to her workshop she wondered how she would feel if Maigraith *had* died. On the one hand, relieved.

And on the other? As though she, Aviel, had fallen and would never recover. Many people could do bad things without a qualm, but she was not one of them. She had done the right thing, saving Maigraith's life.

Yet she knew she was going to regret it.

Late that night, Maigraith took an enemy propaganda poster out of a drawer and sat there, gazing at the sketch of the hero it portrayed. Skald was a big, handsome man who resembled Rulke, though Skald was much younger and a lot hairier. Some time ago she had used the image to locate him and had subsequently created a secret spy portal to check on him.

Seeing his vulnerability and his desperate yearning to prove himself, she had briefly fantasised about seducing him to get back at Rulke – but that would be the pettiest of revenges. Besides, Maigraith was not the seducing type. Even if she used illusion to give herself the outward appearance of a siren, inside she would remain the cold, inhibited woman she had always been.

But could she use Skald to rid herself of her rival?

The more she had spied on him, the more he'd aroused her curiosity, especially his astounding escape from Flydd through a gate powered by partly drinking his own life. It bespoke both a superhuman need to succeed and a terror of the disgrace of capture.

She had also spied on him as he lay on Durthix's chart table, stripped naked and bleeding from every orifice while Dagog tried to terminate the life-drinking spell, and the Merdrun's best healers struggled to haul Skald back up the precipice of death.

The first thing she had done after recovering was to spy on him again. Skald was desk-bound and chafing; he craved danger because it temporarily quieted his inner demons. But there was only frustration in his present work, and he was ripe for an offer. Maigraith would give him another couple of days to learn the meaning of despair.

48

CAN WATER BE PUMPED FROM A DRY WELL?

S kald had been right. The tower could not be completed in time, or even if he'd had twice the available time. Doing it by mechanical means was out of the question; it would take years. It could only be done in time by using magic, but the magical power needed to lift hundreds of massive iron beams to the top of Skyrock and assemble them there, and to cut the six hundred-foot-wide tunnel through the base of the pinnacle, was far beyond what could be drawn from the field.

And even if those works could be completed on schedule, much greater power would be needed to operate the secret devices and mechanisms required for the True Purpose on the Day of All Days, Founder's Day. It could only come from the node deep below Skyrock.

Skald met the chief miner, a small, lopsided fellow, on the Fourth Level below Skyrock, which was as deep as Skald was allowed to go.

'No further, Super.' The pores of the chief miner's grey skin and the wrinkles around his pinkly inflamed eyes were infilled with rock dust, and there was dust on his cap and his eyebrows, and down the bridge of his flat nose. He had no fingers on his left hand, just the thumb, and his left shoulder hung three inches below the right. 'Ain't safe for the likes o' ye.'

Skald did not want to go lower. The confinement, the close, dusty air and the weeping walls roused long-suppressed horrors from his early childhood: darkness, his two older brothers holding blankets over his head so he could not breathe, kicking and screaming in pure terror –

With an effort, he crushed the unworthy emotions. His brothers had died in minor battles years ago; they could not hurt him anymore. 'How long to clear the rubble out from the roof fall, and the bodies?'

The chief miner picked grey sludge out of his nose with a pointed thumbnail. 'Safer to leave them there ... bad luck, though.'

Skald wasn't going to tempt fate any further. 'How long?'

'Two days,' said the miner. 'Or three or four. Could be more roof falls, or fissures gushin' water that's gotta be pumped out, or bad air. Never know what yer gunna find underground.'

'I need it done in two days,' said Skald. 'And the node reached three days after that.'

'It'll take as long as it takes.'

'I could have you killed,' Skald said, already feeling desperate.

'Next chief miner will tell you the same. And the one after that.'

He was probably telling the truth, though you could never tell with the enemy. 'What if I bring in a second crew?'

'There are miners enough, and all hungry for *paid* work.'

To get the best out of key workers, they had to be paid, though that wasn't a problem. The Merdrun had an endless supply of purloined treasure and no other use for it, since they did not value gold or jewels. 'What about a third crew?'

'No room. Gotta haul all the rock back up the shaft.'

'Dig a new shaft.'

The chief miner rolled his inflamed eyes. 'That'd take *weeks*. And the more miners you got, the more fresh air you need. Bad air, killin' air, lies in low places, and the deeper you go the worse it gets, and you can't smell it. Got to have fans to get rid of it, and they take power too.'

'But all these problems can be solved.'

The chief miner sighed ostentatiously. 'Super, the closer we get to the node, the rottener the rock becomes.' He picked the other nostril and held out the grey, quivering muck. 'It's like this, sometimes.'

Skald stepped backwards, disgusted. 'Why?'

'You'd know better than me, bein' a sus-magiz.'

'Have a guess.'

'Guess the great node is eatin' away at the rock.'

'Does it affect people who get close to it?'

The chief miner shrugged with his good shoulder. 'People are softer than rock.'

Skald assumed that meant yes – but if a crew of miners became ill from exposure to the node, another crew would replace them. 'I'll send two more crews, and find power to drive the fans,' he said rashly. 'And there'll be a great prize for the crew who can get to the node in five days.'

'Double is more likely,' the chief miner said dourly.

He probably expected to be killed when the job was finished. It was what the Merdrun had always done, but now Skald could see how corrupt they had become, how that would taint their True Purpose.

Pain stabbed through his inner organs as he plodded back to the shaft and climbed over the wicker side of the lifting basket. A pair of emaciated female slaves wound the winch and the basket slowly rose, swinging from side to side and thumping into the broken walls. The surface seemed so far away, and the frayed ropes symbolised life and death. Like this impossible task.

They would never do it in time. He had to find another source of power – but there was no other credible source.

When he returned to the tent where he worked, Sus-magiz Pannilie, who ranked fifth below the magiz and was vastly Skald's superior in talent and experience, was waiting. A lean, compact woman, darker than most Merdrun, with pink scaly patches running up her arms and throat, and almost covering the lower third of her face, including her lower lip. A failed spell cast on her by a rival sus-magiz years ago, it was rumoured. Other rumours said a bitter former lover had done it.

'You called for a report on power,' she said brusquely, picking at the scaly skin on her lower lip until it bled. 'We're drawing everything we can take from the field, and it's not nearly enough.'

'You can't squeeze any more out of it?'

'Can water be pumped from a dry well?'

'What about fields further away? Why can't we draw power and store it – as the enemy does with their sky galleon?'

'Suitable crystals are very scarce; we can't store enough power to make any difference. Don't you know anything about the nature of power on Santhenar?'

'Only what I've read in Flydd's *Histories*. But I've got to explore all possibilities.'

'The only possibility is the node.'

'I've ordered two more mining crews in. One of them *might* reach the node in five days.'

'Mining always runs behind schedule. When is it *likely* that they'll reach the node?'

'Ten days.'

The blood withdrew from under Pannilie's dark skin, leaving the upper part of her face a sickly grey but the pink, lower third unchanged. She turned away. 'Then it's hopeless.'

Paradoxically, the despair of this immensely competent and experienced sus-magiz strengthened Skald's own resolve. 'I swore to complete the tower and tunnel, and get the power we need, by the appointed day,' he said quietly. 'There must be a way.'

She grimaced and went out. Skald still did not know what the inside of the tower was meant to look like once complete, so he headed up the hill to see the deputy architect. She was a slave; all the designers and artists were.

The design tent was set on a knoll overlooking the front of the officers' compound and, unlike all the other tents, was circular with a high central peak, not unlike a circus tent. The deputy architect turned out to be surprisingly young, and Skald stopped in mid-step, staring at her.

'Have we met before?' he said.

'No, Superintendent. My name is Uletta.'

She was a big woman, tall and broad-shouldered, with heavy thighs and muscular arms, nicely hairy, and broad feet and hands. Her nose was long and blunt, her ears large, and her jaw strong enough to crack nuts. Skald, to whom delicacy of face or figure was a sign of weakness, thought her beautiful.

'The – the former Superintendent of Works and the Chief Architect have been killed by a rock fall,' he said, feeling a trifle breathless. 'I'm in charge of completing the project in time. And powering it.'

'We have been told.' She did not look upset. 'And you wish me to show you the plans and designs.'

'At once.'

They spent hours going over the structural drawings for the tower and tunnel. Skald was quick to understand them, for he could look at a plan and visualise it in three dimensions, but his head was throbbing and his damaged inner organs were pierced with shard-like pains. If he did not rest, he was likely to do more damage.

But time was desperately short and he did not take well to inaction. Few

Merdrun did; they lived on their feet and mostly died on their feet. Even mating and childbirth were more often than not done standing up.

'Do you also want to see the decorative designs, artwork, embellishments, motifs and symbols?' said Uletta.

Skald did not need to see them yet, but working with her created feelings that he had never felt before and did not have words for. He felt a little light-headed, almost delirious. 'I need to know everything.'

They worked late into the night, after all the other slaves had been escorted to their compound and locked in. Near midnight, Uletta rolled the second last set of drawings and took them back to their rack.

Skald was admiring her massive backside and heavy thighs, her glossy black hair and quick, confident step – she was not cowed like most of the slaves – when a dreadful pain tore through his belly. His head and torso grew boiling hot, yet his hands were freezing. He put his head between his legs but the dizziness did not go away. He was going to faint! And no Merdrun soldier ever fainted.

'Superintendent?' said Uletta. Merdrun did not name themselves to slaves, even important ones; they went by rank or title only. 'Are you unwell?'

He could not answer. The pain grew, dizziness rose until it overwhelmed him, and he toppled.

He was vaguely aware of Uletta catching him, laying him on his back on the floor and putting her coat under his head. Her cool hands touched his forehead and throat.

'You're burning up,' she said. 'And your heart is beating so fast it's liable to burst.'

'Merdrun – don't die – burst hearts!'

'Maybe you'll be the first.'

She soaked a cloth, laid it outside the tent for a few minutes to cool, then bathed his face and neck, opened his shirt and felt his chest and middle. Her heavy bosom swayed, inches from his face. He winced when she touched his belly.

'Something must be wrong inside you,' she said.

'Tore my inner organs – escape – Flydd. Nearly died.'

She stepped backwards, staring at him. 'You're the Merdrun's great hero, Skald Hulni?'

Slaves weren't supposed to talk to Merdrun this way. They were supposed to be submissive and speak only when spoken to.

'I – am – Skald.' It was all he could manage.

Her eyes glowed. It was as if she admired him, which was preposterous. He was an enemy.

'You found Flydd's *Histories*. You took Mechanician M'Lainte and a ... secret weapon. You drank from your own life to evade capture,' said Uletta.

'Capture is dishonour.'

'But you're also a *sus-magiz*. Are you addicted to drinking lives, like ...?' She checked over her shoulder, lowered her voice. 'Like your evil magiz.'

'No!' Perhaps because he was so weak and vulnerable, he craved her good opinion.

'You have never drunk a life?' she said sceptically.

'I had to,' he whispered. 'Pass the test ... you become sus-magiz. Fail – you die.'

Why was he being so indiscreet? No slave should know such secrets.

'You're burning up.' She took the cloth out to cool again. Skald lay there, pain jagging through him, and felt sure he was dying.

'Cold,' he said. 'Very cold.'

Uletta came back and ran her hands through the fur on his chest, raising goose pimples all over him. She fastened his shirt, sat him up and went to put her coat around his shoulders, but it wasn't wide enough. She got his own coat from a hook and put it on him. 'Better?'

'Yes.'

'I'll help you to your tent.'

'No!' he cried.

'Why not?'

'You're a slave.'

'Good of you to remind me.'

'It would undermine us both. Me for needing help, you for helping an enemy. And it might cause the magiz to notice you, Uletta.' A thrill surged through him as he said her name. Slaves were either addressed by their job title, if they were important, or as, 'Slave!' if they were not. 'You do not want the magiz to notice you.'

She trembled. 'He might drink *my* life.'

Skald closed his eyes. The thought was awful.

'*I* could never care for a man who drank lives,' she said softly.

He did not know what to make of that. 'I feel a little better. Show me the designs for the stone carving and engraving, and the great crystal wall mosaics.'

It was well past midnight when they finished. Skald did not thank her, for that was not the Merdrun way. He nodded and withdrew to a late dinner, a quick bathe, and bed. As Superintendent of Works he had his own tent in the officers' camp, which was hard to get used to. In his childhood he had slept in a dormitory. Once he became a soldier, and even a sus-magiz, he had bunked in the barracks with everyone else. Having his own space felt wrong.

There was still work to do, but if he drove himself too hard he would collapse and Durthix would replace him. Then, because Skald knew too much, he would be killed.

He blew out the lamp, collapsed on his camp stretcher and lay in the dark, raking through the astounding events of the day. How had he, a lowly captain and sus-magiz who had failed to complete his last mission, ended up as Superintendent of Works, responsible for driving thousands of workers and tens of thousands of slaves to do the impossible? It did not seem real.

And Uletta liked and admired him, but why did she seem familiar?

What did it matter? She was a slave and an enemy. It had been a pleasant few hours, though. He was looking forward to seeing her again tomorrow.

But when tomorrow came, and the day after, it was impossible to get back to the design tent. There were too many supervisors to cajole or threaten, too many documents to read and understand and act on, and too many frustrations. Skald could no longer succeed or fail based on his own strength, quick thinking and iron determination – he depended on thousands of others, competent and incompetent, and on gaining enough magical power to get the work done in time.

But no more power could be taken from the field, and by the end of each sixteen-hour day he was screaming with frustration. Every day the work fell further behind, and the time could not be made up. He was going to fail and let his people down. His oath, sworn by the sacred Founder's Stone, would be null, a disgrace so enormous that he would have to commit public suicide, and his name would stand, on the Tablet of Infamy, four steps higher than his father's.

There came a tiny *pop*, and air whispered across his face – *warm air*. Skald sat up, frowning. It had felt like a gate opening, though there was no evidence for one.

'My name is Maigraith,' said a woman's voice, quietly. 'You may know of me as the Numinator, though I no longer go by that name. You have a problem that you can't possibly solve by Founder's Day.'

Skald stiffened. He knew who she was, and her reputation. What could she want from him? 'How can you know such deadly secrets?' he whispered.

'Irrelevant. I'm the one person in the world who can help you.'

'I will never betray my people.'

'I wouldn't ask you too.'

'Then what – what's the price?'

'One you will be happy to pay.'

49

HE'S NOT THE MAN HE WAS

'Where are you?' Skald whispered. If Durthix discovered he was secretly talking to one of their greatest enemies, he would be executed on the spot.

'Far away,' said Maigraith. 'I'm using an untraceable spy portal, which I invented. Any attack you make through it will rebound on you.'

What could she want with him? And what if Dagog found out? He was always sneaking around, listening at tent flaps. Looking for his next life to drink.

'You are aware that Rulke, who has come back from the dead, was once my consort?' she said.

'Yes.'

'And that he dwells in Alcifer, with a coarse, grasping trollop named Lirriam.'

'His bed partners are of no interest to me.'

'They are to me!' Maigraith's control slipped a little; her voice rang out. 'Rulke and I swore to each other, forever.'

Skald saw where this was going and could not have cared less. 'Go away and don't come back. I need my sleep.'

'Not as much as you need to complete your work in time for the Day of All Days.'

He choked. How did she know about that?

'If you succeed, it will make you. And you crave success, don't you, Skald? You're desperate to prove that you're not like your cowardly father.'

Skald's short hair rose on his head. How could *she* know what drove him so desperately?

'I am not prone to hyperbole,' Maigraith added.

'What's the offer?'

'Rulke out of the war.'

His heart lurched. Rulke was the Merdrun's greatest fear, for he had twice defeated them in the distant past and they were still scarred by those defeats.

'How?'

'I can show you a secret way into Alcifer, known only to me.'

'To what purpose?'

'To capture his strumpet and use her as a bargaining chip to keep him out of the war.'

'Why would we want that?'

'You're starved for magical power, and if Rulke joined with Flydd and fought against you, the cost in power would be more than you could sustain. But the poor, blind fool cares about the trollop and, to ensure her safety, Rulke will agree to not fight on the side of Santhenar.'

'The Rulke we knew of old would never agree to blackmail.'

Maigraith seemed to hesitate, as if unsure how much to tell Skald. 'The wound that nearly killed him has changed him. He's ... not the man he was.'

'Yet you still want him?'

'We swore!'

'This can never work. He'll swear bloody revenge. He'll try to rescue Lirriam.'

'He won't dare.'

'Why not?'

'He's emotionally scarred.'

Emotionally! Skald squirmed. 'How so?'

'Long ago he was deeply in love, and his betrothed was used to trap him. He tried to rescue her but failed and she was put to a cruel death; he was sent to the uncanny prison of the Nightland, where he remained for a thousand years. He won't try that again. Think about it. I'll contact you soon.'

She was gone. Skald's instincts were to report her offer, but if he did the matter would be taken out of his hands. Would Maigraith really betray Santhenar and work on the side of the Merdrun? He doubted it. And yet, from Flydd's *Histories* he knew how obsessive she was. In a jealous rage she might well hatch a plan to rid herself of her rival. But could she be trusted?

What did he have to lose?

Everything, if Dagog discovered he was having secret talks with the enemy.

Several days after the grim meeting in the ruins of the Governor's Palace, Flydd, Nish, Maelys and Karan boarded the sky galleon. Clech was staying behind to help Persia collect a small war chest, and locate those useful people who had survived. Flydd planned to pick them up on the way back.

The sky galleon headed due west for the long flight across the Sea of Perion to Nixzy, the principal city of those Aachim who had not yet gone home.

'Though I'm damned if I know what to say to Issilis when we get there,' said Flydd.

Having lived with the Aachim for years after her father was killed, Karan held little hope of getting aid from them. They had always been isolationist, backward-looking and slow to make decisions in a crisis. Why would now be different?

Flydd had locked the controls and was sitting at his table, using a yard-square mica sheet as a power patterner, to visualise how and where power was being drawn from the field. A variety of yellow pinpoints of light were dotted across the square, as well as several larger yellow patches.

'The power patterner only sees medium and large power draws,' he said to Nish. 'But it may indicate that the enemy are up to something we don't know about. See the bright, blurry glow at Skyrock?'

Nish did not reply. He was staring at the far side of the sheet, a good three feet away, where there was a circular, dark yellow glow.

'Is that –?' he said.

'Alcifer,' Flydd said absently. He started and leaned across to look down at the little bright circle. 'Why is Rulke using so much power?'

'Alcifer's a big place.'

'It's never lit up like that before. Something must have changed.'

'Maybe's he's finally recovered.'

'But ... he must be using half as much power as the enemy are at Skyrock.'

'He's afraid they'll attack; he's readying Alcifer's defences.'

'Or hiding like a terrified hermit crab,' sneered Flydd.

Karan saw her chance. 'What if Rulke's preparing to leave? No one knows what uncanny weapons he's got there.'

'Why would he leave?' said Flydd, studying the strawberry-shaped glow at

Skyrock through an eyeglass.

'He's the last of the Charon!'

'So?'

'The others went back to the void where they came from, *to die*. What if he plans to abandon Santh and join them?'

'It fits,' Flydd mused. 'There's nothing to keep him here now. Why would he stay?'

'If he abandons Alcifer, and all its secrets and weapons fall into the hands of the enemy –'

'I know what you're trying to do, Karan.'

'Doesn't mean she isn't right,' said Nish. 'Given how little hope we have of getting help from the Aachim, we'd be fools to ignore Rulke.'

Flydd sat for a moment, staring into nowhere, then thrust the mica sheet aside and ran to the controls. 'Twenty-eight days gone. Thirty-six remain, if we don't count the day they put their plan into effect. Alcifer it is – and let's hope it isn't a trap.'

Skald's heart grew more leaden every day. Failure was never mentioned, yet it was clear that Durthix and his senior generals were losing hope that the True Purpose could be achieved. Dare he tell them about Maigraith's offer? Skald wasn't sure he would survive it.

But their need for power was now so desperate that he had no choice. Three days after Maigraith first spoke to him he went to General Chaxee in the command tent, and was shocked to see that she wasn't on her feet. She was slumped on a canvas chair, rubbing the stump of her missing arm and talking to Senior Sus-magiz Pannilie.

Skald, quaking inside, reported that his work could not be done in time.

'We *will not* speak of failure,' said Chaxee. 'The tower and portal tunnel must be ready.'

'With respect, General, it's impossible. We don't, won't, *can't* have enough power.'

'Why not?'

'The closer the miners get to the node, the rottener the rock becomes, and that makes far more work: much bigger tunnels are required, three times as much rock must be hauled out of the way, and more timber framing is needed to stop the roof from falling in. Besides, the miners can only work for an hour at a time, so close to the node. It's eating them away, as it eats the rock away.'

'Send in more miners.'

'There isn't room for them to work.'

'I should have you executed for incompetence, Superintendent, and put someone in charge who can get it done.'

'Perhaps you should,' said Skald, and meant it. Things were that bad.

'We tried and we failed, General,' said Pannilie, tearing a long strip of pink, scaly skin off her arm. 'Durthix must be told that none of us, nor generations of Merdrun for centuries to come, are going home.'

Chaxee's broad face crumpled, but she was not a senior general for nothing. 'Very well.' She heaved herself to her feet, one-handed.

'But there may be another way to get power,' said Skald.

'How?' she said dully.

'If you will come with me to Durthix and Dagog, I'll put it to everyone.'

Neither man looked pleased to see them. 'I gave instructions that there were to be no interruptions,' said Durthix, who looked worn out and discouraged.

'Skald thinks there may be a way to gain the power we need,' said Pannilie.

'If Skald had done his job we wouldn't be in this mess,' said the magiz.

Skald had to be bold and confident, otherwise Durthix would send him away. 'We were in this mess before I was asked to do the job, Magiz. But if you'll hear me, High Commander, there might be a solution.'

Durthix directed a soul-crushing glare at him. 'Five minutes. Not a second more.'

'Three nights ago, I was contacted, via an undetectable spy portal, by Maigraith, the former –'

'We know who Maigraith is,' growled Durthix.

'And you did not report this, you treasonous dog,' hissed Dagog. 'I've drunk lives for less, Sus-magiz.'

You've drunk lives for the sheer joy of killing a defenceless human being, you swine! Skald thought.

'I'm reporting it now.' He had to be quick or he'd lose the chance, and probably his life as well. 'Maigraith, embittered that Rulke broke his promise to her and has, apparently, taken a much younger lover, Lirriam –'

'Who is this woman?' said Durthix.

'Just a bed partner, but Maigraith wants her gone and has made me an offer.'

'Go on,' said Durthix in a dangerous voice.

Skald swallowed. 'She knows a secret way into Alcifer. She will gate me there, and anyone else I need, to seize Lirriam and carry her away to captivity, as a bargaining chip to keep Rulke from entering the war on the side of humanity.'

Durthix sat up at that, and so did General Chaxee. 'If Maigraith knows so much, I wonder she doesn't do the job herself.'

'If Rulke discovered she was trying to get rid of his lover it would destroy her hope of getting him back.'

'True,' said Durthix. 'And having Rulke neutralised would greatly relieve us. But how do we know Maigraith can be trusted?'

Skald reminded them about her well-known obsessiveness and presented the arguments she had given.

Durthix rubbed the thick black stubble on his chin. It sounded like leather being sandpapered. 'Far-fetched ... yet appealing.'

'It's too risky,' said the magiz, scowling.

'The risk is mainly to Skald and his squad,' said Durthix, 'And the reward is a great one: it could allow us to fulfil the True Purpose after all.'

'If we were to carry out this sortie and it failed, as is overwhelmingly probable, we would have made an enemy of a neutral.'

'Rulke has never been neutral. Charon and Merdrun have been enemies ever since Stermin forced us to choose at the Gates of Good and Evil. He's just biding his time, waiting to strike.'

'In any case,' said Dagog, 'Skald is still as weak as an *old human*. He can't lead a squad on such a desperate enterprise.'

Skald wasn't giving this chance up. 'Maigraith made the offer to me,' he said quickly. 'She will only make a portal available, and reveal the secret way in, *to me*.' This wasn't true, but it might have been.

'Why would she specify *you*?' snarled the magiz.

'Apparently I remind her of Rulke. In looks, and in daring.'

The magiz's stinking, brown-stained fingers clamped around an imaginary throat.

'Besides, I have an idea,' said Skald, 'that could tilt the balance from risk to reward ...'

Durthix's eyebrows rose. He rubbed his chin again and signed to Skald to continue.

'General Chaxee believes Alcifer contains a Source, independent of nodes and fields. If we could steal it –'

'Must we listen to the ravings of this disordered mind?' exploded Dagog.

'Enough of your negativity, Magiz!' snapped Durthix. 'Superintendent, how would you find this great Source in so vast a place?'

'When Maigraith made her offer, I said neither yea nor nay. I had no authority. Neither did I state our price for undertaking so risky an endeavour on her behalf. But if you agree, High Commander, the price I would ask of Maigraith is the Source itself – where it lies and how it can be taken.'

Durthix let out his breath in a great gust of air. He leaned back in his chair, folded his arms across his chest and studied Skald, thoughtfully. 'What do you say to that, Magiz?'

The magiz wanted to tear the idea down. Skald could see the battle raging in him.

But he surprised. 'As much as any Merdrun, I want our True Purpose to be fulfilled. If this mad scheme offers hope of completing tower and tunnel in time, and powering the secret devices to be installed therein, then I say yes. The risk, as my *most junior* sus-magiz points out, is more than balanced by the reward.'

'I say so too,' said Durthix. 'Skald, you may negotiate with Maigraith. If she agrees, what will you need? I'm mindful that you're too weak to fight or use powerful Arts.'

'Ten soldiers and a sus-magiz,' said Skald, who had already thought it through. 'And a senior sus-magiz with a field scanner capable of locating the Source – in case Maigraith tries a double-cross.'

'That all?' grunted Dagog. 'I can hardly spare a junior sus-magiz.'

'Plus a highly accomplished artisan, experienced in the making, use and repair of devices that draw on the field.'

'Why?'

'To safely remove this mighty and perilous Source. The mechanician, M'Lainte, would be ideal.'

'Not a chance!' Dagog's voice rose. 'High Commander, I cannot spare her.'

'M'Lainte is required elsewhere,' said Durthix. 'Name another, Superintendent.'

'The former geomancer, Tiaan,' said Skald. She was the only other artisan whose name he remembered from Flydd's *Histories*. 'She created the first thapter, and she's known to be sound in a crisis.'

'All right,' Dagog said grudgingly. 'When will you speak to Maigraith?'

'She usually contacts me after midnight. If she does, I'll try –'

'Don't try,' said Durthix. '*Succeed!* Your squad will be made ready. If Maigraith agrees, you can be gated to her within the hour.'

50

ANOTHER WEAKNESS IN HIS PLAN

To Skald's surprise, Maigraith agreed to his terms. 'You may have the Source, if you can find it. I know nothing about it. But ...'

'You have a price,' said Skald.

'Always. Rulke must not be harmed. I'll make sure he's out of the way.'

Skald hid his relief. Taking Rulke on could not end well.

'Is your squad ready?' she asked.

'They're outside.'

'Call them in.'

'A gate is being prepared. What's the precise destination?'

'I will make the gate.'

Skald had not expected this. What if Maigraith was in league with Rulke and planning to attack Skyrock through the gate? How could he tell? He could not read her.

If she was, Skald would soon be dead. He called his team in: Pannilie, nine soldiers and a sergeant, then Tiaan, who was gagged and had her wrists bound, and Ghiv, the junior sus-magiz. The tent was cramped with fourteen people in it, and Pannilie was not happy.

'This isn't the plan, Skald,' she hissed.

'Maigraith gave me no choice.'

'She can't be trusted. I'm calling it off.'

'No, I'm leader!'

'Dagog instructed me to take charge if I deemed it necessary. And I do.'

Skald hesitated. This was undermining his self-confidence and his authority, and any argument with her could only make it worse. They didn't trust him.

But as Pannilie turned to go out, Maigraith's little voice portal transformed into a gate and he was jerked into it. Pain stabbed through his middle, he took a double blow to the head as if someone had slammed their palms against his ears, and he was disgorged into a circular pavilion in a dusty park, surrounded by crumbling stone buildings in what he assumed to be the abandoned city of Thurkad. Pannilie came through backwards, slammed into him and lost her footing, and the rest of the squad landed on top of them.

The guards sprang up and assumed defensive positions, facing out, blades at the ready. Pannilie rose slowly, holding her left wrist, which was starting to swell.

Maigraith stood by the pavilion. A stringy woman, a foot shorter than Skald and not half his weight, yet she was one of the most powerful people on Santhenar. He began on introductions, but she said abruptly, 'Names are unnecessary.'

She was staring at him. Was she thinking about Rulke, and the subtle ways that Skald resembled him?

'You look bigger in the flesh,' she said quietly.

The left side of her face might have been carved from stone, for it was quite rigid, and the tip of her nose drooped, crone-like. How could *she* imagine that she could get Rulke back?

She nodded to Tiaan. Skald supposed that they had met before. Tiaan appeared to have lost a lot of weight recently. Most of the slaves had. Mid-thirties, but with streaks of grey in her ragged dark hair. A determined jut to her neat jaw was contradicted by the desolate look in her eyes. No wonder – she had three children, the youngest only five, and had been abducted in front of them.

Doubtless she feared for her children, and that she would never see them again. While drinking Tataste's life, and afterwards, Skald had lived such emotions. He relived them almost every night now.

Pannilie stalked past Skald and caught Maigraith by the arm. 'This is not the plan.'

A bright yellow nimbus formed around Maigraith and Pannilie was hurled backwards, off her feet.

'I deal only with Skald,' Maigraith said arrogantly. 'Touch me again and you die.'

Skald caught his breath. Pannilie was a powerful sus-magiz and not used to being treated with contempt. Could she accept it from an enemy, an inferior? She rose slowly, flexing her fingers. Surely she did not think to take Maigraith on? Or was that the magiz's real plan?

Skald caught Pannilie's eye and shook his head. She fought inner demons, then her face set hard and she turned away, picking at the scab on her lower lip.

'This way,' said Maigraith indifferently. 'The route is complex and you will be in darkness.'

She led them to a small stone table on which a number of maps were held down by an fist-sized geode, one side broken open to reveal purple crystals inside. Skald quickly committed the maps to memory. It was part of the training of every Merdrun officer and he was good at it.

Maigraith created her gate and it opened whisper-quiet; no boom, no popping, no discharges of lightning or gush of air. No Merdrun could have done it.

'Go in,' she said. 'The gate takes you to the secret entrance. Once there, be quick to your destination. I've lured Rulke out of your way, but ... no one can master him.'

'And when we're done?' said Skald.

'Return to the secret entrance *with Lirriam*, and the Source if you find it, and the gate will bring you back here.'

But would it? He needed to trust her, just as she needed to trust him. She could not risk Rulke seeing her. But could he trust her once she had Lirriam? He doubted it. He had to be ready for a double-cross, though he could not imagine what he would do if it happened.

Skald took hold of Tiaan's bound wrists and led them through the gate, which opened in the dark next to a yard-high drainage outlet. A cast iron cap, almost rusted through, lay to one side. He bent his head and went into Alcifer.

The dark was as pitch, though from faint echoes made by their footsteps he sensed a large space. The air was stale. He dared not use a glowglobe or any form of the Art to make light here. If Rulke detected them the mission must fail.

Tiaan gave off waves of terror, the slave's lot. Her life was utterly dependent on his whim, and this was a very dangerous mission. They might all die here.

Skald recalled the first map to mind and located himself on it. 'Take hold, squad.'

Behind him, as Senior Sus-magiz Pannilie caught hold of his belt, Skald sensed her fury and frustration. Did she think they were being led into a trap?

Was she right? Her experience could not be ignored, but neither could they back out. If they returned without Lirriam, he did not think Maigraith's gate would open, and Alcifer's defences would not allow any Merdrun to make a gate here.

The soldier behind Pannilie caught her belt and so on, down the line. Pannilie had the field scanner in her pack and would use it to locate the Source as soon as Lirriam was taken.

Skald took Tiaan's slender wrist with his left hand. She did not resist; she would have seen slaves killed for the slightest of reasons, or no reason at all. She whimpered; he was hurting her. He loosened his grip and moved forwards in the dark, free hand extended. The rest of his superbly trained squad matched him step for step.

Maigraith's route maps had shown the location of stairs and other key features, and the size and shape of rooms and passages, but not their function. Skald knew where they were but had no idea what each part of Alcifer was for.

Their soft soles made no sound as they moved across the large empty room, along a narrow passage with a high ceiling, through a metal door that stood open, and up fourteen steps.

Skald stopped at the top and everyone stopped with him. They were in the citadel of the Merdrun's greatest enemy and there could be unseen defences anywhere. Unseen pits and traps, guard beasts, spells that could be set off at a touch, mechanisms to sever or crush or impale, poisons released from the walls.

Pain touched him in the belly, low down, a warning not to do too much. He wasn't a warrior anymore; he did not have the strength for it. It was hard to accept.

'Anything, Pannilie?' he said softly. She was highly adept at sensing the aura of mancery.

'Nothing,' she said curtly.

Sweat ran down his nose. She was a danger too. Did her secret orders allow her to cut him down if things went wrong? That would be just like the magiz.

Ahead, faint light came in through a small, rectangular window. Skald looked out and saw clusters of slender towers, red or black, in groups of three and seven and nine. Some were hundreds of feet high, others only a couple of levels.

Beyond, starlight silvered a series of domes, the largest hundreds of yards across. Sweeping aerial walkways ran from one cluster of towers to another, and to the domes. There were bowl-shaped lakes and perfectly laid out gardens that surely must have maintained themselves while Rulke was in stasis. Alcifer was a beautiful, terrible place, powered by unknown magics, and no Merdrun could have designed so much as an outhouse here.

Skald felt a shiver of fear. What would Rulke do to trespassers?

They continued. Until they found Lirriam, they would speak as little as possible. Rulke might have sensing devices or protective wards, and servants and guards.

The first task was to follow the route to Lirriam's quarters, where Skald hoped to find her asleep. Pannilie would cast a paralysis on her, then bind and gag her. The guards would watch over Lirriam while Skald and Pannilie located and secured the Source, and then they would race back to the gate.

A simple plan but it could go wrong in so many ways, Rulke being the most obvious. If he detected them, or realised that he had been lured away, the mission must fail.

Skald would have liked to gate the Source directly to Skyrock, but only Rulke could make gates inside Alcifer and, the moment they emerged from the secret entrance, Maigraith's gate would take them back to Thurkad. It was her means of ensuring there was no double-cross. And of getting her hands on her rival.

The mission could also fail if Lirriam and Rulke were together. Maigraith was sure they were lovers and it was likely to be true – after so long under the stasis spell, a lusty man like Rulke would have a lot to make up.

Taking a Source through a gate might also be dangerous. Had the magiz considered that? Perhaps he thought it was worth the risk.

They were creeping along a tube-like passage now, so low that Skald, the soldiers and the tall junior sus-magiz had to bend their heads. The oily smell was stronger here and he wondered what mechanisms this incredible city held. It had been designed for Rulke in ancient times by the incomparable Aachim architect, Pitlis, and it was utterly unique.

Skald wished he could see more of it, because Merdrun were not great builders. Their main structures were cramped communal houses, on the barren rock that was their home world, and temporary fortresses elsewhere.

As they exited the passage his belly throbbed, more strongly than last time. In the olden days he had ignored pain; now it indicated trouble ahead. And he was already tiring. The warrior who had raced miles up the mountainside from the Sink of Despair a few weeks ago, and felt only exhilaration, was gone forever. Was he falling as quickly as he had risen?

There was still a long way to go: five more passages totalling half a mile in length, and hundreds of feet of stairs. They had entered at the lowest point in Alcifer, and according to Maigraith's maps Rulke's living and working quarters were mostly high up.

On they went, and on. Every so often the pain hacked at Skald's belly, worse each time, and his legs were weakening. He wasn't far from the point where he would have to will himself to take each step.

He stopped and everyone stopped with him. Tiaan gave a little cry and he let go of her wrist; he had been crushing it again. Her terror washed over him in waves.

He wished it had not been necessary to bring her, a slave who must hate him and all Merdrun. She was another weakness in his plan, but no Merdrun knew powered mechanisms the way she did, and he needed her to safely remove the Source.

Would she? He had made it clear that her life depended on doing it faithfully; it was her only hope of seeing her children again. But what if she did not believe him?

Tiaan, he knew from Flydd's *Histories*, was clever, creative and unpredictable. At the end of the Lyrinx War, in despair at the ruin wrought by powered magical devices, she had destroyed all the nodes, and the fields with them. But her self-less act had backfired, gifting Santhenar to a monster, Jal-Nish Hlar, who with the power of his sorcerous Tears had become the invincible God-Emperor.

If Tiaan thought she would be put to death once she was no longer needed, she might do anything. Another thing to worry about.

Skald stopped at a closed door. 'We're close. Take a minute.'

Behind him, he heard tiny movements in the darkness as the twelve Merdrun shifted their weight, scratched itches or made sure weapons were to hand. He closed his eyes. Even in pitch darkness it helped him to visualise his location: on Maigraith's third map now, in the uppermost levels of the centre of Alcifer. He oriented himself and mentally traced the route she had marked to Lirriam's room.

'We go.'

He eased the door open and they passed through into a hall, dimly lit by starlight filtering through high windows. He paused so everyone's night sight could adjust, then went on, around a corner, and something hard struck him in the chest. A man, hurrying the other way, carrying a large jug.

He let out a shocked cry and dropped the jug, which spilled icy water down

Skald's front and shattered between his boots. Skald tried to grab the fellow but was too slow, too weak. The man threw himself backwards and ran.

Pannilie cursed and tried to get past, but with Skald and Tiaan blocking the narrow passage there wasn't room. She shook a glowstick to light.

The man roared, 'Rulke! Enemy intruders!' and darted around the corner.

51

PUT A KNIFE TO HER THROAT

Pannilie blasted a paralysis spell at the running man but only caught his lower left leg. Skald heard him stumble, then hop away, roaring, 'Rulke, Lirriam, intruders! Rulke, come quickly!'

Pannilie knocked Tiaan aside, ran to the corner and blasted along the dark corridor.

'Get him?' said Skald.

She turned and her contempt burned him. 'Why didn't you grab the oaf? If he's roused Rulke, we fail!' She ran and the soldiers raced after her.

The least of Skald's troops would have taken the man down in a second. Shamed, he grabbed Tiaan's wrist. She resisted; the man's escape must have given her hope.

'Come!' he hissed, and yanked her arm.

She let out a small cry and lowered her head in submission. He dragged her after Pannilie and, a minute later, where the corridor ended in a T-junction with another corridor, saw Pannilie outside the door Maigraith had identified as Lirriam's. Pannilie blasted the heavy metal door off its hinges, driving it halfway across the room, *thud*. A cry and the sound of someone falling.

'Secure Lirriam!' she snapped. 'Troops, guard the corridors.'

The sergeant lifted the door away. Lirriam, who was naked and must have risen from her bed, was unconscious on the floor with an oval bruise rising on her forehead and a trickle of blood coming from her left nostril. The nine soldiers took up their positions, well back along the corridors. Skald went in. The square, plain room was empty apart from a bed and a side table with a unlit lamp.

He studied the woman in Pannilie's light and caught his breath. Lirriam's hair was astounding, unique, impossible, for it shimmered in reds and blues, greens and blacks, ever-changing as if it were made from strands of precious black opal. Her fingernails and toenails were also opaline, glistening, extraordinary. He had never seen anyone like her. Where had she come from?

It did not matter; she was a soft, curvaceous woman, with neat, symmetrical features and small feet and hands, and therefore no threat. Merdrun beauty was founded in size and strength, and her delicate looks, creamy skin and modest stature were signs of weakness.

What does Rulke see in her? he thought contemptuously. She belongs in one of the enemy's salons, chattering inanely to others as superficial as herself.

A silver chain hung around her neck. Her right arm was broken above the wrist and the slender bones had torn through her skin.

'Should we do a temporary healing?' said Skald.

'The broken arm will make her easy to control,' said Pannilie, who was studying Lirriam thoughtfully. 'If Rulke heard the outcry earlier, he'll be on his way.'

And they would fail! 'What do we do?'

'I can't take him on face-to-face. But if he doesn't know I'm here, I might strike him down from concealment …'

'Yes!' said Skald. 'Go, hide!'

Pannilie handed him the light, and a ring with a chunky red jewel embedded in it. 'When you want me to attack, rotate the jewel half a turn anti-clockwise.' She gave the field scanner case to Sus-magiz Ghiv and slipped away.

Skald cut Tiaan's bonds. 'Dress her.'

He lifted Lirriam to a sitting position. Her skin was silky and soft but, underneath, the muscles were as hard as his own, and she bore a number of scars, evidence of old wounds. He sat back on his haunches. She was not what she seemed.

Tiaan pulled a loose red blouse on Lirriam, taking care with her broken arm, and did up the fastenings, a line of triangular ebony toggles that curved from her left shoulder to the right side of her waist. She drew blue, knee-length pants up Lirriam's legs. She moaned and her eyelids fluttered.

'Put a knife to her throat,' Skald said to the sergeant. 'If Rulke comes the threat must be immediate – *but under no circumstances will you harm her.*'

The sergeant repeated the order and drew a foot-long knife. Skald said to Ghiv, 'Use the field scanner. Find the Source.'

Ghiv slipped away.

Skald sent three soldiers down each corridor to keep watch, and the remaining three down the long arm of the T-junction, then paced outside Lirriam's doorway. Everything depended on Rulke now. If he had been alerted, they would probably die here and the mission would fail.

On active duty in the past, Skald had rarely felt fear. Going into combat, where the stakes were life and death, and his size, strength and superb training gave him the advantage, had exhilarated him. But he knew what would happen if he had to pit his useless body against the greatest warrior of all.

Rulke would annihilate him.

A muscle spasmed over Skald's right eye, and again. His knees were wobbly, and it was hard to draw enough breath. He was afraid! Not afraid of dying, never that. Afraid of breaking in battle and running like a coward. Afraid that his mother would be proved right about him. He stiffened his courage, as he had been doing since he was a little boy.

I am not my father! If I have to face Rulke, if I must die, I will die bravely, doing my duty.

The mantra made him feel better, but he had to survive. The True Purpose rested on him getting the Source back to Skyrock. He had to find a way.

Without warning, with no sign at all, Rulke materialised next to Skald. He choked and took an involuntary step backwards. Now, *now* he was afraid.

Rulke was barefoot and wore only a robe belted at the waist, gaping to reveal a broad, muscular chest and a long, ropy purple scar across his belly and side. Another, faded scar ran almost parallel. He did not appear to be armed.

He was the biggest man Skald had ever seen, topping his own height by half a head, and his shoulders were a handspan wider. Rulke was more than four thousand years old; he had defeated most of the enemies he had ever faced and outlasted all of them; and he was probably the greatest living mancer on Santhenar. Skald could never have been his match.

Rulke raised his right hand and pale blue lights brightened along the ceilings of each corridor, reflecting off the drawn blades of Skald's troops.

'Stay!' said Rulke, and they went still.

Paralysed, Skald thought, *or petrified.* Everything depended on Pannilie now.

Pain tore through his belly, worse than before, but he had to try and take the initiative. 'We have Lirriam.'

'How did you get in?' said Rulke mildly.

'A secret entrance.'

Skald studied him in the bright light. The healed wound still restricted Rulke and he moved so as to favour that side. Was that why he had not come to Santhenar's aid?

Rulke's gaze settled on Tiaan. He gestured at her and the gag fell away. 'Who are you?'

She looked him in the eye. 'The mother of three children, the youngest five years old.'

'That's not why you're here. What is your name?'

'Tiaan Liise-Mar,' she said reluctantly.

'Tiaan?' he said, as if riffling through the names of hundreds of people he'd read about recently. 'The great artisan and geomancer. The destroyer of nodes and fields.'

'I was sick of the ruin of war,' she said quietly. 'I wanted an end to it.'

'There is no end to war. It's part of the sad human condition.'

'I was young and stupid,' she cried. 'I've a far more important purpose in life now.'

'What greater purpose can anyone have,' said Rulke, 'than to protect their children? I have not fathered many, and all are dead. It makes me a failure.' He looked down at Skald. 'Name?'

Skald told himself that he was in charge here, though it did not feel that way. 'Captain Skald Hulni. I am also a sus-magiz.'

'Never heard of you. What do you want?'

'In exchange for Lirriam's safety,' said Skald, 'I want the Source.'

'You're overly bold for a midget.'

Skald was a big man by any standards, but he must not let himself be provoked. He waited.

'What makes you think Lirriam matters that much to me?' said Rulke. He glanced towards her doorway.

He could not see her from where he stood, for which Skald was thankful. Whether Rulke cared about her or not, in Alcifer she was under his protection.

'If you're wrong,' Rulke added, 'every one of you is dead. You do know that?'

Skald did but he was determined not to show it. This was as much a battle of wits and wills as it was a battle of strength. 'If we were wrong,' he said, 'and you were capable of it, you would have killed us already.'

'Only a fool, or a callow captain on his first mission, imagines he knows what his enemy is thinking. I could take days killing you, *Captain Sus-magiz* Skald. Weeks! There's nothing I don't know about death. I've looked back on it from the other side.'

52

GET MY POTION MADE

Late on the thirtieth day after the invasion began, the sky galleon raced through the vast pall of smoke above Booreah Ngurle, the Burning Mountain, then skirted Worm Wood not long after dark. Before midnight it was whispering over the dry plains and hills of Rencid.

Flydd had flown almost non-stop for two days and nights, yet he looked brighter and more determined than when they had left Roros, and there was no sign that he was affected by aftersickness. What a remarkable man he was. Karan had done nothing the whole time, yet she was exhausted.

'Only fifty leagues to go,' he said, yawning and rubbing his eyes. 'But what am I to say to Rulke? What appeal will move him?'

His lips moved as if he were rehearsing a speech. He shook his head, thought for a while then rehearsed another, which appeared to satisfy him no better than the first.

Karan did not try to sleep; she knew it would be fruitless. Within hours she and Llian might be reunited – assuming she could prevail on Rulke to let him go. What would *she* say to Rulke? And to Llian, after all she had done to him? What a bitch she was! What had he ever seen in her?

Everything had to change now. She would go to him humbly and beg his forgiveness.

But would he forgive? Could he?

Being a great chronicler and teller, as well as a legend from the past, Llian would be very attractive to the opposite sex – look how Thandiwe had pursued him. If he'd had enough, there would be a myriad of younger, kinder, better women to choose from. Women who would not keep him at a distance, forever put him down and keep terrible secrets from him.

Karan wanted to tear her hair out. And even it was failing her. Her magnificent, fire-red hair had always been her crowning glory, but yesterday she had discovered several grey threads there.

~

Aviel already regretted saving Maigraith's life, because her *much better idea* involved conspiring with an enemy, Skald, via a spy gate. Aviel knew his name because she had seen an enemy propaganda poster about him on Maigraith's table, and the conspiracy had to be about getting rid of Lirriam.

And it was partly Aviel's fault. If she had let Maigraith die, an innocent woman would not be in mortal danger.

When Maigraith's door opened and closed after midnight Aviel followed her, down the empty streets to a dusty park scattered with weeds and pocked with smelly ferret burrows. Two avenues of trees had once intersected at a round pavilion in the centre of the park, but many had died and had been cut down for firewood.

Even in daylight the park was a depressing place. It was a few nights after the full moon, half of whose dark face was now showing, and a dry wind hissed through the treetops and rattled the dead twigs like finger bones. Nothing good could come of such a night.

Maigraith went to a small stone table in the pavilion, the wind whipping her greying hair about her hollow cheeks. She stroked the outside of an egg-shaped geode and spoke, too quietly for Aviel to hear.

Maigraith slipped three fingers into the geode and a small, subtle gate formed in front of her. It was misty and Aviel could not see what was on the other side. Nothing happened for twenty heartbeats, then a big Merdrun was ejected from the gate. Skald, and he did not look well. A female sus-magiz was hurled out next, backwards. She slammed into Skald, bringing him down, and a file of soldiers in leather armour landed on top of them. A woman in slave's rags and a junior sus-magiz, a tall man with butterfly ears and big, startled black eyes, completed the party.

Maigraith closed the gate. The soldiers stood guard outside the pavilion, facing out, their faces a ruddy brown in the eerie moonlight. Maigraith spoke quietly to Skald and the senior sus-magiz, then led them to the table and laid down a number of maps. They fluttered in the wind.

Skald picked up the top map, stared at it as if memorising it and handed it to the senior sus-magiz, who did the same. Skald asked Maigraith a question; Aviel didn't catch it. Maigraith replied curtly and they walked back to the point where the gate had opened. The guards joined them. Maigraith created a new gate, smaller than the first, and they bent over and shuffled through. She went last.

Aviel was wondering if she dared follow, and thinking that she did not, when the gate closed. It did not disappear, though – its outline shimmered and twinkled in the air.

She scurried across to the table. The maps, held down with the geode, were drawn in purple ink and labelled in red in Maigraith's small, neat hand. They showed sections of a city, though it was nothing like any city Aviel had seen, full of towers and aerial walkways and paths that looped back on one another.

She was studying the lowest map when a bony, age-spotted hand caught her upper arm and squeezed. Maigraith had come back so quietly that the gate had not flared when it opened. It was gone now.

'Do you think I don't know you've been spying on me?' she said coldly.

Aviel gulped.

'It's lucky you haven't finished the rejuvenation potion, mouse. Well, go on, ask me.'

'What's this place?' Aviel looked down at the maps.

'Alcifer, what else would it be?'

'I don't understand why you're sending the enemy there.'

'You're not capable of understanding, you stupid little stickybeak. Hobble back to your workshop and get my potion made!'

Aviel went, but there was nothing she could do, since the next step had to be done precisely sixty-six hours after the previous one and there were still eight hours to go.

She unwrapped a chunk of cake she had baked in her workshop furnace and opened her grimoire, but could not concentrate. Was Maigraith a traitor? Presumably she was conspiring with the enemy to get rid of Lirriam, but what did the Merdrun get out of it?

There was no way of knowing, unless ... No! Aviel was not going to spy on Maigraith again. It was too risky. There was nothing she could do, anyway.

The over-baked cake looked like conglomerate rock and was just as hard. She mashed it to chunks in an agate mortar and pestle and picked at the crumbs, thinking. Maigraith did not trust anyone. She would follow Skald's troop, and Aviel could not let them destroy Lirriam.

She stuffed a handful of cake in a pocket, filled her water bottle, returned to the dusty park, hid behind a triple-trunked tree with black stripes across its pale bark, and waited, shivering, though it was a warm night. A quarter of an hour later Maigraith appeared, wearing a dagger on her left hip and a small pack on her back.

She recreated the gate and passed through, though this time it remained open, as if she might need to return in a hurry. Aviel hesitated. What could she possibly do, anyway? Nothing. There was no point. If she followed an armed troop of enemy, she would most likely be captured, tortured and killed.

Go back to bed. It's not your problem.

But Aviel could not stand by. She dug deep for her courage and followed, quaking with every step.

Maigraith entered Alcifer through a hidden opening that only appeared after she put her right palm on the wall in front of her, and made her way along dark passages using the faint glow of a tiny, covered globe. She had lived here for a long time, mourning her lover and steeping herself in the city he had loved, and needed no map to tell her where to go.

Aviel had to keep up; if she lost Maigraith, she would never find the way out. But before they had gone far her ankle was tormenting her, and she bitterly regretted being such a *stupid little stickybeak*. Too late now.

In a large open space, faintly lit by starlight through a translucent skylight, Maigraith pocketed the globe and settled down to wait. An oval opening in the floor allowed her to look down on the level below, though Aviel could not see anything from her own hiding place. Was Maigraith watching for the intruders, or for Rulke?

The minutes ground by. Why would the Merdrun care about Lirriam, when Rulke had shown no signs of intervening in the war? Or were they after *him*? He was their ancient enemy, after all.

But Maigraith would never allow them to take the man she loved. Was that the real reason she was here – to ensure his safety?

53

DARE HE RISK ALL TO GAIN ALL?

S kald's strength was waning, the forbidden emotions rising to undermine him. He fought them back. 'I too have looked back from the other side of death,' he said quietly. 'You don't scare me.'

'Ah, but I can.' Rulke turned and called, 'Llian!'

The man Skald had crashed into earlier came down the long corridor, struggling to walk straight. His left leg was still affected by Pannilie's paralysis spell.

'Thank you for the warning,' said Rulke.

'Not as useless as you think,' Llian said pointedly. 'You might remember that, when –'

'Don't push your luck. I can send you back to your prison as quick as blinking.' Rulke pointed at Llian's leg and he stood upright again. 'This Merdrun calls himself Skald Hulni. What do you know about him?'

'He's the junior officer who found Flydd's *Histories*.'

'That all?' said Rulke.

'All I know,' said Llian.

'Then get out of here. There's nothing you can do.'

Llian stared at him, then turned and walked into the darkness.

Tiaan took a deep breath. 'Skald captured M'Lainte near the Sink of Despair. And a secret weapon the scrutators lost long ago.'

Skald gaped at her. 'That's Top Secret.'

'What one slave hears,' she murmured, moving a little closer to Rulke, 'we all hear.'

'Anything else?' said Rulke.

'Skald almost succeeded in assassinating Flydd, who was trying to recover my old thapter near Ashmode. Skald drank part of his own life to get the power to escape.'

'What an enterprising little chap you are,' said Rulke to Skald. 'And you want me to give up the Source, an incomparable reservoir of power, in exchange for one single woman?'

Skald did not reply.

'What are your people building at Skyrock? And why in such desperate haste?'

'Who said anything we do is in haste?'

'You've spent the last ten thousand years honing your battle skills in place after place, against race after race. Any of the worldlets you attacked would have made a better home than the barren rock where your civilians have been hidden all this time, but they stayed where they were.'

The stabbing pains in Skald's belly spread. Rulke was too clever, and he saw far too far.

'Until a month ago,' Rulke continued, 'when you attacked Santhenar with your entire army, keeping nothing in reserve. You captured a few large cities and strategic places, only to abandon them two weeks later and take your army, and your civilians young and old, to live in hastily erected camps surrounding the great rock pinnacle at Skyrock, a place so high, cold and barren it could never support three hundred thousand Merdrun. And there's only reason to go there.'

'What?' croaked Skald. How much more did Rulke know?

'To tap the power of the Skyrock node, the greatest on Santhenar. Now you're cutting the pinnacle down and shaping it into a rather familiar tower, heedless of how many workers and slaves die in the process. Your people are engaged in the most desperate enterprise of their existence – *that's* why you need more power, and ever more. That's why you're here now, Skald.'

Skald swallowed. Did Rulke also know *why* they were doing it? He would do everything he could to thwart them.

Rulke glanced at the broken door, anxiously, and Skald realised that he actually cared about the woman with the opaline hair. Skald's stomach throbbed, more painfully than before.

'Lirriam had better be unharmed.' Rulke took a step towards Skald.

With an effort, he held his ground. 'When we blasted the door in, it struck her. She's not badly –'

Rulke backhanded Skald in the mouth, knocking him down. He sprang through the doorway and, in mid-air, blasted the sergeant, who fell dead as a stone. Rulke bent over Lirriam, speaking softly. Her eyelids fluttered but her eyes did not open.

Skald wiped blood off his mouth and controlled his fury. Backhanding a Merdrun officer was a mortal insult, as Rulke well knew. But if Skald attacked, Rulke would kill him.

Rulke whirled, jerked Skald in by the breastplate and dumped him on the floor, then beckoned to Tiaan. She came in, bright-eyed now. He heaved the sergeant's body out, forced the metal door back into its frame and used his thick fingers to smooth the metal so that it fused there, immovably.

Skald was at Rulke's mercy now and the entire mission rested on the edge of a blade. Was there anything he could do to save it?

'Hold her shoulders down,' Rulke said to Tiaan, and she did so.

He stroked Lirriam's opaline hair and she gave a little sigh. He stretched her right arm out, held her forearm above the break, took hold of her wrist and pulled slowly and steadily. Her lips drew back, baring her teeth, though she did not wake. The broken bones withdrew beneath the skin and the wrinkled flesh smoothed out.

He manipulated her arm this way and that for several minutes, then said, 'Hold it, here and here.'

Tiaan held Lirriam's forearm. Rulke clamped a hand around the breaks and subvocalised a healing charm. Skald sensed the aura from it and felt a wash of heat.

Rulke wrenched the side table apart and fashioned a splint from two flat lengths, which he bound together with strips torn from the bedcovers. He probed Lirriam's nose, which was not broken, wiped the blood away and examined her bruised foot and ankle. Though his back was turned, Skald knew Rulke was aware of his smallest movement, and he dared not attack.

'Put her boots on,' Rulke said to Tiaan.

When she had done so Rulke rose and, without any change of expression, backhanded Skald across the left cheek, knocking him sideways. Another calculated insult. A warning pang struck him, low in the belly, and he was stricken by the fear that he had already failed. He felt an overwhelming urge to tear the door open, abandon his troops and run for his life. He fought it.

I am not my father! If I have to die, it will be on my feet, facing my enemy.

Rulke caught Skald by the shirt, held him up and backhanded him with the other hand, then swapped hands and backhanded him on the left cheek again, and let him fall. 'Got anything to say, boy?'

Tiaan, who had the sergeant's knife and, clearly, knew how to use it, wore an enigmatic smile.

Skald's cheeks throbbed. He put the pain aside. The insults were harder to overcome but he had to. He had made a monumental blunder. How could he have thought to steal from Rulke, who had fought hundreds of battles and defeated or outwitted all manner of cunning enemies, with so few at his back? Skald's squad, tough and experienced as they were, were insignificant to a mancer of Rulke's power.

Behind his back, he rotated the red jewel on Pannilie's ring. She was the only advantage he had.

'How did you get in?' said Rulke.

Skald did not want to mention Maigraith. If she was lurking about, she might, just possibly, intervene in his favour. 'Secret door. Our spies found it. South-west drain.'

Rulke looked disbelieving. He also looked as though he was considering battering Skald to death. The way Skald felt, it would not take much. He clutched his belly, no longer trying to hide the pain.

'What's the matter with you?' snapped Rulke.

Skald did not answer.

'When he returned from trying to assassinate Flydd,' said Tiaan, 'blood was running from every orifice.'

'The life-drinking damaged you,' said Rulke. 'Why on earth did they send you?'

Sweat flooded down Skald's chest and sides. 'I pleaded for this mission.'

'But you'd done great things.' Clearly, Rulke was intrigued by him. 'You'd earned a rest.'

'When he was a boy, his father was executed for cowardice under fire,' said Tiaan. She seemed to take pleasure in saying it.

'And it tainted your life, didn't it? You're desperate to prove yourself.'

Skald did not answer. Why hadn't Pannilie attacked? Or was she waiting for Rulke to unseal the door? Yes, that had to be her plan.

'Heroes have short lives,' said Rulke. He eyed Skald shrewdly. 'I wonder how your magiz feels about your fame.'

Skald maintained a blank face but knew Rulke was not fooled. He prised at the jammed metal door, tore it open at the top and peered out.

Skald braced himself. It would have been the perfect time for Pannilie to blast him in the face, but nothing happened. *Pannilie, come on!*

What if the magiz had given her other orders? Had she used the diversion to go after the Source? If she fled with it, Rulke would annihilate Skald and his troop, and he would die a failure.

An idea surfaced, one so reckless that it could not possibly succeed. But he had nothing to lose now. He kept his head low while he considered it, in case his face gave him away.

One of the sus-magiz spells Skald had learned during his convalescence was called Rupture and, if targeted by a master, it could tear open one of an enemy's vital organs, or an artery or vein. It was too difficult for a sus-magiz of his experience, though. There was no way he could attack with it.

Could he use it on himself? Targeting would be much easier; he could tell from the pain if the spell was working. And no need to attack a vital organ – anything that had a dramatic effect would do.

But he had damaged himself so badly inside that such a spell might kill him. Dare he risk all to gain all? What did he have to lose? Rulke might cut him down at any moment.

Skald did not have much power left but the spell required subtlety, not strength. He turned away, clenched his fists and, as Rulke wrenched the door out of its frame with a squeal of tearing metal, Skald cast a small Rupture spell on the pit of his own stomach.

It felt as if his belly had been torn open with a barbed hook. He doubled over, clutching his middle and moaning.

Rulke propped the twisted door against the wall, heaved Skald upright and studied him dispassionately. 'That the best you can do?' He shoved Skald aside.

Another wave of agony tore through his middle, starting low and moving up, then his guts heaved so violently that blood exploded from his mouth, splattering the lower wall, the floor and Rulke's bare feet.

Rulke sprang backwards, stumbled and clutched at his side, wincing. He recovered, checked outside and said to Tiaan, 'Go first.'

She went out into the hall. Rulke carried Lirriam out, holding her tenderly in his arms. He beckoned Skald, who was clinging to the foot of the bed, spitting out blood. The pain was worse than the aftermath of his life-drinking spell and he was sure he was going to die.

But before he did, he had to bring down his enemy. He drew power to deny the pain and divert the needed strength to his legs. If he could just stay on his feet another minute …

He staggered through the door, moaning and dribbling blood. Rulke set Lirriam down on the floor and checked the corridors. Skald lurched past, turned and lowered his head and, using all the strength in his massive thighs, drove his skull into Rulke's recently healed scar, slamming him backwards into the wall.

Rulke's face contorted in agony, though he made no sound. Skald kept pushing with his legs and battering with his skull until he felt Rulke's scar tear open. He doubled up and fell.

Skald ducked aside, clouted Tiaan over the head and snatched her knife, and pressed the blade to Lirriam's throat. 'Move and she dies,' he gasped.

Pannilie appeared at the far end of the hall. She touched the three soldiers there and the paralysis spell on them broke.

'Bind Rulke and Tiaan.' She pointed to the other six guards and freed them, then ran towards Skald. 'Then Lirriam.'

The soldiers raced up. Two held Rulke down while they tied his wrists and ankles and gagged him. They were binding Tiaan's wrists when Lirriam's eyes sprang open. She took hold of the silver chain around her neck and jerked a black, irregularly shaped stone out from between her breasts.

Clutching it in her left hand, she reached across with her right arm and took hold of Rulke's shoulder. '*Incarnate!*' she said. 'Away, *away!*'

A dark red spark lit in the centre of the stone and a gate sprang into being around her, though it was unlike any gate Skald had ever seen before. It made no sound and its edges, indistinct and foggy, wavered in and out. A lobe extended from the gate and began to creep around Rulke.

They were going to escape! Skald struck out instinctively, hitting Lirriam's splinted arm and knocking her hand away from Rulke's shoulder. Pain stabbed him. Another mouthful of blood surged up. He swallowed it.

Lirriam cried out in agony and the gate, which had enclosed the top half of Rulke's body, peeled away with a squelching sound. It was drawing tightly around her when Pannilie dived at Lirriam, reached through the opening in the gate, broke the silver chain and wrenched the black stone out of her hand.

'Rulke!' wailed Lirriam. She sounded tormented, desperate. 'She's got the Waystone!'

Rulke heaved at his bonds but could not free himself. Pannilie pressed the stone to the black glyph on her own forehead, winced, and subvocalised a spell that Skald did not catch.

She touched the stone to the edge of the gate, which crept around Lirriam.

In a commanding voice, Pannilie said, 'Skyrock! To the guards at the gate of the officers' compound!'

Skald saw, through the gate, the blue and white spirals of the partly completed tower. Rulke tore one hand free, wrenched off the gag and hopped towards Lirriam, but he was too late. The gate vanished, carrying her with it.

Pannilie pointed the stone at Rulke and attempted to enclose him in another gate, but no gate formed. She touched the stone to the glyph on her forehead again, wincing as smoke rose from it and from the fingers holding the stone. She turned her glove inside-out to enclose the stone.

Three guards caught Rulke and two held him while the third gagged him, tightened the bindings around his wrists and blindfolded him. Blood ran down his side.

'This is a mighty object,' Pannilie said quietly. 'The moment I tried to look inside it, it burned me.'

'Whad ...id it?' Skald's mouth was full of blood again and it was oozing down his chin. He tried to swallow but it would not go down.

The Waystone now glowed deep crimson inside. She weighed it in her hand. 'It's incredibly heavy.' Her eyes narrowed as if she had realised something important. 'Where's Ghiv? Did he locate the Source?'

'Don't know.'

She gazed at the Waystone and smiled, then turned and ran.

Skald forced some blood down. 'Pannilie?'

She did not look back. Was she planning on gating the Source directly to Skyrock? That had to be it – the magiz's revenge. Skald slumped to his knees, panting, and a clot slid out of his open mouth.

A few minutes later Ghiv appeared from the other direction. 'Captain, what happened?'

'Rubdure zpell. You know id?'

Ghiv shook his head.

With supreme concentration, Skald focused on his innards and did his best to cancel the Rupture spell. It made no difference to the pain, which was unrelenting. He cleared his mouth. 'You see Pannilie?'

'No.'

'Find – Source?'

'Not yet, but it's up above us. Somewhere.' He studied Skald, frowning. 'You look dreadful. Better wait here.'

'No!' said Skald. 'Coming.'

Ghiv took the field scanner, a triangular box with a pale grey, illuminated glass plate on the top side, out of its case. A red pinpoint of light was spiralling near the apex of the plate. Looking down at it, he headed down the corridor to their left, and then up a steep flight of metal steps. Every step sent a spike of pain through Skald. Twenty-six spikes. He could not go much further.

Behind him three soldiers led Rulke, bent double and with a rope around his neck. The middle of his robe was red. Three more guards followed, weapons drawn. Another two supported Skald and the last man watched Tiaan.

Her slave's apathy was gone; she looked fascinated by everything around her. Did she miss the challenge and drama of playing an important role in the war against the lyrinx? She must. And perhaps she could sense the Source from here.

She had been one of the heroes of the Lyrinx War, Skald reminded himself. Brave, bold, an original thinker and a brilliantly creative artisan. He had to watch her.

At the top, where a passage opened out into a space some six yards by ten, Ghiv helped Skald to a bench. Two guards forced Rulke to the floor and the others stood around him.

'Where is it?' said Skald.

Ghiv jerked a thumb upwards. 'Somewhere up there.' He put the field scanner down. The red point of light was jerking all over the place. 'Scanner's no use, this close.'

Skald drew on his dwindling power to try and ease the pain. He could go no further in this state. 'Take Tiaan and three guards. Bring it down.'

They went down a narrow corridor made of grey metal, and at the end Skald heard them climb a long ladder. He was slumped on the bench, breathing through his nose, when a dreadful thought struck him. Maigraith was a loner who did not trust anyone, and she was a master of illusion who knew Alcifer well. She would not be far away.

The pieces fell into place. She wasn't a traitor and she would never let him take the Source. He, Skald, was just a tool, the means to get Lirriam without revealing herself.

But Lirriam was now at Skyrock. When Maigraith found out she would believe that Skald had double-crossed her.

54

HE WOULD HAVE TO BE CARRIED

Aviel heard soft footsteps coming their way. There was just enough light to see Maigraith rise into a crouch, her right hand extended. The senior sus-magiz crept past, looking through each doorway. An object in Maigraith's hand gave out a small white flash, the sus-magiz grunted and fell, and something slipped from her right hand and clattered across the polished black marble floor.

Maigraith recovered the item, a small but clearly heavy black stone. She raised it high as if in exultation, then dragged the body into a side room and closed the door.

The cold-blooded way she had killed the sus-magiz hit Aviel in the guts. It wasn't right to extinguish a living person from ambush. Had she done it for the stone, which Aviel had seen around Lirriam's neck through the spy portal? Or did Maigraith plan on killing all the Merdrun once they took Lirriam?

Maigraith returned to her hiding place. Half an hour passed but no one else appeared. She rose and began to pace, casting anxious glances this way and that, perhaps fearing that the Merdrun had betrayed and eluded her.

The floor quivered, and again. A few seconds later there came a distant crash.

Maigraith let out a small cry and darted down the left passage. Aviel went after her. More crashes and thuds were followed by the groan and squeal of metal on metal, as if some gigantic mechanism, not used in centuries, had been forced into motion. What was going on?

❧

The sky galleon hurtled low over the Sea of Thurkad. Karan could see moonlight reflecting off the swell, not far below. But two days had passed since they'd detected that massive draw of power at Alcifer. What if they were too late? What if Llian was gone? Or dead?

'How are we to get in?' Flydd muttered. 'Rulke will have locked Alcifer down tight.'

'Go to the front doors and knock,' said Nish. 'We're not coming like thieves in the night; we're offering an alliance.'

'And he doesn't know our cupboard is bare as a bone,' said Maelys.

She alone among them looked refreshed and ready; she had just risen from her bunk after a night's sleep. Lucky her!

'I'm afraid,' said Karan, scratching herself.

The sky galleon did not carry enough water for bathing or washing clothes, and she still wore the gear she had put on before they left Roros. In the curtained-off space she shared with Maelys, Karan had a quick wash with a cloth, changed her clothes and scrubbed her teeth, fruitlessly ran a brush through her tangled locks, scowled at the three grey hairs and went up to the deck.

They were close; the dark outlines ahead were the eastern shore of Meldorin and the mountains a few miles inland of their destination. And there it was, less than a mile away, its myriads of towers, aerial stairways, sky gardens, arches and domes and pools picked out in red-tinged silver by the light of the moon. The astounding city of Alcifer, designed and built for Rulke by Pitlis the Aachim, the most brilliant architect who had ever lived. And the biggest fool, to have trusted the Great Betrayer ...

Karan had been there with Llian only three months of her life ago, involuntarily gated from Carcharon at the end of Cumulus Snoat's short, bloody uprising. They had gone close to dying there when Thandiwe had trapped Karan, at Maigraith's behest.

'There's a clearing not far from the front doors,' Karan said to Flydd, pointing.

'Something's going on.' Nish was studying the glows on Flydd's power patterner. 'Rulke's using a lot more power than he was two days ago.'

'Pray it's because the bastard is finally ready to fight,' said Flydd dourly.

But fight who? Did he know they were coming? Probably.

❧

Skald stank of rancid sweat and old blood. And failure.

The guards paced around Rulke, never taking their eyes off him. Was Maigraith close by? Would she try to free Rulke, so as to earn his gratitude? She would need to kill Skald and his entire team first, so they could not reveal her real plan.

How could he turn the situation around? Kill Rulke and try to get away with the Source? It was tempting, because Rulke's escapes were legendary – he had even got out of the impregnable prison of the Nightland. No, Durthix and the magiz would want him alive. Besides, Skald needed Rulke as a hostage, his passport out of here once they found the Source. Could they get away with it? Cold logic told Skald that he and his squad were going to die here.

He could hear Ghiv and the three soldiers tramping across metal floors high above, going up and down ladders, and lifting and closing hatches. Tiaan's bare feet made no sound. She would know the Source the moment she saw it. Being a brilliant geomancer, she might even sense it.

Another spasm struck his abused guts. Utter determination had got him this far, but blood loss had gravely weakened him. He slumped sideways against the wall, able to do nothing but endure ...

Time had passed. Ghiv was yelling at him.

Skald forced his head upright. 'Y-yes, Sus-magiz?'

Ghiv's head, with those massive butterfly-wing ears, was extended down through an open hatch above him. 'Found it!'

At last! Skald drew more power from himself, knowing he would pay later. Or not, if it killed him. Right now, death was the only friend he had.

He rose, shaking and shivering and drenched in cold sweat. The six guards were still pacing. Rulke had not moved.

Walking was bad. Climbing the first ladder was worse. And going up the long ladder beyond it, which must have been thirty feet high, caused him such agony that several times Skald considered letting go. *No, never give up!*

He drove himself on and up, into a small, windowless chamber whose walls, floor and ceiling were grey, featureless metal. Tiaan was bent over a six-lobed container, a yard across and a yard and a half high, made of black metal whose surface was embossed in complex, angular patterns. The device was clamped to the floor at the base of each lobe. He collapsed into a curved copper seat, panting, and felt a hideous squelch beneath him.

Everything blurred ...

When he could focus again, Tiaan was staring at him and there was an unnerving light in her eyes. Was she forming a plan to attack them? He could not think; his mind seemed to be shutting down. But at least the pain was less. A good sign – or a bad one?

'It's the Source,' she said.

Skald sighed. He had begun to doubt they'd ever find it. 'Any sign of Pannilie?'

'No,' said Ghiv.

Skald had a bad feeling about that. There would be no rescue. If the True Purpose was to be saved, he had to do it. 'Free it.'

Tiaan released the clamps and gave one side of the Source an experimental heave. It did not budge. Ghiv took hold as well and between them they lifted their side a couple of inches.

'It'll take six to carry it,' he said. 'And eight to lower it down safely.'

'Eight to lower it ...' It was a struggle to think the numbers through. 'Then six to carry it all the way to Maigraith's gate ... One to ... to help me walk.' Skald rubbed his throbbing temples. 'Only leaves two to guard Rulke and Tiaan.'

'Kill him,' said Ghiv. 'An oath given to an enemy can never be binding.'

'He's Maigraith's great love,' Skald hissed. 'If we threaten Rulke, we're dead.'

'And maybe she's planning to double-cross us.'

Why had he gone along with her plan? Why had Durthix allowed it? Skald reminded himself of what was at stake. The Source was worth all their lives. It was worth ten thousand lives.

He lowered himself down the long ladder. The rungs were slippery with the blood he had lost on the way up. Across to the hatch and down the shorter ladder below it. Rulke was still doubled up on the floor, bound and gagged and blindfolded, and the red patch on the front of his robe was larger than before.

Rulke must not be harmed, Maigraith had said. If she found him in this state, she would annihilate Skald and the rest of his squad.

Was she nearby? He had to know, but this part of Alcifer was a confusing maze of narrow, metal-walled corridors and small compartments linked by steep steps and ladders. What had its designer been thinking? It was like being trapped in a machine.

He sent all but one of the guards up to lower the Source down, then plodded along the narrow hall to the left. He had no idea what he would do if he ran into Maigraith.

Fail and die, probably.

55

YOU'RE A PEARL BEYOND PRICE, CHRONICLER

Llian had been shadowing Rulke's captors for more than an hour, keeping as close as he dared in the gloom and trying to think of a rescue plan, but nothing had come to him. There were far too many guards.

Then Skald reappeared, staggering like a reanimated corpse, and sent all but one of Rulke's guards up to bring down the Source, whatever that was. Llian had to act; there would never be another chance.

He crept along a dark, narrow hall. There were hatches in the metal floor at intervals, and compartments of various shapes and sizes along the metal-clad walls. Another series of hatches ran along the low ceiling. Llian could not imagine what this part of Alcifer was for, or why Rulke needed such a vast city for himself.

Perhaps, when it was designed long ago, he had imagined it being full of his people. Now it was an empty relic. Was it a constant reminder of plans gone so terribly wrong that the Charon, in many ways the greatest of all the human species, were now just a heartbeat from extinction?

Llian peered around the corner. In a well-lit open area some twenty yards away, Rulke lay on his side on the floor, his wrists and ankles bound with thick cord. The last guard stood back, watching him. Rulke was the Merdrun's age-old nemesis, the only enemy they had ever feared, and if Skald got him to Skyrock he would be put to death.

Llian had no weapon save the knife he used to cut up his dinner, and if he attacked the guard he would die. The only advantage he had was his Teller's gift. Could he lure the man away? It wouldn't be easy. Merdrun were nothing if not faithful to their duty.

Whatever he did, he had to be quick. Once Skald returned with the other eight soldiers there would be no hope of a rescue.

A feeble plan came to Llian, and at the darkest point of the hall he lifted a hatch in the floor, stood it on edge against the wall, climbed onto it and heaved up the heavy hatch above. He carried the floor hatch further along the hall and laid it down where it was almost invisible in the gloom. He came back, sprang up and caught the edges of the open ceiling hatch, and with an effort pulled himself up into the cavity. It was completely dark here, warm and dusty and still, though he could feel faint vibrations from far away.

Every Teller could mimic voices; it was part of their training at the College of the Histories from the day they entered at the age of twelve. Students, when telling tales great or small, were expected to create a unique voice, accent and manner of speaking for every character in the tale, and Llian had been one of the best.

At the age of sixteen, in his retelling of the Great Tale, *The Death of Magister Rula*, he had given a distinct voice to each of the 173 characters in that monumental tale. He had recreated Rula's final, defiant speech, and her subsequent assassination, so convincingly that ugly old Wistan, the Master of the College and Llian's lifelong enemy, had been moved to tears.

But to induce a Merdrun guard to leave his post, Llian would have to give the performance of his life. He prepared for a minute, put his head down through the hole, looked back towards Rulke and the guard, who were out of sight from here, and held on with both hands.

'What are you doing, Maigraith?' he boomed, using Skald's deep voice and injecting a note of alarm into it. 'Stay back!'

'You betrayed me!' Maigraith, speaking with barely suppressed fury. 'You knew I wanted Lirriam. You gated her to Skyrock to thwart me.'

Llian had heard her speak many times, back in the past, though the intervening centuries must have changed her voice and he had not heard it as it was now. He made it hoarse and a trifle reedy, an old woman's voice, but kept the precise enunciation and the hint of formality that showed it was not her native tongue. He prayed it would be good enough to fool a common soldier, a man who had only learned the basics of the common speech of Santhenar.

'You never had any intention of letting me take the Source,' Skald said coldly.

'You'll never know, Merdrun, because you're not leaving Alcifer alive.'

Llian imitated the sounds of a magical attack by Maigraith, an echoing *boom* ending with a whipcrack, and a return blast from Skald, a bang and a sizzling crackle.

Llian stood up in the ceiling, jumped and landed with a thud like a falling body. He let out a cry and a grunt, waited a couple of seconds, then put his head down through the hatch.

'*Guard!*' he cried in Skald's voice, this time injecting pain and fear into it. 'Maigraith's taken my secret sus-magiz's key. She can break into Skyrock with it. I've got to get it back or we're lost!'

Llian was gambling here, but sus-magizes were bound to have secrets, devices and magics that common soldiers knew nothing about, and feared. And soldiers were expected to obey a sus-magiz's orders instantly, without questioning.

'Guard!' Llian bellowed, putting more pain into Skald's voice, and a hint of terror. He picked up the heavy metal hatch, held it vertically above the diagonal of the opening, and waited.

The guard came running, then slowed and crept forwards, looking around warily in the dim light. Llian was hoping he would fall through the hole in the floor, but he stopped a couple of yards back.

'Sus-magiz?' he said.

Llian's arms were aching. The guard was eyeing the open hatch. He would see nothing; the dark was absolute down below. He came forwards another yard, bent and peered down. 'Sus-magiz, are you down there?'

Llian dropped the heavy hatch cover and the metal edge struck the Merdrun across the back, flattening him. He was hurt, and perhaps stunned where his jaw had struck the floor, and he was lying partly over the hole, but did not fall through.

Llian was afraid to get close but there was no choice. He sprang down, landed beside the guard and tried to shove him down the hole. The Merdrun's right hand caught Llian's ankle and heaved. He fell, one knee striking the top of the guard's head and driving his face into the floor again.

He must have been dazed, otherwise he would have killed Llian by now. Llian pulled free, sprang and grabbed the guard's ankles. He was heaving the man backwards to bring his head and shoulders over the open hatch when the guard kicked with both feet, catching Llian in the groin.

He doubled up in agony, knowing he was going to die. But the guard's kick had driven his own body the other way; his head and shoulders slipped through the hatch, then his torso. His left hand caught the edge of the hatch and held him.

Llian staggered forwards, picked up the guard's feet, holding them to the side this time, and heaved. The guard's legs went through the hatch, but his grip held and he swung from his left hand. He was immensely strong; Llian could not have done it for a second. The guard's right hand clamped on and he pushed himself up.

'Like hell!' Llian cried.

He swiped with one foot, kicked away the fingers of the guard's left hand, lost his balance, swayed wildly and landed with his left foot on one side of the hatch and his right foot on the other. He swayed the other way, almost fell in, and by accident his boot heel came down on the fingers of the Merdrun's right hand. Bones cracked and he lost his grip.

The guard fell a long way before he hit bottom.

Llian threw himself backwards and landed on his back with his legs handing down through the hatch. He lifted them up and to the side, rolled over and scuttled like an injured crab back to where Rulke lay, still bound but now free of the gag and blindfold.

Rulke was laughing as Llian sawed through the ropes with his table knife with one hand, while holding his groin with the other.

'You're a pearl beyond price, Chronicler. I thought I'd seen every ineptitude you had to offer, yet you keep surprising me.'

'When the time comes,' said Llian, wincing with every movement, 'remember who your real friends are.'

~

Skald had checked along twenty corridors and inside more than a dozen metal-walled rooms, but there was no sign of Maigraith. He was peering down a ladder into a dark, tank-like space when he heard yelling, a distant cry and the thud of a body fallen from a considerable height. He staggered back along the dark corridors, sick with dread.

The soldier who had been guarding Rulke was not at his post. Severed ropes lay on the floor next to a smear of blood where Rulke had lain on his side.

And he was gone!

You arrogant fool! Skald thought. *A man of Rulke's skills can't be stopped by binding him and stopping his mouth. He might be able to cast spells by wriggling a little finger, with a mumble, even a thought.*

There was no possibility of getting away with the Source now.

His grossly abused belly throbbed. He doubled over, clutching his middle, but the pressure forced thick muck up into the back of his throat. He could not breathe! He choked and lumps of clotted blood exploded out of his mouth and splatted onto the metal floor, where they quivered like little brown jellies. He tightened his sphincter until it ached but felt blood dribbling out there, too. He was a wreck, not even a shadow of a Merdrun warrior now. A disgusting ruin.

'Ghiv?' he croaked. 'Ghiv?'

No answer. Had Rulke taken him already?

Skald was staggering, one knee-trembling step after another, towards the first ladder when, with a groaning of enormous hinges, the squeal of metal on metal, and a shuddering of the floor beneath him, the metal walls to either side lifted, moved apart and folded away, revealing other walls, also lifting and retracting to form a huge open chamber.

It must have been sixty yards long and forty across, with a full-length balcony, a good sixty feet up, on the far side. A massive glass skylight, a hundred feet above the floor, ran down the centre of the ceiling.

And in the centre of the chamber stood – no, it hung in the air a couple of feet above the floor – a mighty construct. He recognised it instantly because it had a similar shape to the thapter that had crashed, though this construct was three times as big. A long ladder ran up the side facing him, to a closed hatch.

The construct was made of midnight-black metal, shaped into alien, impossible curves. The base was also black, but corrugated, with a cavity in the centre that glowed blue-white and radiated heat. The long front – he assumed it was the front, though Skald reminded himself that where Rulke was concerned any assumption was dangerous – sloped up steeply near the top, where a small platform was surrounded by a curved metal coaming, waist-high. Below it, a line of large crystal portholes, oval in shape, ran around the front and sides.

So that's what Rulke had been up to over the past month – repairing and testing the construct. He must have made two of them long ago, the small one that he had used at the end of the Time of the Mirror, and a large one. And the large one had been hidden here for the past 224 years, concealed as part of Alcifer. It must be powered by the Source, and Skald was prepared to bet that Rulke was inside the construct now.

What would he do? Fly to Skyrock and try to rescue Lirriam? Then destroy the half-built tower? With such a massive craft he could knock the top off, ensuring that it could never be completed and ruining their hopes of achieving the True Purpose.

This was a disaster and Skald would be blamed for it. He lurched towards the ladder. He had no plan, but he had to get into the construct.

He was on the third rung, and clenching his sphincter desperately, when there came a bellow of fury, a hatch opened below the line of portholes and a Merdrun guard was hurled out. His arms windmilled as he fell, he landed on his head, kicked three times and went still. Two more guards followed, then the other six, though the last three fell as though they were already dead. Skald's soldiers, mighty warriors though they were, must have been powerless before Rulke's fury.

Two had survived the fall but with broken legs and other injuries. They were no use now.

The construct rose several feet in the air, shaking Skald off the ladder, but dropped and hit the floor with an impact that rattled the walls and shook ribbons of dust down from the ceiling. The great craft rose again and settled gently, the floor creaking under its weight.

The taste in his mouth was bitter. He had wasted precious power on this fiasco of a mission. He had lost Tiaan, their second-most valuable artisan slave, plus ten soldiers and a sus-magiz. And probably Pannilie as well, a senior sus-magiz who could not be replaced. But far, far worse, he had reminded Rulke as to why he had always been the Merdrun's implacable enemy, and now he had the means to ruin their plans and their ten-thousand-year-old dream.

Skald had failed utterly and would die in disgrace, and generations of Merdrun to come would curse his name – Skald Hulni, the incompetent fool who had caused their True Purpose to fail.

What else could you expect from the son of a stinking coward?

Maigraith slipped through a tall doorway and disappeared. Aviel, creeping after her, made out a vast chamber with a glass skylight across the ceiling. She could see starlight through it, and the half-dark moon, now declining towards the western end of the skylight. The light, such as it was, would not last much longer.

Nine Merdrun soldiers were sprawled on the floor as if they had been dumped there from a height. Two were still moving but neither could get up. To their left loomed a construct akin to the one Karan had used to carry them to the future, though this one was far larger, and a slender metal ladder ran up the side.

Aviel crept around the shadowed base of the left-hand wall, keeping as far from Maigraith as possible. She was staring at the construct in dismay; clearly, she had not known of its existence. Perhaps she feared that Lirriam was inside and Rulke was planning on leaving with her. Aviel hoped so; it would serve Maigraith right.

The construct rose a few feet, dropped and hit the floor with a crash that shook the walls. Again it rose, six feet this time, fell, and the impact opened a crack across the floor. The left-hand half of the floor, on which the construct stood, tilted and one of the bodies slid down and fell through the crack. Maigraith let out a shrill cry. The floor tilted back and the construct settled.

Near the bottom of the ladder a big man rose unsteadily into the light, then crawled behind the remaining bodies. Skald, though he was a shaking, bloody wreck. Aviel glanced at Maigraith, who was gazing yearningly at the top of the construct and did not appear to have noticed him.

Aviel was too low down to see into it. She edged along the side wall to a metal staircase that spiralled up to a door near the ceiling, and crept up until she was above the top of the construct. Rulke was at the controls. Llian, the big-eared sus-magiz and the female slave were inside.

Where was Lirriam?

The sky galleon landed hard in the clearing near Alcifer. Karan, Flydd, Nish and Maelys raced to the enormous front doors and Karan pounded on them with the hilt of her knife. It made little sound on the thick metal. She grabbed a chunk of fallen stone and slammed it into the door.

'Rulke, let us in!' The soft sandstone crumbled. She tossed it aside.

'He could be half a mile away,' said Flydd. 'He'll never hear us.'

The ground shook, and a few seconds later Karan heard a distant crash. 'What was that?'

'Sounded like the top fell off one of the towers,' said Nish.

'We've got to get in,' said Flydd.

'Can you blast the doors in?'

'You greatly overestimate my powers.' There came another shudder and another crash, louder than the first.

Flydd turned, looking back the way they had come. 'Get out of the way. Well away!' He ran down the path.

'What's he doing?' said Karan.

Nish pulled her aside. 'I'd have thought that was obvious.'

Shortly the sky galleon soared over the trees, dipped, raced along the broad path, a few feet up, and hit the doors at the speed of a cantering horse. They burst in.

Flydd moved the sky galleon backwards. Metal screamed and tore, and the left door fell off its hinges and hit the paved path with an almighty clang. The right door was dragged backwards down the path for twenty feet.

He slammed the sky galleon down and scrambled over the side. 'Come on!'

They raced after him, down an immense hall, too dark to see much, and left up a broad, curving white staircase. 'Sounded like it came from up here.'

Considering he had recently recovered from Skald's assassination attempt, Flydd was remarkably quick. Karan started to run up the stairs, but pain shot through her left hip and she had to slow to a hobble. Nish passed her, taking three steps at a time.

Maelys came up beside Karan. 'Need a hand?'

There was another crash, louder and closer. 'No,' she panted. 'Yes! I'm really worried. About Llian. He's ... not good in a fight.'

Maelys gave Karan her shoulder and she managed a bit more speed. Several flights up they reached another corridor, turned a corner and passed into a large open area, dimly lit by moonlight coming through an enormous skylight. They were on a long balcony overlooking a hall large enough to accommodate a thousand people.

'I don't believe it!' whispered Flydd. 'Why didn't he say anything?'

'Maybe, after all this time, he wasn't sure it would still work,' said Nish.

Karan looked over. 'Rulke made *two* constructs.'

'And the big one has been hidden here all this time.'

'I heard long ago that the whole city of Alcifer was a construct –'

'So did I,' said Flydd, 'though I never believed such a thing was possible. And it wasn't. So *that's* what he's been up to for the past month – getting this beautiful craft ready to defeat the bloody bastard Merdrun. Oh, this is glorious! With Rulke and that construct we can win the war.'

The key to happiness is always to hope, *and never to* expect, Karan remembered Persia saying in Roros.

56

HIT THE BASTARD!

Skald lay prone behind the bodies of his troops, longing to join them in death.

A slim figure flitted through the deep shadows on the far side of the hall and stopped, staring upwards in an attitude of despair. It had to be Maigraith. Rulke would not see her from the construct, though she might see his head and shoulders through the portholes.

She had no way of knowing that Lirriam had been gated to Skyrock. She probably assumed that she was in the construct, about to escape with Rulke. Maigraith would try to prevent it.

The construct rose a few yards and hovered. She extended a thin arm towards it. Was she planning to kill him, in a jealous rage? No, she was far too controlled, and far too obsessed with him.

Skald was crawling backwards when a creamy glow formed at Maigraith's fingertips, zipped up, and Rulke's head was driven backwards as if he had been punched in the jaw. But the air between him and Maigraith rippled like a mirage and she fell to one knee, mouth opening and closing. Her attack had set off a counterattack.

The construct dropped, hitting so hard that the whole building shook. The floor cracked in front of Skald at an angle to the main crack and a triangular section fell through, carrying the rest of his troops with it. If he had not moved it would have taken him too.

The construct tilted sharply and he saw into the cabin as Rulke toppled off his seat, evidently stunned by Maigraith's attack. He landed on Llian, who went down as well, but the construct righted itself and Skald could no longer see them.

Nor Maigraith. He prayed that she had fallen through the broken floor.

Then he saw a chance to tear victory from the hooked fingers of death – if he could get inside before Rulke recovered. He scanned the hall more closely. Maigraith was doubled up near the side wall, heaving.

Skald reached the ladder and dragged himself up, spitting blood, and in through the side hatch. He was at the round end of an egg-shaped cabin, dimly lit by dark red light coming from strips set in the walls and ceiling. Directly ahead, the seat Rulke had fallen off was made of curved copper, with narrow slots in the base and sides, and a high backrest of serpentinite, the green rock polished to an oily sheen. Another seat, a plain one made of white metal, was fixed to the floor beside it.

Skald assessed the threat. Rulke lay on his face, unmoving. Llian was on hands and knees, swaying, dazed. Maigraith's stunning spell must have clipped him. Tiaan stood six yards away at the pointy end of the cabin. Sus-magiz Ghiv was tied to a ring embedded in the wall beside her.

In front of the copper seat, a black metal stalk sprouted from the floor and spread out to a yard across at the top, like a mushroom with a bite out of it. Two glassy plates covered most of the top. A third, smaller plate was set in the bite. Coloured lights, shapes and patterns danced across each plate. Between the bite and the copper seat a thick grey tube rose from the floor, curving towards the seat and branching into five control rods, each ending in a knob carved from a different kind of rock.

'How did Rulke get free?' choked Skald. He had to know.

'I called the guard away,' said Llian, and smirked.

Skald wanted to blast him dead but dared not waste the power. He would not have thought the pain could get worse, but it had. He grabbed a handle on the wall, clung to it and cast an endurance spell on himself. It made no difference.

Llian struggled to his feet.

'Stay back,' said Skald, 'or die.'

Llian laughed mockingly.

Not even this fool is afraid of me. How did it come to this? Skald blasted at him, so feebly that Llian only slipped to one knee.

Skald was failing rapidly. He stumbled to Rulke, knelt on his back and put his hands around the Charon's throat. Could he drink Rulke's life? What a feat that would be; what a life! With that much power he might even heal himself, and if he got back to Skyrock he would suck the magiz as dry as the corpses left behind at the Sink of Despair.

He checked on Tiaan, whose eyes were dark, staring holes now. Her mouth was twisted in horror. Or was it terror?

It took all Skald had to initiate the life-drinking spell, but nothing happened. Had he failed? He tried again, the spell went to completion, and power surged out of Rulke's chest and into Skald.

Immense power. Every blood vessel burned as if his heart pumped molten metal; every nerve fibre stung like the touch of a red-hot wire. So much power that he was temporarily paralysed.

But the spell must have erased Maigraith's stunning charm, because Rulke roused and heaved Skald off. Rulke tried to get up but Skald's spell had its hooks deep in him now and he fell down on his back, shuddering violently.

'Llian?' he choked. 'Tiaan? Do something, or we're all dead!'

Llian rose but just stood there, not knowing what to do. Tiaan ran to Rulke, whose heels were drumming on the metal floor. Skald tried to ward her away but the scalding power flowing into him would not allow him to move.

She scrambled under the mushroom-shaped control binnacle, looking up. Hidden lights made red and yellow patterns on her face, constantly changing. She reached up with both hands, twisted and pulled out a mechanism.

The light was too dim for Skald to see it clearly though it contained a variety of crystals, a pair of wire coils and three glass flasks, one half full of quicksilver, the second containing a swirling green gas and the third, shaped like the bottom half of an hourglass, a red powder. He watched dumbly; he had no idea what they were for and could not guess what Tiaan intended.

She touched one crystal, then another and another, her long fingers caressing the facets of each before moving on. She started, bent and plucked a long, blade-like orange crystal free. At her touch, a series of glyphs on one crystal face lit a brighter orange.

She ran to Rulke and slammed the point of the crystal down against his bare chest, between two ribs. It went in half an inch and he arched up so that only his head, shoulders and heels touched the floor.

Pain speared through Skald. What was she doing? What would happen if Rulke was killed in the middle of the life-drinking? Skald could not bear to think. Neither could he move.

Tiaan pushed the crystal in a bit further, mouthing a spell unfamiliar to Skald. Geomancy, he assumed. The crystal glowed like the inside of a furnace, the orange light streaming between her fingers, then she wrenched it out and the link of the life-drinking spell came with it, causing flames to flicker around her fingers. She whirled and hurled the crystal backhanded at Skald. It dug into his forehead and the link attempted to attach to him.

He could not go through that again. He knocked the crystal aside and tried desperately to block the spell. It took most of the power he had drawn from Rulke. His forehead throbbed and he felt a curving welt across his Merdrun glyph, like a deep burn. The spell tried to reattach. Again he blocked it, draining himself further. It was hard to move now. Hard to think, for his blood vessels flowed ice and his nerve fibres were numb.

If Rulke recovered, it was all over. Skald had to find more power, but Llian was not magically gifted and would not hold much, and what Tiaan had just done meant she was too valuable. Attacking Rulke again was out of the question. It had to be Ghiv.

Skald cast the life-drinking spell, which was still trying to embed itself in him, at the helpless sus-magiz. Ghiv was too inexperienced to defend himself and slumped in his bonds, eyes accusing, mouth gaping, as Skald tore his life from him. It was a monstrous betrayal of one of his own, but necessary. *One for All!*

Rulke was rising. Skald had to finish him now or he never would. He went at Rulke again and they wrestled like old men, lurching and staggering and cursing feebly, each trying to use disabling spells on the other with what little strength they had. Skald tried to knee Rulke in the groin. Rulke blocked it with his own knee and head-butted Skald across the welt on his temple. Agony speared through him.

From the corner of an eye Skald saw Llian coming, carrying the leg of a wooden table. It looked heavy enough to brain Skald.

'Hit the bastard!' said Rulke. 'Stove his head in.'

Llian danced around them, the table leg upraised, but afraid to swing because Rulke and Skald were too close together. Skald dared not attack Llian. If he did, Rulke would defeat him in a moment.

'Chronicler!' gasped Rulke. He was staggering, almost falling, but he managed to heave Skald around. 'Hit him *now*!'

Llian swung the club with all his strength and Skald knew he could not avoid it. But as he swung, Rulke stumbled and fell into the path of the club, which thudded into the top of his head.

'This how you convince me to give you our tale?' Rulke said thickly, and fell to the floor, unconscious.

'Hit *Skald*, you cretin!' shrieked Tiaan.

Skald could barely stand up. He felt so very weak. Llian swung the table leg. Skald ducked, a trifle late, and it glanced off the side of his head. A painful blow but not enough to bring him down. Llian swung again. Skald fended it off with his forearm, losing a long strip of hairy skin. He was failing fast but could not allow himself to be beaten by such an oaf.

Llian, slightly off-balance, raised the club once more and Skald knew he could not avoid it. He stumbled forwards, bent at the knees, then drove his head up under Llian's chin, hurling him onto his back. His head hit the floor, and he lay there, blood running from a corner of his mouth.

Skald kicked the club out of his hand, bound and gagged Rulke and went back to Tiaan, who looked terrified now. And well she might be. If Skald was going to die, he would take all his enemies with him.

He slumped over, gasping. 'How – you do that?'

She looked blank.

'How did you eject the life-drinking spell? Speak or die!' said Skald.

Her brown eyes showed the blank desperation of a slave who had seen too many slaves killed, knew she was going to be next, and could do nothing about it. 'Once a geomancer, always a geomancer,' she said. 'I was the best.'

'Can you fly this craft?'

Hope flared in her eyes but faded just as quickly. He pointed to the copper seat. She sat on it.

'Th-the controls look – similar to thapters I once flew,' she whispered.

'Then fly it!'

She did not move.

'Or die.'

She looked around for the orange crystal, retrieved it, wiped Rulke's blood off and reinserted it in the mechanism. Her fingers worked mechanically, her mind elsewhere. She put the mechanism back where it came from. 'Th-this construct is much – bigger. I may not be strong enough.'

Skald stood beside her, supporting himself on the white seat. 'Once you've learned how to fly, how could you forget?'

'You're a fool!' she snapped. But the flash of spirit died. 'Knowing *how* to fly is

the easy part. B-but coordinating mind and hands – and eyes – takes a lot of practice. I haven't flown in fourteen years. Besides –'

'*What?*' Skald could allow nothing to thwart him.

'Drawing great power through a controller burns the mind. Y-you develop
protective scars when you do a lot of flying ... But they fade.'

'You're saying that even if hand and eye *can* control this huge craft, the power
may burn your mind so badly that –'

'Yes,' she said with a disturbing hint of satisfaction.

Was she telling the truth? Or exaggerating the difficulty, hoping she could
seize the construct if he weakened? Skald could not tell. He had to find a way to
control her.

'Llian,' he said. 'Sit with Tiaan. If she falters, hold her up.'

Llian rose shakily and sat on the seat to Tiaan's right. She leaned forwards on
the copper seat and took hold of the black and green knobs, eyes closed. Nothing
happened. She lifted her left hand, touched the red knob, then the blue-white
one, and settled on the last, the sulphur-yellow knob, which she pulled towards
her. The patterns of light on the glassy plates went out, reappeared, and a hum
emanated from the belly of the construct.

'What are you doing?' said Skald.

'Sensing my way into the controller, so we can become one.'

Truth or lie? He could not tell. 'How long will that take?'

Tiaan shrugged. 'I've never flown anything this big before. But if I get it
wrong, and the mechanism fails while we're flying ...'

Skald relived the thapter plummeting from the sky, smashing to bits on that
desert hilltop and burning so fiercely that the rocks beneath it must have melted.
Dare he trust the True Purpose to a woman who had not flown in fourteen years,
might not have the strength for it, and could well take the noble way out if she
realised she was never going to see her children again?

It was Tiaan or nothing. Tiaan or failure and unbearable shame. He had to
make it worth her while.

'Get us to Skyrock,' he croaked, 'and I will personally see that you are sent
home, unharmed, to your children.'

She turned warily, though her eyes glowed with an impossible hope. 'On
your word?'

'By our sacred True Purpose, I do so swear.'

57

I DON'T CARE IF I DIE

Maigraith was Skald's biggest obstacle now, if she had recovered. She could not know he had captured the construct, and if she thought Rulke was flying away with it, and Lirriam, there was no telling what she might do.

While Tiaan sensed her way into the mechanisms, Skald dragged his corpse-like body up to the lookout platform and peered over the coaming. Maigraith was still in the shadows by the side wall, but she was sitting up now and had Lirriam's black stone in hand – Skald could see the distinctive deep red glow inside it. She must have killed Pannilie.

What did Maigraith intend to do with the stone? Make another gate? Lirriam had made a gate effortlessly, but Pannilie had not succeeded in making another. Could Maigraith make one *inside* Alcifer? Probably.

She rose and moved stealthily towards the ladder.

Skald put his head down through the hatch and hissed at Llian. 'Pull up the ladder. That handle, there! Turn it!'

Llian was slow to react.

'Now! Or die!'

Llian stumbled to the side of the cabin and turned a handle shaped like a windlass. The flexible ladder retreated into a slot in the curving metal side of the construct. Tiaan pulled back on one of the levers in front of her and the massive craft rose a few yards.

Maigraith ran forwards, but propped, evidently realising that she was in mortal danger if it fell again. She headed for the side wall and scrambled up a spiralling metal stair until she was level with the cabin of the construct.

She was going to attack, and Skald did not have the strength to stop her.

Aviel watched in increasing dismay as Skald entered the construct and, after a titanic struggle with Rulke, took control. Now Maigraith was creeping up the stair below her. If she came high enough she would see Aviel, who dared not move again.

Maigraith stopped at a height where she could see into the cabin. She was gazing at Lirriam's black stone, perhaps trying to fathom how it worked. She touched it to her forehead. Her head rocked back. The stone glowed a darker red in the centre, as if a flame burned inside it.

Skald was a bloody, lurching wreck; it would not take much to strike him down. Then Maigraith would be free to find Lirriam and kill her. Aviel had to stop her.

Maigraith leaned out over the railing, her right arm out-thrust and her bony fingers pointing at Skald. The only weapon Aviel had was her metal water bottle, which contained a couple of pints of water. She unclipped it, rose slowly, aimed carefully and dropped it.

The water bottle fell twenty feet and struck Maigraith on the head. She toppled, slid head-first down the tight spiral of the stair and onto the floor, her feet coming to rest on the third tread.

She wasn't moving. Had Aviel saved Lirriam by killing Maigraith?

Aviel scrunched up on the step, wrapped her arms around her head and rocked back and forth. Why couldn't she ever do anything right?

As the construct rose in the air, Karan had a very bad feeling. 'Xervish, that's not Rulke at the controls.'

'It's Tiaan!' cried Nish. 'What the hell is *she* doing here?'

And Llian was seated beside her. Karan's eyes stung. He was alive!

'Rulke's on the floor,' said Maelys. 'Tied up.'

'There's the assassin, up on top,' said Nish. 'Skald's forcing Tiaan to fly the construct.'

Karan squinted at Llian. Why was he sitting so close to her? Suspicion burned; she could not prevent it. Was his arm around her? Yes, it was! 'Stop them!'

'I haven't got the power to stop a construct,' Flydd said dully.

Tiaan was a brilliant woman. Attractive, too. Llian would certainly be drawn to her. 'Block her power. Or daze her. Do *something!*'

Flydd sighted along his staff but swore and lowered it.

'What's the matter now?' Karan shrieked.

She had to stop this before it went too far. Or had it already? Tiaan was a legend of the war with a thousand tales to tell, and the way Llian was looking at her they might have been lovers. Were they? *He's mine!* she wanted to shriek, but Llian hadn't been hers for a long time, and it was mostly her fault.

'If I do anything to stop Tiaan,' said Flydd, 'the construct is liable to fall out of the air. And from that height it'll tear through the floor and keep falling. Perhaps bring the whole building down –'

Karan had a flash of the thapter plummeting towards that rocky hilltop, crashing and burning.

'I can't do anything,' said Flydd. 'It's over.'

'No, look!' Nish was pointing to Skald. 'He can barely stand up. Blast him down and the construct is ours.'

It'll always be Rulke's, Karan thought. *But if we rescue him, he'll be grateful. And when I get my hands on Tiaan –*

She cut the thought off. Llian was the wronged one, after all. But even so –

Flydd sighted on Skald, who was partly concealed by the coaming. Karan held her breath.

He blasted. Skald disappeared.

'Got him!' Karan yelled.

Flydd didn't say anything.

'You did get him, didn't you?'

~

Skald was bracing for Maigraith's attack when she fell, slid down the spiralling stairs and lay still. He turned and saw four people on the balcony on the opposite side of the hall, and one of them was Flydd. Had he taken her down?

Skald's nemesis, Karan, was beside Flydd and they were only fifty feet away. Had Skald been at the controls he would have slammed the construct into the balcony and smashed it to bits, completing the assassination mission he had failed at last time, and triumphantly ending the resistance.

But he could do nothing, and Flydd was raising his staff. Pointing it.

Skald ducked below the coaming. The construct was rising rapidly now. Tiaan was planning to splatter him against the glass roof and fly away, to freedom. What a prize that would be for the enemy.

No time to descend the ladder. Skald dropped through the hole in the platform and pulled the hatch down.

It slammed with a clang, his weight tore his fingers off the handle, and he fell and hit the floor hard. Agony tore through his belly. He heaved up another clot of old, brown blood. Had it been bright red and fresh, it would signal that he was dying.

The coaming shattered the glass roof, hurling shards and metal everywhere. Skald lay on his side and attempted to cast a healing on his guts.

Had it worked? He could not tell, though the pain was enough to make the most stoic of Merdrun scream. He fought it down and checked on Llian, who looked shifty. He wasn't much of a threat, but Skald immobilised him and he fell off his seat. Skald could not afford the least of distractions now.

Tiaan was staring at him in horror.

'To Skyrock,' choked Skald. 'If you want to see your children again, do exactly as I say. I don't care if I die, and if my people can't have the construct and the Source, no one can.'

She seemed to take the message.

As the construct tore through the skylight. Maelys dived to one side and Flydd to the other, but Karan just stood there, too numb to take it in. Tiaan no longer mattered. Llian would soon be in the enemy's hands and they would kill him, slowly and cruelly, because he had helped to thwart them in their previous invasion.

Nish jerked Karan sideways so hard that they both fell. A yard-long triangle of broken glass speared through the space she had just vacated and shattered on the floor of the balcony. It would have cut her in two. She stared at it, shuddering, unable to move. Unable to think clearly. How had it all gone so wrong?

'Back!' yelled Flydd. 'Roof's caving in!'

Nish dragged her away and around the corner. A falling beam struck the balcony, breaking the front half off and tumbling it down into the gloom below. He let out a string of oaths, most of which Karan had never heard before.

'If we'd been five minutes sooner ...' she said. 'Even *two* minutes.'

'They might crash,' said Nish. 'Tiaan hasn't flown in years. Might not have the strength for it.'

'Llian is on board!' she snarled.

'Sorry! Didn't think.'

She felt unutterably weary. It had all been for nothing, yet again. Where had he met Tiaan, anyway? How long had it been going on? She tried to tell herself that it was irrelevant now, but the agony kept cycling.

'It's ... alright,' she mumbled. 'Saved my life.'

Flydd supported himself against a wall. 'How did Skald get in?'

'We got in.'

'But Alcifer was designed to protect against Rulke's enemies, and the Charon's greatest enemies have always been the Merdrun. He would have had the very strongest defences against them.'

Nish shrugged. 'What does it matter?'

'It matters.'

Flydd went back around the corner to the point where the front of the balcony had broken off and stood there, staring through the dust towards the far wall. Karan crept up behind him, as far as she dared. The remainder of the balcony was cracked in a dozen places.

'What is it, Xervish?' she said.

'Someone was crouched on the stair, in the shadows. Trying to hide.'

She edged up beside him. 'I wasn't looking that way.'

'In my line of business, you have to notice everything.'

He turned, fists clenched by his sides, eyes closed as if trying to recreate the scene. 'It was Aviel!'

Karan looked down. The stairs had torn away from the wall and there was no sign of anyone on the floor. 'What would *she* be doing here?'

'There's only one way she could have got here – by coming with Maigraith. Or following her.'

'Why would –? Ah!'

'Ah, indeed. Maigraith knows Alcifer backwards and she can make gates where no one else can. She must have let Skald in.'

'Why would she betray Rulke to his enemies?'

'She wouldn't. It must've been part of a plan that went badly wrong.'

'What do we do now?'
'We haven't lost yet. Come on!'

Maigraith's arm moved; her right hand reached out and gripped the side of the stair. She was alive! Aviel did not know whether to be glad or sorry.

The construct rose abruptly, and she saw what was going to happen. She scrambled down the turns of the stair, the structure quivering underfoot, and grabbed Maigraith just as the great craft struck the roof.

Where to shelter? Under the stair? No, it might collapse. There, a door in the side wall. She yanked it open, got Maigraith through with a series of heaves, kicked it shut behind her and crouched with her arms up over her head.

A monumental crash as tons of glass and metal hit the broken floor outside. A metal beam tore the door off its hinges, speared past within inches of Aviel's left shoulder and embedded itself in the far wall. Splinters of glass peppered her back and arms. Outside, metal tore with an ear-stabbing groan and something massive hit the hall floor and rolled away, clicking and clacking. The staircase, she thought. Was the whole building going to collapse?

The crashing and clanging stopped and there was silence apart from her heavy breathing. Her back and right shoulder stung in a dozen places. She picked out blood-tipped splinters of glass and flicked them away.

Maigraith sat up, rubbing her head. She looked even older and more wretched now.

'Lucky the *stupid little stickybeak* followed you,' Aviel said. 'Or you'd be dead.'
'What happened?'
'Construct burst up through the skylight.'
Maigraith gave her a sharp glance 'Who was flying it?'
'A woman. Mid-thirties. Olive skin. Short, dark hair.'
'Tiaan, I expect. What about Rulke?'
'After you cast that stunning spell on him, and it backfired, it gave Skald the chance to get aboard.' Aviel wanted Maigraith to be in no doubt that her folly had caused all this.
'And?'
'He must have overcome Rulke.'
'What – about – Lirriam?' Maigraith said savagely.
'I didn't see her.'

Maigraith laid her head on her arms and wept, but after a minute she stood up, shakily, and wiped her face. She looked older than ever, and harder.

'You saved my life again,' she said to Aviel.

'Yes.'

'I'm not grateful.'

'I never expected you would be.'

'Skald betrayed me,' said Maigraith.

'And you betrayed him. You're even.'

Maigraith rubbed the top of her head. 'Something hit me.'

Aviel tried to keep her face blank. Her water bottle was buried under the fallen ceiling. Nothing could be proved – not that proof mattered to Maigraith. 'When the roof fell in, debris went everywhere.'

She picked out a shard curved like a skeet's throat-ripping talon, and held it out.

Maigraith gave her a deeply suspicious look. 'Take me home. Then get that dammed rejuvenation potion done!'

As Aviel led her away, a dreadful thought struck her. By knocking Maigraith out, and allowing Skald to get away with the construct, had she given the Merdrun the weapon that would win them the war?

58

CAN'T DO IT ANYMORE. WANT TO DIE

Though Skald felt sure he was dying, he could not relax his iron self-control. If by some miracle Tiaan managed to keep this massive construct in the air, and he delivered it and the prisoners to Skyrock, his father's cowardice would be forgotten. Not even the magiz could touch him then.

But it was so very hard. Every bone from the top of his skull to the ends of his toes throbbed as though nails had been hammered through it. Every organ felt as if it had been torn open – even his eyeballs. All he wanted was to fall down and close his eyes and let everything go.

The temptation must be resisted. If his watch on Rulke faltered, even for a minute, the Great Enemy would find a way to free himself.

Endure! You can do it. You must! This saves the True Purpose. This proves you.

Llian was tied up and no threat, but Tiaan was another matter. In the Lyrinx War she had been brave, daring, an original thinker with a conscience, and she knew constructs inside and out. She would have recognised this one from its exposed parts long before Rulke moved the walls that had concealed the whole, and she probably had a plan to seize it and take it to Flydd.

Or to deny it to the Merdrun if her plan failed?

Her face had lit up when Skald gave his word to free her and send her home, but the joy had not lasted. Perhaps she thought the Merdrun could never be trusted. Given the casual atrocities they had inflicted on so many cities, so many people, she was right to think so, and it made her dangerous.

Only Tiaan and Rulke could fly this mighty craft and, if she lost hope, she could destroy it in a moment by releasing her mind-link to the controls. Skald would not have time to free Rulke before the crash turned them all to jelly.

How could he ensure she followed orders? Another Merdrun might have threatened her children, but the thought sent Skald back to the basement and the sad little bodies of Tataste's daughter and son, still clinging together in death. Innocents, dead because he had killed their mother. His eyes stung, and the forbidden emotions that had passed to him as he had drunk her life almost overwhelmed him.

It reminded him of the horror in Tiaan's eyes when he took the life of Susmagiz Ghiv. She was afraid of dying that way.

'I will keep to my promise – as long as you fly directly to Skyrock,' he said. 'But if you decide to end us all, know that I will drink your life on the way down.'

Her short hair stood up; her soft mouth twisted. 'I – I will fly true. For as long as I am able.'

Skald perched on the seat beside her, where he could also watch Rulke and Llian, and drew on the power stolen from Ghiv to strengthen himself. He could not numb the ever-growing pain, though. Nor the fear that, despite all he had done, he was going to fail.

'What's the plan?' said Karan, struggling to keep up as they ran back to the sky galleon.

Flydd did not reply until it was in the air and racing north-east. 'Skald can only be heading for Skyrock, many hours away. We're going to shadow him.'

'And then?'

'Fly above the construct and force it down,' said Nish.

'Too risky,' said Flydd.

'Why?'

'Use your imagination, Nish!' Flydd snapped. 'Tiaan's got to channel a staggering amount of power to keep it in the air. Far more power than she would ever have channelled flying a thapter, and I won't do anything to make it worse for her. Besides, I'll be astounded if she lasts an hour.'

'What do you mean by *lasts*?' Karan said quietly.

'Falls unconscious; has her mind burned out; has a stroke; drops dead,' said Flydd. 'They amount to the same thing.'

'The construct crashing and killing everyone inside.'

'If she sees her end coming, she might bring it down to the ground first. That's my hope; my only chance.'

'Skald's a desperate man,' said Maelys. 'He'll destroy it rather than letting us get it.'

'He was in a bad way,' said Flydd. 'He might collapse before she does. And if he does, we take it. We'll stay well back. Hopefully he won't realise we've followed.'

Only an hour had passed, of the eight-hour flight to Skyrock, and already Tiaan was showing the strain. Her skin had a grey-green tinge and a tremor in her right hand made it difficult to use the controls.

'What's the matter?' Skald said to her.

'Aftersickness,' she said in a whisper.

'So soon?'

'Swore off – Art – many years ago.' She was struggling to control the construct and talk at the same time, not a good sign. 'Power – burning. Head splitting. Can't think.'

'Then how are you flying?'

'Instinct and muscle memory,' she croaked. 'Can't last.'

Was her job impossible? Probably, but he had come too far to give in now.

'I'll cast a healing on you,' he said. 'It'll lessen the headaches and the nerve burning. And then a strengthening spell.'

Tiaan choked, her right arm shook, and the construct shuddered in the air.

'It's safe,' Skald said hastily. 'We who would be masters of war must also master healing.'

He cast a healing spell, followed by the strengthening spell. The grey-green tinge faded and her right arm steadied, but now his arm developed a tremor, as if her weakness had transferred to him.

It can't be done, he thought. *Let everything go – you can still die with honour.*

How he wanted to, but he had to keep going. Even if they only got halfway to Skyrock it would be a mighty achievement, surely enough to make up for the family's shame.

No, he had to go all the way, though not for himself. He was a true Merdrun, and in the end his paltry wants and needs did not matter. What mattered was the True Purpose, and if he failed, it too would fail.

Skald made another agonising trip up the ladder, forced the hatch up and hauled himself out onto the battered lookout platform. And gasped. They were high up and the wind bit into him like daggers grown from ice. In the past, cold had not troubled him, but he was so weak now the chill was creeping along his bones. A few minutes up here would finish him.

He turned to go down and started violently. The sky galleon! Flitting from one cloud to another, perhaps a mile behind. Shadowing him. Gone again.

Skald's teeth chattered as he tried to work out Flydd's plan.

The sky galleon appeared again, a little closer. Had his nemesis spotted him up here? If Flydd had, he might blast Skald off the platform to his death.

He scrambled down. It felt like a cowardly act, but he had to stay alive. A row of hooks on the far side of the cabin held three coats that could only belong to Rulke. Skald put on the heaviest but it failed to warm him. He was too far gone.

He resumed his place beside Tiaan, holding himself upright by gripping the edges of his seat. He could not be beaten by that scrawny old runt of a man.

What would Flydd do next? Skald could not think it through; it was taking all his mental capacity to support Tiaan and maintain the watch on Rulke and Llian. Both had recovered now and Rulke's unblinking eyes were fixed on Skald. He shivered.

On they flew. An hour later Skald was forced to renew the spells on Tiaan, and every hour after that. Was Flydd still following? There were no portholes in the rear wall of the cabin and Skald dared not go up to the lookout. Flydd might be close behind, waiting for the chance.

No, he would want the construct whole, and its passengers alive. He would not attack while it was high in the air. But later, as the ground rose towards the Ramparts of Tacnah and the Great Mountains beyond, a chance was bound to come.

On and on and on Tiaan flew, now towards the rising sun.

By the end of the seventh hour, when Skyrock was still a hundred miles away, Skald's healing and strengthening spells no longer had any effect. Tiaan was shivering and twitching, her face was swollen into a balloon, her red eyes leaking bloody tears.

The construct had gone close to crashing three times in the night, and twice more this morning, and the last time she had only saved it a few hundred feet above the ground. If she lost control again, nothing could save them. He dared not go lower, because that would give Flydd the chance to force the construct to the ground, and Tiaan lacked the strength to climb higher.

And the more power Skald used to support her, the less there was to keep him going.

Endure! For the True Purpose. One for All!

But not even the True Purpose moved him now, and there were still fifty miles to go. And he had used every skerrick of the power stolen from his sus-magiz.

Tiaan was shaking uncontrollably, and moaning. 'Let me go. Can't do it anymore. Want to die.'

Skald wanted it more than she did, but one thing drove him on. His desperate need to rise above the taint of his father's cowardice.

He lifted Tiaan out of the copper seat, fell onto it and heaved her onto his lap. It took all his strength; he was weaker than a Merdrun boy. She shuddered and wailed and tried to get away. He held her until she gave in, then returned her hands to the controls and drew on the last of his own magical power to strengthen her and alleviate her pain.

'Keep going,' he said. 'I've got you. Not long now. You'll be all right.'

But *he* wasn't. With no power left to numb the pain, the agony in Skald's bones and his belly came back redoubled, and doubled again. Then the bleeding started anew. How much blood had he lost now? He was sitting in a puddle that squelched with every movement and oozed through the slots in the copper seat.

Ten miles to go. The land had risen steadily as they continued east, the construct now only eighty feet above the ground. Flydd would strike soon. Skald wished they were higher but Tiaan could barely channel enough power for level flight.

'Flydd's right behind us,' Rulke said suddenly. 'He's moving in for the attack.'

Skald whirled. Rulke had worked the blindfold and gag free, and his dark Charon eyes, still fixed on Skald, seemed to be mocking him for a fool and a failure.

Skald did not ask how he knew. 'What's he going to do?'

'If I were him, I'd force the construct down. It'd probably survive a crash from eighty feet, and I might, too. But you and Tiaan won't.'

Her eyes were closed and she was making an awful keening sound, like a mother over a dead child. Skald held her upright with the insides of his arms while his hands enclosed hers on the knobs and he tried to sense out, beneath her convulsive shuddering, the instinctive movements she made to keep the massive craft in the air.

But he had almost no power left. He'd lost.

Or had he? A possibility occurred to him, a tiny one, almost hopeless. He had to take the chance.

Skald extended a shaking arm towards the one victim who could not possibly resist him and cast a feeble little version of the life-drinking spell, all he had strength for.

But how could Llian's life be enough?

59

HAD HE BURNED HER MIND OUT?

They shadowed the construct for what remained of the night and the first hours of daylight, creeping ever closer.

Flydd was an automaton at the controls, muttering to himself as he waited for a chance to attack. 'Now? No, not yet, *not yet.*'

Karan watched the construct's wavering flight with increasing terror. Five times it had fallen from the sky and she had been sure everyone inside it was going to die. Five times Tiaan's geomantic genius had managed to save it, though the last time it had only been seconds from destruction, and it was clear that she could not do it again. Judging by the construct's erratic path and jerky motion, she was almost done.

It was even lower now, barely skimming the higher hills as it crossed the rising ground towards Skyrock, no more than ten miles away.

'Xervish,' said Karan, 'if you leave it any longer –'

'Still too high.'

A skin-crawling horror struck Karan, then a sickening pain that grew steadily worse until she wanted to vomit. She slumped to her knees, palms pressed to the sides of her head, shaking it.

'Karan?' Flydd said sharply.

She did not reply; she could not. Was she being attacked? How could she be, so far from anywhere? What was going on?

Mummy, Mummy, Skald's drinking Daddy's life!

How did Sulien sense such things from so far away? But it gave Karan the answer she needed. The pain, the sickness and the cold horror was coming through an involuntary link to Llian, and she had no choice but to break the link in case the spell jumped to her, then to Flydd.

It meant rejecting Llian all over again, but there was nothing else she could do. She did not know how to block a life-drinking spell.

Don't worry, Sulien, she sent. *We'll save him.*

But Sulien was gone and Karan could not find her. 'It's Skald,' she said limply. 'Drinking Llian's life. Xervish –'

'I've got to risk it,' said Flydd. 'Brace, everyone.'

Karan slumped sideways onto the floor, still holding her head. She felt very cold, very weak. Flydd accelerated until the bow half of the sky galleon was above the rear of the construct, then cut the power. The sky galleon dropped sharply, the keel hit the top of the construct with a clang and a shock that made Karan's teeth vibrate, and both craft fell.

For a moment, Karan thought it might be best if Llian was killed in the crash. Occasionally, she had heard, people did survive a partial life-drinking, though they were never the same afterwards.

～

Llian screamed as the spell sank deep into him. His eyes were bulging from their sockets, his tongue bloody and protruding, his mouth a rip across his blanched face.

That's for freeing Rulke! Skald thought. *How dare you try to thwart* me!

Skald had begun to wrench the life out of Llian, and it proved surprisingly strong. Skald was anticipating the ecstasy to come when the link was brutally severed. Llian fell down, heels drumming on the floor, fists opening and closing spasmodically. Skald slumped forwards against Tiaan, gasping.

'You – will – not – touch –my – Teller,' grated Rulke.

How had he broken the spell while his hands were bound? Skald could not imagine, and dared not try again. But the trickle of power he had taken from Llian might be enough. He heaved Tiaan upright, held her hands with his own and jerked on the left-most knob. The rear of the construct kicked up and there was a grating sound, then the weight of the sky galleon was off them.

Crash, scum! Skald prayed. 'Tiaan, go!'

Her eyes were closed; she was completely out of it. But her hands made the necessary movements and the construct streaked away.

∼

Flydd was forcing the construct down when the bow of the sky galleon was driven up so sharply that it tumbled backwards in the air, slamming Karan, Maelys and Nish against the rear wall of the cabin.

Flydd cursed and clung desperately to the controls as the sky galleon stood on its stern in mid-air, kept tumbling backwards and went upside-down. It was out of control and they were only sixty feet above the ground. Fifty feet! They were going to crash.

Karan braced herself as she hit the ceiling. Flydd needed help but she was too weak. It felt as if part of Skald's spell had come across the link and attached to her.

Was Llian dead? She had no way of knowing.

Nish sprang, caught hold of the control binnacle and supported Flydd while he tried desperately to right the craft, which was now plunging bow-first towards the ground. But with so little altitude, Karan did not see how it could recover.

Flydd fought the controls and had the sky galleon almost levelled out when the front of the keel struck earth with an almighty thud, kicking the bow up again and hurling Karan and Maelys across the cabin. The keel hit a second time, carved a gouge across the ground for a hundred yards, struck a shelf of rock, the sky galleon skidded sideways, righted itself and slid the other way, and stopped.

Flydd, who had a badly cut lip and a large bruise on his right cheek, staggered to the cabin door, heaved it open and looked east. As Karan came to her knees the construct wobbled across a ridge a mile away and was lost to sight.

He cursed. 'We'll never catch them now. Skald's beaten us.'

'They might have come down on the other side,' said Nish. 'If they did, we can take the construct before anyone from Skyrock can reach them.'

Karan lay on the floor, wrapped her arms around herself and closed her eyes. *Llian, whatever you've done, I forgive you. Just be alive, and whole again. Or ... if he's drunk too much of you ... die peacefully.*

∼

There was no further sign of the sky galleon. Skald prayed that it had crashed and Flydd had been killed, though he did not think it likely. He had read all about the scrutators, and they never gave up.

Seven miles to go. The pain grew ever worse as the last of the stolen power dribbled away, and his mission felt as impossible as ever. If Flydd had saved the sky galleon, he could still win.

Five miles. *You must do it. You can.*

'Flydd's coming fast,' said Rulke with a savage smile. 'You've lost, you pathetic little man.'

He was still tied up, his middle was covered in blood and he did not seem capable of attacking, so why did he seem so happy?

The worry intensified Skald's pain. He glanced at Llian, who was doubled up on the floor, fists clenched. There was blood on his bottom lip and his eyes were vacant. He would cause no more trouble, at least.

How close was Flydd? Skald could not leave the controls to find out.

Could he outrun the sky galleon? Skald felt sure the construct was the faster craft, but if he forced Tiaan to channel any more power it would kill her – unless he could take part of it through himself. But to do that he would have to drink part of his own life again, hideous though that had been last time.

There was no alternative. He cast the spell on himself and sipped from his life force. The tearing pain inside him grew even more unbearable, though the heat searing through his arteries and along his nerve fibres partly counteracted it.

He pushed the power lever forwards and the construct accelerated a little. Tiaan screamed and slumped sideways. Had he burned her mind out? There must be something left, otherwise the construct would have crashed. He could move the controls, but only Tiaan could channel the power where it needed to go.

Only four miles now and, in what had to be a mirage, the beautiful blue and white twisted columns of Skyrock appeared above the hills in the distance. Not a mirage, a miracle!

'He's still coming,' said Rulke mockingly.

Skald braced himself for Flydd's next attempt to force the construct down. He could still win.

～

'We're gaining on the mongrel,' said Nish.

'Not fast enough,' said Flydd.

'Can't you get any more speed out of this thing?' said Karan, chewing on her knuckles. She was feeling a little better now. The construct was less than a hundred yards ahead. Llian was so close. But if Flydd did force it down, and overcome Skald, what would she find inside? Perhaps it would be better if it crashed …

'When we hit the ground, something must have jarred loose in the drive mechanism. This is the best I can do.'

'Can we catch them?' said Maelys.

They gained a few more yards, but now the upper half of the tower of Skyrock was visible in the distance.

'Touch and go.' Flydd made a complicated series of movements and the sky galleon accelerated a little.

Just three miles more. *Endure!*

Two miles. Skald wanted nothing more than to set the construct down and allow oblivion to claim him.

Don't give up yet. Even this close, Flydd could snatch the craft, and victory, before help could reach Skald from Skyrock.

The sky galleon was only five yards behind the construct now, both craft racing sixty feet above a dry, stony valley scattered with blue-grey bushes and tall yellow clumps of spear grass.

Four yards.

Three.

Karan's gnawed knuckles were bleeding, her heart thundering as if she had just climbed the great tower of Katazza again. She tried to convince herself that Llian was alright, that Skald's life-drinking spell had failed. That things could go back to normal.

'What you going to do?' she croaked.

'Nudge it out of the air,' Flydd said, his bony jaw clenched.

'Crash it?'

'Yes.'

'Could kill everyone inside.'

'Yes.'

'Once we cross the next ridge,' said Nish, 'we'll be in the bowl around Skyrock. Where they have an army of 150,000, Xervish.'

'I know!' snapped Flydd. 'Shut up and let me concentrate.'

Two yards. One.

Flydd tickled the controls and the battered bow of the sky galleon slammed into the left rear of the construct.

60

MUMMY, I'VE GOT TO BREAK MY PROMISE

One mile. Another minute and they would be safe.

Crash!

Something struck the construct so hard that it hurtled off at a tangent, spinning so fast that it was dizzying. Llian sat up, wild-eyed, and projectile vomited.

The spinning slowed. They were hurtling towards a massive rock outcrop at the top of the ridge and Skald did not know how to get the craft back under control. Only Tiaan could – if there was anything left of her mind.

'Tiaan!' he yelled in her ear. 'Do something.'

She made that terrible keening sound again. Her hands moved the controls minutely, the construct stopped spinning, lifted and shot over the rocks, so close that bushes scraped across the corrugated bottom. Then they were over the ridge and heading down the bowl-shaped valley surrounding the pinnacle of Skyrock.

Ahead he could see the triple rings of scaffolding and work platforms, and on them, tens of thousands of workers and slaves. All looked the same as it had yesterday. Had it only been yesterday that he had left? It felt like a lifetime ago.

A stranger's lifetime.

~

Flydd groaned. Karan watched desperately as the construct spun towards the rocks, knowing it was going too fast for anyone to survive the impact. At least it would be quick.

But with only seconds to go it straightened out, lifted, and the base of the construct smashed through a patch of bushes on the top of the ridge, setting some of them on fire, and it wavered away.

'How does the swine keep doing it?' said Nish between his teeth.

Flydd followed. On the other side of the ridge the enemy's vast encampment appeared before them. To either side, the clusters of tents, some surrounded by palisade walls, occupied a good fifth of the sides of the bowl. And at its centre, the vast, spiralling blue and white tower.

Karan stared at it, cast back in time and greatly disturbed. 'It reminds me of the great tower of Katazza.'

'It's an ancient design,' Flydd said absently. 'Goes back to the dawn of the Charon and Merdrun.'

'Xervish, pull back!' Nish yelled. 'They've got catapults, javelards and ballistae, and they're already tracking us.'

'Not while there's a chance of denying the construct to them,' Flydd said through bared teeth. 'I'll kill everyone inside it, if that's the only way.'

Karan moaned.

'If Llian, Rulke and Tiaan fall into the enemy's hands they'll suffer a worse fate. And if the Merdrun get the construct, Santhenar is lost. It's all or nothing, Karan.'

'Once a scrutator, always a scrutator,' said Maelys, who was sitting on the floor with her hands folded in her lap. It was almost as if she would welcome oblivion.

Flydd coaxed more power out of the sky galleon and streaked across the great camp, cutting across the diagonals of the construct's erratic path. Heading directly for it as if to smash it out of the sky. And there was nothing Karan could do about it – or anything.

~

From the corner of an eye Skald saw the sky galleon hurtling at them. Flydd was no longer trying to take the construct. He wanted to destroy it.

Tiaan whimpered and slumped forwards. She was no longer controlling the craft, which lurched and plunged towards the tower. It was going to slam right into it and Skald could not bear to think of the ruin that would cause. No True Purpose then; it would set his people back hundreds of years.

'Wake, Tiaan!' he cried.

She did not stir. Perhaps she never would wake.

He lifted her again. His hands, after following her movements for so many hours, made the necessary movements of the levers and the construct turned. But they were not safe yet. It only flew because she was still subconsciously channelling power to the controls, and if she fell unconscious, or had a seizure or died, the power would stop flowing and they would crash.

Though Skald had barely enough strength left to stay upright, he directed the lot into a healing spell to keep her alive. The broad road running up the slope from Skyrock, between the slaves' and officers' compounds, appeared before him and he pointed the construct at it and cut off the controls.

The construct slammed into the ground, hurling sprays of gravel out for fifty yards to either side and tossing Skald, with Tiaan enfolded in his protecting arms, off the seat. It skidded along for several seconds then came to rest, the structure creaking and groaning, and finally going silent.

~

The construct was safe on the ground. Skald had beaten them, and Llian and Rulke were now in the enemy's impregnable camp. If there was anything left of Llian. The taste in Karan's mouth was bitter.

Crash!

A javelard spear, a good fifteen feet long, tore through the port side of the bow. Two more spears passed overhead, the second one ripping away part of the cabin roof, and a boulder hurled by one of their mighty catapults thudded against the keel, rocking the sky galleon. It was fine shooting; deadly shooting.

'Xervish!' Nish roared. 'It's over! Get us out of here, now!'

Flydd gave them a blank-eyed stare, then jerked savagely on the controls and the sky galleon hurtled away. It was hit by three more spears and two other rocks before it cleared the ridge and passed out of sight.

~

Skald had never made friends, his family shame had seen to that, yet to his aston-ishment a powerful bond had formed between himself and Tiaan over the past eight hours. He actually *cared* about her.

He laid her tenderly on the floor, wound down the ladder, then clawed his way up to the platform and, on hands and knees, looked over the crumpled coaming and out on a scene of chaos. Terrified workers and slaves were running in all directions. They had never seen anything like this gigantic metal craft.

'Call High Commander!' Skald gasped. 'Send – Durthix.'

He was already running down the road from the officer's compound, followed by the magiz, who did not look pleased to see Skald alive. They scrambled up the ladder, and in.

'Maigraith betrayed us,' Skald said in a wisp of a voice. 'Source too heavy to carry. It – it was there – power –construct. I – I took it. And Rulke – and a Teller, Llian. Secure them. Artisan Tiaan needs – best healer. Gave her my word – send her home – unharmed.'

'You did *what*?' cried the magiz.

'Swore by – True Purpose. Only way – get construct here.'

'Durthix?' said the magiz, practically foaming at the mouth with rage.

'Not now, Magiz!' snapped Durthix.

Tiaan was unconscious. Blood oozed out from beneath the nails of her clenched fingers, and from a bitten tongue, and even her tears were red. She was probably going to die, burned inside from channelling so much power, and if she did, it would scar him. He had grown surprisingly close to her over the past eight hours, as they'd acted as one to bring the construct safely home.

Rulke was sitting up, smiling, though he was surely putting on the act of his life. He had to be neutralised, and there was only one way to do that.

'Pannilie gated Lirriam here, yes?' said Skald.

'Ten hours ago,' said Durthix.

'Has she been harmed?'

'Not yet,' Dagog said ominously.

'Don't lay – finger on her. Put – secure prison,' said Skald. 'Treat – courtesy.'

'To what purpose?' said Durthix, not even challenging Skald for daring to issue orders to his high commander.

'Ensures – Rulke's cooperation.'

Durthix gave the necessary orders, checked that Llian and Rulke were secure, and set a dozen guards and three sus-magiz to watch each of them. Four stretchers were called for.

'Where is Senior Sus-magiz Pannilie?' said the magiz.

'Think – Maigraith killed her,' said Skald.

'And your troops?' said Durthix.

'Dead – at Rulke's hand.'

'What about the junior sus-magiz?' said the magiz.

'Drank – life,' said Skald. 'To escape.'

'Yet again he returns with every one of his squad dead,' said the magiz. 'Durthix –'

'Skald has returned with treasures undreamed of,' said Durthix icily, 'and I won't hear any more of your malice.'

By now thousands of Merdrun troops, and many gaping slaves, had gathered around and, strangely, Durthix did not order them away. The stretcher bearers arrived and Tiaan, Rulke and Llian were taken to the healing tent under heavy guard. Rulke still wore that disturbing smile. Durthix gestured to the last stretcher.

But Skald could only think about his father, executed for cowardice. *Had* he been a coward, or were the charges trumped up by a malicious rival?

Skald would never know, but he had to go the rest of the way, unaided. 'Will walk. Finish what – I started, High Commander.'

'Are you *sure*?' said Durthix.

Skald knew he was a gruesome sight. Blood and vomit were splattered all down his front, and the back of his pants was saturated in congealed blood. He could barely stand up, and every step sent jolts of agony through his middle, but he had to do this.

Endure!

The Merdrun parted to form an impromptu honour guard, and only once they were inside the black command tent did Skald allow Durthix to take his arm.

'Now will you –?' said Durthix.

Skald found an ounce of strength, hopefully enough to deliver his report. 'Source powers construct – is mighty. Supply power – until node tapped. Progress?'

'Another week should do it,' said Dagog sourly.

'Construct – even greater prize,' said Skald.

'It's no use to us if Tiaan dies,' said the magiz. 'And I expect she will. No other pilot has the strength to fly such a mighty craft.'

'Rulke does. Cares greatly – Lirriam. Her, hostage – he'll obey.'

'Spell it out,' said Durthix.

'Construct can lift timber – metal – stone – even sections of iron tower – top of Skyrock. Finish tower – *twenty* times faster.'

Durthix stared at the roof of the tent, his fists clenching and unclenching by his sides. 'Yes,' he said quietly. 'Yes!'

Skald swayed, grabbed a tent pole and clung to it desperately.

'You have done well, Captain,' said Durthix. 'Hasn't he, Magiz?'

'Sus-magiz Skald has exceeded all expectations,' said the magiz with bitter heartiness.

'And on the Day of All Days, after our Great Purpose has been achieved, you will receive the highest honour of all.'

Skald found a little more strength, enough to speak clearly now and to say all that needed to be said. 'The only honour I need, High Commander, is that which comes from having done my duty. *One for All!*'

He saluted and collapsed.

~

An hour later Flydd landed on a bare hilltop where any pursuit would be visible from miles away, and they lit a campfire and choked down a grim breakfast. No one spoke. Everyone was exhausted after days of flying and the sleepless night. There was nothing to say, anyway.

'Rulke was our last hope,' he said finally. 'And now the enemy have him, plus a construct the like of which the world has never seen. They can't be beaten.'

It fired Karan up. 'I'm not giving up, so get up off the scrawny arse I've twice saved for you, *and find a way.*'

Flydd looked at her blankly, then climbed to his feet and turned away. Had he finally succumbed to the despair he so feared?

'Got to sleep.' He trudged towards the battered sky galleon, his scrawny shoulders slumped.

'I'll take the first watch,' said Maelys. 'I don't feel too bad. Go on, all of you.'

She pocketed the Mirror of Aachan, pulled her coat around her and climbed onto the javelard platform. Nish followed Flydd up into the sky galleon.

Karan remained where she was, sipping her tea and staring into the fire. And then it happened –

Mummy, Mummy, they've got Daddy!

'Sulien?' Karan whispered. 'How do you know that?'

I sensed it. I – I'm sorry, Mummy, I've got to break my promise. Daddy's hurt, and they'll kill him if I don't do something.

No! Don't do anything. Stay where you are. Stay hidden.

But Sulien was gone. She would try to probe the enemy, and they would find her.

And kill her to protect their secret.

The End of

The Perilous Tower

The Gates of Good and Evil quartet concludes in

Book 4, *The Sapphire Portal*

Subscribe to my newsletter for free books and special offers, preview chapters, news and other great stuff.
https://www.ian-irvine.com/join-my-newsletter/

Chapter 1 of *The Sapphire Portal* follows.

FIRST CHAPTER OF BOOK 4, THE SAPPHIRE PORTAL

'Proud of yourself, Chronicler?' said Rulke.

After half a day as prisoners in the Merdrun's camp, and lengthy secret talks between Rulke and their captors, he and Llian had been returned to the construct. Its power controller crystal had already been removed to ensure that it could not be operated, and the construct searched to make sure there were no spares.

Llian flushed. His earlier, daring rescue of Rulke had been utterly negated by last night's failure.

'How does it feel to singlehandedly turn victory into defeat?' Rulke said disgustedly. 'To give my construct to the enemy – and lose the war we stood to win?'

'You know I'm not a man of action, yet –'

'You can say that again! But Skald was on the verge of collapse. You only had to whack him.'

'I hit him twice while you were wrestling him. But –'

'And then you knocked *me* unconscious.'

Even in Skald's gravely weakened state he had been more than a match for Llian. There was no point saying that, either.

'I'm sorry,' said Llian. 'I failed you.'

'Again!' Rulke said relentlessly.

'What are you –?'

Rulke put a finger to his lips. 'Someone's coming.'

The construct quivered as a group of Merdrun climbed the ladder, led by a senior sus-magiz and a group of artisans, and entered the cabin. The sus-magiz, a pipe-thin, flat-headed fellow who looked as though he were half human and half snake, examined the controls, while the artisans opened every door and compartment and noted what was inside.

Two hours later, after they were gone, High Commander Durthix entered, along with the magiz, Dagog, a repulsive little man who stank of rotten meat.

'Well?' Durthix said to Rulke.

'You need my cooperation,' said Rulke, folding his arms. He was a half-head taller than Durthix, and broader across the shoulders, and Durthix did not like it. In the Merdrun army, size mattered.

Durthix gave a derisive snort.

'You have no pilot capable of flying this craft,' Rulke added, 'and you can't complete your True Purpose without it.'

Durthix started. 'Why do you say that?'

'Tiaan is gravely ill, burned inside, and will never fly again. M'Lainte does not have the strength to fly a construct and neither does any other pilot on Santhenar, save myself. You need my aid and you need it now.'

The magiz whispered, 'High Commander, don't let him speak –'

Durthix waved Dagog to silence. 'Lirriam is imprisoned in a fortress without doors or windows. She will be hostage for your good behaviour, Rulke.'

Rulke stepped forwards and stood chest to chest with Durthix. 'And who will be hostage for *your* good behaviour?'

'How dare you!' the magiz exploded. 'High Commander –'

Llian gagged. The stink of rotten meat was overpowering in the closed cabin, and it issued from every part of Dagog.

'Not now, Magiz!' snapped Durthix.

He stared into Rulke's eyes but could not break his gaze. Llian sat in the background, recording everything in his perfect Teller's memory. The contest, deadly though it might become, was fascinating.

Rulke smiled grimly. 'Your people and mine have been enemies for aeons, Durthix, and there can never be trust between us. Unless I can monitor Lirriam's health and safety, I *will not* cooperate.'

'Then she dies!' the magiz blustered, 'and you will feel such tortures –'

Rulke picked Dagog up in one hand, spun him around and booted him across the cabin. Dagog scrambled to his feet, his face purple in outrage, and thrust out his bony right hand.

'Try it and you're dead,' snapped Rulke.

Dagog's eyes went entirely white. Rulke had made a dire enemy. Durthix, scowling, signed to Dagog to stay back.

'If Lirriam dies,' said Rulke, 'I have nothing to lose ... and I can extinguish myself in a moment.'

'You wouldn't,' said Durthix.

'I'm the last of my kind. I was preparing to go back to the void to die when I sensed her out there, and my beacon led her to Santhenar. If I lose her, I'll have nothing left.'

'If she died, you'd want revenge.'

Rulke's smile flashed again. 'My best revenge would be thwarting you – and blowing your stinking magiz to shreds.'

'High Commander,' said the magiz, and now there was a whine in his voice, 'call his bluff.'

'Why don't I call yours?' said Rulke. 'You have one chance to complete the True Purpose, Durthix. The time window is but weeks away, it's only eight hours long ... and after it closes it won't reopen for 287 years.'

With an effort, Durthix controlled himself, but Llian was a master at reading faces. Durthix was shocked at how much Rulke knew, and must be wondering what other dangerous secrets he was privy to.

Rulke squared his shoulders. 'There's only one way to complete Skyrock in time – if I fly the construct for you.'

'High Commander, that would be madness!' said the magiz.

'I will permit you to *see* Lirriam once a day, remotely,' Durthix said to Rulke, 'to reassure yourself that she hasn't been harmed, but you will not be able to communicate with her. In return you will fly the construct strictly according to the requirements of my Superintendent of Works. To ensure that you do, the controller crystal will be removed at the end of each day.'

'I accept your terms,' said Rulke. 'Though I have one additional requirement.'

'What's that?'

'Llian.'

This, Llian had not expected.

Durthix turned and looked down at him with curled lip. 'What about him?'

'He remains in the construct,' said Rulke.

'To what purpose?'

'His incompetence keeps me sane.'

The magiz giggled, a sound both incongruous and alarming, and another blast of rotten meat assailed Llian's nostrils.

After the Merdrun had gone and Rulke had checked everywhere for spying devices, and destroyed several, he began to prepare dinner, whistling a merry tune. It was not the first time he had been unexpectedly cheerful in the last half day.

Llian sat down and thought through the incidents. 'Aha!' he said.

Rulke quirked an eyebrow at him.

'How dare you blame me!' said Llian. 'It was *you*, all along.'

'Your ramblings are more opaque than usual, Chronicler.'

'When you and Skald were wrestling last night, and I was dancing around with the table leg, trying to get a clear go at him, you *deliberately* stumbled into the path of my club.'

'Why would I do such a thing?'

Why indeed? It was the one question to which Llian had no answer. Then inspiration struck.

'You wanted Skald to defeat you and take the construct to Skyrock because Lirriam means everything to you. It was your one chance of getting her back.'

'That would be desperately reckless,' said Rulke. 'And I'm not a reck–'

'Cobblers! You're famous for reckless daring – like the time you led the Hundred out of the void to Aachan and almost single-handedly took the Aachim's world from them.'

'I was young and impetuous back then.'

'You were also recklessly bold after you freed yourself from the Nightland. And you still are – you thrive on impossible conflicts. What if Tiaan had been unable to control the construct, and it had crashed?'

Rulke shrugged. 'There was no other way to save Lirriam.'

'We could all have been killed.'

'It was a strong possibility, even though I was subtly channelling power to the controls. If I hadn't, Tiaan would have been dead before the construct reached the other side of the Sea of Thurkad. No old human could channel that much power, and live.'

'A wonder Skald didn't realise what you were doing.'

'He has an overly high opinion of himself. And I was banking on the Merdrun's lack of experience with our mech-magical devices. Even so, it was a dangerous night; it could easily have gone wrong.'

'It still can. You've made it possible for them to realise their age-old goal, whatever it is. What are they going to do to us then?'

'I don't know, Chronicler, but I had to risk all to gain all.'

'Or lose all.'

'Or lose all,' Rulke repeated soberly. 'Everything – the fate of the Three Worlds and four human species, and you and I – rests on my gamble.'

Another question occurred to Llian. 'Your original construct could make gates and jump from one place to another. Can this one?'

'I wish it could, but there isn't a field on Santhenar that can deliver enough power, these days. Get to bed. You had a hard night.'

'I'm afraid to go to bed,' said Llian.

Rulke looked around sharply. 'Because Skald began to drink your life?'

'Yes. And he started on you first. Are you –?'

'You may want to relive it, Chronicler, but I do not.'

Llian did not want to relive it either, but when he lay on his hard bunk in the dark he was hurled back to that ghastly moment – the worst of his life.

The blind terror of seeing and feeling his life force being drawn out of him and into Skald. The unnatural cold that had crept through Llian's body, the deathly weakness and unbearable pain, and his utter inability to do anything to save himself.

The revulsion that had come from experiencing the emotions and the foulness of a mind that could do such things to another human, and enjoy it. A mind that revelled in the power while he fed on his victim's helpless terror.

It was sickening to experience, second-hand, the ecstasy that Llian's precious life was giving to Skald. And he had been shaken by the realisation that Skald might use up, or even waste, the power gained from drinking his entire life, in a few moments of sorcery.

Worse still was the emptiness of the soul that had followed. People were monsters and life was futile.

Worst of all, Llian could not stop imagining it happening again, his terror conflicting with an inexplicable desire for Skald to begin drinking his life anew, and for the sick union with another human that could be gained in no other way – even if the life drinking went all the way to completion.

OTHER BOOKS BY IAN IRVINE

BUY EBOOKS

BUY AUDIOBOOKS

THE THREE WORLDS EPIC FANTASY SEQUENCE

THE VIEW FROM THE MIRROR QUARTET

A Shadow on the Glass

The Tower on the Rift

Dark is the Moon

The Way Between the Worlds

THE WELL OF ECHOES QUARTET

Geomancer

Tetrarch

Scrutator

Chimaera

THE SONG OF THE TEARS TRILOGY

The Fate of the Fallen

The Curse on the Chosen

The Destiny of the Dead

THE GATES OF GOOD AND EVIL

(sequel to The View from the Mirror)

The Summon Stone

The Fatal Gate

The Perilous Tower

The Sapphire Portal

A Wizard's War (shorter Three Worlds stories)

ABOUT THE AUTHOR

Ian Irvine, an Australian marine scientist, has also written 34 novels and an anthology of shorter stories. His novels include the Three Worlds fantasy sequence (**The View from the Mirror, The Well of Echoes, The Song of the Tears and The Gates of Good & Evil**), which has been published in many countries and translations and has sold over sold over a million copies, a trilogy of eco-thrillers in a world of catastrophic climate change, **Human Rites**, now in its third edition, and 12 novels for younger readers.

BUY EBOOKS

BUY AUDIOBOOKS

Printed in Great Britain
by Amazon